THE CLASH

The Krishnan stepped forward in a fencing stance. Reith bored in, lunging, thrusting, and parrying. The swords clanged and whirled, spattering raindrops. Once Reith slipped on the mud but, straining every sinew, recovered before his antagonist could take advantage of the error.

Reith feinted at the Krishnan's midriff. The Krishnan whipped his blade around in the parry in seconde, turning his hand from supine to prone. But Reith had been well drilled in the counter to this maneuver: he doubled and drove his sword into the Krishnan's chest...

The KRISHNA SERIES from L. Sprague de Camp
and *Ace Science Fiction:*

L. SPRAGUE de CAMP
CATHERINE CROOK de CAMP

THE BONES
OF ZORA

ACE SCIENCE FICTION BOOKS
NEW YORK

This Ace Science Fiction Book contains the complete
text of the original hardcover edition.
It has been completely reset in a typeface
designed for easy reading, and was printed
from new film.

THE BONES OF ZORA

An Ace Science Fiction Book / published by arrangement with
the authors

PRINTING HISTORY
Phantasia Press edition / 1983
Ace edition / August 1984

ISBN: 0-441-07012-4

Ace Science Fiction Books are published by The Berkley Publishing Group,
200 Madison Avenue, New York, New York 10016.
PRINTED IN THE UNITED STATES OF AMERICA

To Dr. Nicholas Hotton III, Ruth Olmstead Hotton, and "Ozymandias," whom we jointly discovered in the Permian beds of Wilbarger County, Texas, on April 27, 1982.

CONTENTS

AUTHOR'S NOTE

This story is the latest in my series about the fictional planet Krishna, a satellite of the star Tau Ceti. These novels, all of which have a *Z* in the titles for easy recognition, take place in the 22d century. Their chronological order is: *The Queen of Zamba, The Hand of Zei, The Hostage of Zir, The Prisoner of Zhamanak, The Virgin of Zesh* (a novella), *The Bones of Zora,* and *The Tower of Zanid.* For reasons of publishing expediency, *The Virgin of Zesh* and *The Tower of Zanid* were published in a single volume, although the first of these takes place before *The Prisoner of Zhamanak* and the second after.

While the reader may pronounce the names in the story as he likes, I have the following renditions in mind: *a* and *á* as in "add" and "wad" respectively; other vowels as in Spanish. Among consonants, *k* and *q* as in "keep" and "quote" regardless of adjacent sounds; *gh* = French uvular *r; kh* = German *ch; '* = a glottal stop or cough; others as in English. Words ending in a consonant or a diphthong are stressed on the last syllable; others usually on the next to the last. Hence Qirib is "keer-EEB" (with a guttural *k*); Sadabao is "sad-ab-OW"; Mishé is "MEE-sheh"; Sainian is sigh-nee-AN; Bákh is close to (Johann Sebastian) Bach. The Portuguese name of Herculeu Castanhoso is "air-koo-LEH-oo kush-TAH-nyew-soo."

THE BONES OF ZORA

I.

THE CAUSEWAY

The hooves of the four ayas clattered over the flagstones of the causeway traversing the great Koloft Swamp on Krishna. The first two six-legged, horned riding animals each bore an Earthman; the other two, led by ropes, carried bundles of gear wrapped in canvas.

Mounted on the sorrel aya, the younger rider, the lean, carrot-topped Fergus Reith, peered suspiciously into the rank, rainbow-hued vegetation that crowded in from the sides. Then an arrow whistled past his head.

"Doctor Marot!" yelled Reith, sweeping out his sword. "Run like hell! *Byant-hao!*"

A swarm of naked, hairy, tailed Krishnans erupted from the many-colored tree trunks that lined the causeway. They brandished weapons with heads of stone, along with a few steel swords and axes obtained by trade or theft.

More arrows whistled; one struck the aya led by the other Terran. The animal bucked and jerked at its lead rope. The rider of the bay aya, a big, black-haired, middle-aging man, inclined to stoutness, braced himself in his stirrups and held on. But a Koloftu, waving a rusty steel blade, slashed the rope through.

1

Spurred, Reith's aya bounded forward; his led animal galloped after. Aristide Marot, slower in starting, pounded behind,
gripping his saddle.

Shouting and waving, Krishnans with tails ran out on the
causeway in front of Reith. His aya snorted, tossed its head,
and tried to stop; but Reith savagely spurred it. As the beast
plunged through the group, Reith swung at the nearest foe on
his right. The hairy Koloftu skipped back with simian nimble-
ness; but another, ridden down, rolled screaming under the
aya's hooves.

Past the interceptors, Reith craned his neck. Marot was close
behind Reith's led aya; but the professor's pack animal was
down on the causeway with Krishnan savages swarming over
it, stabbing and hacking. Blue-green blood poured from its
wounds and spread out over the flagstones.

"God damn!" yelled Reith. "There go our tent and cooking
gear! Step on it, Doctor Marot!"

"Step?" gasped Marot, bouncing on his aya's back. "Oh,
a colloqui—" He broke off to clutch his saddle and heel his
beast to greater effort.

The Krishnans were now in pursuit at amazing speed. Even
at full gallop, the ayas barely drew ahead. If one of the Terrans'
animals stumbled, or if a rider fell off, the tailed ones would
surely get them.

A thrown spear clattered on the causeway behind them.
Arrows whistled; one struck the cantle of Marot's saddle and
stuck in the wood. Marot yelped before he realized that he was
unhurt. Looking back, Reith saw his companion was still with
him, and the Krishnans at last were falling back.

The pair continued their gallop until their pursuers shrank
to specks and faded from view. At last Reith held up a hand
and gentled his lathered mount to a walk. Marot pulled up
alongside his companion. He had wrenched the arrow out of
his saddle and held it up.

"A point of polished chert," he said. "It will make a fine
souvenir." He spoke fluent but French-accented English. "A
centimeter higher, I should have been hit in the *fesse* and have
to eat standing."

"Lucky you didn't get it in the kidneys," said Reith in tones
of exasperation. "I thought I told you to wear your sword?"

With a guilty smile, Marot said: "I am sorry, Mr. Reith. I
forgot; so it is packed. It would be of little use anyway. I am

no hero out of Dumas *père*, but a peaceful scientist. I find it hard to take these medieval weapons seriously."

"Well, now you see what happens when you don't."

"What good would it have done, when that monkey-man cut the rope?"

"If you'd taken a swing at him, he'd have been too busy for rope-chopping. I hope you don't mind eating cold food and sleeping under the stars for the next few days. Not to mention losing the stuff I packed to turn us into Krishnans."

Marot sighed. "All right, I was wrong. Now are you happy? As for cold food, I have put up with hardships in the field before. At least, I still have my longevity capsules."

The longevity capsules or "LPs" to which Marot referred were universally used by human beings to retard aging. By consistently taking them from early adulthood on, the human life span could be approximately tripled. Hence, while Reith had lived the equivalent of more than forty Terran years, in appearance and physical condition he was not over thirty. Marot continued:

"Why do the tailed ones attack us without provocation?"

"Because the tailless Krishnans raid them for slaves, so to them the only good tailless person is a dead one."

"We can replace our lost equipment in Mishé, no?"

"I hope so," said Reith. "It'll help that I'm on good terms with the Knights of Qarar. They want me to bring my next gaggle of tourists there, so the Republic of Mikardand can tax their shopkeepers' profits. But getting more gear will take time."

Hours later, Reith pointed. "There's some high ground for our camp. It'll keep us out of the swamp and away from the leeches."

They led their ayas to the hillock, pushing through dense, fernlike green-and-scarlet vegetation, and tethered their mounts. Reith gathered sticks and started a fire with his wooden piston firelighter. Marot said:

"I should think that the authorities would at least let us bring matches. This seems like carrying the technological blockade to absurdity. That Scottish engineer who gave us copies of his maps—what was his name? Strashan?"

"Kenneth Strachan." Reith rhymed the surname with the city of Aachen. "Some say Stracken; some say Strawn; but

Ken, who's a kind of professional Scotsman, gives it the full guttural. What about him?"

"He lectured me on the iniquity of the technological blockade. He would like to abolish it."

"I know. To his way of thinking, if the Krishnans develop nuclear bombs and blow up their planet, that's their worry. But the official line is stricter than ever since the Gorchakov scandal."

"Was that the case of the paranoid security officer who got a female missionary drunk and, when she woke up, told her she was his wife? And pursued her when she fled to that nature cult on an island?"

"Yes. What really shook up the system was not so much their personal conflict as the fact that Gorchakov took a gun with him. That's the worst possible violation of Interplanetary Council rules."

"How did it come out? My informants seemed secretive about it."

"No wonder, since that's Novorecife's biggest black eye. Two other Earthmen fled with the girl. When Gorchakov caught up with them and one of the Terrans tried to protect her, Gorchakov killed him. Then one of the locals killed Gorchakov."

"What became of the missionary?"

"She married the local."

"Is that legal?" asked Marot.

"Depends on where you are. Now help me find some more dry wood. We'll need a pile of it before morning."

As darkness fell, they sat across the fire from each other, slapping at flying pests and trying to heat their emergency rations by toasting them on sharpened sticks. Luminous winged arthropods, scarlet specks like animated sparks, wove looping patterns against the dark. When a real spark flew up, several arthropods would swoop upon it in a futile attempt to mate. Marot said:

"Mr. Reith—"

"Call me Fergus," Reith interrupted.

"Hokay, then call me Aristide, if you please."

"Fine, Aristide. Isn't that the name of some ancient Greek politician, who was exiled for always being right?"

Marot chuckled. "Something like that. Actually, me, I was

named for a Saint Aristide, because I was born on the thirty-first of August. The saint, I suppose, was named for this ancient Aristides. How do you know about such things?"

"I taught school before I got into the travel business and became a tour guide. But you were about to ask something."

"Yes; what was it? Ah, I remember. How much delay will the loss of our equipment cause?"

Reith shrugged, "Maybe ten or fifteen days. I'll try to expedite things; but it'll still take more time than if we had gone the longer, safer route."

"All right; you need not rub it on."

"I think you mean rub it in," said Reith.

"In any case, I hope you can try to catch up our lost time. I do not wish Foltz to get any more of a start on us."

"So that's why you insisted on the route through the swamp, to save a couple of days! What's between you and Foltz? Aren't you both scientists, devoted to the truth regardless of petty personal feelings?"

"Hah! Whoever told you that the scientists were godlike thinking machines, free of normal human failings and prejudices? If someone did, my friend, he misinformed you."

"Well," said Reith, "who is this Foltz? I haven't met him."

"Warren Foltz—a countryman of yours—calls himself a scientist, and he has the degrees and experience. But he has the temperament of a fanatic, which does not mix with the science. He has an unorthodox theory, which he is determined to prove no matter what—would you say skull dodgery?—he has to commit."

"I think you mean skullduggery."

"Hokay, skullduggery. Oh, that villainous *queux!*" Marot clenched a fist. Reith was surprised to see that mention of Foltz actually enraged his usually good-natured companion.

"What's his nutty theory?"

"It was not nutty when Krishnan biology was new to Terrans. Then it was plausible. But, since then, the weight of evidence has accumulated against it."

"But what *is* it?" Reith persisted.

"It is a matter of the descent of the two main classes of Krishnan terrestrial vertebrates, the oviparous Tetrapoda and the viviparous Hexapoda, with four limbs and six limbs respectively. Most of my colleagues and I now believe that they evolved separately from aquatic predecessors, dwelling in different land-locked seas on this planet. But Foltz is determined that the Tetrapoda are merely an offshoot of terrestrial Hexapoda, who have lost one pair of limbs."

"In other words, it's a question of whether the four-leggers branched off from the main stem before or after they crawled out of the water?"

"That is an oversimplification, but you have stated the general idea."

"Seems like a funny thing to get fanatical about. I can imagine getting all hot over a political cause, or a personal relationship, or even a work of art; but not over something that happened a hundred million years ago."

Marot spread his hands with a wry smile. "You do not know some of my fellow scientists, especially those who go to other planets for field work. For that you must—how do you say— go for bust?"

"Go for broke."

"Yes, yes; for broke. It is a lifetime commitment in a way. You get on a spaceship and spend perhaps a year in transit and in the field, and when you return you find that a quarter or half of a century has elapsed, because of the Fitzgerald contraction. If the human life span had not been tripled by longevity medicine, nobody would undertake a round trip to an extrasolar planet."

"How far ahead of us is this Foltz character?"

"They told me at Novo that he left ten days before we did. Were you not there when he was at Novorecife?"

"No; I was running a tour, mostly Arabs and other Middle Easterners."

Marot said: "They told me at Novorecife that you had had adventures on your tours to lift the hair."

"I've had some. On my first tour, everything that could go wrong did, including the kidnapping of my whole tour group. We were lucky to get out alive. The second time, when I had a party of oh-so-polite East Asians, everything went as smooth as silk. The third tour would have gone well except that I had certain—umm—personal difficulties."

"Oh? I have heard rumors of that."

"Yeah. That was the tour that started the breakup with my wife."

"Oh. I am most sorry, Fergus. I did not mean to intrude on painful matters."

"That's okay. I've put it all behind me."

"Was your wife that Krishnan princess they say you married in Dur?"

"No; that was annulled long ago on grounds of coercion."

"You mean you were compelled?"

Reith grinned. "Yes, sir! The Regent of Dur caught us *in flagrante delicto,* and I had the choice of marrying this Krishnan squid or being carved into small pieces, a piece at a time. Nice kid, but no brains. The Regent staged the whole thing, knowing that Vázni and I couldn't produce an egg to hatch and grow up to take Tashian's power away, as a legitimate prince would have done. After a few moons of this world's most exquisite boredom, I escaped."

"Is the—ah—the *poum-poum* with Krishnans pleasurable?"

"Just as much fun as with Terrans, although there are differences in the way they function. They're the only extraterrestrial species you can say that about."

"An amazing example of convergent evolution!"

"Oh, sure! But then, Krishna's the most Earthlike planet we know of; so we shouldn't be surprised to find some pretty Earthlike organisms. But the fact that Earthmen can mate with Krishnan females doesn't mean they're entitled to unlimited free pussy."

"Kitten? Oh, I see. You mean the *foutre.*"

"Krishnan sexual customs vary at least as widely as ours. One of these jaspers hears of a place where the women of the house bed down with male guests as a matter of normal hospitality. So he jumps into an occupied bed in some place where the customs are different, and *khlk!*" Reith drew a finger across his throat.

"I will be most cautious in making advances. But this other wife of whom you spoke, if you do not mind?"

"That's Alicia Dyckman, the xenanthropologist—or xenologist as most people call it." Reith shook his head sadly. "She's the prettiest thing I know of as well as the most brilliant and charming. I first met her the day she got back with Percy Mjipa from the Khaldoni countries, where they'd had hairraising adventures. It was one of those instantaneous things; we practically fell into each other's arms. The first moon of our marriage was wonderful.

"But she insisted on going along on my third tour. Then she interfered with all my arrangements and tried to take over the tour direction. On a thing like that, you can't have two leaders; but that's my little Lish."

"You do not approve of executive women?"

"That's not it at all! I've worked for women bosses and never had trouble. But when I'm in charge, I won't put up with anyone's taking over my job so long as I'm conscious and able-bodied. I don't care if it's a he, a she, or an it. Poor Lish can no more help taking over and setting everyone right than Comandante Glumelin could help his drinking before he took the treatment. It's sad; she's such a marvelous person in other ways. But living with her is like taking a bath in lava."

Marot mused: "They say the new Moritzian therapy can abate self-destructive personality traits, given the time and the money."

"Maybe so; but we've got nothing like that out here in the *matagais*."

"What has become of the lady?"

"On my fourth tour, I flatly refused to let her come along; and when I got back to Novo, she'd flown the coop. I haven't seen her since. She wasn't around Novo when I got back from my last tour, and somebody hinted she'd gone off to shack up with some guy. They wouldn't tell me more; I suppose they were afraid I'd go after him with a sword."

"Would you have?"

Reith shook his head. "Nope. What my ex does is her business."

"I heard a rumor that Foltz had left Novorecife with a woman. Could this have been your former wife?"

"I don't know." Feeling a painful tension rising within, Reith changed the subject. "How about you, Aristide? What's your situation?"

"I am in something of your predicament, my friend. My dear wife decided that she preferred to go off with a younger man, to 'find herself,' whatever that means. I generally know where I am and so have no need to find myself. This fellow was what you would call a drifter, with vague artistic pretensions and an invincible aversion to the work. I could not see his attraction; but I suppose to some, fossil-hunting seems dull, and my little Marcelline said she wanted more adventure and excitement in her life. So off she went, and I have heard nothing since."

"People who go to extra-solar planets, like this one," said

Reith, "rarely have close ties on Terra, because of the Rip van Winkle effect."

"Yes indeed," said Marot somberly. "Things being what they were with me, I had few qualms about cutting my Terran ties." He yawned. "My friend, I am worn out and sore in the *fesse.*"

"Okay, we'll turn in. But we must post watches. The Koloftuma don't move about much at night, but we might get a *shan* or a *yeki.* The best defense is a good, bright fire." Reith paused, listening to the symphony of buzzes, clicks, chirps, trills, and squeals of nocturnal Krishnan life. "Now get that sword out, old boy, and keep it within easy reach!"

Marot fumbled in his gear, saying: "Fortunately the weapon was packed on this aya. I am not used to going armed, since I have worked in several *soi-disant* wild parts of Terra without difficulty. When I went to Texas to dig in the Permian beds there, my friends warned me that Texans were a fierce and dangerous lot. If a Texan disliked my appearance or accent, I was told, he would cry: 'Draw!' and whip out a pistol; and *pan!* one paleontologist the fewer. But I had no trouble; in fact I found the Texans polite and hospitable. Who has been in Chilihagh to report on conditions?"

"Strachan and his partner Lund surveyed the Dashtate of Chilihagh after their work on the railroad in Dur. They had to do it by simple plane-table methods, since Novo wouldn't let them carry proper transits, let alone modern wave-pulse stadiometers."

"I did not meet Mr. Lund."

"He's up in Ruz but expected back shortly," said Reith. "The partnership busted up."

"How?"

"Over a woman. Both made a play for Kristina Brunius, the secretary."

"The tall blonde, is it not?"

"Yes. She picked Sigvard Lund, because he was the only one around she could talk Swedish with. So Siggy and Kristina were married, and we danced Swedish folk dances around them. Strachan went off in a snit on a contract with the Republic of Katai-Jhogorai, so the partnership remained dead. It's silly, because Ken's probably dipped his wick with more females of both species than any other Terran on this planet."

"But what about Chilihagh?" persisted Marot.

"The only other Terran I know of who's been there lately was the writer, Esteban Surkov. At least, that's where he was headed the last we heard of him."

"That is a peculiar name."

"He's a South American—forget which country—of Russian ancestry. He went off to Chilihagh to get material for a book, and then—silence."

"Do you mean he has disappeared?" asked Marot.

"As far as Novo knows, he has. We may never learn what happened to him. I promised Castanhoso to inquire around."

"Are such disappearances frequent?"

"Not unusual. People go off and vanish. Once in a while Novo hears that so-and-so was eaten by a yekí, or was drowned crossing a river, or is the chief of a backward tribe, or has been beheaded for violating some religious tabu."

"Does Novorecife do nothing to protect its people?"

"They make treaties with the nearer states and try to persuade the others to use Terrans kindly. But the Interplanetary Council forbids anything smacking of imperialism, so in the end all Novo can do is to tell the Terran that the place he means to go to is dangerous. If he goes there, he'll be on his own."

"What species of person was this Surkov?"

Reith shrugged in the darkness. "Nothing special; just a little dark guy. He seemed a bit starry-eyed—you know, impractical and absent-minded. Those qualities don't make one a good insurance risk here." Reith yawned. "Okay, do you want first watch?"

"You get some sleep, please. All this talk has awakened me again. Do you mind if I play this for a little?" He held up a flute.

"No; go ahead. It'll put me to sleep."

"Good!" Marot settled himself and tweetled a melancholy air.

Dawn was paling the greenish Krishnan sky when Reith, on watch, abruptly sat up. His ears had caught a faint sound that was not that of the smaller Krishnan wild life. He leaned over and shook Marot.

"Wake up, Aristide!" he whispered. "I think I hear Koloftuma on the causeway."

"Hein? Que diable. . . . Oh, it is you, Fergus. What—"

"Quiet! Our tailed friends must have marched all night to catch up with us. Listen!"

A susurration of guttural voices grew. Then Reith's ears caught the slap of bare feet on the causeway.

"What shall we do?" breathed Marot.

"Keep quiet and hope the ayas don't give us away."

"I thought they did not travel at night—"

"So did I; but I must have been wrong. Now move very slowly to where we can see the road. Keep behind me!"

They crept to the flank of the hillock. Presently a score of Koloftuma came in sight, muttering and chattering. They were armed in the same fashion as yesterday's group, but Reith could not be sure whether they were indeed the same. When sighted, they were already abreast of the hill.

"Damn!" whispered Reith. "Now they're between us and our destination, and in this muck we can't circle round and get ahead of them."

"Why did we not get on the road sooner?"

"Because I'm stupid. Hey, look at that!"

He pointed to Marot's left leg. A leech had inserted its head through one of the eyelets in Marot's boot and gnawed through tongue and sock to reach flesh. It was now engorged to the size of a tennis ball and purple from the blood beneath its tightly-stretched skin.

"Pouah!" said Marot, reaching for the parasite.

"Don't pull it off," said Reith. "Wait here."

Moving silently, Reith returned to the nearly dead campfire. He found a stick whose end could still be blown to redness and went back to Marot, who sat staring disgustedly at the leech. A touch of the glowing end caused the creature to drop off, and Marot stamped it into bloody slime.

The Koloftuma passed out of sight, although their voices could still be heard. Reith said: "The best thing I can think of is to get out on the road and ride straight at them, waving our swords and yelling like hell. My guess is we'll get through again."

"But suppose one of those sacred animals trips on a body and falls?"

"Not likely, with those six legs."

"But suppose—"

"Damn it, have you a better suggestion? Do you want to go back to Novo?"

"No, but—"

"All right, then. Saddle up!"

A quarter-hour later, the rearmost Koloftuma whirled about

at the clatter of hooves. At the sight of two screaming Terrans charging with bared blades, the tailed Krishnans leaped off the causeway and scattered with cries of dismay. The three ayas galloped through unscathed. This time the Koloftuma did not even try to pursue.

II.

THE CITADEL

Travel-stained, Reith and his companion rode into Mishé, a big sprawling city surrounded by a buff-gray wall. At the gateway, decorated with the heads of felons, stood a pair of men-at-arms in spired helmets and chain mail. Having examined the Earthmen's papers, they waved the travelers through.

"Where do we stay?" asked Marot.

"We'll stop at an inn I know to clean up. Later, I may be able to wangle us a berth in the Citadel."

Reith led the way to the inn, identified by the skull of a Krishnan beast above the doorway. Two hours later, bathed at the public bathhouse, shaved, and dressed in clean clothes, the Terrans ascended the sloping pavement to the Citadel. An impressive example of pre-gunpowder fortification, this mesalike acropolis crowned the city. The sides of the hill supporting it had been dug away to a nearly vertical slope and revetted with massive masonry.

Once inside the Citadel, Reith and Marot found themselves among huge, gray, graceless, rough-stone buildings. Here the Guardians—the Garma Qararuma, the knightly caste of Mikardand—lived well and pursued their duties. The gay hues of the knights' tunics and trews contrasted with the drab grays and browns of the commoners' garb. Numbers of these lesser folk went about their jobs in the Citadel, cleaning the streets and performing other humble tasks. They were clad in loose, short jackets, the women in skirts, the men in a triangular nether garment worn like an oversized diaper.

Women of the knightly caste went freely through the streets in bright, calf-length dresses, cut away in front below their blue-green nipples. One such lady, so clad but incongruously wearing a hat of obvious Terran inspiration, approached the travelers. She was pretty even by Terran standards, despite her flattish Krishnan features, her skin with its faint sheen of olive-green, and the pair of feathery antennae, which sprouted from the inner corners of her true eyebrows, over which they lay when in repose. In Mikardandou she said:

"Hail, fair sir! Are you not Master Reit', from Novorecife?"

"Yes," said Reith. "And you are the Lady—ah—Gashigi?"

"Aye; how good of you! And the other *Ertsu?*"

"The learned Doctor Marot." Reith switched to English. "Professor, this is the Lady Gashigi, an old friend."

"Enchanté, Madame!" said Marot, bowing low and kissing Gashigi's hand. She seemed a little startled but not at all displeased.

"He hath fair Terran manners," she said. "Doth he speak our tongue?"

"He is studying it," said Reith.

Gashigi proffered a cigar case to Reith, who said: "No, thank you. I don't smoke, remember?"

Gashigi offered the case to Marot, who accepted a cigar. The lady next produced a small device like a barrelless flintlock pistol. When she pulled the trigger, a hammer sent a shower of sparks into a recess filled with tinder. A flame blazed up, with which she lighted Marot's cigar and hers. Then she shook out the last embers, took a tinderbox from her reticule, and recharged the fire-lighter with tinder.

"Hey!" said Reith. "May I see that device, please?" He examined the lighter. "I haven't seen one of these before."

"One of our commoners invented it," said she. "He was elevated to the Knights of Qarar as a reward."

Reith handed back the lighter. "As pretty as ever, I see. Where did you get that hat?"

"This?" she smiled. "A milliner in town. Hath it a Terran look?"

"Yes. That's why I asked."

"Know you not that Terran fashions are now the rage? It makes the Grand Master furious. He issues sumptuary decrees, forbidding them to us Garmiya, saying 'tis a brazen insult to our ancient ways. But he shall learn with what success he can decree what a woman shall and shan't wear! We have no fewer rights than the female commoners, who wear whatsoever they list!"

"How have you been, Lady Gashigi?"

"I am now head of the savings section of the banking department, so I can vouchsafe sound advice in matters monetary. But interest in finance is not that wherefor I remember you, Fergus!" (She pronounced it "far-goose.") "Ah, how vividly I recall our one glorious night! Were't not for a certain difficulty, I'd invite you and your companion again to monstrate *Ertso* virility. Even so, belike a rendezvous could be arranged in the lower city."

"What's this difficulty?" asked Reith suspiciously.

"You see, Khabur waxed passing wroth. Since you're an off-worlder, he cannot challenge you to battle. Instead, he swears that, if ever he meet you, he'll cut off your nose, your ears, and the other projecting parts of your body."

"Thanks for the warning," said Reith. "Much as I should like to renew so well-remembered an acquaintance, we must go to the Treasurer's Office forthwith and then move on. If we pass through Mishé on our return journey—we shall see. For now, fare you well! Come, Aristide."

"What was that all about?" asked Marot.

Reith translated Gashigi's remarks, adding: "The knightly caste here practices a kind of communism, with property collectively owned. Moreover, they apply the principle to sex. Noble men and women couple with whomever they like. Eggs are hatched in a crèche and brought up by commoner nannies, so nobody knows who's related to whom. These females have the nearest thing to sexual equality on Krishna."

"It sounds," said Marot, "like Plato's *Republic* put to practice."

"I suppose so. They have informal 'relationships,' but it's bad form to take on a new partner before dismissing his or her predecessor. When that happens, the males fight duels, while the females slip daggers into their rivals' ribs or poison into their soup."

"Like our Terran Renaissance," said Marot. "Such arrangements have been tried on Earth with only indifferent success. On both planets, I suspect, many develop proprietary feelings towards their loved ones. They expect strict fidelity from them but demand complete freedom of action for themselves. So conflict is inevitable; and I take it you are involved in such?"

Reith nodded glumly. "Alicia had left a few moons before, and I was—well, you know what it's like. Gashigi assured me this Khabur blug wouldn't mind, since they were about to break up anyway. But things don't seem to have worked out that way."

"My friend—" Marot hesitated. "I would not dream of criticizing your conduct; but I should be happier if you did not take the lady down on her offer."

"I think you mean, take her up; though it makes a kind of sense the other way, too. Have you no curiosity? She included you."

"Absolutely not! I am not amorously adventurous. My one aim is to return to Novo with my fossils intact. Then, *nous verrons.*"

"I was only kidding. Something tells me we'll be better off in the lower city during our stay in Mishé. Khabur's only a so-so fencer, but he's strong as a shaihan."

Reith led Marot to the Treasury Building, where presently they were ushered into the office of the Treasurer of the Order of Qarar. Sir Kubanan proved a rarity, a fat Krishnan, who looked a little like a beardless Santa Claus. A large, golden, dragonlike emblem on the front of his crimson coat identified his lofty rank.

"Ah, Master Reit'!" said Kubanan in Mikardandou, waving his pungent cigar. "We have awaited your arrival with a score of Terran travelers, come hither to see our sights and buy our goods. Instead you appear with but one. Or are the others elsewhere at the moment?"

"No, good my lord," said Reith. "For now, I am guide to the learned Doctor Marot alone."

Kubanan puffed. "And what, may I ask, is the learned doctor a learned doctor of?"

"He studies forms of life that once roamed your world but no longer exist."

Kubanan's olfactory antennae drew together. "If they no longer exist, how then can he study them?"

Reith cleared his throat. "Doctor Marot digs up the bones of these long-vanished beasts."

"Interesting, albeit it strikes me not as a profitable business. We have some such bones in our little museum, if our visitor care to scrutinize them."

Reith translated for Marot. "A museum?" said Marot, becoming animated. *"Mais, c'est la civilisation, donc!* Pray tell Sir Kubanan that I shall be delighted."

Reith did, adding: "Tell me, did another Terran pass through Mishé a few days ago, bound for Chilihagh?"

"Methinks there was a report of such an one, buying supplies. Since he seemed harmless, we hindered him not. What canst tell me of this wight?"

"He is a scientist of the same kind as Doctor Marot. Had he others with him?"

"I wot not. Wherefore your interest in this—was his name Fost?"

"Foltz, my lord. My client and Foltz are colleagues and, in a sense, rivals."

"Well, I trust you to see that any conflict betwixt them shall be carried on beyond the bourne of the Republic."

"Sir," said Reith, "any combat between Foltz and Marot would be fought, not with swords or crossbows, but with the publication of learned essays, wherein each would accuse the other of inaccuracy and misuse of evidence."

"A tedious sort of combat," mused Kubanan. "One could hardly charge admission to witness it. Now that I bethink me, I recall another fact anent Master Felst. He came disguised as a human being, with dyed hair, false antennae, and in civilized raiment, as did all you *Ertsuma* until a few years ago. This seemed prudent, since Chilihagh is a wildish place, unused to Terrans. Would you, too, adopt this masquerade?"

"We meant to," said Reith, "but lost half our baggage to the Koloftuma. Does anyone here sell such cosmetics?"

"Nay, unless you could send to Majbur."

"Then we must trust our bare Terran faces. By the way, do you know anything about another *Ertsu*, Esteban Surkov, who also was bound for Chilihagh and has not been heard from?"

"Nought beyond the fact that he passed through Mishé some moons past. Your Comandante hath written the Grand Master to inquire, but we could add nought to what I have told you. And now, good my sirs. . . ."

* * *

"Let us see this museum before returning to our inn," said
Marot.

"We'd better get the hell out of the Citadel. We don't want
to run into Khabur," replied Reith.

"Oh, Fergus, I beg you! This to me is important."

Reith gave his companion a hard look. "Will you back me
up with your sword?"

Marot hesitated. "Yes, even that. I know the elementary
movements."

The museum occupied another boxlike building. Reith cast
a nervous glance around to assure himself that no jealous Knight
of Qarar lurked nearby.

Inside, they found a collection of curios: the helmet of some
long-fallen king; a model of a Majburo war galley; a badly-
stuffed *pudamef* from the boreal regions. This predator, like
its tropical cousin the shan, resembled a ten-meter, six-legged,
long-necked lizard, with a fanged crocodilian head. Unlike the
shan, the pudamef was covered with thick white fur. Marot
said:

"Were I stranded here, I should apply for the post of curator
in this museum. Nothing is in logical order, and the labels are
mostly missing or illegible."

At last they found the fossil to which Kubanan had alluded.
It consisted of several limb bones and a meter-long, chocolate-
brown skull. Marot crooned with delight as he examined it with
a pocket magnifying glass.

"I think this is one of the Ocnotheridae," he said, "but a
new genus. It is a plant-eating hexapod from a recent horizon.
I wonder if the Order of Qarar would sell this fossil, to take
back to Novorecife?"

"They're terrible people to do business with," said Reith.
"Under their communistic setup, you have to work through
endless interlocking committees to get a decision."

"How old is this system here?"

"I'm not sure, but at least several centuries."

"They appear to make it work not badly."

"Sure, because they ride on the backs of the commoners,
who do all the real work. The knights just supervise and skim
off the profits. The pretext is that the knights shouldn't stoop

to vulgar toil, because they stand ready to fight for the Republic."

"It sounds like the *ancien régime* in my country."

"Aristide, suppose you could buy these fossils, how would you get them back to Terra? The freight charges would be astronomical, in the figurative as well as the literal sense."

"Oh, I would not attempt to ship the whole thing. Back in Novo, I have a lovely little computer. This makes a record of each piece of fossil so accurately that, when I return to Earth, the computer can reproduce the fossil in a synthetic material to an accuracy of ten microns."

"But suppose we find a half-ton fossil of some monster in Chilihagh? How would you get that back to Novo?"

"If it is too heavy for the local wagons, we get a carpenter to build us a sled and have it hauled by those—what do you call those things like six-legged buffaloes?"

"Shaihans."

"But truly, we are unlikely to encounter such a problem. The organisms I seek are near the point of division between major groups. Such creatures are usually small, like mice and lizards."

"How do you ever find the fossil of such a little critter?"

"Practice, my friend. With experience, the searching eye seizes upon a fossil fragment no larger than the joint of your finger."

Marot made a fist and aimed the large ring on his middle finger at the fossil, slowly moving his hand. Reith knew that the gem on the ring was actually the lens of a Hayashi ring camera, and that Marot was running off a strip of miniaturized film.

"You disappoint me," said Reith. "I thought we'd find a skeleton the size of a Terran dinosaur and have to move ten tons of petrified bone."

"Ah, no! Such discoveries are rare. Besides, a complete skeleton is something one can expect only a few times in one's life. Now, what things must we buy in the city?"

"Mainly a tent and a set of cooking utensils. I also want one of those lighters, like Gashigi's. There's the answer to Strachan. The technological blockade will in time become obsolete, because the Krishnans are just as inventive as we are. Now that they've heard of the wonders of Terran technology, they won't rest until they've made most of the same discoveries independently.

"We'll also buy Krishnan clothes to make us less conspicuous. Let's not push our luck; let's get away right now!"

Neither the cooking utensils, which they bought ready-made, nor the tent, which they ordered from a tentmaker who promised it in three days, presented difficulties. At a clothier's, Marot grumbled as he held up one of the large triangles of heavy cloth, which formed the common male nether garment of the region. "I am no longer an infant, in need of a diaper. My natural functions are under excellent control. Is there no alternative?"

"Yes, there are these kilts. You can buy either the straight skirt kind or divided. The latter are the nearest thing they have to real pants here; they're better for riding. Ken Strachan wore a kilt like this one when he was courting Kristina. He marched back and forth beneath her window playing his bagpipes."

"I am not surprised that she chose the other suitor," said Marot.

The divided kilt was a pair of voluminous trousers, coming to just above the knee, low in the crotch and multiply-pleated.

"Looks good on you," said Reith, belting on his own selection, like Marot's a sober dark blue. "When we get farther south, we'll find them wearing oblongs of gauze or nothing at all."

They collected their three ayas from the stable at which they were boarded and took them out into the country for exercise. Returning from their ride, they paused at the livestock market outside the city walls. Reith ordered their three animals washed and rubbed down while he shopped for a fourth aya to replace the lost one. Having dismounted and handed his reins to a groom, he said to Marot:

"I'm not an old aya-trader, but I know a good beast from a bad one. I've dealt with these yucks. They'll think: aha, here come the rich, stupid Terrans! Now we can make a killing!" He turned to the stablemaster and switched from English to Mikardandou, explaining that he wanted to buy an aya. "It will be mainly used as a pack animal, so no fancy hunter or racer is needed. On the other hand, we want one that can be ridden, in case something befall one of our present beasts."

"Methinks we have just what ye need," said the boss. Making a trumpet of his hands, he shouted: "Pustá! Hither, pray!"

Soon a Krishnan groom appeared at a run, leading an aya by the bridle. As the animal trotted past, Reith said to Marot: "If they had crows on Krishna, we'd call that critter crow-bait. When ayas get swaybacked, they do it twice: once forward of the middle legs and once aft." To the stablemaster he said: "How much demand you for this beast?"

"For a gallant Terran like yourself, I'll make a special price of three hundred karda."

"Ha!" said Reith. "For that sorry bag of bones, thirty were too much. At three, I could at least slay the animal and sell its hide at a profit."

"Sir, ye are offensive! If ye be not lief to do business with us, take your custom elsewhere."

"Very well. Come along, Aristide."

"Are you really going to walk out?" murmured the paleontologist.

"Hush! You'll see."

As they neared the gate of the corral, the stablemaster caught up with them. "Depart not so hastily, gentlemen! With a modicum of patience, belike we can find a beast to fit both your crotch and your purse, eh? Come back, I do pray."

Reith let himself be cajoled into returning. More ayas were paraded, more prices bandied. At last Reith cast a receptive eye on a medium-sized roan. "Let us have another look at that one," he said.

As he approached the aya, the animal rolled its eyes, pricked its ears, snorted, and reared its fore-pair of legs off the ground. Reith tried to speak soothingly to it. But the more he tried, the more frantic became the aya's behavior, until he had to jump back lest he be hooked by a horn.

The stablemaster said: "Belike he's unused to the Terran stench—pardon, sir, I meant the distinctive Terran odor. 'Twill pass with usage."

Marot had wandered up behind Reith and, as Reith retreated, strode nearer the frantic animal. The aya became calmer and settled down on all six legs, although it still rolled a wary eye. In broken Mikardandou, Marot said:

"If you put saddle on, I will ride try."

"Hey!" said Reith. "You may get yourself killed!"

"But, as you see, he tolerates me much more than you. I

do not think it is the smell, but your red hair; unlike Terran ungulates, these beasts have the color vision. One of us must prove him ridable; if I am killed, your fee is on deposit at Novo."

"But—but—" sputtered Reith, unable to think of a cogent argument. He had become fond of Aristide Marot and was upset at the thought of losing the amiable scientist.

In a few minutes, the aya was brought back saddled. Marot took a firm grip on the saddle, got a foot in the nigh stirrup, and swung aboard. The aya stood quietly the while, its head and ears drooping. Then the corral gate opened and two Mi-kardanduma, who had been out hacking, rode their ayas in.

As a groom prepared to close the gate, Marot's aya raised its head. Almost unseating its rider, it started with a bound and raced towards the still-ajar gate. The groom had barely time to look around when the beast was upon him. He sprang aside, but the aya's shoulder sent him rolling as the animal thundered through the opening, Marot clutching the saddle.

Shouts of "Stop them!" arose. The runaway aya disappeared in a cloud of dust before the first pursuer could set out.

Reith's three ayas had been led away for their wash. Of the two hackers who had just brought their animals in, one had dismounted from his fat spotted gray. Reith made a running leap and vaulted into the vacated saddle. The hacker still held the reins.

"Give me those reins!" yelled Reith.

"Give them not!" shouted a trader. "These filthy foreigners would rob us!"

Stable hands and aya-owners began streaming out the gate as their beasts were saddled. Reith leaned forward, got a hand on the reins, and wrenched them out of the grasp of the be-wildered hacker. He turned the gray and headed out the gate with the rest. As he neared the main road, a pair of knights in jingling mail galloped past, waving swords and shouting: "Stop thief!"

Reith had a vision of his companion, mistaken for a mis-creant, being carved into gobbets before anyone could explain. He spurred his aya. But the gray was a placid beast, which merely stepped up its canter a little and soon dropped back to a rocking-horse gait. Other pursuers raced past.

After several minutes, this onrush slowed as a tableau blocked the road ahead. When Reith maneuvered his aya through the throng, he found Marot sitting amid a low, spreading bush, which he had smashed in his fall. A trickle of blood ran down his face. The two knights, dismounted, stood above him with naked blades. Others of the posse—grooms, traders, hackers, and chance passers-by—stood about, mounted or afoot, gabbling and gesticulating, indulging the Krishnan proclivity for oratory to the full.

Marot looked up. "I have essayed to explain," he said, "but between their excitement and my poor command of the language. . . ."

Raising his voice, Reith told the Krishnans that Marot had merely been the victim of a runaway. Another rider appeared, leading the truant roan.

"I caught it beyond yon hill," said he. The crowd murmured approval.

"These Terrans seem honest folk," said the stablemaster. "Let us return to the market."

"Are you hurt, Aristide?" asked Reith.

"A little bruised, that is all. When I saw that I could not guide this sacred beast, I looked for the softest spot to fall into."

"Why couldn't you stop it? Lose your reins?"

"No. I could have halted it, I am sure; but when it heard a thunder of hooves behind it, the creature ran faster than ever, regardless of how I pulled and sawed. How to get back to Mishé? I do not wish to try that devil aya again."

"The brute looks good, but he must be crazy. I'll have you boosted up behind me."

Reith asked the spectators for a hand, and a pair of brawny peasants lifted Marot into place. When they returned to the market, Reith asked the stablemaster:

"How much do you want for this nag we've been riding? She seems to suit us."

"Two hundred and fifty, sir."

"Don't be ridiculous! I'll give seventy-five. . . ."

An hour later, the price was set at a hundred and thirty.

Wearing new Krishnan garments, the two set out on the five-day journey to Jeshang. The early part of the ride passed uneventfully save for a rainstorm. They rode through the gently-rolling farmlands of southern Mikardand, along the fine road maintained by the Knights. Traffic was heavy. At the first inn, Marot asked:

"What lies before us?"

"In three days we should cross into Chilihagh, ruled by a dasht, Kharob bad-Kavir. He's quasi-independent both of Mikardand and of Balhib, and he keeps this independence by playing each off against the other. Each has some vague claim to sovranty over the dashtate. But Mikardand had been too preoccupied by internal struggles to press its claim, while King Kir of Balhib thinks he's a flowerpot; so nobody takes him seriously."

At the border, the Chilihagho soldiers, in chain-mail vests over blue tunics, snapped to attention. One looked over the travelers' papers and said: "I understand this not."

"It might help if you held it right side up," said Reith.

The soldier glowered: "Wait here." He disappeared into a hut and emerged with an officer sporting a silvered cuirass. The two conversed earnestly, in a dialect that Reith had trouble following. The officer studied the Terrans and said:

"Aye, these must be the twain whereof we were warned. Seize them!"

Before either Reith or Marot could act, soldiers grabbed their arms and relieved them of their weapons.

Reith raised his voice: "What is this? We are harmless travelers. . . ."

"A brace of Balhibo spies, more like," growled the officer. "Ye think to befool us by having your smelling-antennae amputated and your hides and hair dyed to look like Terrans? How simple ye must deem us!"

"We are as Terran as you are Krishnan!" said Reith. "We have no scars from that amputation. We are well-known at Novorecife. We speak Terran tongues—Portugese, French. . . ."

"All that can be faked," said the officer. "We have a short way with spies, sent by the mad King Kir to subvert our holy land. Which prefer ye, hanging or beheading?"

"What—what—" stammered Marot. "Are they indeed about to kill us?"

"Shut up!" snapped Reith. "I'm thinking. What external difference between men and Krishnans can't be faked?"

Marot frowned. "Since they are oviparous, like the other Tetrapoda, they have no navels."

"Good! Captain, if you will enter the hut with us, we can demonstrate our Earthly nature to your satisfaction."

"Think not to cozen me with sweet talk! But come on; the regulations give you the right."

In the hut, Reith and Marot bared their bellies. "Behold!" said Reith. "Here's proof of being born alive from Terran females."

The captain peered. "Those little hollows could be made by surgery. Now, would ye liefer be hanged—"

"Curse it, listen!" shouted Reith. "You know, the sexual organs of male Terrans differ from those of males of your kind. Drop your pants, Aristide!"

The captain peered again. "Ugh! what great, repulsive. . . . But meseems ye speak sooth. Resume your garments, *Ertsuma*. Now get ye hence, and the quicker the better!"

They rode off, leaving the captain fuming as if he wished he could find some other charge against them. Marot said:

"We have worried because we lost the means of disguising ourselves as Krishnans; and here we are suspected of being Krishnans disguised as Terrans! I wonder who warned that officer to watch for us? Could it be my esteemed colleague Warren Foltz?"

"Hmm—maybe you've got something. Perhaps Foltz put in a bad word for us with Baron Kharob's flunkeys. No, hold on! If he's ahead of us, how could he know we're following him? He'd left Novo before you arrived and hired me as guide."

"I made a reservation on the *Amazonas* well in advance, before Foltz left Terra. He could have learned that I should arrive soon after him. From what he knows of my work, he could have guessed that I would seek the fossil beds of Chilihagh."

"Well, you'd better sharpen that sword of yours. This guy seems to be playing for keeps."

"I do not doubt that he hoped to have us killed at the border," said Marot. "Foltz is a man with a cause, one of those who consider all rules suspended when they act on behalf of their cause."

As they wended southward, the travelers saw the everyday costume for both men and women become a simple wrap-around kilt, of thin material since this was summer. The upper body was covered, if at all, by a simple oblong of cloth, casually pinned over one shoulder.

Kharob bad-Kavir, Dasht of Chilihagh, proved a cadaverous Krishnan, clad in rusty black. When Reith explained their mission and requested a digging permit, a worried-looking Kharob said:

"Alas, good my sirs, you come too late. Your predecessor, Master Foltus—Follets—the other Terran hath obtained from me, a ten-night past, exclusive permission to excavate what he calls the Zorian beds of this realm. He gave solemn assurance that nought he should uncover would in any wise cast doubt upon the truth of our reformed religion."

"Deign to tell us about this religion, Your Altitude," said Reith. "Word of it has not yet reached Novorecife."

"It hath been the True Faith here for a score of years. 'Tis the worship of Bákh, whom we know to be the only God, as proclaimed by the *Book of Bákh,* given by an angel in person to our High Priestess."

"Where does that leave the other Varasto deities, my lord?"

"There is a debate in the temple whether they be angels, or demons, or even mere figments. Some maintain that they be the creations of crafty priests to cozen the simple, or magnified memories of heroes of yore. Bákh hath promised our High Priestess further revelations—so she saith—to clarify these details. To receive this authentic doctrine, she hath gone to her summer retreat in the hills.

"I strive to serve justice and to remain friends with Novorecife. So it grieves me to reject your petition. But I have given my word and seal."

"How could Foltz's work affect your religion, my lord?"

The Dasht explained: "Our High Priestess, the holy Lazdai, would fain have straitly examined Master Foltus to make sure that nought he found could cast doubt upon the manner of Bákh's creation of the world, but that she was away when he passed through here. Ere I extended permission to go digging, she would likewise examine you, were she in residence.

"Be not downcast, good my sirs. Jeshang, albeit smaller than Mishé, hath its share of sights and entertainment. Tarry a few days, I pray, ere returning northward. But promulgate no heretical opinions! Her Holiness hath been energetic in the extirpation of heresy."

* * *

"For all Kharob's boosterism," growled Reith, "this looks like the dullest little jerkwater town on Krishna. What now?"

"I am thinking, my friend," said Marot. "Did he not say he had given Foltz exclusive permission to dig in the *Zorian* beds?"

"He sure did. Please explain what the Zorian beds are."

"Do you know the work of the geologist Yamanuchi?"

"I've heard of him, but that was long before I came to Krishna—at least half a century ago."

"The lapse of time is inevitable, because of the years it took him to come here, to do his work, to return to Terra, and to publish his reports. *Alors,* Yamanuchi made a preliminary survey of the geological formations of the area west of the Sadabao Sea. He blocked out a rough chronology of these beds and named a series of periods after the places in which he found them exposed. One period he called the Zorian, after a ranch in the watershed of the upper Zora River, which joins the Zigros here at Jeshang."

Reith asked: "Did Yamanuchi collect any fossils?"

"No, although his report said that in the Zora region he saw fossils lying on the surface. He traveled alone, light, and fast. He wore complete Krishnan makeup, as did all Terrans working on Krishna then. Being Japanese, he found it easier to play the native than we big-nosed Westerners ever could. I assume that Foltz has read Yamanuchi's report."

Reith mused: "Paleontology's not my line; but it seems to me you fellows often disagree as to how the geological past should be divided up."

"But yes! Centuries ago, the Americans divided the old Carboniferous into the Pennsylvanian and the Mississippian, but some European geologists still cling to the old nomenclature."

"Well, why couldn't we claim something of the sort with the Krishnan—"

"My friend, you are a genius!" Marot did a little dance step. "Let us go back to that *taudis* of an inn, so that I can go over my papers!"

In their room, Marot spread sketches and diagrams across the floor. "Here," he said, "is a copy of Yamanuchi's sketch of the Zora beds. The strata of the Zorian period dip to the north and disappear beneath those of a much later perod. Here is the Zora River, on some maps called the South Branch of the Zigros.

"Now, if we divide the Zorian exposure into halves, the lower and older would extend from here to the river—unless the normal sequence has been reversed by an overfold or an overthrust fault. In that case, *nous sommes foutus*. Anyway, I suspect that critical fossils will be found in the lower Zorian, which from an evolutionary point of view somewhat corresponds to our Devonian. What shall we name our new period, the *ci-devant* Lower Zorian?"

Reith said: "Why not call it the Kharobian, after the Dasht? Otherwise, even if he lets us in to dig, he might make us wait around for the High Priestess to get back, to put us through a theological wringer."

"Magnificent! Flattery conquers all. Today I shall plan my argument, and we will see the Dasht again tomorrow. By the way," said Marot pensively, "as a youth I saw a cinema with a title similar to that of this ranch to which we are going. It was, I think, 'The Mark of Zora,' about a noble swordsman in California, centuries ago, who went about in disguise, carving his initials on the persons of evildoers."

Reith laughed. "That was 'The Mark of Zoro,' not 'Zora.' 'Zorro' is Spanish for 'fox.' You must have seen the thirtieth remake of that old movie. I saw it, too, back in my school-teaching days."

Marot mused: "As a child I once phantasized about that kind of buckle-swashing. But you would make a better Zorro than I."

Reith shrugged. "Not me! I've been forced into a couple of sword fights on Krishna, and I've managed to avoid being killed. I much prefer to avoid all shedding of blood, especially my own."

When Marot, in halting but adequate Mikardandou, had made his presentation, Dasht Kharob gave the Krishnan equivalent of a smile. "I am gratified by the proposal of you gentlemen from afar," he said. "To have my name preserved in your learned books as that of a whole bygone era! But stay! The True Faith of Bákh avers that Bákh created the universe in three days. Yet you imply that these rocks were formed over many centuries, or ever human history began. How reconcile you this divergence?"

Marot: "My lord, if Bákh be omnipotent, then cannot he

make each day as long as he pleases? Equal to hundreds, thousands, or even millions of years?"

Kharob frowned. "I am no theologian. Were Her Holiness here, she would doubtless have somewhat to say on the subject; but I find this talk of millions of years a thing to fuddle the brain. By the way, Bákh is here preferably alluded to as 'it,' being sexless."

"I beg Your Altitude's pardon," said Marot. "I will try to remember."

"Now then," said the Dasht, "I take it you wish a permit, like unto that of Master Foltus, giving you the exclusive right to dig in the Kharobian beds of Chilihagh?"

"Yes, my lord," said Reith and Marot together.

"Very well, Master Ráu!" The Dasht spoke to his secretary. "Prepare a permit of the sort described. Gentlemen, if you call upon the morrow, your permit will await you. And now—"

"My lord!" said Reith.

"Aye?"

"Have you heard anything of another Terran, named Surkov, who may have passed through Jeshang before Foltz? A writer by trade?"

"Yea, I recall the wight," said Kharob. "He was bound for the same lieu whither you and your companion are headed. But his motive differed. He spake of how, on Terra, there was once a race called kaoboz, or perhaps kaboiz, who lived by rearing and selling beasts like unto shaihans. Although the true kaoboz no longer rode their plains, herding their kaoz when not slaying one another in feuds, they left behind a rich folklore. Surkov wished to find a place on this world where such a culture still existed, so we sent him to Zora. Beyond that, I know nought."

The next day, Reith and Marot picked up their permit, stamped with the seal of the Dashtate. Kharob said: "Understand, gentlemen, this merely extends *my* permission. I cannot command the local landowners to let you trespass on their demesnes. You must make your own arrangements with them."

"Who owns the land around Kubyab?" asked Reith.

"The owner of the largest ranch, Zora, is Sainian bad-Jeb. Knowing you have my favor, I think not that he'll make difficulties. For the others, you can inquire at the tax office or in Kubyab."

Leaving the palace, Reith and Marot decided to wait till they got to Kubyab, the village nearest the fossiliferous beds, before hiring any help. "This Dasht," said Reith, "seems a well-meaning sort but under the thumb of his High Priestess. It was smart of you, about those millions of years equal to a day."

"Thank you, my old one. I was brought up a Catholic, so I can still split a theological hair or two. I do not doubt that this High Priestess has heard of the progress that the Terran religions, especially the Christians and Muslims, are making on Krishna. So she decided to—how do you say—take a leaf from their tree?"

"Take a leaf from their book."

"Ah, yes. So she whipped up her own monotheistic theology and a sacred book full of recondite doctrine. Thus she has elevated Bákh from a mere Krishnan Jupiter or Odin to Sole God. The next step may be the wars of religion. I do not care to be caught in one of those."

"But say," said Reith, "won't Foltz raise holy hell when he learns you've broken his monopoly by a verbal sleight-of-hand?"

Marot shrugged. "Doubtless he will. But I hope by then to have finished my digging and be enroute to Novo with my fossils. So let us get an early start tomorrow!"

III.

THE RANCH

A faint orange of dawn appeared through the cracks in the shutters as Reith and Marot began packing for their journey. Then came a timid knock on their bedroom door. As Marot started for the door, Reith held up a cautioning hand.

"Hold it!" he whispered. "On this world, you don't fling open a door to just anybody."

Drawing his dagger halfway, Reith shot back the bolt and pulled the door open a crack. Outside stood a small Krishnan wearing priestly garments.

"Master Reese?" said this one in a stage whisper. "Let me in, pray! I am in peril dire."

The Krishnan appeared unarmed; but then, his voluminous clerical habit of gray kilt and high-buttoned jacket could easily hide a dagger. Reith said over his shoulder in English: "Get your sword, Aristide, just in case." He turned back. "All right, come in. Who are you?"

The little Krishnan ducked a bow. "Nirm bad-O'lán, a humble servant of Yesht."

"Who is Yesht?" asked Marot.

"The old Varasto god of the underworld," Reith replied. Turning back to the priest, he asked: "Are you, then, a priest of Yesht?"

"Aye, my lord. That's wherefore I am in peril."

"Explain, pray."

"Sir, since the High Priestess Lazdai came to power, the Bákhites have striven to suppress all rival cults and to force their creed upon all Chilihaghuma, on pain of cruel punishment. Now, on the pretext that we Yeshtites practice human sacrifice, she hath persuaded the Dasht to outlaw our holy cultus and declare forfeit the lives of its votaries."

"What do you want of us?" said Reith.

"I've heard that in some Terran lands, governments are forbidden to interfere with religion."

"Yes; that's the case in my native country. But why—?"

"Then, sir, I can count upon your sympathy, can I not? I must needs flee Jeshang. Learning that you twain are on the way to Kubyab, I bethought me that I might join you."

"In what capacity?" asked Reith.

"Oh, I can offer prayers for your safety and by divination warn you of bad luck and stormy weather."

"Does your cult in fact practice human sacrifice?"

"Nay! That is a vile falsehood," said Nirm indignantly. "Never would the god of justice countenance the shedding of innocent blood."

"We have heard of such rites at the Temple of Yesht in Zanid."

The priest raised his hands. "For aught I know, that may be sooth. The worship of Yesht in Balhib is independent of that in Chilihagh. We know little of their practices, for we and they are not on terms of friendship. Belike the Balhibuma have fallen into evil ways."

"If I understand him," said Marot in English, "this little Krishnan seems worthy of our sympathy. Could we not let him join us?"

The Yeshtite peered in anxious incomprehension from one Terran to the other. Reith said: "No, sir! Now that we're on the good side of the Dasht, it's our business to stay there. Besides, we don't even know if this lad is telling the truth. He might be a plant."

"A plant? He does not look like a vegetable—"

"I mean, he may have been sent, perhaps by the Dasht, perhaps by the Temple of Bákh, to see if we're playing a double game."

"Such suspicion! And you once called me paranoid because I accused Foltz of plotting to impede us."

"You may have been right about Foltz. It just means we must be wary of everybody: Foltz and this little fellow both. In several years on Krishna, I've had more narrow squeaks than I like to remember. So I don't take more chances than I can help." To the Krishnan, Reith said: "It grieves me, Father Nirm, but I fear we cannot accommodate you."

"Oh, good my lords, I beg you—"

"Leave off the begging, for it will do no good. For one thing, we shall work in the western part of the Dashtate, where the Bákhites could still lay hands upon you. When we're finished there, we shall return through Jeshang, where your enemies could seize you. I fear, my good Nirm, that you ask the impossible."

The Krishnan's shoulders drooped. "Ah, me! Then I may end up in Lazdai's Kettle after all."

"What's that?"

"The Cauldron of Repentance, it is called, wherein convicted heretics and unbelievers are boiled to death."

"Why don't you quietly quit the priesthood and take up some less risky trade?" suggested Reith.

"What, abandon my holy faith from motives of self-interest? That were base and cowardly! I may not be Qarar reincarnate, but I can face my doom with becoming dignity!"

The little Krishnan turned to leave, then froze as another knock, more emphatic, rattled the door. "'Tis the priests of Bákh, come to hale me hence!" he whispered. "Save me!"

"Get under the bed," said Reith.

As Nirm scuttled beneath the bed like some great gray cockroach seeking shelter from the housewife's broom, Reith stepped to the door and again opened it a crack. Before him stood a Krishnan in a black-and-white habit, similar in form to Nirm's garb.

Ostentatiously yawning, Reith mumbled: "What is it? What—who are you? You awoke me. . . ."

"Your pardon, my masters," said the one without. "Have you seen a small knave slinking about in garb of an outlawed priesthood?"

"No, we have seen no one," said Reith, smothering another yawn. "My fellow *Ertsu* and I were sound asleep until you knocked."

"None hath sought admission to your chamber?"

"If any knocked earlier, we failed to hear it."

"Then, forgive the intrusion. Bákh bless you!"

The Krishnan made a benedictory gesture and departed. Closing and bolting the door, Reith turned to Marot. "It was a priest of Bákh all right, and I don't mean Johann Sebastian. Our little fellow had better stay under the bed for a while, till we're sure the other priest has gone for good."

"Who is this Qarar of whom he spoke?"

"The Krishnan Herakles. There's a whole cycle of legends about his labors—six according to some, nine according to others. Qarar is supposed to have slain assorted monsters and impregnated an astronomical number of females, including a she-yeki."

"I find impregnating a female of my own species quite sufficiently taxing," said Marot. "Do you ask me to gratify a lioness or a she-bear as well!"

Reith peered under the bed. "Come on out, Nirm. Why don't you go somewhere where your cult still flourishes and you'd be welcome?"

Nirm crawled out and dusted himself. "The Temple of Yesht in Jazmurian is said to retain the pure worship. But how can I get thither? A riverboat leaves in two days, but the fare is twenty karda. Because of the persecution, the offerings of the faithful have been meager; and my entire wealth is sixteen karda." He withdrew the small hoard from his purse and displayed it.

Marot took four silver coins from his purse. "Here, my friend, take these," he said, ignoring Reith's disapproving frown. "But do not, I pray you, tell anyone from whom they came."

"I understand, my lord!" said Nirm, dropping to his knees and touching his forehead to the ground before the scientist.

"Come, come," said Marot. "Terrans do not like such excessive homage. Get up, I pray!"

"I am eternally grateful! I shall offer prayers to Yesht for you all the rest of my life!"

"That's fine," said Reith, "but right now we'd rather see you on your way. Change into ordinary garb, and get aboard your boat as soon as you're allowed." He opened the door, and the priest, glancing nervously about, disappeared.

"I hope they don't boil the poor little devil," said Reith. "But half the Terrans who get killed on Krishna do so as a result of well-meant interference in Krishnan affairs. My former wife is such a meddler; if it hasn't killed her yet, it probably will. So don't let your generous heart lead you down that garden path."

* * *

Reith had calculated that the journey to Kubyab would take three days. They spent four days on the road, however, because for most of a day a storm imprisoned them in their tent. It began as a sandstorm. A black wall of sand and dust swept across the sky and sped towards them. Preceding the storm were clouds of whirling black specks, flocks of bat-winged bijars and aqebats fleeing the storm.

Reith and Marot hastily set up their tent, driving the pegs extra deep against the anticipated gale. Before they had quite finished, the air began to churn with flying sand. For the next several hours they huddled inside, hearing the howl of the wind and wondering how soon the bellying canvas would be whirled away. Then thunder boomed, and the sand gave way to a downpour, beating against the tent walls like a regiment of drummers. During lulls, they peered out to see whether their ayas had broken loose; but the animals stoically stood in a clump, facing down-wind, with lowered heads and closed eyes.

When the storm was over, the floor of the tent was a morass of mud. Although there were but a couple of hours left of the long Krishnan day, Reith and Marot packed their soggy gear and moved on in hope of finding a drier spot to spend the night.

The farther west they went, the sparser became the vegetation. Between rare stands of trees, mostly along creeks, stretched open terrain. The Krishnan equivalents of grasses and herbs, plants with stems and leaves of green and blue and gold and crimson, provided a ragged cover for the red, clayey soil.

On the evening of the fourth day, they rode into Kubyab. As they ambled down the unpaved main street, Reith remarked: "I take back any nasty things I said about Jeshang. Compared to this godforsaken place, Jeshang is a metropolis!" He hailed a belated pedestrian. "Good my sir, can you direct us to an inn?"

The Krishnan looked around, warily studied the strangers, and answered; but his local dialect was spoken too fast for Reith to follow.

"Slowly, I pray!" said Reith.

At last the Krishnan made Reith understand that there was no such thing as an inn in Kubyab. Reith then asked: "Then where can travelers pass the night?"

"I can put you up in my house," said the local, "for a price."

"How much?"

The Krishnan hesitated, then said: "Half a kard for each, and another half-kard for stabling and feeding your beasts."

Marot began in English: "That seems reason—" but Reith cut him off saying: "Too much for a pair of poor travelers. Make it a kard total, including the beasts."

The Krishnan paused, then said: "Be ye not *Ertsuma?* We see few hereabouts."

"Yes, we're Terrans. How about the price?"

"Everyone knows that Terrans are richer than Dákhaq. So why would a pair of great, rich lords like you be stingy with a poor countryman like me?"

"Because you wrongly think Terrans have bottomless purses and therefore quote us far above the customary rate. I'll tell you: Make it a kard total, and my friend and I will answer all your questions about our own far-off world."

"That be a canny offer. I'll take it, fair sirs. Come hither, pray."

The house proved a two-room shack. The Krishnan introduced a slatternly wife and three dirty children. He indicated that the guests should have the only bed in the house; he and his family would sleep on the floor in the other room.

When they were alone, Marot asked: "Why did you screw that half-kard out of the poor *paysan*, Fergus? My Institut would never have noticed it."

"Because I've dealt with such people. If you take the first offer, they think you're half-witted and they can cheat, rob, or murder you with impunity. If they think we're sharp fellows, alert for any tricks, they're less likely to try them. All the same, we'd better stand watches tonight."

Supper consisted mainly of what Terrans called "live spaghetti," a form of edible Krishnan worm with the disconcerting roperty of continuing to wriggle after boiling for hours in the countryman's big iron pot. Marot sighed.

"When I get back to France," he said, "I shall sit down in a good restaurant and eat myself into my grave. I am no great gourmet, and I try to adapt myself and not complain, but this! *C'est épouvantable donc!*"

"What saith he?" asked the householder, whose name was Hendová.

"He praises your food," said Reith. "He says he has never eaten aught like it."

The Krishnan simpered. "Oh, come, sir, ye know I be but

a simple countryman; but my wife will be glad to hear it. . . ."

Afterwards, Reith and Marot sat for an hour answering questions about the planet Earth. The oldest child built a fire on the hearth, since in these drier lands the temperature rose and dropped sharply between day and night. At length Reith asked:

"Where does Squire Sainian bad-Jeb live?"

"The squire?" answered Hendová. "Why, in the big house at the north end of the village! 'Tis the biggest house for many a hoda around. Ye maun have seen it—but I forget, ye entered the town from t'other end."

"Is the squire at home?"

"Aye. He passed me on the street, in's carriage, but yesterday."

"We need to hire some folk to help us. Can you recommend any?"

"How many, and what would ye have them for?"

"We need two workers, to dig and haul earth and do camp chores. Then we should like a couple of trustworthy men who can handle arms, to serve as guards."

Hendová paused, chin on fist. At last he said: "I cannot serve you. I'm the town's carpenter; my apprentice is sick; and I'm tardy on orders. My cousin Doukh is to be had; he's strong as a shaihan. But ye maun keep at him, since he's as lazy as an *unha* in's wallow. As for the other—well, old Girej is still hale, an ye can keep him off the drink. Had ye come a moon earlier, ye'd have had a wider choice."

"What happened then?"

"Why, t'other Terran hired six of our best men—the best not rooted in their present tasks, ye wite."

"By the other Terran," asked Reith, "do you mean Warren Foltz?"

"Aye. He had some such outlandish name, but I couldn't put my tongue to it."

"How about the guards?" asked Reith.

"There again, we had two retired soldiers, who'd fit your desires like the skin of a *qasb*, but t'other Terran hired them both."

"The first thing tomorrow, will you take us to the two you named as workers?"

"Aye, if ye start early. I maun be at my bench by sun-up."

Reith and Marot passed an uneasy night, disturbed by many-legged Krishnan scuttlers, which got in under their blanket with them and had to be chased out or squashed.

When Reith knocked on Sainian's door, he heard sounds of movement within; but for long minutes the door remained closed. Then it opened suddenly, and Reith found himself confronting three armed Krishnans. In the middle stood a lean, elderly person with a sword. Like other Terrans, Reith found the age of a Krishnan hard to judge; but the network of fine, small wrinkles on the swordsman's face and the paling of his hair to the gray-green of light jade gave evidence of many years' passage.

The other two, flanking the aged Krishnan, were young males clad in the costume of the Chilihagho shaihan-herd. Beneath the triangle of checkered cloth worn like a diaper and serving the function of riding breeches, they wore lace-trimmed white pantelettes tucked into high, soft boots. Large silver spurs, with star-shaped rowels, were attached to these boots by loops of silver chain. Above the waist they wore leather vests that left bare their arms and part of their chests. On their heads were large, floppy, yellow straw hats with meter-wide brims, low skull-hugging crowns, and ribbons tied under the chin. Each bore a cocked crossbow, aimed at Reith's midriff.

"You are right, Fergus," murmured Marot. "One does not fling the door open to anyone."

"What would ye, Terran?" said the oldster in the center.

"Good-morning, sir," said Reith. "Are you Sainian bad-Jeb?"

"What if I be?"

"The Dasht referred me to you. He's given permission to my companion, the learned Doctor Marot, to dig for buried bones in his realm; but he advised me to ask your permission before entering your land."

The Krishnans exchanged puzzled glances. The elder one said: "Strange. Within a ten-day, another *Ertsu* hath told the same tale and made the same request. Ye be the third set we've seen within the year. Who are ye?"

"My name is Fergus Reith. I work out of Novorecife, guiding visitors from Terra about your fascinating planet. I am now under contract to guide and protect Doctor Marot."

Sainian mused: "This other wight averred the Dasht had

given him the exclusive right to dig for bones—an occupation that, if it be true, goes far to prove Terrans a mad race; unless, that be, 'tis but a pretence to disguise a hunt for treasure. Kharob's no ninny; how could he so brazenly contradict his own words, unless one permit or the other be a forgery? Let me see yours."

Marot produced the paper with Kharob's signature and seal. Sainian frowned. "This seems in order, albeit I am no scholar adept at detecting forgeries."

"If you will note," said Reith, "the other fellow got exclusive right to dig in rocks and soil of the Zorian Age, whereas our permit applies to terrain of the Kharobian Period. There is thus no conflict."

"Rocks are rocks; soil is soil. Wherein lies the distinction?"

Marot said: "Please excuse my bad Mikardandou; but the Kharobian layers of rock are the older and lie beneath Zorian. If I may show a map. . . . Here! Zorian beds extend approximately from here to here; the Kharobian from the latter line to river Zora."

"Certes, that's my land," growled Sainian. "I think not that this other Terran, clept Folt, said aught of Kharobian beds. But ye shall have permission—save that of any gold, silver, or jewels ye find, I shall have half."

"Agreed," said Reith.

"Speaking of names," said Sainian, "what said ye yours was?"

"Fergus Reith, sir."

"Methought I'd heard that name erstwhile. Are ye not the Terran who thrice escaped captivity in Dur—the third time after being forced to wed the Regent's cousin?"

"I am."

"Oh, well, that's different! Come in, come in! Stand not gaping in the doorway, admitting all the flying vermin! I've heard of your feats. Unload your shooting gear, lads."

As the two shaihan-herds turned away, Sainian ushered his visitors into a spacious room, decorated with the heads of Krishnan beasts on the walls and their cured hides on the floor.

"Sit down, sit down," said the squire. "When left ye Jeshang? How fared ye on the road? Where spent ye the past night?"

When he heard of the travelers' bug-infested bed in Hendová's hovel, Sainian said: "Ohé! That's no way to treat eminent visitors from afar. Ye shall move your gear hither. We have a plenty of space, since our silly son went off to Hershid to study art, instead of learning to run the ranch."

"That's very kind of you," said Reith. He and Marot exchanged glances. Marot said:

"Please, Squire Sainian, how long does it take to get from here to beds I showed on map?"

"With a fast aya, not above two hours; with a slower one, up to three."

"Then," said Marot before Reith could protest, "I am desolated, but I fear we must decline. To take away four to six hours from each working day, coming and going, would not leave us the time needed for our work."

Reith subsided. While being Sainian's guest would be infinitely more comfortable than bunking with Marot in a tent, he had to admit that the paleontologist's reason was valid. Sainian replied:

"I grieve that ye won't be here to liven our evenings with tales of far fantastic adventures. But the hour of the repast draws nigh, and ye shall stay now to bare a tooth with us." He turned in his chair and shouted: "Babir! Set two more places. We have visitors. Now, my Terran friends, ye'll have, I trust, no religious or other objections to a drop of kvad?"

The golden kvad was the strongest Reith had drunk; the first swallow almost made him choke. But their host gulped it down as if it were water. By the time the meal was announced, the squire had drunk enough, by Reith's estimate, to have put three ordinary men beneath the table; but he seemed not to show it save to become a little more boisterously hospitable.

"Come, gentlemen," he said. "After the fancy aliment of decadent cities like Majbur and Jazmurian, our plain fare must seem sorry stuff. But 'twill keep your bellies away from your spines."

Reith and Marot sat down with Sainian, the two shaihanherds, and Sainian's wife Ilui. The food, served by the servant Babir, proved excellent. Sainian said: "Ye'll take it not amiss, I trust, that ye received a wary reception enow? One must be careful in these parts. It might have been young Ye'man, from across the Zora; he's lusted for my blood ever since I slew his sire."

"I understand a reasonable precaution," said Reith. "But tell us about Foltz. With whom did he come here?"

"That I know not, for he approached my house alone. A

prim, offish wight, not open like ye twain. I heard he had with him some folk from Jeshang and more hired in Kubyab. I sent one of my shaihan-herds to make sure that, an he found treasure, he'd divide it fairly with me. I'd do the same with you gentlemen, but I cannot spare more men. Two I need to protect my home, and the rest are out on the yearly roundup."

Reith suggested: "You could tell the fellow with Foltz to alternate between Foltz's camp and ours. We shan't be more than a few hoda apart, and we have nothing to hide."

"I'll think on that," said Sainian.

Reith continued: "You said, sir, we were the third set of Terrans to come here in the past year. Was the first man named Esteban Surkov?"

"Aye, so 'twas. The bugger spake of making's living by writing books, as if we'd believe anyone could earn his badr in so fantastical a fashion."

"What became of him?" asked Reith.

"I shot him."

"What?"

"I said, I shot him. I'd warned him against leaving gates open, not once but twice. The third time, a score of my beasts escaped, and one we never did find. So I put a bolt through Master Surkov's right eye and into that mess of pottage he called his brain. Neatest shot I'd made in years! I fain had had his head mounted with those of other beasts I'd slain, but Ilui thought it in poor taste. Ye know how women are. Now tell me how things fare in the lands betwixt here and Novorecife."

For the rest of the meal, the replies of Reith and Marot were subdued; but the squire seemed not to notice. He plied them with questions and urged more food upon them.

"Come, good my sirs," he said, after wolfing down a plateful that would have done credit to a hungry yeki, "stint yourselves not! When ye've camped out a while, ye'll wish ye'd eaten more here whilst ye had the chance."

"Thank you, Squire," said Reith, "but I've reached the point where I can still chew but cannot swallow. And we must be off to the Kharobian beds. Since we don't know the country, we'd prefer not to go blundering about in darkness looking for our site."

"That shall be no problem. I'll send one of my boys to guide you thither, albeit he cannot long remain with you." Sainian turned to one of the shaihan-herds. "Herg, ye'll do that duty.

Tarry not at these Terrans' camp, but hasten back."

As they rose, Sainian said: "This hath been a pleasure, gentlemen. I have not so enjoyed myself since the day I slew the three bad-Faroun brothers. Oh, ere I forget, keep a sharp eye out for a band of outlaws, headed by one Basht. They'd as lief slit your weasand as look at you."

Outside, Herg led his own aya, a glossy buckskin, around to the front of the house. He said: "Master Reese, this is my personal steed. Would ye care to ride him? He'll give you a fine ride, the like of which ye've never known."

Reith realized that all the Krishnans—Sainian, Ilui, and the two shaihan-herds—were staring expectantly at him. He also caught a glint of suppressed mirth in Herg's eyes.

"I'm most grateful," he said. "But I'm not a very skilled rider, and I might in my ignorance mishandle your fine beast. I'll stay with my own, if you please. Come, Aristide. We shall be back soon, with our animals and gear."

As they walked back to Hendová's house, Marot asked: "Why did you decline the use of that fine mount?"

"These people have a reputation as great jokers. I'm sure that, if I'd forked that cayuse, the beast would have gone crazy and either bucked me off or run away the way that other did with you. They were hoping for something like that; and if I'd broken my neck, that would have added to the fun."

Half an hour later, they returned to the squire's house prepared for the journey. Sainian waved them off, calling: "Forget not to close any gates ye pass through!"

"Little danger of *that*," muttered Reith.

Leading their pack ayas, Reith and Marot rode with Herg. Doukh and Girej followed on foot, leading a small aya on which they had loaded their personal possessions and a folded tent. Hiring them had occasioned a long haggle, since the villagers had demanded extra pay because of the danger of outlaws. When Herg asked them if they knew "the place on the riverbank where the tax collector was slain," they assured him that they were familiar with the spot and urged the others to ride on ahead.

"We shall be with you ere sundown," said Girej.

Red Roqir was low in the west, banding the greenish Krishnan sky with scarlet and gold, when the travelers reached the area that Marot had chosen. The paleontologist said:

"Fergus, let me pick the place of our camp. I have done this before." He asked the shaihan-herd in Mikardandou: "Master Herg, how high does the Zora rise during floods?"

"Let me think," said the Krishnan. "In the third year of Dasht Kavir, it came to the top of yonder ridge." He pointed. "That's the highest whereof I've heard."

Marot walked his aya to the ridge and cast a sharp eye along an imaginary contour line. "Wait here!" he called, and spurred his mount to a trot. Back and forth he went, and up and down the shores of the river. A quarter-hour later, as the sun touched the horizon, he returned.

"I have a suitable place," he said. "Follow me, please."

Reith thought that the paleontologist had shrewdly picked a site safely above high-water mark but still within easy walking distance of the river. The earth was mostly bare, a reddish clay formed by the disintegration of shale, and littered with sandstone pebbles and an occasional boulder. It sloped down in a long, easy incline to the river on either side, and from the top of the slope rolled gently off into the distance. Away from the river, plants grew more thickly. Many were spiky or thorny multi-colored herbs and bushes, with stretches of bare red soil between.

There was no sign of Doukh or Girej. Reith shouted for them, but only silence answered. As Roqir slipped below the skyline, Krishnan night life began its endless symphony of chirps, squeaks, and buzzes.

"It looks as if we'll have to put up our tent ourselves," said Reith.

"Need ye a hand?" said Herg.

"Thanks," said Reith.

When the tent was up, the Krishnan said: "I maun be off to Kubyab. The chief'll send a man down to see how ye fare betimes."

"Good-night," said Reith, then to Marot: "Those two so-called workers aren't here yet."

Marot shrugged. "Perhaps they got lost, or changed their minds, or met with an accident."

"Maybe I ought to go back along the trail to look for them."

"Do not think of it, I beg you! Casting about in strange country in the dark would merely get you lost, also."

Reith was not unhappy to let himself be argued out of a nocturnal search, although his overdeveloped sense of responsibility nipped him. He and Marot cooked a simple meal.

Reith poked his head out of the tent the next morning and saw a family of slender-legged Krishnan herbivores drinking on the far side of the river. When he opened the flaps and emerged, the creatures looked up, snorted, and bounded away up the bank.

Later, Reith set out on the sorrel aya to cast back along the trail for signs of the camp workers. He moved slowly, staring about to fix in his mind the contours of the land, and halted now and then to consult Marot's map. It was easy to get lost in this roadless, rolling country with few obvious landmarks. He passed a herd of Sainian's shaihans, massive pied brown-and-white beasts, munching away at the scanty vegetation. The animals stared dully at him and resumed their repast.

An hour later, Reith came upon Girej and Doukh, sprawled on the turf with an empty bottle beside them. Their aya was tethered nearby. Reith dismounted and, holding his reins, stood over the recumbent forms. Both breathed; Girej even snored. Reith nudged the huge Doukh with the toe of his boot. The Krishnan awoke, looked up, and grinned sheepishly.

"What in Hishkak are you doing here?" barked Reith. "We expected you at the camp last night."

"Well, sir," grumbled Doukh. "'Twas this way. After we'd walked for an hour, we stopped to rest our feet. And old Girej had a bottle to strengthen us for the rest of the journey. I drank but a few swallows; but the miching losel finished it off ere I could stop him. Then there was no getting him to's feet to travel on."

"Why didn't you come on yourself, with the aya?"

"Why, sir! Think ye I'd leave a comrade lying insensible drunk in the wild, where a kargán or a yeki could come upon and devour him? What sort of rudesby think ye I be?"

"Well, get him up now," growled Reith. "He's had time enough to sleep it off. This'll cost you two each half a day's pay."

At length Reith and the workers straggled in to camp, Doukh leading the pack aya and Girej mumbling: "Oh, my poor head!"

Marot came running up, puffing. "Fergus! I think that I have found a promising bed!"

Reith dismounted, handed his reins to Girej, and gave the two Krishnans their orders. He said to Marot: "Show it to me, old boy!"

Scientist and guide walked a hundred meters upstream. Pointing with his geologist's hammer, Marot said: "This patch of gravel is the mouth of a former stream bed. Under the pebbles is Z—I mean Kharobian sandstone. Luckily it is soft near the surface. These pebbles have been carried down from fossil-bearing beds higher up. I know because they include many fossil fragments." Marot bent and picked up an apparent pebble. "See!" he said. "It is a fragment from the dorsal spine of a piscoid, which on Terra we should call a fish. It is not of course related to our fishes, but has evolved along parallel lines. Here is another."

Marot showed a second pebble to Reith, glanced at the two specimens through his magnifying glass, and tossed them away.

"Aren't you going to save those?" asked Reith.

"No. I can collect a basketful any time. Since they are not *in situ* and are not connected with the rest of the skeleton, they would tell me nothing that I do not already know. But they point the way to possible significant discoveries."

For the next hour they wandered back and forth about the area. Marot found several small fossils: a curved, reptilian-looking fang three centimeters long; an unidentified vertebra; and a teardrop-shaped stone which, he explained, was a coprolite—the fossilized turd of some bygone aquatic creature.

Reith was roaming over a patch of red sandstone more or less free from its overlay of pebbles when, in a little depression, he noticed a streak of pale gray amid the brownish red of the rock. Looking closer, he saw that this material had a certain regularity, like that of a string of beads.

"Aristide!" he called. "Would you look at this? I don't suppose it's anything at all, but you might...."

Marot approached. *"Hein!"* he said. "I assure you, my friend, it certainly is something. It is a vertebral column. Here is a vertebra that has become detached from the matrix." He picked up what to Reith looked like an ordinary dark-brown stone. "Let us look further."

Marot squatted over the streak and, with a whiskbroom, began cleaning the coating of dust from the disintegrated sandstone of the surface.

"Ha!" said the paleontologist. "This is a rib. And here is

another." As further streaks came into view, Marot poked at the crumbling surface with a dull old sheath knife, swept away the loose fragments, and poked some more.

"This is remarkable luck," he said. "We might have spent a moon poking about without finding a thing."

"What can I do to help?" said Reith, keeping his excitement under control.

"Oh, go walk around here and bring me anything that looks like a fossil."

Marot laid out the tools of his trade: a geologist's hammer, with one sharp and one squared-off end; a whiskbroom; a blunt knife; and a small pick, about half the weight of a normal pick, with an eighty-centimeter handle.

"What do you call that little pick?" asked Reith.

"That is a Marsh pick," said the scientist.

Reith frowned. "Seems like a funny kind of tool for dredging a swamp."

"No; it is not that kind of marsh—*un marais*. This pick is named for the great American paleontologist, Othniel Charles Marsh, who designed it three hundred years ago. In the nineteenth century, he it was who furnished the convincing fossil proof of the organic evolution of all organisms.

"This Marsh was also, I regret to say, something of a scoundrel. He was accused even of stealing or destroying the fossils of rival paleontologists, to rob them of the credit for their discoveries. I would not kill a man, even to prevent a crime of less than murder against me; but such a man, if I found him destroying knowledge, I would kill!" Marot shook a fist.

Reith started off, head bent and eyes on the ground. During the next hour, while Marot poked and swept, Reith picked up several pieces that looked interesting. Some, on presentation, were pronounced mere stones. Some turned out to be fossilized plant stems. One was a nearly complete dorsal spine, and three were teeth.

Then Reith brought back a peculiar-looking piece, which resembled petrified bone; but Reith could not imagine what part of any creature it might be.

"That is a piece of skull!" cried Marot. *"Mais, c'est magnifique!* See, here is part of the orbit. Where did you find it?"

"Let's see—I think. . . ." Reith walked uncertainly to a spot a few paces away. "I think it was about here. But to me, every patch of pebbles looks pretty much like every other."

"That is close enough. Pile some stones one upon another to mark the place, and see if you can find more fragments. That piece of skull may be from our specimen here."

Reith built his little cairn, resolving, if he ever found such a thing again, instantly to mark the spot in this manner. Then, as he began turning over stones, he found part of a jaw with teeth attached, and another piece of skull. When Marot looked up to identify this last find, Reith asked:

"Aristide, supposing these are from the same animal, what sort of critter would it have been?"

"At this stage," replied Marot, "I can give only the educated guess. It is a fishlike or salamanderlike creature, perhaps a meter in length. It had a very simple construction, as far as we can tell; no strange horns, or spines, or other ornaments. Now continue with your hunting; you appear to have the luck of the beginner."

As the long Krishnan day wore on, Marot continued his digging and Reith his search for surface finds. Reith thought he began to recognize the distinctive colors and textures that distinguished fossils from ordinary stones. At least, of the finds he brought to Marot for judgment, the percentage of fossils seemed on the increase. When he brought another specimen, Marot said:

"Look here, Fergus."

The Frenchman pointed to a depression he had dug in one side of the specimen. Here could be seen a cluster of small bones, just breaking the surface.

"If I do not let my hopes deceive me," said Marot, "this is a set of limb bones; but I cannot yet tell whether they are the bones of a genuine leg, or the base of a lobed fin, or something in between. It is well that I have a strong heart, or the suspense would kill me. It is time we went back for lunch. Hand me that aya hide from the pack, please."

Marot spread the hide across the specimen and weighted the corners with stones. "This will make it easier to locate again and will protect it against accident. Now let us go."

They were finishing lunch when Doukh called: "Master Maghou, someone comes!"

Two figures on ayas appeared, looking like mushrooms under the enormous yellow straw hats. They wore the clothes of the Chilihagho shaihan-herd. As they came nigh, Reith perceived that one was indubitably a Krishnan; the other, he suspected, was a Terran in disguise.

Marot pointed to the leading rider, saying in an undertone: "That is Warren Foltz." He raised his voice: *"Allô,* Warren! You ought to have come an hour sooner, and we should have given you the lunch. There is still some salad, which I made myself...."

Foltz swung down from his saddle, took off his straw hat, and stepped close to Marot with his face grimly set. Reith moved nearer to his client in case Marot should need help.

The newcomer, Reith saw, was carefully made up to look like a Krishnan. Foltz's skin had been stained or powdered to give it the faint olive-green cast of the true Krishnan humanoid. His straight hair, black at the roots, had been dyed a bluish green. Elfin points had been affixed to his ears; and from his forehead, at the inner ends of his eyebrows, sprouted a pair of feathery antennae, like extra movable eyebrows, in imitation of the olfactory organs of natives of this world. Otherwise the newcomer was a strikingly handsome man of about Reith's age, slim, well-built, and dark-complexioned. Foltz grated:

"Aristide! Will you kindly explain how, when the Dasht gave me exclusive rights to dig here, you are horning in? We saw the smoke from your fires."

"Excuse me, Warren," said Marot pacifically. "The Dasht gave you the exclusive right to dig in the Zorian beds. We have the exclusive right to dig in the Kharobian beds. There is thus no conflict."

"What in hell are the Kharobian beds? I never heard of that horizon."

"You will, dear colleague. The time has come for a more detailed subdivision of the Krishnan geological past."

"Meaning that you just thought up this sub-period to get around my permit? Where is your permit, anyway?"

"One moment." Marot disappeared into his tent and emerged with the hand-written screed on native paper. As Foltz reached for it, Marot snatched it back. "Oh, no! You shall not lay hands on this paper. I will hold; you read."

Scowling, Foltz bent forward and read. At last he said: "And what if I go back to Jeshang and tell the Dasht he's been the victim of a barefaced swindle?"

"It would be your word against mine. If I may hazard a guess, the Dasht would decide that Terrans are too much trouble and order both of us out of his barony. Or perhaps he would turn us over to the priesthood of Bákh, to be tried for heresy and boiled to death. Would you like that?"

"Think I'm crazy?" Foltz stood chewing his lip.

"In any case," said Marot, "this ranch covers an enormous area. If we both worked for ten Krishnan years here, we could not more than scratch its surface, geologically speaking."

At last Foltz conceded: "I've got to hand it to you, Aristide. It was a damned clever move. Serves me right for mentioning 'Zorian' in my petition, thus limiting the scope of my dig. Tell you what! To show there's no hard feelings, why don't you and your friend here—excuse me, sir, I don't know your name?"

"Mon dieu!" cried Marot. "Where are my manners? Dr. Warren Foltz, Fergus Reith. Mr. Reith is my guide and guardian. I tell him I wish to go to a place, and presto! by magic he whisks me to that place."

"The tour guide?" said Foltz. "I've heard of you, Mr. Reith. So why don't the pair of you come over to my camp before sundown for a drink and a bite? We picked up a pretty good cook in Jeshang." Foltz added directions.

"It is most kind of you," said Marot. "Is it hokay with you, Fergus?"

Reith's heart had begun to pound. At Foltz's camp, he would learn whether Alicia was with Foltz, as rumor had led him to suspect. The thought roiled unbearable emotions. In a sudden panic, Reith was on the verge of refusing the invitation, to avoid a confrontation. But then, he thought, Aristide was simple-minded in some ways and needed someone to watch over him in the enemy's camp. That thought tipped the balance.

"Sure, we'll be there," he said with affected casualness.

IV.

THE SITE

Reith and Marot went back to their specimen. For most of the afternoon, the paleontologist pried and picked and swept, while Reith wandered about looking for more detached fossils. He found hardly any, for the ferment of emotions aroused by the impending visit kept distracting him from the task at hand. Over and over, he found himself rehearsing the things he would say to Alicia if they met. At last Marot called:

"Fergus! Look at this.... You see, now I have its whole flank exposed. In this flank are two limbs. See there and there? Both terminate in a process that is not quite a leg. I believe those little things are partly-calcified cartilagenous rays, evolving into webbed feet. Krishnan cartilage differs chemically from ours—that in the human nose, for example—and therefore fossilizes better. Do you realize what you have done?"

"Nothing wrong, I hope," said Reith.

"On the contrary, you have provided the clutching argument—"

"You mean 'clinching,' don't you?"

"Yes, yes, the clinching argument in the dispute with Foltz! See?" In his excitement, the portly Marot did a little dance step. "This creature has two limbs on a side, not three. And it is a true transitional form: a piscoid in the act of turning itself into a salamandroid. So the division between the Hexapoda and the Tetrapoda must have taken place before this emergence."

"You mean the division between the four-leggers and the six-leggers happened while these 'legs' were still just fins?"

"That is the idea."

Reith frowned. "Are you sure all the land-living—ah—Tetrapoda of today are descended from this guy? Could it be that his line died out, and then a branch of the six-leggers lost a pair of legs, the way Foltz claims?"

Marot sobered. "That will doubtless be Foltz's argument. Of course, we never have all the fossils we need to settle, beyond all doubt, the question of who descended from whom. But this guy, as you call him, is a weighty argument on my side. I shall name the species after you, Fergus—something *reithi.*"

"Thanks. I'll call him 'Ozymandias,'" said Reith. "You know: 'Round the decay of that colossal wreck. . . .'"

"Ah, yes. That was some nineteenth-century English poet, was it not? Byron? Tennyson?"

"Shelley. Are you going to dig the whole skeleton out, bone by bone? Some of those bones look pretty small and fragile."

"You are right," said Marot. "This skeleton must be taken whole back to Novorecife, along with the additional fragments we have found."

"You mean in one solid rock? That'll weigh a couple of hundred kilos, won't it?"

"I do not think so. I shall mark out a block, and our stalwart helpers can earn their pay by digging a trench around the specimen and prying the whole loose from its matrix. Then I shall chip away at the block from various sides until I begin to strike bone, to reduce the weight to a minimum. Finally, I shall haul the block out of the pit and load it on one of our beasts." Marot climbed out of the depression and shouted: "Doukh! Girej! Come here, please!"

Marot explained to the Krishnans what he wanted done, scraping a groove around the specimen with the pointed end of his geologist's hammer to show them where to dig. For the rest of the afternoon he hovered over them, anxiously watching lest they cut too close to his find.

The afternoon sun scorched the riverbank and the laboring men. Stripped to the waist, Reith said, "I'm going to get one of those super-cowboy hats they wear here. How about you?"

Marot shrugged. "I have been so absorbed that I have not noticed the heat. Anyway, Roqir does not burn the flesh so severely as our own Sol, because of the deeper atmosphere."

"You swarthy Latins," said Reith, "can take the sun better than us pale-skinned Nordics. Redheads like me just burn and peel."

Later, Reith interrupted the scientist again: "Aristide, if we're going to Foltz's camp, we'd better start getting cleaned up."

"Ah, yes. I had forgotten in the ecstasy of finding this beautiful specimen. That will be all the digging for today, my good fellows."

An hour later, as Roqir sank in the west, Reith and Marot, freshly washed and in clean khakis, rode in to Foltz's camp. They found this camp much more impressive than their own. Five tents stood amid evidence of much work done in the time since Foltz arrived. They saw tables on which fossils were being cleaned and sorted, piles of fossil-bearing rock awaiting attention, and a pile of discarded rock fragments. Reith thought that Foltz's party must include about a dozen people.

The two armed guards, wearing vests of rusty chain mail, had been lounging before the main tent. As Reith and Marot appeared, the guards scrambled up and stood at attention with drawn swords resting against their shoulders.

Foltz emerged from the main tent, saying *"Rabosh dir!"* ("At ease!") to the guards. Then he came forward, shouting: "Ma'lum! Take charge of these gentlemen's ayas!"

As the visitors dismounted, Foltz extended a welcoming hand to each in turn. "I'm glad you came. Sit at that table, will you?" He raised his voice again. "Daviran! Serve us kvad."

When the drinks were poured, Foltz raised his mug: "To all the fossils on Krishna!"

The kvad was the same fiery stuff that Sainian had served them. Marot drank, then raised his mug again: "To the truth to which they will lead us, whatever it be!"

Foltz drank to that one, but silently. After the first gulp, Reith sipped slowly. Marot, he feared, was in such a euphoric mood that he might get tight and blab about his find. Reith resolved to stay sober and keep an eye on the Frenchman, who seemed to have forgotten his own warnings about Foltz's fanaticism.

"The truth," said Foltz, "will turn out to be *my* theory. You'll see."

Having finished his first mug of kvad, Marot smiled craftily. Foltz signaled Daviran to refill the vessels: Marot's; Reith's, still more than half full; and his own, empty. Taking another gulp, Marot said:

"Perhaps and perhaps not. If you saw the specimen that we found today, you might not be so chickensure."

Foltz looked puzzled, then laughed. "You mean cocksure. What's this marvelous specimen?"

Reith wanted to shout: "Shut up, you damned fool!" He glanced beneath the table to be sure of kicking the right ankle, then nudged Marot's leg with the toe of his boot.

Marot said: "Aha, do you not wish you knew? In any case, I cannot tell more, because it is only partly exposed. But from what I have seen, it will drive the screw in the coffin of your theory."

"I must come over and have a look," said Foltz.

"You will be welcome at any time," Marot laughed. "Just think of the irony! La Rochefoucauld could not do better. Here I, an established paleontologist of wide experience, come across light-years of interstellar space to dig up Krishnan bones. Then, the first day, what happens? A rank amateur—excuse me, Fergus, but that is what you are—finds what may be the most crucial specimen in the whole field of Krishnan evolution!"

"Congratulations, Mr. Reith," said Foltz. "If, that is, this find turns out to be as critical as my enthusiastic colleague seems to think. But brace yourself for disappointment. Scientists have gone wrong in such extrapolations before. I have firmly established the Hexapod ancestry of all Krishnan land vertebrates beyond—"

Marot interrupted: "Oh, *quel sottise!* You are an incorrigible self-deceiver, Warren—"

"On the contrary, it's you and the other fuddy-duddies who—"

"Please, gentlemen!" said Reith loudly, since the discussion promised to become an open quarrel. "Let's shelve the technical argument. Most of it's over my head, anyhow. There's plenty going on in Krishna to talk about. The nomads of Qaath are threatening—"

"Damn it, I—" began Foltz.

"But I insist—" began Marot.

The flap of the main tent parted, and out stepped a slender, striking woman of delicate features and golden-blond hair. She had almost reached the table when her gaze met Fergus Reith's. She stopped as if she had run into an invisible wall. Her lips parted silently.

"Lish!" said Reith, setting down his mug and rising.

"Fergus!" she said. After a second's hesitation, she stepped forward again. She and Reith shook hands.

"You know each other?" asked Foltz, glancing sharply from one to the other.

"Yes," said Reith.

"I do not know the so-charming Mademoiselle," said Marot. "Pray, present me!"

"Oh, ah," said Foltz. "Alicia, this is my colleague, Aristide Marot. Doctor Marot, my secretary, Dr. Alicia Dyckman. She does for me what Mr. Reith does for you: translating, dealing with the locals, buying, hiring, and so on."

Marot kissed Alicia's hand, but she barely acknowledged the gesture. Her eyes were on Reith. She said: "Warren didn't tell me who was coming over to dinner. Did you know I was here?"

"I thought you might be," said Reith. "I was braced for it."

"Sit down, everybody," said Foltz. "One more round and we'll eat." He looked alternately at Reith and Alicia, his eyes narrowed thoughtfully. At last he said: "Things begin to fall into a pattern. Alicia, is Mr. Reith by any chance that former husband of yours?"

She nodded, staring uncomfortably at her knuckles.

Foltz continued: "You never mentioned his name; at least, not—so I didn't know—I mean, I didn't plan this as a surprise—"

"I'm always delighted to see an old friend," said Reith. "Lish, how are you doing? How come you're not barging around on your own, collecting anthropological data on the Krishnans?"

"They didn't renew my grant," she said. "At least, the letter failed to arrive on the ship it should have. I wasn't quite broke, but if I'd waited around for more grant money and none came...." She shrugged. "When Warren offered me the job, I took it. Of course, I've been collecting my own data in my spare time, as well as keeping his records and coping with the Krishnans. How about you?"

"Still running guided tours, and in between times recovering from the last one and planning for the next. The job is really getting too big for one man to handle, but a couple of Krishnans I've tried to break in as assistants have pooped out."

"What was their difficulty?"

"One could never be on time, which is fatal in my trade. The other couldn't learn English well enough to be understood, let alone any other Terran tongues."

"Drink up!" said Foltz. "Here's dinner."

As the party progressed, Reith asked Foltz: "Did you have any trouble with the Bákhites?"

"No. Luckily, when I was in Jeshang, High Priestess Lazdai was up in the hills, filling her venom sacs. Did you?"

"No; she was still on vacation." Reith turned back to Alicia. "Tell me, Lish, where were you all that time during the last year, after—after we—after we lost touch? When I got back from my tour, you'd dropped out of sight. Not even Herculeu knew where you were."

Having finished his dinner, Marot took out a large cigar. He glanced at Reith and Alicia, utterly absorbed in each other and oblivious of their table companions. Foltz sat quietly frowning.

Marot rose. "Warren, my old one, let us take a little walk and a smoke to settle our stomachs. Perhaps we can do ourselves some good by pooling our observations of the local geology."

Foltz glowered, hesitated, then rose and walked off with Marot. Alicia told Reith:

"I went to Katai-Jhogorai to study their family system. It's an extreme example of disjunctive marriage, in which there's no connection between the practical ends of the union and affection between spouses. So long as the marriage serves its politico-economic functions, neither spouse cares how many love affairs the other has or who fathers the eggs; like royal marriages in pre-industrial Europe. One who demands exclusive sexual rights to another they consider a barbarian.

"The system fascinated me, and I might be there yet. But

I ran into trouble and had to leave in a hurry."

"What happened?"

"You know that slavery is a sore subject there? Some anti-slavery societies have sprung up; but the masses fear and hate them. Shortly before I arrived, a mob lynched an abolitionist who spoke out of turn.

"One of these societies heard that Terrans were anti-slavery and sent a delegation to me, to try to enlist my support."

"Oh, oh!" said Reith. "I know what's coming."

"No, you don't! I know what you're thinking: There goes Alicia, meddling in Krishnan affairs and putting all the Earthmen on the planet in danger."

"I didn't say anything of the kind!"

"You didn't have to; I know you too well. No, I flatly turned down these good people and forbade them to use my name in their propaganda."

"Then what—?"

"They went ahead and used it anyway, publishing a synopsis of their interview with me. Then the soup was in the fire—"

"You mean, you *did* sound off on slavery, but supposedly off the record?"

"Well, they asked some straight questions, so I thought I ought to give straight answers. I thought I could trust them. I couldn't very well pretend to be pro-slavery, now could I?"

"You could have refused to discuss the subject at all. Lish darling, you're incorrigible, and it'll kill you yet. Let's be thankful you got out of that one with a whole skin."

Marot and Foltz returned to the table. Foltz sat down heavily and tossed down another drink. He said: "Renewing old acquaintance, I see. That's okay, so long as you don't go getting ideas."

"I beg your pardon?" said Reith, giving Foltz a coldly level stare.

"I said, don't go getting ideas."

"Ideas about what?" Reith's muscles tensed themselves.

"About Alicia, you—" Foltz seemed to have been about to say something like "you fool!" but choked it off. "She's my secretary, and I won't let anybody come between us."

"I believe the lady will have the last word on that," said Reith sharply.

"Not this time she won't." Foltz's speech showed the first traces of the thickening induced by alcohol. "I know she's no dewy-eyed innocent, what with you, and that black African, and the President of Qirib, and I don't know who else; but for here and now she's my—my—"

As Foltz groped for a word, Reith began slowly to rise, like an uncoiling spring. Alicia sent frightened glances from one to the other. Then Marot spoke up loudly:

"I fear that we must be going, my friends. We have had a long day. I most sincerely thank you, Warren."

"Oh, ah," said Foltz, recovering his self-possession. "Must you go? Think you can find your way back?"

"I am sure of it. Golnaz is nearly at the full, and we can always go down-grade until we strike the river."

"Sure," said Reith, also clapping on the mask of civility. "With these six-legged critters, you don't have to worry about their stepping into a hole and going arse-over-teakettle with you. Goodnight, Lish."

He and Alicia shook hands again, but continued their clinging handshake, murmuring: "When can I see you. . . ." "I want to hear more about. . . ." "Whatever happened to. . . ."

At last Marot touched Reith's elbow, saying: "Come along, Fergus. *Faites une bonne nuit!*"

Recalled to the present, Reith gave Alicia's hand a brisk squeeze and turned away, mounting his aya without further words.

When they had ridden away from the camp, Reith said: "Good thing you broke that up, Aristide. In another minute we'd have been kicking and gouging. The most damned uncomfortable dinner party I ever sweated through; like dining with the headsman the night before he shortens you."

"Ah, yes," said Marot. "I only regret that you did not shut me up more quickly when I talked indiscreetly of our find. When shall we learn never to commit these gaffes? But to speak of more pleasant matters, I was much impressed by your Alicia."

"Not mine any more, I'm sorry to say."

"I am still impressed. She seems to have more virtues than any one woman ought to have: the beauty, the intelligence, the charm, the energy. . . ."

"You'd have to know her better to perceive the less admirable ones, which are not really faults but virtues carried to extremes."

"As an example?" queried Marot.

"She should be the greatest xenologist in the galaxy. But a xenologist should know how to be quietly inconspicuous—to blend into his background. Lish is about as inconspicuous as a sunflower in a coal scuttle. She's also bossy, dogmatic, contentious, and hot-tempered. She has a touch of the missionary attitude; instead of just accepting the Krishnans as they are and studying them, she *will* try to set them right and convert them to Terran ideals. As a result, she's *persona non grata* in several Krishnan nations, and she's lucky she hasn't been killed."

"Without doubt you have reason. It is also plain to the eye that you and she are not—how shall I say—not altogether emotionally detached."

"No, worse luck. I'm afraid the old fires are just banked, not extinguished."

"Fire banked?" said Marot uncertainly. "Oh, you mean *le feu est couvert.*" With a sigh, Marot shook his head. "It is a spectacle to make angels weep; two good, decent people who love each other but are prevented by a clash of personalities from living together. But this Foltz displays a proprietary attitude toward her. Do you suppose they are—ah—"

"If he's screwing her, you can be sure it's by consent. If he used force, she'd kill him in his sleep."

Broodingly Marot said: "Have a care, my old one. I can see the making of a fatal triangle—a fine melodrama, like one of those Italian operas where everybody stabs everybody."

"Better worry about your own fatal triangle," said Reith.

"How do you mean?"

"You, Foltz, and Ozymandias. That's as likely to cause violence as mine."

Reith spent a restless night, troubled by memories of the times he and Alicia had been together and by dreams of making passionate love to her.

The following morning, Fergus Reith parted the tent flaps to see a gray dawn lightening an overcast sky. An hour later, the work of blocking out Ozymandias was well under way when Doukh looked up from his task to say: "Master Reef, yonder comes someone!"

Following the Krishnan's pointing finger, Reith looked, and his heart seemed to turn over inside his ribs. Alicia, in khaki shirt and shorts, was running towards the excavation. As she came nearer, Reith saw that she was not only dirty and disheveled but also bore a black eye and several visible bruises about the face, arms, and legs.

"Good God, Lish! What's up?" cried Reith.

"Warren b-beat me up!" she sobbed, throwing herself into Reith's arms. "I ran away, and I've been wandering in circles half the night trying to find you." Her speech was thickened by a split and swollen lip.

Marot cleared his throat. "Fergus, my friend," he said, "perhaps you and this little lady would prefer to discuss matters by yourselves, *hein?*"

"He's right," said Reith. "Come this way, Lish, and tell me about it. Did you say that bastard beat you up?"

"Y-yes."

"I'll kill him, and I don't mean just punching his nose. But tell me the whole story."

"Well, after you went away, Warren and I got into a fight. He was furious at what he said was the way you and I had eyes for nobody but each other through dinner, and how we held hands and cooed at each other in saying good-night. He accused me of being still in love with you."

"Are you?" Reith asked on sudden impulse.

"That's not a fair question, right now. I'll admit you'll always be someone special to me. Anyway, one thing led to another, and I told him a few home truths about himself."

"Using your tongue as a scalpel to skin him alive. I know your talents."

"Don't be mean! I couldn't bear it. What tore it was when I told him how much better in bed you were than he. Then he really lost his temper and began punching and kicking. I'm stronger than I look, but he's stronger yet. When he'd battered me around the tent, he tried to rape me.

"I won't kid you, Fergus. I've been sleeping with him ever since this expedition started; that was part of the agreement—"

Reith sorrowfully shook his head. "Doesn't sound quite like you, Lish."

"I know; it looks as if I were for sale to the highest bidder. But it was neither for love nor for fun; it was that or starve. He made it plain at the start: no fucky, no jobby."

"Good lord, that's practically rape anyway. But I don't see—no talented *Ertsu* need starve on Krishna. There are always jobs to be had among the natives—"

"Ah, but it's one thing for a man like you to apply for such a job, and quite another for a personable Terran woman to do so. I've been offered jobs by several Krishnan bigwigs; but every offer had the same string attached as Warren's.

"What you don't understand is how low I felt. I'd fallen down on my job, been kicked out of Katai-Jhogorai with my work half done, lost my grant, run out of money, and thrown away the best man I was ever likely to get. So, what did I have to lose? Warren looked pretty good on first contact, and I thought I might be able to build the relationship into something useful. I was a fool, of course."

"Sweetheart, you need never starve on Krishna while I have one arzu to rub against another."

With tears in her eyes, Alicia threw her arms around Reith and buried her face in his chest. "Oh, darling. . . . But you weren't at Novo then. Even if you had been, I couldn't have asked favors of you after the way I'd treated you.

"Anyway, to get back to last night: After he'd beaten me half unconscious, he came at me with lance in rest. But this wasn't lovemaking; it was plain sadism."

"How did you get out of that? You said 'tried.'"

"I kneed him in the crotch. If I'd only had a good sharp knife or sword, I'd have given him a sex change free of charge. . . . Anyway, while he was still doubled over, I ran out. Then I tried to find your camp, but I got lost."

"You knew about where it was, and you always had a keen sense of direction."

"True; but I hadn't been over this way. And then the overcast crept across the sky, so I couldn't steer by the moons and stars. After dawn, I recognized the slope of the land; and I knew that if I kept going down-slope, I'd come to the Zora."

Reith said: "First, let's get you cleaned up. Come on in this tent, where I've got my first-aid kit."

"I have stuff like that, too; but it's back at Warren's—oh, my God! All the notes I've been taking on Krishnan sociology are still in Warren's tent!"

"Hold still, darling. This will sting. . . . Better forget your notes for the present."

"But I must go back and get them—"

"You're not going anywhere. If I get a chance later, I'll get them for you." For once Alicia forwent an argument, to Reith's relief. All too well, he knew her tendency to respond to any opposition with a fierce, intransigent belligerence. He continued: "What gave Foltz the idea he had exclusive rights to you? Did he consider you his betrothed or something?"

"No; he never even suggested a permanent relationship, legal or otherwise—not that such a proposal would have interested me, once I got to know him. It was just plain, old-fashioned jealousy. You might read my Ph.D. thesis, on the proprietary component of the human sexual drive. Warren doesn't care for anyone but himself and his career. His idea is, what's mine is mine, and what's yours is negotiable. And he viewed his secretary-mistress as much his as his geologist's hammer."

Later, outside the tent, Reith sat down and began sharpening his sword on a whetstone, with long, careful strokes. Alicia, cleaned and tidied, followed him out. She asked:

"What are you doing?"

"I told you I'd kill that guy. When this is sharp enough to shave with, I'll ride back to his camp and have at him."

"Do you mean that, Fergus?"

"Of course. I'll bring his head back on the point of my snickersnee."

"But that's crazy!" She looked up as Marot approached. "Aristide, talk sense into this chivalrous idiot! He's acting like one of his nuttier tourists!"

When Reith's plan had been explained, Marot said: "I sympathize, my friend. An ancestor of mine killed a man in a duel on less provocation. But let us see if the means you propose will lead to the desired result, or if they will be—how do you say—contraproductive. First, have you any idea how good a fencer Foltz is?"

"No. Do you know, Lish?"

"I suspect he's quite good. He has some padded jackets and wooden practice swords, and he and the guards fence with them."

"Furthermore," continued Marot, "you propose to assail this villain alone, when he has eight or nine Krishnans, including a pair of armored guards, at his call. You would have only me, and I am no warrior; I do not think our Krishnans would be of help. Even if you wounded Foltz, one of his retainers would stab you from behind. Then who would be left to protect the lady?"

"Fergus needn't pick a fight with Warren," said Alicia. "He

said he'd kill both of you, the first chance he got."

"Then again," continued Marot in his calm, professorial manner, "suppose against all odds that you succeed. Dasht Kharob was very insistent that there be no combat between Foltz and me, and I am sure he would feel just as strongly about you and Foltz. Unless the winner quickly escaped across some border, he would find himself arrested by the men of the Dasht. By then, the High Priestess may be back on her throne, looking for a chance to question the victor on the orthodoxy of his theological views—with the help of the red-hot pincers."

"I hate to admit you're right," growled Reith. "But suppose Foltz brings his whole gang over here and attacks us?"

"Then we must fight or flee, as circumstances dictate. Meanwhile, I urge that we finish our work as soon as possible. If you and I aid our Krishnans with the picks and the shovels, perhaps we can break the block out this afternoon and be on our way back to Kubyab before nightfall. Once there, I think we can count on the good squire for help. Meanwhile, the charming little Doctor Dyckman had better catch up on her sleep."

"Aristide!" she said sharply. "I *hate* it when people call me 'little'! I'm a hundred and seventy centimeters, which is well over average height for American women."

"A thousand pardons, my lit—my tall dear."

An hour later, Alicia was asleep in the Terrans' tent. Reith and Marot, stripped to shorts and boots, worked on the excavation along with the two Krishnans. Although Roqir was still hidden by the overcast, the day turned steamy-hot. To aggravate their problems, a few centimeters below the surface, the ruddy sandstone became harder and more resistant to the picks, slowing the excavation.

Reith stepped back for a breath, drew his forearm across his sweat-bathed forehead, and looked up. "More visitors!" he exclaimed.

Two riders in wide straw sombreros approached at a gallop. One was the shaihan-herd whom Sainian had posted at Foltz's camp; the other, Warren Foltz.

As they neared the excavation, Foltz pulled his aya to a halt with a savage jerk, sprang to earth, and tossed the reins to the shaihan-herd. Reith noted that Foltz wore his sword. Reith felt for his own and then realized with dismay that it was back in his tent. He cursed himself for stupidity.

Foltz stepped close to Reith, barking: "Where's Alicia?"

"What business is that of yours?" said Reith.

"She's my woman, that's what business it is, and I'll have her back!"

"She's nobody's woman. She can go where she likes and live with whom she pleases."

"Oh, yeah?" said Foltz. "We'll see about that." He looked around. "I'll bet she's in one of those tents. I'm taking her back, and don't anybody try to stop me if he knows what's good for him!"

"What saith the Terran?" asked Girej. "We want no part of this dispute."

Foltz turned and started for the tents. Reith bounded around and got in front of him. "Keep away from those tents!"

"Gentlemen!" said Marot. "You must not carry this further. Fergus is correct about the rights of Doctor Dyckman."

"Out of my way, Reith!" snarled Foltz, drawing his sword and pointing it at Reith's naked midriff. "I don't want to kill you, particularly; but if you try to stop me I will!"

Reith spied Marot's Marsh pick lying on the red, pebble-dotted soil. He snatched up the tool and again confronted Foltz.

"Think you can fight with that? Ha!" said Foltz. "Okay, sucker, don't say I didn't warn you!" He threw himself forward in a fencing lunge.

Reith parried the lunge with the head of the Marsh pick, batting the blade aside with a clang. He tried to get in a return blow at Foltz's head, but the awkward implement moved too slowly in his hands. He had to whip it around to parry another thrust. Then came another, which he barely avoided.

Reith was aware of movement behind Foltz. He was watching his antagonist too closely to note peripheral details but heard a solid thump. Warren Foltz swayed and collapsed, his sword clattering on the pebbles. Marot stood behind the fallen man, holding in both hands his geologist's hammer.

Reith knelt to examine the body. A wound on Foltz's scalp oozed blood, but his pulse was regular. Reith cautiously probed the scalp around the wound; there was no indication of a broken skull.

"What'll we do with him?" said Reith. "I'd like to cut the bastard's throat, but I suppose that would cause more trouble than it's worth. Besides, it wouldn't seem right."

Marot replied: "I suggest that we tie and gag him until we are ready to depart."

The shaihan-herd, who still sat his mount, spoke: "Sirs, what do ye? My master told me not to meddle in the privy quarrels amongst the Terrans. At the same time, I was to succor Master Folt when, because of's ignorance, he got into trouble. Lives he yet?"

"He lives," said Reith. "He'll probably recover—perhaps in an hour or two."

"I'll take care of him," said the shaihan-herd. "Pray hold these."

As he spoke, the Krishnan dismounted and handed the reins of the two ayas to Reith and Marot. He picked up the unconscious Foltz and slung him across his saddle, so that his head and arms hung down on one side and his legs on the other. With the lariat that had been coiled on his own saddle, the shaihan-herd secured Foltz in place. Then he remounted, took both sets of reins, and set out at a walk. The two animals passed over the nearest rise and out of sight.

"Thanks, Aristide," said Reith. "He'd have let daylight into me otherwise."

Marot shrugged. "What is a friend for? But I do not know that we were clever to let that cowboy take him away. We should have tied him up and kept him here until we left, as I proposed."

"I'm afraid you're right. When the Krishnan took over, I didn't think fast enough."

"But look," said Marot. "The day is more than half gone, and the weather does not look good. Let us return to our muttons."

"Belt on your sword! We've got to wear them and sleep with them, even when they're in the way."

Alicia appeared at the entrance to the tent and came towards them, moving briskly even though the signs of her recent encounter with Foltz were still visible. "Has anything happened while I slept?" she asked.

"*Grand dieu*, has anything happened!" exclaimed Marot. "We had a visit from your former employer, who tried to kill Fergus."

"*What?*"

"Let Fergus tell you the tale. Me, I must push some more

work from these *soi-disant* workers."

Marot turned back to the dig. Reith, who had been examining Foltz's sword, narrated the events of the man's visit. Alicia cried:

"Oh, you beast! Why didn't you wake me up, at least after the Frenchman stunned him?"

"If you'd been here, darling, you might have gotten between us and been run through by Foltz or whacked with my pick. So it's just as well."

"Male bigot! I seem to miss all the fun. But, after Aristide hit him, why didn't you kill him? You earlier wanted to ride to his camp and skewer him."

"I know. I thought of it, but it might have caused complications with the Dasht and, later, with the administration at Novorecife."

"Nonsense! All you had to do was put your point against his throat and push, and say it was self-defense. Or quietly take him away and bury him, and say nothing to anybody."

"Sainian's cowboy was watching, so the story would have gotten out. Besides, killing an unconscious man goes against the grain."

"Oh, you sentimental idiot! You're as bad as Percy Mjipa! He's a magnificent fighter and brave as a pride of lions, but his squeamishness almost got us killed three times in the Khaldoni countries."

"Percy!" said Reith to the heavens. "Where are you now that we need you?"

"He's off being Terran consul at Zanid."

"I know. I'm sorry, Lish, but if you want a cold-blooded killer, don't waste time on me."

"Then let me tell you what your attack of knight-errantry will cost us. When Warren recovers, he'll come back loaded for bear. You'll wake up to find yourself full of arrows and bolts, without a chance to use that nice shiny sword. He's a grade-A hater. If you think he'd spare you because you spared him, you're kidding yourself."

"If he's such a creep, how come you ever took up with him?"

"Mainly, because he had a job for me when I had to have one or starve. To be fair, Warren has his good points, even though he's a bastard in other ways. He's a handsome devil and can be charming. He's a hard worker and honest according to his lights. But when he gets a fixed idea, he'll break a leg, no matter whose, to prove it.

"Of course, I should have caught on to Warren's nature sooner. He hit me once before, a slap in the face when we quarreled. But he seemed so truly sorry that I forgave him."

"Well," said Reith, "we've got to dig out Aristide's fossil and be on our way before Foltz tries anything more. I'd better lend a hand with the picks and shovels. You can help, too."

"How? I'd be glad to."

"By scraping away the spoil as we dig the trench around the block. Otherwise it keeps sliding back down in."

The block came loose as the light began to fade. Marot said: "Much as I wish to be off, I do not see how we can part before tomorrow. So let us eat, go early to bed, and be up before daybreak."

Alicia was sitting by the dying fire, asking the two Krishnan workers about life in Kubyab and scribbling notes in English shorthand, when Reith beckoned Marot into their tent. In an undertone he said:

"I can't very well ask her to bunk in with the Krishnans, although they have more room than we do. Three in here would crowd us badly. Shouldn't you and I both move—"

"But my friend!" exclaimed Marot. "It is I alone who shall move in with our workmen. You shall remain. Do you think I am made of stone?"

"Well—ah—"

"It is the only practical plan. Four in the larger tent would be too many. But please have a care for my papers and specimens."

"Of course!" said Reith. He went out and spoke to Alicia: "We keep farmer's hours here, you know."

"That suits me. It's been a rough day."

"Okay. Aristide has given up his mattress to you."

"Darling of him." As she tied the tent flaps closed, she asked: "Is that one his?"

"Yep," said Reith. Like any old married couple, they stripped without ceremony or self-consciousness. But, when Reith turned down the lamp, Alicia slithered in under Reith's quilt. At once, without words or hesitation, they began kissing and fondling, avidly and hungrily, with a kind of desperate ardor. It was as if by the intensity of their lovemaking they hoped to wipe out all the unhappy memories of the past year. Presently Reith whispered: "Ready?"

"You just bet!... Boy, *you* certainly are! Just be careful of my bruises, dearest love!"

From the other tent came the plaintive sounds of Marot's flute and the snores of the hired hands.

As they lay side by side in the darkness, Reith heard a smothered sniffle. Alicia angrily wiped away a tear; he knew how she hated displays of feminine weakness. But then came a sob and a torrent of tears. She buried her face against Reith's chest, murmuring:

"Oh, Fergus, what a fool I've been! I should have known that good men like you don't grow on trees."

Cradling her in his arms and stroking her hair, Reith felt wetness trickling down his own cheeks. He longed to tell her how much he loved her and wanted her back. But his basic caution, together with a lively memory of their battles before the break, held him silent. Before he dared commit himself again, he wanted to observe her, to make sure that the other, the unlovable Alicia, the termagant into which she sometimes unpredictably metamorphosed, had been banished for good.

After Alicia had cried for a while, she said in a choked voice: "Fergus dear, you don't suppose—I mean—could we possibly—"

"We'll see how things work out," said Reith.

She lay silently for a time before saying: "I suppose that's the best I can hope for now. Whatever happens, you'll always have a special place in my heart."

"And you in mine."

"You know I wasn't without experience before I met you, but you're the *only* one I've ever really enjoyed making love with."

Reith thought it tactless, but entirely characteristic of Alicia, to bring up her sexual adventures before and after her marriage. She had a compulsion to confess to any act of hers that the hearer might take as to her discredit. Yet her allusion sent waves of intense curiosity through Reith's mind. He wanted to know all about her relationship with Foltz. When and how had they begun? Was it true that Foltz had failed to give her pleasure, or had she said that merely to flatter her former husband?

Reith sternly repressed his curiosity, not wishing to embarrass or offend her. She plunged on: "In spite of what Warren said, it's not true about me and Percy Mjipa. We were *not* sexually intimate, even though we were cooped up naked together, and with his huge strength I couldn't have prevented him. Percy's a genuine man of honor. Nor was it true about the President of Qirib, either."

"What's this about President Vizman?" said Reith. "I knew you'd met him on your way to the Khaldoni countries, but. . . ."

"What gave Warren the idea that Vizman had screwed me? The poor dope fell genuinely in love with me."

"That's easy to do," said Reith.

"I've been propositioned by more Krishnans than I can remember; but Vizman and King Ainkhist were the only ones to offer honorable marriage; and with the king I'd have been just the head of a huge harem. Vizman was unmarried, and the Qiribuma are monogamous; so he wanted to make me the First Lady of Qirib."

"Well, obviously. . . ."

"Obviously I didn't accept. Vizman's a nice enough fellow as politicians go, but I hadn't the least desire to be his consort, or mistress, or anything other than a friend of another species."

Reith felt himself tensing, as if he were facing an invisible foe; but he kept his voice even. "Well? What happened?"

"I explained, as gently as I could, that we'd have to remain just friends. I had my own life to lead and would not join my fortunes to those of any Krishnan, no matter how exalted."

"At least," said Reith with a sardonic edge to his voice, "you wouldn't have had to worry about your career's being interrupted by pregnancy."

"Let's not revive that old argument, darling! There wouldn't have been any more career—of my kind, anyway. Vizman wanted to buy me an egg on the adoption market, so I'd have a little Krishnan to raise. When I said no, loud and clear, the poor fellow was quite cut up, accusing me of racial prejudice. But he still writes me and sends little gifts.

"Anyway, that's how the story got around. Vizman did offer an unusual inducement to marry him."

"What was that?"

"I stayed several days at his palace, and we had long discussions, mostly about Terran laws and institutions. He'd heard that most Terrans regarded slavery as wrong, and he wanted to know our reasons. So I told him—and don't accuse me of meddling in native affairs!"

"I wasn't going to," said Reith.

"Anyway, when I presented all the arguments, he came around to the anti-slavery point of view."

"I thought there were only a few slaves in Qirib?"

"Several thousand, mostly in the mines of the Zogha Range. I don't suppose they like it better than slaves do elsewhere. Vizman had to move cautiously; but he promised that, if I accepted his proposal, he'd abolish slavery in Qirib within a year. I feel a little guilty about turning him down, when I think of those poor slaves."

"If you'd accepted him," said Reith, "you wouldn't have met me in Novo after Percy rescued you. And we wouldn't have had—whatever we had."

Alicia began to sniffle again. "Now you're thinking, maybe that would have been just as well! Oh, Fergus, for all my bluster about being self-sufficient, I sometimes feel as if I were standing naked in an icy wind. Hold me tight!"

He cuddled and stroked her until she calmed. At last he said: "Good-night, Lish darling," and settled himself to sleep. Outside, a flash of lightning illuminated the crack of the tent flaps. Rain began to drum on the canvas.

V.

THE DIG

As Reith peered forth from his tent, a small voice behind him said: "How's the weather?"

"Drizzling." He turned to see Alicia, barely visible in the pre-dawn light, throw off the quilt and stretch. Through a yawn she asked:

"What does one use for a bathroom here?"

"We haven't given the matter much thought. There's a thicket on the river bank, about fifty meters downstream."

"Do you know what I need, Fergus? A good bath. I haven't had a decent bath in a ten-night, and you don't exactly smell like roses either."

"Little wonder," said Reith, "the way I've been kept hopping. Tell you what! I'll meet you at the river in ten minutes, with a bar of genuine soap."

A quarter-hour later, they stood waist-deep on the sandy bottom of the Zora, splashing, soaping, and scrubbing each other. In the course of this play, they somehow found themselves in each other's arms and, inevitably, began hugging and kissing. At last Alicia drew back and giggled:

"My goodness, and in this cold water, too! I wouldn't have believed it possible, you old satyr!"

"It's been a long time," said Reith. "Well?"

"I'm just a poor, weak, helpless woman, at your mercy."

"About as helpless as Jengis Khan," he said as they waded ashore hand in hand. They dried each other off and started for the tent. At the entrance, Reith paused.

"Wait!" he said. "I should have asked sooner: are you safe? You couldn't have brought your FMs with you."

"I took my last one three days ago," she said. "So I couldn't get preg for another thirty days anyway. Come on!"

Later, Alicia sighed: "Fergus, you're wonderful! How could I have been such an idiot?"

"We all do things we regret later. Speaking of your FMs, I wonder, considering how adamant you were about not mixing children with a profession, why you never had yourself sterilized, as so many career women do?"

"I once intended to, but Lucy McKay warned me away from it."

"The one you learned anthropology from?"

"Yes, the famous xenathropologist. She had herself sterilized young, for the usual reasons—"

"The usual reason," Reith interrupted with a trace of scorn in his voice, "is to be able to screw around *ad libitum* with impunity."

"If you think I considered a tube job for that reason, you're wrong, whatever Lucy's purposes. But sometimes a woman is put in a position where she has little choice; and accidents will happen."

"She can always say no, unless there's actual force—"

"That's what you think, but I know better! I've been through it three times, beginning with my doctorate. The old creep made it plain that either I gave him his or flunked my oral. And then there was—"

Reith put up a hand: "I know; I know. Please, Lish, don't confess again. But—"

"Anyway, the year after Lucy had herself fixed, she fell desperately in love with a man who wanted a family and wouldn't marry any girl who couldn't give him one. She never really got over it. When I knew her, she'd been through eight husbands and at least a hundred lovers but was still unhappy. So I've left that option open, just in case I should change my mind. Fergus dearest, have you a spare clean toothbrush I could borrow?"

* * *

As the only gourmet in Reith's party, Marot had taken over the cooking. While he lit a fire and juggled his supplies to put together a tasty breakfast of native ingredients, Reith shaved with a hand mirror. When the paleontologist called the others together, Reith and Alicia fell ravenously upon their food. Marot explained:

"I must reduce the block containing our specimen, so that we can hoist it to the back of an aya. When I need your muscle, Fergus, I shall call. *Amusez-vous donc!*" he added with a knowing twinkle.

"He must think I'm a superman," muttered Reith as Marot and the Krishnans trailed off.

"You're superman enough for me," said Alicia. "If you were any superer, you'd wear me out. Let's get at the packing."

As they worked, they talked and gossiped and laughed and paused for kisses. When their task was done, Reith cast an uneasy glance at the leaden sky, saying:

"It'll be just our luck to slog back to Kubyab in another downpour."

When all was ready for departure except for striking the tents, Marot and the Krishnans appeared for their midday repast. Marot said: "The work is finished. Let us eat before we go."

As Marot finished mixing one of his salads and Reith was frying squares of shaihan steak, a rider appeared against the sky. He came down the long slope at a canter, drew up, and sprang lithely from his saddle. Beneath the brim of the floppy straw hat, Reith recognized the shaihan-herd Herg, who had guided them to the site.

"Good morrow, sirs!" said Herg. "The squire hath sent me to see how ye fare, and what treasure ye've found."

"I will gladly show you my treasure," said Marot, looking up from his salad-making. "The rest of you, eat! I shall take Master Herg to the dig."

When the paleontologist and the shaihan-herd returned, the Krishnan wore a puzzled frown. "Is it that these bones turned to stone have magical or medicinal properties?"

"No," said Marot. "We seek them only to give us knowledge. This knowledge, we hope, will explain life on this world and on ours as well."

Herg shook his head. "I shall never understand *Ertsuma.*"

"Your fellow beings speak enviously, do they not, of the wonders of Terran machines and devices? The reason we have them is that certain Terrans first sought out the knowledge needed to make them."

"That idea bears thinking on," said Herg. "But now I maun tell you ye'll soon have company."

"Eh?" said Reith. "Who's coming? Foltz and his people?"

"Nay—at least, not that I wot of. The party whereof I speak is a priest of Bákh, one Behorj bad-Qarz, with guards and attendants numbering a score in all."

"How do you know this?" said Reith, looking sharply at Herg.

"I passed them on my way hither. They sought your camp, so I gave them directions and continued on."

"Why didn't they come along with you?"

"The Reverend Behorj, being aged, travels but slowly. They'll be here within the hour."

"What do they want?"

"A guard told me a rumor hath reached Jeshang, that these diggings by you and Master Folt may cast doubt upon our holy scriptures. Father Behorj comes to inquire."

"Aristide!" said Reith. "Can we load the pack aya quickly and be off for Kubyab before they arrive? We'll try to avoid them—"

"It will take half an hour at least, including the securing of our specimen." Marot shaded his eyes with his hand, peering up the long slope from the river. "Master Herg, do you see figures moving on the skyline?"

"Aye; 'tis indeed the priest's party." Herg looked up at the lowering sky. "I smell more rain, and the squire commanded me to visit Master Folt along of you. The master hath withdrawn Ghirch from that camp for duty with the roundup. So fare ye well!"

Marot said to Reith: "You see, my friend, it is too late to flee. They would arrive while we are still struggling with our block. We must face them with such equanimity as we can muster."

"You have the most training in that kind of argument, so you'd better handle the Reverend Behorj," said Reith.

Herg swung into the saddle and spurred his aya up the long slope.

"I want my say!" said Alicia. "The Bákhites are making the same mistake that most theological religions on Earth have made. They try to impose their own doctrine on everyone."

"Of course!" said Reith. "A monopoly of the supernatural means more wealth, power, and glory for them."

"There must be some who take a less narrowly selfish view!" Alicia persisted. "I want to warn them that all they'll accomplish is to start a cycle of bloody wars."

"Good Lord!" said Reith. "You're out of your mind, Lish. These people won't listen to your reasoning. They'll take your talk as evidence of heresy and boil you in Lazdai's Kettle."

"But it's wrong, when you see people taking a disastrous course, not at least to tip them off. Don't worry about me; I'll flatter old Behorj and have him eating out of my hand."

"Dear lady," said Marot, "such a course would cause you trouble at Novorecife, even if you avoided difficulties here."

"I don't care. I'm merely doing what's right; somebody's got to."

"It would be a flagrant violation—" began Reith.

"Oh, fishfeathers! I'm not leaking technological secrets. I'm not doing anything Terran missionaries don't do all the time, and Novo tolerates *their* meddling in native affairs."

"Novo has to, because of pressure from the national governments," growled Reith. "But it's still dangerous meddling. Not long ago, the Reverend Jensen's head was sent to Novo packed in salt. And I just won't allow you to run such a risk."

Alicia jumped up. "Don't tell me what to do, Fergus Reith! You're not my husband, and I wouldn't let you stop me even if you were."

"That's one reason I'm not," barked Reith. "Since it's my hide you're risking along with your own, you will *not* attend this inquisition. You'll stay in one of the tents, as quiet as Aristide's fossils, until these priests have gone."

"I'd like to see you make me! I'm not going into your damned tent, and—what are you doing?"

Reith, who had risen, said to Marot: "Aristide, fetch me a length of rope, and bear a hand."

Reith seized Alicia's wrist, spun her around, and grabbed her other free arm. She screamed, kicked, and clawed; but with Marot's help, Reith tied her wrists behind her back. Then with another turn of the rope he lashed her ankles together.

"I'll kill you for this!" she panted.

Marot mopped his sweating face with a bandana. "She is strong, that one. I would rather tie up a wildcat."

"Sorry about this, Lish," said Reith. "If you had your way, we'd all be killed. Now for a gag. Aristide, can you sacrifice that handkerchief?"

Soon they carried Alicia, writhing and gurgling, into the larger tent and laid her on one of the pallets.

"That *petite* must be horribly uncomfortable," said Marot as they emerged. "I hate to treat her thus, but I comprehend the necessity."

Reith looked up the slope. Herg was just riding past the approaching priestly party. The shaihan-herd exchanged brief waves with the newcomers and vanished over the skyline. The priestly procession plodded slowly downhill.

As the visitors neared his camp, Reith saw that a boxlike sedan chair was slung on poles between two ayas in tandem, guided by a groom on the back of the lead animal. The party included six mailed guards, several Krishnans in the garb of shaihan-herds, and several others clad in uniforms of black and white. Reith guessed these to be acolytes or servants of the priest.

The procession halted before the tents. One of the attendants dismounted, handed his reins to another, and ceremoniously opened the door of the litter. He reached inside and took out a stool, which he placed on the ground.

The priest, whose apparel resembled that of his minions save that his diaperlike nether garment was scarlet instead of black, and he wore a red-and-white turban, lowered himself stiffly from the litter. Supporting himself by a staff fitted with a brazen finial of intricate design, he surveyed the Earthmen. Reith and Marot bowed. In slow, careful Mikardandou, Marot said:

"I am Aristide Marot, from the planet Terra. Have I the honor to address the Reverend Behorj bad—" He whispered fiercely to Reith, "What was the rest of his name? The patronymic?"

"Bad-Qarz."

"The Reverend Behorj bad-Qarz?"

The priest gave the Krishnan equivalent of a smile. "That is so, my son. I take it you have been apprised of my coming?"

"Yes, Your Reverence; but only after we had finished our

midday meal. Had we known the time of your arrival in advance, we should have prepared a repast for you. As it is, may we offer you any refreshment?"

"Thank you, my son; but we have already dined along the road. Know you the purpose of this visit?"

"As I understand it, you wish to ascertain whether our researches bear upon your holy religion."

"Quite right. Where can we hold this discourse?"

"Doukh, set up three camp chairs and a table, quickly. Your Reverence, this other Terran is my guide, the intrepid Fergus Reith."

"My client flatters me," said Reith.

Behorj and the Terrans seated themselves. The priest leaned forward and fixed sharp black eyes on Marot, saying: "Tell me, in your own words, what you do here."

Marot: "We seek the remains of beasts that once roamed your planet but no longer exist, save as petrified bones and teeth embedded in the rocks."

"Mean you that there once abounded monsters, like those whereof the legends tell, and that these have utterly vanished?"

"I believe that to be true, Your Reverence. Of course, we Terrans have as yet explored but a fraction of your planet's surface. It may be that creatures we believe extinct still dwell in places that we have not seen. I can only reason by the analogy of my own world, where hundreds of species have become extinct, many in recent centuries as a result of hunting or the occupation of their habitats. But what, Reverend Sir, has this to do with the Gospel of Bákh?"

Behorj paused before answering. "The first chapter of the *Book of Bákh* tells how, after Bákh had created the universe, the divinity established life on each planet where conditions favored its survival. Bákh presented a pair of each species to the first human pair and recounted the names of each, saying: 'These creatures I have made to share the world with you forever. Have a care that ye take no more of each kind than ye need, lest the breeding stock be depleted to vanishment.' Now, if Bákh intended each species to last for all eternity, how could it permit any to become extinct?"

"Your Reverence, your question lies beyond my competence. I do know that many life forms have disappeared from my own world, where Bákh presumably established them with similar intentions. As for this world, it would not surprise me

if the people, being weak and sinful like those of my own
Terra, have disobeyed the commands of Bákh."

"Why should Bákh permit such flouting of his desires?"

"I do not know, Your Reverence. Your question has given
generations of Terran theologians deep concern, and no fully
satisfactory answer has yet transpired. Does the religion of
Bákh accept the philosophy of Kurdé the Wise in matters of
logic?"

The priest's antennae rose with surprise. "Know you the
words of Kurdé?"

"I have read some of his treatises," said Marot. "He can be
compared to a philosopher on Terra, one Aristoteles, who flour-
ished centuries ago. Both sages found that a statement of fact
cannot be both true and false at once. Does the doctrine of
Bákh agree with that?"

"Aye, it doth. But what hath this to do with the question
of extinction?"

"This, Your Reverence. If men of science find the remains
of a creature, and diligent exploration of the planet fails to find
any living specimen thereof, then we must infer that extinction
has indeed taken place. In such a case, the doctrines of Bákh
must be reinterpreted in the light of this discovery. Following
Kurdé, a beast cannot be both extant and extinct at once. Is it
not so, sir?"

"Is there not the possibility," said Behorj slowly, "that these
petrified bones be not the remains of living creatures, but shapes
formed by natural causes—the inherent generative powers of
nature? Or perhaps they have been lodged in the rocks by evil
spirits that serve the demon Yesht, in order to deceive the
faithful?"

Marot shrugged. "When your world has been completely
explored and studied and both its living forms and those found
fossil have been catalogued, then perhaps the answers to these
questions will transpire. Meanwhile, let Your Reverence be
assured that we Terrans have no desire to disturb established
doctrine."

As the leaden gray of the overcast darkened, distant thunder
rumbled. An attendant approached and bowed. "Your Reverence, if we fain would reach the other Terran camp without a
soaking, we had best move on."

"All in good time," said Behorj, waving the servitor away.

"Do Terran doctrines of the Creation agree with the Truth of Bákh?"

"If Your Reverence will tell me the tenets of your faith, perhaps I can judge."

"The *Book of Bákh* reads thus: 'In the beginning, chaos abounded. Wearying of confusion, Bákh gathered all the chaos into a single lump, which it compressed down to a size no greater than the head of a pin. Then it spake a magical word, and the pinhead burst, casting all the matter of the universe far and wide to form stars, planets, and all other heavenly bodies.'"

"Why, yes!" said Marot. "It is a belief held in esteem among Terran astronomers. It is the Doctrine of the Great Explosion—in Master Reith's native tongue, the 'Big Bang.'"

Lightning flared purple among the lowering clouds, and thunder rolled closer. Behorj said: "I fear we must part, much as I have enjoyed this discourse. I shall report your piety and humility to the High Priestess, good my Doctor."

Reith and the Frenchman rose and bowed as the aged priest got slowly to his feet and, supported by his staff, tottered back to his litter. They silently watched as the procession formed up and started up the slope.

"Whew!" said Reith. "You sure handled that one, Aristide. Doukh! Pack up these chairs and table, and quickly, please."

"I feared the priest would ask me something really dangerous," said Marot, "like creation versus evolution. I have not actually read Kurdé; only an article about him in a French journal. So I was—how do you say—buffing?"

"Bluffing."

"Thank you. We can thank Bákh for the coming storm, which sent the priest on his way. At least Bákh, unlike the Judaeo-Christian God, seems to have been a conservationist."

"Shall we load your specimen and start despite the rain?"

"I wish we could, but I do not think that practical. This clay, when wet, becomes extremely slippery; and if we were caught in a downpour along the road, we should probably get lost."

"Hey!" said Reith. "I've got to untie Alicia. She'll be mad enough to scratch my eyes out, but she'll get over it by to-morrow. Here comes the rain!"

A few big drops spattered as Reith peered up the slope to

make certain that the Bákhites were out of sight. Reassured, he walked briskly towards the larger tent.

"*Holà!*" cried Marot. "We have more visitors, down along the river. I think I see Foltz at their head."

Reith whipped around. Foltz and nine mounted Krishnans were galloping along the north bank of the Zora, their sombreros flopping. Behind them fluttered yellow rain capes of some sort of waxed cloth.

"They're out for blood," muttered Reith. "Damn! Alicia was right; we should have killed that skite."

As the rain thickened to a downpour, Doukh and Girej exchanged a few words, sprang to their feet, and ran away downstream.

Marot handed Reith his sword but shook his head. "Two cannot fight ten. One must be realistic."

"We can take a couple with us," grated Reith. "Don't trust them, whatever they say. They'd rather kill us without resistance, but kill us they will."

Now the riders were upon them. The column swerved to one side and coiled around itself. Reith and Marot stood at the center of a ring of galloping ayas, from whose hooves flew clods of russet mud.

"Halt!" shouted Foltz. The Krishnans pulled up, their animals skidding on the wet clay.

"Do you give up?" said Foltz.

"No," said Reith. The rain fell harder, running off the brims of the riders' hats like ragged veils.

Foltz made a hand signal. Four Krishnans dismounted and unstrapped crossbows from their saddles, cocked them, and placed bolts in the grooves. They pointed their weapons at Reith and Marot.

"Surrender!" barked Foltz.

Reith muttered: "Guard my back!" He hurled himself straight at Foltz, his sword extended before him. He had not gone three strides when a lariat snaked out of the air and looped around Reith's legs, bringing him down prone in the mud. Several Krishnans piled on him, punching and kicking.

"Tie them up!" said Foltz.

Marot yelled angrily as he, too, was roped. Reith's wrists and ankles were lashed together. Foltz dismounted.

"Master Foltz!" cried one of the Krishnans on foot. "Come see this!"

By craning his neck, Reith perceived that the Krishnan who spoke was standing at the larger tent. Foltz hurried over. Presently he emerged leading Alicia, who was rubbing her arms. Foltz dragged the girl to where Reith lay trussed and kicked him in the ribs.

"For this," he said, "I'm going to kill you, Reith." He addressed Marot. "I passed your dig, Aristide. You'll never ruin *my* career with false inferences from scattered finds!" To his Krishnans he said: "Find me a hammer!"

"*À dieu ne plaise!*" said Marot in a tearful voice. "He means to break up my specimen!"

Someone handed Foltz a geologist's hammer and the Marsh pick, and he started towards the dig. Alicia walked with him, pulling at his arm and arguing; but Reith could not hear the words over the chatter of the Krishnans and the drumming of the rain.

Some Krishnans followed Foltz; others remained to guard the captives. The rain-muffled sounds of pounding rock came to Reith's ears.

"This time," muttered Marot, "we must kill Foltz when chance permits. I am a man of peace; but to destroy scientific knowledge is worse than to murder a human being."

"Chance is unlikely to permit," muttered Reith. "Lish was right. It's one of her more irritating traits."

"What is?"

"Being right, about killing that bleep."

"I know, my friend. But it is also my fault."

"How? I don't see—"

"If only I had hit him with the pointed end, he would now be a rigid."

"A what? Oh, you mean a stiff."

"Ah, yes. We could have quietly buried him. . . ."

The bellow of thunder and the howl of the wind muted the sound of the blows on Marot's fossil. The Krishnans moved about, talking and gesturing. A garrulous species, given to oratory, each seemed to try to shout the others down. The arbalesters retreated to the tents to protect their weapons from rain, but the others remained. As lightning sent lavender tentacles snaking through the clouds, the herd of ayas was led away. Misery silenced the captives.

Then a Krishnan gave a shout and pointed. Twisting his neck, Reith glimpsed, beyond the curtain of rain, mounted figures moving. The four crossbowmen boiled out of the tents, hastily recocking their weapons. Amid the gabble, Reith thought he caught the words: "Basht's gang!" He remembered Sainian's warning against the bandit chieftain.

Crossbows snapped, though the rain drowned out the thrum of the quarrels. From one of the newcomers came a scream.

All was confusion. People ran hither and thither, slipping on the mud and sometimes falling down. Swords flashed from scabbards; contradictory orders were shouted. Reith had a glimpse of Foltz, charging towards the camp with his sword out.

A mounted man pounded past, so close that Reith feared being trampled. To his astonishment, as the wind blew back the rider's rain cape, he glimpsed the black-and-white habit of an attendant of the Bákhite priest.

Nearby, two fought savagely on foot until one slipped in the mud and fell. Reith saw the other's blade rise and fall again and again, until the cries of the fallen man died away to a gurgle.

The fighting swirled away downstream. At last a feminine voice said: "Hold still, Fergus, and I'll cut you loose."

It was Alicia, wielding a dirk taken from one of the sprawled bodies. She severed Reith's bonds and then freed Marot.

"Now what?" she asked breathlessly.

Sitting up and rubbing his extremities, Marot said: "They've all gone downstream, *dieu merci!*—those on their feet, that is. Where are my sacred eyeglasses? Ah, there!" He picked his glasses out of the mud. "Fergus, you and Alicia go find us mounts. Then come to the dig."

"What are you planning?" said Reith, scraping mud off his face.

"You will see. I know what I do." The paleontologist limped off upstream.

"He'll collect his specimen if it kills him, and us. too," growled Reith. "But we've got to catch some ayas. Come along!"

Reith picked up his sword, which lay naked in the mud, and trotted towards the shrubs to which their ayas were tethered. There he found not only the expedition's four animals but also ten others. A Krishnan in a rain cape barred their way with a sword.

"*Ohé!*" said this one. "Who loosed you?"

"Out of my way!" cried Reith. "I'm collecting my animals."

"Nay, ye shan't! I command these beasts until Master Folch relieves me. Get ye hence and threaten me not! Must I spit you?"

The Krishnan stepped forward in a fencing stance. Reith bored in, lunging, thrusting, and parrying. The swords clanged and whirled, spattering raindrops. Once Reith slipped on the mud but, straining every sinew, recovered before his antagonist could take advantage of the error.

Reith feinted at the Krishnan's midriff. The Krishnan whipped his blade around in the parry in seconde, turning his hand from supine to prone. Reith had been well drilled in the counter to this maneuver, he doubled and drove his sword into the Krishnan's chest.

While Reith's blade was still fixed between his opponent's ribs, the Krishnan made a weak slash at Reith's sword arm. As the blade bit into the leather of his jacket, Reith felt the sting of a cut. He snatched his own blade back.

The Krishnan tottered forward, muttering, and crashed to the ground. Reith wiped the blue-green blood from his blade on the fallen one's garments. Battered and exhausted, he picked his own party's ayas out of the herd and gathered up their reins, saying: "Let's go, Lish!"

Reith and Alicia led their four beasts to the remaining tent. They saddled the animals, working furiously with rainwater running down their faces and little by little washing off the mud. They hastily gathered such gear as had not been scattered, smashed, or stolen. All his and Marot's extra clothing had disappeared.

Reith recovered his razor case, his igniter, and Marot's spare eyeglasses. Not seeing Marot's sword, he detached one from a corpse. He tossed everything he could find on a pair of blankets, tied up the corners of the blankets, and loaded the bundles on one of the ayas. Then he and Alicia led the animals to the dig.

They found Marot sitting on the ground in the rain, whistling a cheerful French tune as he worked, methodically going through a pile of rock fragments ranging in size from tennis balls to fists. Foltz had broken the fossil-bearing slab into about two dozen pieces but had not had time to pulverize the fragments. A few of the stones Marot tossed aside; the rest he laid on the shaihan hide stretched out before him. He looked up, saying:

"One little minute and I shall be finished."

"For God's sake!" said Reith. "What are you doing?"

"Recovering most of my specimen, which Foltz broke up.
I have sorted out the pieces with bone in them and discarded
the rest."

"God damn it!" Reith exploded. "Stop fooling around and
come along! D'you want our throats cut after all?"

"Just three more pieces," said Marot unperturbed. "Ah,
there we are!" He gathered up the corners of the hide. "Help
me to tie this up and load it on our faithful beast. If I ever
have another chance to kill Foltz. . . ."

A quarter-hour later, they wrestled the bag, now securely
tied and weighing about forty kilos, up to the back of the pack
aya. It took the combined strength of all three to hoist the
awkward bundle into place. Marot and Alicia held it balanced
while Reith hunted for more rope to fasten it to the pack saddle.
Then the aya shook itself, the bundle got away from them and
clattered to the ground, and they had to start over.

When the job was finally done, Reith raked a forearm across
a forehead coated with a mud of clay, rain, and sweat. "Ready
at last?" he gasped.

"Hokay. *A bord!*"

They walked their mounts up the slope away from the river.
As they neared the upper level, there was a lull in the rain.
Turning back, Marot said:

"Look, my friends!"

From this elevation, they could see a place on the nearer
river bank, a few hundred meters downstream from Reith's
camp. There stood a cluster of people, afoot and mounted, with
their yellow hats and rain capes bright against the dark, drab,
rainswept ground. The figures were too small to identify; but
Reith could make out perhaps five or six standing with bound
hands. Surrounding them, afoot and on ayas, stood the attendants of the Reverend Behorj, weapons at the ready. A couple
of bodies sprawled nearby.

"That ends Monsieur Foltz's dig," said Marot in tones of
grim satisfaction. "Can you see if he is among the living,
Fergus?"

"Not from here, especially as he's in Krishnan disguise."

* * *

"What on earth happened?" said Alicia as they rode off. "Foltz's gang seemed to be fighting Behorj's escort, but how could that be? It makes no sense."

"It was Behorj's escort," said Reith. "Foltz's gang mistook them for bandits and started a fight; all one big blunder. Now I'm one solid bruise from the manhandling Foltz's people gave me. What about you? I saw Foltz lead you away towards the fossil, and I thought you were trying to persuade him to come back and cut our throats."

"Oh, you idiot! I was furious at you, of course; though I admit Aristide handled the priest better than I could have. But I wasn't mad enough to ask Warren to kill you. After all, you were once my husband; and I'm still fond of you, even if you do get my back up at times."

"Then what were you doing, pulling at his arm and bickering with him?"

"I was trying to save you two, silly, and dissuade Warren from breaking up the fossil. Paleo isn't my line; but as a fellow scientist I can imagine how Aristide felt. But Warren said he was going to smash the fossil, which he said he had a moral right to do; and then come back, kill you two, and bury you.

"He also said he would take me back, whether I wanted him or not. If I'd be a good girl, know my place, and never argue, he might not have to discipline me. I suppose he meant more beatings."

"Anyone who can stop you from arguing, my dear ex, deserves a medal."

"Don't be nasty!"

"Sorry, my dear; I didn't mean that. You saved our hash this afternoon."

"And you saved mine yesterday, and I love you for it. Oh, Fergus, your arm's bleeding!"

Reith glanced at his right hand, down which a trickle of blood had run. "Just a scratch from that poor Krishnan devil I killed. We're in a hurry; it can wait till we get to Kubyab."

"You must let me clean—oh!" cried Alicia. "I have a simply divine idea!"

"What's that?"

"Warren's camp is empty. Let's ride back there so I can scoop up all my notes and things!"

"Good God, woman! We escape death by the skin of our

teeth, and you want to dally to recover some sociological scribble! No!"

Alicia's lips tightened, her eyes flashed, and Reith feared she would fly into one of her rages. Instead, with a visible effort, she controlled herself. She guided her aya close to Reith's and caught his hand, looking up with little-girl appeal. Muddy, disheveled, and rain-streaked though she was, he still thought her the prettiest thing on two planets. She pleaded:

"But Fergus! It's only a little detour, and we have hours of daylight yet. And I want those notes more than anything— more than anything but one—in the world. I'll—I'll do anything you ask."

Marot cleared his throat. "My friend, I am willing to take the small additional risk. I know what the little Alicia suffers over the loss of research materials. Permit me to add my plea to hers."

"Suppose we run into armed men?"

"Then we can retreat. What is the English saying, nothing ventured, nothing obtained?"

"Okay; but if it lands us in the soup again, don't blame me." The party changed direction towards Foltz's camp. "It strikes me we're in the soup already, in one way. Foltz's Krishnans have about cleaned us out of cash."

"When was that?" asked Marot.

"When we packed up, I looked for those bags of coins we had to pay the help, but they were gone. I've got a few karda in my money belt, but that wouldn't feed us for three days in a big city like Jazmurian. They got my good clothes, too. How about you two?"

Alicia said: "I left Warren with nothing in the world but the clothes you see."

"I was not carrying money," said Marot. "Will not that tessara around your neck get us credit on Novorecife?"

Reith held up the green rectangle of jadeoid, on which was inscribed his name and occupation in several Krishnan languages. "It might work in a real city like Mishé or Majbur; but I doubt if these Chilihagho yucks would trust it. They'd know nothing about Terran credit out here in the boonies."

Foltz's camp proved empty. Alicia found her papers; then she wanted to collect her clothes and other possessions. She took so long that Reith said:

"Lish! Foltz's gang may come back any minute. Come along!"

"Just one minute. . . . I can't find my. . . ."

"Come *on* Alicia! Aristide, help me collect her!"

"You must come, my dear," said Marot. "Otherwise we shall have to compel you again."

"Oh, damn you men!" she flared. Returning to the pack aya, she stowed a small bundle as well as her notes. "Pretending to be strong and heroic, and really being scared of your shadows! You've collected your things; why can't I have mine? Well, aren't you going to help me tie this stuff in place?"

"Such a gracious request!" murmured Reith, but he bent to the task. Then he was startled by an unearthly screech of fury from Alicia. She was looking at a table on which lay specimens wrapped in cloth. She darted to this table and snatched up a strip of azure goods, letting the fossil bone fall.

"No wonder I couldn't find my one decent dress!" she cried. "That son of a bitch cut it into strips to wrap his damned fossils! And out of sheer spite! I'll boil him in oil!"

Angrily wiping away a tear, she mounted her aya. During the long ride to Kubyab, she sulkily refused to speak to either companion.

VI.

THE BARGE

When, hours later, the fugitives drew up at Sainian's ranch house, the clouds had begun to break. A few golden spears of late-afternoon sunlight pierced the western overcast. Sainian cried:

"By Qondyor's iron yard! Ye look like the survivors of a battle!"

"We are," said Reith.

"Herg rode in this afternoon, telling of a brabble of some sort amidst the rainstorm. He seemed confused as to who fought whom. Come ye in, get dry, eat, drink, and tell me all! The only fee I ask is a good story to bedazzle my copemates. Come in!"

"Master Reith is wounded, sir," said Alicia.

"A wound?" said Sainian. "Let me see. . . . Ah, I perceive that Terran blood be red, even as I've heard. Strange. Your cut reminds me of the scratch I got when I slew that shaihan-thief. Ilui! Fetch a poultice and a bandage. But first we must rid him of the mud. Babir! Fill the tubs!"

Sainian turned Reith and Marot over to the servant Babir, while Ilui took charge of Alicia. Babir led the men to a small room containing an enormous wooden tub, which he filled with bucketfulls of water.

"You go first, my friend!" said Marot. "No, no, I insist! You have had the more strenuous day."

Knowing that Marot would argue all night rather than yield a point of politeness, Reith let himself be persuaded. He lowered his tired body into the tub, wincing at the cold.

"At times like this," he said, "I miss the hot running water at Novo."

When Reith had bathed, and Marot had bandaged the minor wound, Reith said: "I don't like having you take a bath in used water, but if we ask Babir to empty it, that might take an hour."

"Think nothing!" said Marot, stepping boldly into the cold water. "In a little French hotel, when a family orders a bath, the papa bathes first, then the mama, then the children, all in the same water. No true Frenchman would be so extravagant as to pay for three full tubs when one will serve."

Babir put his head in, saying: "Be ye gentlemen finished? The squire asks if ye need raiment."

"All we own are those muddy work clothes we arrived in. We should certainly appreciate a loan," replied Reith.

"Then, quotha, ye shall be clad from his supply."

Laid out on the bed, they found two fine woollen suits. Each consisted of a pleated kilt and a pearl-gray sleeveless jacket with large brass buttons. One kilt was a sober blue; the other, gaudy with stripes of scarlet and gold. Reith would have preferred the blue; but he was compelled to adopt the other when the red-and-yellow could not be let out at the waist far enough to accommodate Marot's girth.

"Not bad," said Reith, surveying himself in a metal mirror. "Oh, Babir! Would your master mind if we rested an hour before joining him? We've had an exhausting day."

An hour later, clad in their new splendor, Reith and Marot followed Babir to the living room, where Sainian and a burly Krishnan waited. Their host said: "These be the *Ertsuma* whereof I told you. Maghou is the stout one; Reef, the lean. Sirs, this is my old friend and distant cousin, Captain Sarf bad-Dudán, of the barge *Morkerád*."

After amenities and a round of kvad, Reith asked: "Where does your ship run to, Captain?"

"Up the Zora to Kubyab, down the Zigros to Jazmurian. This is the head of navigation for vessels larger than a skiff. We make one regular stop, at Jeshang, and as many flag stops as requested."

"How do you work your way upstream?"

"By shaihans on the towpath, same as ye do on the Pichidé. We have sails but seldom use them on the upstream passage."

"What cargo do you carry?" persisted Reith.

"Now, now," said Sainian. "All that can wait. Tell us how went your hunt for ancient bones, and how befell the battle."

Reith was well into the tale of their dig when Alicia came in with Ilui, the rancher's wife. The sight brought Reith's tale to a halt. Alicia had not only been scrubbed but also provided with a filmy violet dress, cut below the breast in the manner seen in Mishé. The captain broke the silence, saying:

"By Bákh's mercy, Sainian, this Terran frail's a well-found vessel. Pity 'tis she be not a human being; she'd lay many a fine egg for one of our lusty swains."

"You flatter like a courtier, sir," said Alicia, with a smile that brought Reith's heart into his throat.

Ilui said: "Like ye the dress, Master Reef?"

"I'm dumb with admiration."

"Ah, ye do but blandish our poor rustic fashions. Methinks 'tis not the dress but its occupant that doth kindle your admiration."

"Let's say, they complement each other," said Reith. He was about to ask whence the costume came, but Sainian had poured a second round, saying:

"Pray proceed with your story, Master Reef. I am agog to hear it."

The tale of the Terrans' adventures continued through dinner. Afterwards, as all but Reith and Alicia lit strong cigars, Reith said: "We need your advice, squire."

"Do but ask."

Reith told of the loss of their cash. "Were this one of those decadent cities you speak of, I could borrow enough to get us back to Novorecife on the strength of this token."

Reith drew the chain of the tessara over his head and handed the green slab to Sainian, who said: "Nought like this have I seen; nor, I'll wager, hath any of the villagers. Another time, I'd lend the money without asking more than a handclasp to secure it. But ye come when we have but little coin in the house—barely enough to pay my shaihan-herds till more comes in."

"When will that be, sir?"

"After the next shaihan-drive—in two or three moons. Meanwhile ye are welcome to stay here, for I fain would hear more tales of distant places and strange adventures. Shaihan-ranching's the only life for me; but betimes it grows monotonous. We've had no variety since I drowned that rascally peddler in the aya trough."

Reith shook his head. "I fear we cannot accept your generous offer, sir. We must get back to Novorecife to meet the next incoming ship from Terra. I have a flock of tourists coming in; while Doctor Marot has a berth reserved on the return passage."

"Then I know not. . . ."

Captain Sarf blew smoke. "Ye escaped the rogues on ayas, did ye not?"

"So we did."

"If they haven't been foundered, they should fetch you enough to get you home."

"It's a Hishkak of a walk from here to Novorecife, tak-ing—" (Reith paused in calculation.) "—at least a solid moon of hik ing. I might be able, but I doubt if my companions could do it."

"Besides," said Sainian, "I've examined those beasts. They should bring a good five hundred karda. Methinks that sum's not to be had in Kubyab, an ye turned every villager upside down and shook him."

"Is the railroad from Jazmurian to Majbur running?" asked Reith.

"Aye," said the captain, "or 'twas the last I heard."

"Do you carry passengers?"

"Aye; we can sleep up to ten."

"What's the fare to Jazmurian?" asked Reith.

"Thirty-five a head. Oho, I see whither blows the wind! Let's say, I'll bear the three of you to Jazmurian at a special rate: one hundred for the three, plus carriage for your beasts. That were an additional fifty."

"Fine, if we had the hundred and fifty karda," said Reith.

"Since Sainian seems to trust you," said Sarf, "I'll do the like. Let ye and your beasts ride with me to Jazmurian. There ye can sell them, pay me what ye owe, and buy your way homeward."

The squire interrupted. "Why ask the Terrans to pay for shipping ayas to Jazmurian, when the beasts were useful here? I'd say, leave the animals and board the *Morkerád*. I'll give you a letter to my agent in Jazmurian, praying him to advance four hundred karda to you and pay my cousin Sarf the hundred for your passage. The agent can deduct the debt from the profits due me after the next shaihan sale. Four hundred should see you safely back to Novorecife."

"Admirably thought on!" said Sarf. "What say ye?"

"An excellent idea," said Reith. He was struck by the informality of the arrangement. In Mishé or Majbur, there would have been an endless haggle, paring sums down to fractions of a kard, followed by written contracts with witnesses, bonds, and guarantees. He continued:

"I agree with all my liver. Permit me, squire, to thank you for your courtesy to strangers."

Sainian waved a hand. "I've lent money many a time and oft, mostly to shaihan-herds when, at the end of a drive, they'd squandered their pay on drink, gambling, and their other great pastime. Never have I lost an arzu. Nay, that's not quite sooth. One lown sought to cheat me of money I'd lent him for a house." The squire puffed smoke.

"What happened to him?" asked Reith, suspecting that he already knew the answer.

Sainian made a negligent gesture with his cigar. "I slew him."

"When you can, will you please pay Doukh and Girej whatever I owe them, and deduct it from the sum your agent is instructed to advance to me?"

"Aye; though methinks ye owe those poltroons little, since they fled from the fight."

"I can't blame them; the odds were great, and they weren't fighters."

Captain Sarf arose. "Ye'll forgive me, cousin, but I maun get home, where my good wife awaits me."

"Captain!" said Reith. "When does your ship sail?"

"Day after tomorrow, soon after dawn. I'll look for you at the pier. Good-even, all!"

When the captain had taken his leave, Sainian chuckled. "Sarf hath a double comfort, with a wife at either end of 's voyage. Thus he never wearies of either."

Alicia said: "I thought the Chilihaghuma were monogamous?"

"So they be, like unto the other Varasto nations, saving the promiscuous knightly class in Mikardand and the loose-living Balhibuma. But since Sarf's wives dwell in different jurisdictions, he's not like to be called to account."

Reith suppressed a yawn. "I trust you'll excuse us, too, sir. It's been a long, hard day."

"Indeed it hath! I see the learned doctor hath fallen asleep in's chair. Then to bed, my friends. And—ah—there's a little matter. . . ." Sainian hesitated.

"Yes?"

"As ye've seen, ye have two rooms, with one large bed and one small. I know not the Terran custom in a case like unto yours. . . ."

"Don't worry, squire. We have our arrangements all worked out."

"Ye relieve my mind; I feared embarrassment. How were ye fain to pass the morrow? I can take you on aya-back for a fifty-hoda tour of the ranch. . . ."

"Thank you, squire," said Alicia sweetly, "but after today's adventures, I'm sure we shall be happy to do nothing at all and let our cuts and bruises heal."

"I grasp the nib. Remain bedded the livelong day, an ye would. Rise when ye will, and Babir shall feed you."

Reith and Alicia took the larger room. After Reith had closed the door, she put her hands on his shoulders and gave him a long, vigorous kiss. "Darling Fergus, I'm sorry I was beastly again this afternoon! You were right as usual. You were a real hero."

"Huh!" he grunted. "I feel anything but heroic. All day, events were one jump ahead of me, and I've been too stupid to catch up. I'd be dead now but for your cutting us loose and the blunder of Foltz's gang."

"How do you mean?" She sat down on the bed and pulled him down beside her. Morosely, Reith explained:

"A hero wouldn't have let Foltz catch him without a sword. When Aristide conked the fellow with a hammer, I shouldn't have let that cowboy drag Foltz away. I should have at least tied him up until we were on our way to Kubyab. We were much too casual and dilatory about Foltz. We should have killed him, as you said. Failing that, we should have cut and run, fossil or no fossil, as soon as Herg told us of the priestly party, or even sooner. As a hero, I'm just a poop."

Alicia clasped him around the neck and spoke, punctuating each sentence with a kiss: "I won't have you speak of the man I love that way! . . . You were wonderful, and you know it! . . . You were brave enough to face Foltz unarmed, . . . and to kill that Krishnan with the ayas. . . . But for you, Foltz would be beating and raping the hell out of me right now. . . . And he made just as many bungles as we did. . . ."

Between the praise and the kisses, Reith's spirits began to revive. Alicia found him staring at her with a look she knew of old. "Fergus, don't tell me you want it *again,* after all we've been through today? How can you, with all those bruises?"

"It's that topless dress, darling. The sight of you in it would give carnal thoughts to Aristide's fossil. Where did you get it?"

"Ilui gave it to me. It's one their daughter left behind when she married and moved away. I'm so happy to be able to dress up again! I had one good blue dress, which I'd have worn the other night if I'd known it was you coming to dinner; but Warren cut that one up." She stood up, turning her back to him. "Please, could you undo those little buttons?"

As Reith struggled with the loops, she added: "What I missed most about being husbandless was having nobody to help with clothes that fasten down the back. There!" She gave him a smile pregnant with meaning. "Give me a few minutes, and we'll see if you can rise to the occasion!"

When Alicia returned to the bedroom, she found Reith sound asleep. She kissed his ear lightly, put out the lamp, and slid under the covers. After all, their host had invited them to spend the whole next day in bed.

The following day Reith and Alicia, smothering yawns, emerged for a very late breakfast. Marot had finished his, and the others of the household had long since departed on their various tasks.

The three Terrans set out for a walk about Kubyab, responding to the villagers' stares with amiable greetings. At that instant Reith felt that he loved everybody, with a few exceptions like Warren Foltz. They encountered Doukh, who began volubly to excuse his flight from the field of battle.

"Never mind," said Reith. "If we'd had better sense, we should have run for it, too. But you'll have to wait a while for your money."

Chewing a grasslike plant stem, Doukh looked past Reith, saying: "Here comes the priest of Bákh ye spake with yesterday."

A startled glance showed the Reverend Behorj's litter swaying between its ayas, and the rest of the priest's entourage riding behind. "Into this alley!" snapped Reith. "Quickly!"

"But what—" began Alicia as she was dragged into a narrow, muddy lane.

"Don't argue!" said Reith in a low, tense voice, tugging his companions along the alley. "Over here, in the shade!" He flattened himself against a house wall, whence he could watch traffic passing on the main street with little chance of detection.

The litter lumbered past. Then, guarded by the mounted priestly escort, six bound captives shambled past afoot. One was Warren Foltz. Beside Reith, Alicia uttered a faint squeak.

"Hush, darling!" breathed Reith. "The less that lot knows about us, the better." For once Alicia forbore to argue.

As Roqir's red shield thrust its rim above a thicket of trees downstream, the three travelers boarded the *Morkerád*. They stood in the bow and watched the loading of heaps of hides, baskets of farm produce, and sacks of iron ore. Two local workers carried Marot's shaihan-hide bag of fossil-bearing stones, slung from a pole, up the gangplank. The team of shaihans, which had pulled the boat upstream, were stabled in a pen in the stern, whence the light westerly breeze wafted their pungent odor the length of the riverboat.

At last Captain Sarf and his four riverboat hands cast off and pushed the craft free of the pier. Two of the hands clambered to the roof of the deckhouse and broke out the triangular sail; while the other two, manning a pair of sweeps, maneuvered the boat out to midstream, where the current ran swiftest.

Reith and Alicia remained at the rail. Alicia had her arm through Reith's and clutched his elbow as if she feared that, should she slacken her grip, he would plunge overboard or fly away like a winged arthropod. Ever since leaving Sainian's ranch house, she had clung to Reith like some timid, helpless ingenue. Knowing that she was anything but that, Reith felt both amused and gratified.

"Sainian was a generous host," said Reith, glancing at his companions. Like Reith, Marot wore the kilt and jacket which the squire had insisted on their keeping. Alicia had packed away her seductive gown; but her khakis, like those of the men, had been washed and mended by Babir.

"Yes, darling," said Alicia. "The squire's a sweetheart so long as you keep on his good side. The minute you don't— *khlk!*" She drew a finger across her throat.

Marot said: "The mores of this country differ much from ours. I gather that to these people, to keep one's word and meet one's obligations are important; but homicide—if that is the right word—is no great matter. We were fortunate not only in escaping Foltz and his troupe, but also in avoiding offense to our recent host through ignorance of local customs and tabus."

"I wouldn't dare bring a party of tourists to Chilihagh," mused Reith. "If they didn't run afoul of the state religion, they'd accidentally insult some cowboy and be walking around without their heads."

"Speaking of religion," said Marot, "what shall we do at Jeshang? Priestess Lazdai will probably be back on her throne. She may wish to question us further."

"We'll stay aboard," said Reith, "and keep strictly out of sight—and I hope, out of mind as well."

"How long is this journey, Fergus?" asked Alicia.

"About a hundred and fifty kilometers to Jeshang and something more than that to Jazmurian. With a favoring wind and no stops, we could sail to Jeshang in two days. In practice it takes three, because this tub stops at a lot of little private piers along the way."

The day drifted lazily by. The *Morkerád* passed placid marshes, whence aqebats rose squawking to flap away on leathery wings. At other times the river quickened its pace between steep brown bluffs. As they continued down-river, the plant cover thickened and trees became larger and more numerous, presenting a polychrome of trunks clad in bark of crimson and emerald and gold.

"These colors pertain to cross-fertilization," Marot explained. "Krishnan plants lack the true flower, but those bright-hued tree trunks perform the function of flowers. They permit the flying arthropods, which here have the color vision, to find the species they are designed to pollenate."

Now and then wild Krishnan herbivores, surprised at their drinking, scrambled up the riverbank and bounded away. A family of bishtars, standing in the shallows, held its ground and continued to scoop up hectoliters of water plants, which they stuffed into their huge pink mouths. This Krishnan elephant was a colossal, barrel-bodied beast on six columnar legs, with an elongated, tapering, tapirlike head ending in a short, bifurcated trunk or pair of trunks. Its vast hide was clothed in short, glossy, white-spotted purplish-brown hair. A pair of small, trumpet-shaped ears completed the ensemble.

By mid-morning the Terrans, lulled by the slight motion of the hull as the wind on the sails varied and by the gentle slapping of wavelets against the hull, went into the deckhouse to sleep. They found accommodations minimal: a stack of pallets, from which any passenger might choose one to spread out on the floor. The Captain had a private cabin, but for the others there was no privacy. Reith realized that intimacy with Alicia would be impossible before Jazmurian. Perhaps, he thought, that would be just as well; a few days' rest would be welcome.

When Reith and his companions emerged from the deckhouse, Marot dragged out his bag of fossil fragments. He also brought out his geologist's hammer, which had somehow survived the journey. With this and a pocket knife, he began going through his fossil-bearing stones, examining each to see what fragments of rock might be tapped or pried loose from the bone. He explained:

"This task awaits me sooner or later. If I do it now, perhaps I can reduce the weight of the mass till I can take the whole sackful back to Earth. Scientists would naturally prefer the original material to plastic replicas, no matter how accurate."

"How will you ever put all those pieces back together?" asked Reith.

"The computer in Paris will take care of that. If you put one piece in the machine and run a hundred others through on the conveyor, the machine will pick out the piece whose fracture surface matches the piece you are testing. It is, one might say, an electric jigsaw-puzzle solver."

Leaving Marot to his work, Reith saw that the *Morkerád* was angling towards the south bank. On a small, rickety pier stood a Krishnan signaling with a white square of cloth on a pole. Two crewmen leaped to the pier to snag lines around wooden bollards. They held the boat against the pull of the current while Captain Sarf climbed on the pier, conferred with the flag-waving Krishnan, and received a small package from him. The captain leaped back to the barge, the lines were cast off, and the vessel pulled away.

They stopped again around midday, when the Terrans were eating on deck, and made a third stop before sunset, to take on another passenger. The newcomer proved a short, middle-aged, black-clad Krishnan who paid his fare, stared hard at the Terrans, and silently moved to the other side of the boat.

At dinner, the Terrans joined the others in the deckhouse, where the cook had set up a folding table. As they took their places, Alicia addressed the newcomer: "Good-evening, sir. I am Doctor Alicia Dyckman; may I know your name?"

The Krishnan stared at his plate and said: "I care not to hold converse with godless *Ertsuma.*"

"That simplifies things," said Reith in English. "We leave him alone, and he leaves us alone."

"But I only wanted to pick up a little data—" Alicia began.

"Which he obviously doesn't want to give. So pipe down, darling. We have enough problems."

Alicia's eyes flashed anger, but she pressed her lips together and resolutely remained silent.

The second day passed like the first, a long panorama of wild scenery with occasional stops at shabby little piers, while the Krishnan passenger ostentatiously ignored the Terrans.

On the afternoon of the third day, the quays of Jeshang hove in sight. As soon as the *Morkerád* was tied up, the Krishnan passenger stepped briskly ashore. Looking back at the three Terrans, all now clad in their shabby fossil-digging khakis, he snapped:

"Ye shall see what befalls heretics in the holy Dashtate of Chilihagh!"

"A real friendly fellow," said Alicia. "I'm a brass monkey if he's not on his way to make trouble for us."

"If he goes to the Bákhite temple and makes charges. . . . Oh, Captain!"

"Aye?" said Sarf, supervising the unloading of cargo. "What would ye?"

"When do you mean to sail?"

"Tomorrow morn, Bákh willing, as soon as we finish loading."

Later Alicia said: "He seems to like us. When he finishes loading, I'll tackle him about hiding us."

When the last basket, jar, and crate had been carried ashore, Alicia went to the captain and spoke earnestly and long—so long that Roqir sank behind the trees and Reith became uneasy. At last she returned, while Sarf hastened down the pier towards the town.

"I had some trouble with him," she said. "But I got what I was after. Now he's gone off on a drinking date with some cronies."

"What did he say?" asked Reith and Marot together.

"Any friend of his cousin Sainian is a friend of his; so he'll help. We talked about ways of concealment in case the priests come aboard looking for us. The only way that makes sense is to hide us among those big bags of ore in the hold."

"What shall we do with the ore, while we're tied up in the sacks?" asked Reith.

"That's the problem. Sarf said that, much as he wished to befriend us, he couldn't dump three bagfulls of good ore overboard to make room for us. He'd show up at Jazmurian three bags short. I suggested dumping the ore in some corner of the hold, but the idea horrified him. He runs a neat little ship.

"He proposed that one of us go ashore and buy three bags of the same design for us to hide in. He even lent me the money and gave me directions to the ship chandler's shop, three blocks west along the waterfront. I'll go if you like—"

"Not you!" said Reith. "This is a tough neighborhood, and some of the local hooligans might think it fun to gang-bang a Terran woman. Since I speak the best Mikardandou, I'd better go."

"I should go, too, to guard your back," said Marot.

"Hm." Reith hesitated. "Yes, I guess you'd better. Be sure to wear your sword!"

They found the chandler's shop, just as the proprietor was fastening his shutters. "Closed for the night!" he snapped.

Wanting to yell with frustration, Reith turned a dangerous red. Marot whispered: "Let me, Fergus." Then to the chandler he began: "Sir, do you know Captain Sarf bad-Dudán?"

"Aye, an old customer. What of him?"

"He has sent us hither on an urgent errand. He carries a load of ore in sacks. Three sacks have burst, spilling fragments about the hold. He begs—"

"He never bought those sacks from me!" said the chandler. "My sacks have only the best canvas and are double-stitched. He must have picked them up from one of those cheap-Jack dealers in Jazmurian."

"In any case," Marot resumed, "he begs you to sell him three of your superior sacks to confine the spilled ore before he makes delivery." When the chandler hesitated, Marot added: "He instructed me to tell you that it is a desperate emergency. He hopes for the sake of future transactions that you can accommodate him."

"Oh, very well," growled the chandler, folding back his shutters. "What size?"

"I know not the exact dimensions," said Reith, "but they hold—" In English he asked: "What's thirty kilos in Mikardandou pounds, Aristide?"

"About fifty, I think," replied Marot. Reith translated.

"That were a Number Four heavy-duty," said the chandler. "Come inside." He rummaged among piles of canvas, coils of rope, racks of tools, and jars of paint and tar until he found what he sought. He slapped down three sacks of heavy, dun-colored canvas. "One kard fifty, an ye please."

"A moment," said Reith, fumbling for the money. "Aristide, wouldn't you like a real bag for your fossils instead of that stiff, awkward hide?"

"You are right, Fergus." When the chandler had added a fourth bag to the pile, they paid and left with sighs of relief.

Back at the ship, in the gathering dusk, they found a big-eyed Alicia at the rail. She looked pale and shattered. "Fergus!" she called in a half-whisper.

"Yes?" said Reith.

"Do you know what happened while you were gone?"

"How should we? Tell us!"

"A Bákhite priest and four armed guards came aboard. After some argument with the crew, the priest cornered me and told me Her Holiness, High Priestess Lazdai, desires forthwith the presence of you and the bone-seeker."

"Did he say what for?" asked Reith.

"Only something about 'further questioning.'"

"What did they say when they saw we weren't here?"

"I explained that you two had gone ashore and might not be back until morning, and they'd have to comb all the taverns to flush you out. Then, I said we were wearing our oldest clothes, and it wouldn't be fitting to come before the High Priestess in such condition. I don't know which argument carried the most weight; but they went away, stating they'd be back at sun-up to escort us. I was to tell Captain Sarf to delay his sailing until it's been decided whether to let the Earthlings continue their journey."

"Sarf'll love that," said Reith.

"If he finds out," said Marot. "Perhaps the beautiful Alicia will forget to pass the word. You know women." He winked.

"Aristide," said Reith, "I never suspected you of being such an intriguer."

Marot shrugged. "What is a diplomat but an honest man sent abroad to lie for his country?" He turned to Alicia. "But, my dear, why did they not seize you and carry you off? They could have held you as a hostage to assure our appearance."

"I don't know. I suppose the warrant was based on the original dossier for the expedition, and that mentions only you two. I'd be listed in Foltz's dossier."

"Proving," said Reith, "that bureaucracy works the same everywhere."

At sun-up, a priest of Bákh and six guards appeared at the foot of the gangboard. Longshoremen were already loading bundles and cases of cargo; but at the sight of priestly vestments, they hastily stepped aside. The intruders marched up to the deck, where Sarf awaited them.

"Where are they?" barked the priest.

"Whom seek ye, sir?"

"Feign not stupidity! Where are the Terrans you have aboard, who yestereve were summoned by Her Holiness?"

"Oh, the Terrans!" said Sarf. "They've gone ashore. So eager were they to see Her Holiness that they waited not for their escort. They thought to meet you on the way."

"A likely tale!" sneered the priest. "Search this vessel, men!"

For an hour the guards prowled, opening bundles, peering under benches, and poking into corners. Reith, curled up below deck in total darkness, could hear them tramping about, gabbing and prying. His sack, tied at the top, stood amid the other sacks of ore, as did the sacks containing his companions and Marot's fossils.

Sounds, muffled by the canvas, implied that a couple of the guards were investigating the ore sacks. Reith caught snatches of speech: "Nay; this one, too, holds nought but lumps of stone...." "How shall we know the petrified bones from the ore? In this light, all look alike...." "If we catch the *Ertsuma*, we'll make them tell us. Go on, open another...." "Oh, Hish-kak! That's my tenth, with never a sign of Terrans or their bones...."

Presently these sounds died away. Straining his ears, Reith heard faintly from above the voice of the guard: "Your Reverence, we've searched every nook and cranny in vain."

"Opened you all those bags in the hold?"

"Aye, sir; we examined every one. There were at least fifty."

The priest's voice was heard directed at the imperturbable captain: "Bákh curse you! Why detained you not these suspects?"

"None so commanded me, Reverend Sir; and none told me that the Earthmen were suspects."

"This whole investigation hath been bungled. Sending out that easygoing old fool Behorj, and failing to hale the alien female back to the Temple when Qásh had her cornered on this tub...."

The voice sank to a mutter and then to silence. Booted footsteps on the gangplank told of the guards' departure.

"Fergus!" came a faint, high voice, muffled by the heavy cloth. "I'm smothering!"

"For God's sake, Lish, *shut up!* They may come back. We stay mousey quiet until the ship's at sea again."

He heard a little snort of suppressed laughter. "Some sea!"

Another endless hour dragged past. Overhead could be heard the footfalls of longshoremen, the shouting of orders, and the sounds of crates and other containers being moved.

At last these sounds quieted, and Reith heard the gong strokes that signaled the ship's departure. Hard on the last sonorous stroke came the sound of running feet and an excited, unintelligible rush of speech.

The slight motion of the boat on the bosom of the current and the faint creaking of her timbers showed that the *Morkerád* was at last under way. Wind thrummed against the sail. Foot-steps approached, and the lashing atop Reith's sack was untied.

"Ye may come up for air now," said Captain Sarf, grinning.

Alicia and Marot, their hair disordered, stood blinking in the half-light from the hatchway overhead, while their sacks lay crumpled about their feet.

"Many thanks," said Reith. "If I can ever do you a favor...."

"The biggest favor whereof I bethink me," said Sarf, "is to go quietly back to Novorecife, boasting to none how ye gulled the mighty priesthood of Bákh. If ye did, the story would spread and make life chancy for me, the next time I put in at Jeshang."

"I promise." When Alicia and Marot had added their pledges, Sarf said: "Come up on deck and greet our new passenger. Ye'll find her friendlier than that sour-faced pietist."

On deck, they found a young Krishnan female carrying a box with a handle, which Reith recognized as a portable incubator. The captain introduced her as Qa'di bab-Gavveq.

"Ah, how thrilled am I to meet true Terrans!" she gushed. "Oft have I heard tales of their ways and wonders, but hitherto I've seen them only at a distance."

"Enchanted!" said Marot, kissing the girl's hand. "Whither are you bound, may I ask?"

"Jazmurian, sir. I do pursue the father of my egg here. This liverless wight hath fled thither to escape the wedding that he promised."

"What will you do when you locate him?" murmured Marot.

"I shall obtain a court order, binding him to pay the child's support and to post a bond lest he think to slip away again. I am not without friends, and I'll show the losel!"

She launched into a catalogue of the iniquities of her seducer. After a few minutes of this verbal downpour, Reith and Alicia glided quietly away, leaving Marot to bear the brunt of her confidences.

"Fergus," said Alicia, "I thought you ought to know."

"Know what?"

"When Sarf untied you, you said you'd be glad to do him a favor. Well, I said something similar. He told me I could indeed do him a favor—in the bunk in his cabin tonight."

"Yes?" said Reith, his face studiously immobile.

"I turned him down."

"Why?"

"*Why!* Fergus, you stupid idiot! Having just found you again, do you think I want to ruin my chances for good and all? Don't tell me you wish I'd taken up with the captain's offer. That would be cruel."

"I didn't mean that at all." He slid an arm about her waist. "In fact I'm delighted. I have my share of old-fashioned jealousy, too. On the other hand, you're a free, single, independent woman who, as you've said, can do as you like."

Unexpectedly, Alicia began to cry, burying her face in his shirt. Alicia was not one to cry easily. "All right, throw my past up to me!" she sobbed.

"But I didn't—"

"Oh, yes you did! You're thinking: here's this dame I was once silly enough to marry, who's been screwed by all and sundry. Now she's dangling the hook in front of my nose, with her personal person as bait—"

"Nothing of the sort. I've told you—"

"But for now anyway, you're my one-and-only whatever-it-is, as long as you want me. What would you call an ex-spouse with whom one is having a love affair?"

"Let me think. Ah! Before I left Terra, a fad word was going round: 'amorex,' meaning one who is a lover of his or her former spouse. Okay! You're my amorex, darling. Give me a kiss and dry those tears. There, now!"

"I was never promiscuous, and I was never unfaithful while we were married. I was forced to let that old professor and King Ainkhist and Warren Foltz take their pleasure of me; so you could call it constructive rape. . . ."

"I know darling; you've already told me all about it, more than once. You're a compulsive confesser. Let's not hear any more about your amatory adventures, which don't amount to much anyhow. Compared to most people nowadays, we've both been pretty abstemious. Instead, let's think how lucky we are that Sarf didn't decide to cut his risk by pitching us overboard tied up in those bags."

"What a gruesome idea!"

"Yes. The thought came to me in that sack, with no way to get out and no way to defend you. It made for a nasty couple of hours."

"I suppose he has too much regard for his cousin Sainian." She pulled away and wiped the backs of her hands across her cheeks. "I hate being a silly, sentimental *feminine* female! I'd better go rescue Aristide. That egg-layer is beating his ears off, and he's too polite to tell her to go jump in the Zigros."

VII.

THE LANDING

All next day, Alicia subjected herself to Qa'di's confidences, taking endless shorthand notes. Glad to be relieved of that chore, Reith and Marot stood with elbows on the rail and watched the riverbank slide past. Marot said:

"Your Alicia is a most amazing woman. It is too bad that you and she could not—what is the expression? Make a do of it?"

"Make a go of it. Yes, it is too bad. We're one of those unlucky couples who can't live happily together and can't live happily apart, either." Reith stared moodily at the water wafting by. "I suppose each of us should have put more effort into trying to please the other. I'm often blunt, tactless, and dictatorial; while she has a temper that would make the surface of Roqir seem cool."

"She appears to retain a very warm affection for you, and I perceive that you entertain similar feelings. Is it likely that you two might make another attempt?"

"I've thought of that, and I'm sure she's thinking the same thing. I suppose that, having sampled the competition, she's decided I'm not quite the gloop she thought when she ran out on me." Reith sighed. "It would take careful thought. I don't

107

intend to re-fight old battles, and one bath in lava is enough. So please, Aristide, don't try to play Cupid. It's something we have to work out for ourselves." Reith set his jaw and stared at the scenery. After a while he said: "We sure had luck that time! Those guards were told to look into all the sacks. So they opened a few, failed by chance to find us, got bored, and went back on deck telling the priest they'd opened them all."

Marot chuckled. "You have reason. We owe our lives to the fact that the Krishnan nature exhibits the same frailties as the human."

"But say! The Bákhites had orders to search the ship not only for us but also for your fossils. How would they know about them? Foltz thought he'd destroyed the specimen."

"He did not finish the job. After they captured him, he must have guided them back to the dig. Not seeing the pieces, he drew the obvious inference."

"Why should the Bákhites be so hot after these bones?"

Marot shrugged. "I suppose they think the fossil crucial evidence against their creation myth, which it is. In Darwin's day, people spoke of 'missing links.' Anti-evolutionists said: where is the link between apes and men? In time, not one link but whole chains of them were found.

"Ozymandias is a 'missing link' as important in its way as were *Australopithecus* and other ape-men. It shows how the transition from aquatic vertebrates to terrestrial ones took place on Krishna. If the Bákhites could destroy it, they could continue for a while to preach their Creation myth without fear of confutation."

"If Earthly experience is any guide," said Reith, "they'll go right on preaching their myth and collecting followers, regardless of scientific evidence."

As Roqir sank scarlet behind the forest, Reith wandered past Alicia and Qa'di. The Krishnan female was still chattering, but Reith observed that Alicia had ceased taking notes. She cast an appealing glance at Reith.

"Come along, Lish," he said. "Ship's passengers should walk at least a kilometer a day to keep in shape."

She rose, saying in English: "Thanks for the rescue. That girl had begun to repeat herself for the seventh time. I think I have all the data I can squeeze out of her, and she's a frightful bore."

"I suspected as much."

After walking, they stood at the rail, watching the green water. There was a stir on the surface, a splash, and a flash of leathery gray hide. Waves marched out in expanding rings from the center of the disturbance.

"An 'avval, I think," said Reith.

"That thing between a crocodile and a sea serpent?"

"Yes. The Zigros is not safe for a swim."

"I'm glad to have you watch out for me," she said, pressing against him.

Looking down at her, Reith suppressed a smile. Her last sentence was not in the least characteristic of the headstrong, belligerently independent Alicia he knew. It did not take a shrink to understand why she had said it; she was the world's most incompetent liar. Instead of voicing his thoughts, he slid an arm around her and kissed her; she responded warmly, squeezing him and flattening herself against him.

Aft at the tiller, with a cigar cocked at an angle in his jaw, Captain Sarf watched them. Spreading out from Novorecife, the Terran custom of kissing had been enthusiastically taken up by Krishnans. Alicia said:

"I know what's on your mind, Fergus Reith."

"I haven't said a word—"

"But you'll just have to wait till Jazmurian. I won't make love with people looking on. Unless, that is, we could persuade Captain Sarf to lend us his cabin."

Flattered and amused but also a little taken aback, Reith thought: My impetuous little darling was never one to wait demurely for others to take the initiative; whatever she wants, she goes straight for, hammer-and-tongs. He said:

"I doubt if he would, especially since you turned him down."

"Are you too embarrassed to ask? Well, I'm not!"

In fact, Reith was embarrassed. He said: "You're not afraid of anything, are you? Okay, I'll try to live up to my rôle as hero. I'll take a deep breath, suck in my guts, and ask. Come along!"

Reith halted in front of Sarf. "Captain, would you mind—that is—I wonder if we might borrow the use of your cabin for, say an hour while you're out here on deck?"

Sarf's olfactory antennae rose. "Wherefore would ye that? I like not strangers in my privy domain."

Reith reddened. "Well—ah—Doctor Dyckman and I have

a matter to discuss in strict privacy, and that's the only private place on the ship."

"Ohé!" Sarf gave a coarse, gobbling laugh. "So ye be fain to jig on my pallet, eh? I offered the same regalement to the learned doctor, but she renied me."

Reith scowled. "I said, she and I have an important matter to discuss; nothing more."

"As if ye were but a pair of savants discussing the fat doctor's petrified bones? Ha! I've watched the pair of you, slobbering on each other in that uncouth Terran fashion."

Reith's emotions flared up from mere anger to homicidal fury. Holding himself in check, Reith grated: "If it's any affair of yours, Captain, Doctor Dyckman is my former wife, and...." He caught himself before blurting out that they might resume that relationship. He was not yet ready to commit himself. "Will you lend us your cabin or not?"

Captain Sarf drew a big puff on his cigar, took it from his mouth, and studied it. "I'll tell you. Ye may use my cabin wherein to futter your heads off—provided that the lady concedes me the same privilege there tonight."

Reith and Alicia exchanged glances, angry and appalled. Stiffly, Reith said: "Forget it, Captain. That would be quite against Terran custom. Come along, Lish; we haven't yet walked our kilometer."

Next morning, Reith and Alicia strolled about the deck, avoiding Qa'di and watching Marot patiently chipping away at his fossils. After the midday meal, the *Morkerád* put in at the village of Qantesr, larger than Kubyab, where a floating bridge spanned the Zigros. While the *Morkerád* tied up at the pier, the bridge tenders cranked away at the winches that hauled the string of supporting boats against the shore to allow the ship to pass.

Several Krishnans were gathered on the pier, together with a scattering of crates, bags, and jars. As the crew made the ship fast, Alicia said:

"Fergus, I'm going ashore for a while."

"What for?"

"I want to ask some questions of these folk, and I want to feel solid ground beneath my feet and breathe some clean air. This tub is pretty stinky, with the smell of the shaihans blowing over us day and night."

"How can you do any real research in the short time we'll be here?"

"Sarf said he'll be here most of the afternoon. They have to load a lot of stuff, and he has some deal on with one of those people on the pier."

"I don't think you should go," said Reith in his tour-guide voice.

"Why not?"

"I don't know how safe it'll be ashore. You know, Lish, you attract trouble the way honey does flies. You might have an accident, or run into some tough characters, and we'd never know what happened to you. So do stay aboard."

"No, I won't! I've decided to go."

"Oh, darling, do show some sense! We're still in Chilihagh, and the priests of Bákh are looking for us."

"Pfui! There's been no sign of a priest since we left Jeshang. Besides, there's a question about the Chilihagho inheritance law that I simply must ask while I can. I was an idiot not to think of it sooner."

"Ask Sarf."

"I did, and he doesn't know. I'm going!" she proclaimed.

"Don't be silly, darling! Do stay aboard, please! Bákh knows you've got enough data in those notebooks for a shelf of treatises."

"I tell you, I'm going, and that's that! As you said yourself, I'm an independent woman, free to go where I like."

"Then I'll come with you. Wait till I get my sword."

"No; I don't want you! You'd only be in the way."

Despite his efforts to control it, Reith's voice grew more dictatorial. "I'm responsible for you and Aristide, and I won't let you take foolish chances. We've been through enough already."

"You're not my husband any more, and it wouldn't matter if you were. *I* never signed a contract making you my expedition leader. I'll go where I wish, and if I get raped or murdered, that's my tough luck!"

She started for the gangway. Reith stepped in front of her, spreading his arms.

"Out of my way!" she cried.

"I won't let you!" shouted Reith.

"You can't stop me, you bossy bully!"

"Oh, yeah? I'll show you who—"

Alicia put both hands against Reith's chest and shoved. As she had said, she was stronger than her graceful build implied. The muscles in her slender limbs were hard; she had been a champion tennis player in her college days. Reith was thrown against the rail, which struck his buttocks. The momentum of his stagger over-balanced him, and his legs flew up. He executed a backflip and plunged into the water between the *Morkerád* and the pier.

"Man overboard!" bellowed Captain Sarf. "Ye there, Gamrok! Drop him a line!"

Marot appeared around the corner of the deckhouse in time to see Reith hauled out of the water. *"Quel contretemps!"* he exclaimed.

Alicia, standing on the gangboard, paused as Reith, dripping emerald slime, reached the level of the deck. She took a couple of steps and put out a hand to help him over the rail; but he ignored the proffered assistance.

"Fergus!" she said. "I'm sorry. I didn't intend—I mean—"

Reith coughed up some Zigros water. Retching and coughing, he rasped: "The hell . . . you didn't!"

"Oh, be a bastard, then!" she snapped, and marched defiantly ashore.

"My friend," said Marot, "what can I do?"

"Get me a towel, will you, old boy?"

Knowing that these subtropical Krishnans had no nudity tabu, save where Terran missionaries had striven to implant one, Reith stripped and hung his dripping garments over the rail. Qa'di, drifting nigh, remarked on Reith's pubic hair. Since Krishnans lacked this anatomical feature, the sight of it often elicited comments from them.

Dried and dressed in his good Krishnan kilt, Reith found his anger cooling. No matter what Alicia said or did, he could not bear deliberately to hurt her, no matter how furious she made him from time to time. If only she would return to the boat before something untoward befell her!

Qa'di moved closer until only a few centimeters separated them. "I would not treat you thus ruthlessly," she murmured.

"Thanks. I'm sure you wouldn't."

"Belike I could soothe your wounded liver?" She cast a meaningful glance towards the deckhouse door.

"Your pardon, lady. I feel unwell today. But let's take time tomorrow to know each other better."

"Good! I shall be here."

For the next Krishnan hour, Reith paced the deck, watched cargo being stowed, and fidgeted. At last the ship's loading was nearly complete, and Alicia was still missing. Reith said to Marot:

"Aristide, that woman has got me buffaloed. Should I go ashore to look for her? If she's lost, we can't ask Sarf to hold his boat indefinitely. If I go ashore, I may get lost, too. It would serve Lish right if we sailed off without her; but I can't do that to a fellow Terran, let alone. . . ."

"I understand your feelings," replied the Frenchman. "I think that we must collect our belongings and place them at the end of the gangplank. If she has not returned when Sarf casts off, we shall have to go ashore, wait for her there, and throw ourselves on the mercy of the inhabitants. There may be places for travelers. Perhaps we can flag down the next east-bound riverboat."

"We're practically out of money," said Reith. "To be stranded broke on Krishna is quite as serious as to be stranded penniless on Earth."

"Some *paysans* might put us up in return for gossip," said Marot, refusing to be discouraged. "Or we may be near enough to Jazmurian so that we can raise credit on the strength of your tessera. If none of these schemes works—how far is it to Jazmurian?"

Reith frowned. "At a guess, twenty to thirty kilometers."

"I am a little old and heavy for such a walk, but perhaps I could do it. Let us gather our things, no?"

A quarter-hour later, when Captain Sarf banged his gong to signal the ship's departure, Alicia came running from the woods, waving a sheaf of notepaper. She sped up the gangboard as the crew prepared to hoist it into the ship and threw a contemptuous glance at Reith and Marot.

"Ready to jump ship?" she said, eyeing their bundled gear. "Do you find my company so unbearable?"

Without awaiting an explanation, Alicia vanished into the deckhouse. When she reappeared, she ostentatiously ignored both Reith and Marot. She attached herself to Captain Sarf, standing beside him where he manned the tiller and remarking on his skill as the ship got under way.

At dinner, she preëmpted the seat next to the captain and continued to give him her exclusive attention, talking, joking, and laughing with all her charm. In that mood, thought Reith morosely, she could talk a bijar out of a tree.

When the *Morkerád* anchored on a sandbar for the night, Reith stood at the rail, drinking in the moonlight on the water and brooding on the mistakes he had made throughout his life. At last he retired to his deckhouse mattress. The other passengers and crew had already bedded down; as the last one in, it fell to Reith to pinch out the candle. Before he did so, he looked around for Alicia's blond head, but failed to find her among the recumbent bodies.

Disturbed and a little alarmed, Reith put out the candle, went out, and made the circuit of the deck. He peered along the narrow walkways between the sides of the deckhouse and the rail, and searched the broader deck between the after end of the deckhouse and the shaihan pen. As he came forward, voices told him that Alicia was in converse with the crewman on night duty. He caught the end of her question: ". . . which has the greater say in your affairs: your father's brother or your mother's brother?"

He found them sitting on the deck with their backs against the forward end of the deckhouse. The lantern in the bow shed a warm yellow light over the deck, and against the deckhouse Reith saw the red spark of the crewman's cigar.

"Seaman Gamrok," said Reith, "I never thanked you properly for pulling me out of the river."

"'Twas nought. Anyway, I saw ye could swim."

"Fergus!" said Alicia, rising. "May I talk with you?"

"Sure, Alicia. Come along."

They strolled aft and stood with elbows on the rail. After a long silence, Reith said: "You gave me a turn not being in the deckhouse with the rest of us. I wondered if you'd decided to take Captain Sarf up on his offer."

"Oh! How could you imagine such a thing?"

"Well, you certainly gave him a pitch, from the time you got back from your safari."

"I was just trying to make you jealous, silly! And I'm sorry about this afternoon. I really wasn't trying to push you overboard."

"If you weren't, it sure was a marvelous imitation."

"I just wanted to get you out of the way and show you I was not to be dictated to."

"You're stronger than you look—all made of steel springs and rubber bands. I hate to think of what would happen to anybody who really vexed you."

"Oh, Fergus! I'm not a robot; I do have feelings, even if I have to act rough and tough to get by in this hard world."

"Yes?" said Reith, in a rising inflection implying doubt.

"Yes. This afternoon I planned to ask you to come ashore with me. I thought, when I'd finished asking my questions, we could find some grassy spot out of sight of the ship and make love. But you spoiled everything by bellowing orders in your drill-sergeant voice."

Reith had been through this sort of thing too often with Alicia to be easily mollified. He said: "Sorry; I guess I owe you an apology, too. I realize I've been trying to take care of you the way I do my tourists. That authoritarian tone is the only way I can keep the fools out of trouble. Well, there won't be any more of that. The next time you want to do something that's likely to get you assaulted or killed, Doctor Dyckman, feel free."

"You're still angry?"

"N-no, not exactly. You should know me better. I don't lose my temper so quickly as you; but when I do get angry, I don't get over it so quickly, either."

"Now let me tell you something, Alicia. I've said this before, but it doesn't seem to penetrate. Whatever you want in life—"

"I know what I want!" she interrupted, staring him defiantly in the eye.

"Whatever it is, you're certain to spoil your chances of getting it, either by your bull-headedness or by your violent temper. What you need is a good shrink."

Her eyes fell and her shoulders drooped. "I suppose you're right, but what can I do? We don't have a first-class shrink on Krishna. Marina Velskaya's a good general practitioner and knows a lot about Krishnan anatomy and diseases, but in psychiatry she's just an amateur. If I went back to Earth for treatment, I'd be gone twenty years of Krishna time, and meanwhile some other woman would grab you."

"Then I guess you'll have to manage on your own. But remember what I've said."

After another pause, she asked: "May—may I have just one little kiss?"

He gave her a brief, brotherly kiss. "Maybe you'd rather I went inside," she said in a slightly choked voice.

"Let's both go in." He opened the deckhouse door for her.

VIII.

THE TEMPLE

Reith and his companions stood at the rail as the sprawled-out city of Jazmurian hove in sight. From the waterfront, its houses seemed to consist mainly of slum dwellings and grog shops; although on higher ground, away from the river, could be seen a hint of costlier edifices, and the sun-sparkle of brass and glass on the temple spires. Downstream, where the Zigros opened out into the Sadabao Sea, appeared the masts and yards of seagoing ships, looking in the distance like a tangle of toothpicks.

"Fergus," said Alicia, "where can we stay until we get our finances in order?"

On the last two days of the voyage, she and Reith, while not unfriendly, had treated each other with a certain formal reserve. Reith felt he must soon decide about their joint future; and, being a methodical man, he meant to consider and weigh all possibilities. While having Alicia as his amorex was great fun, he doubted that, in the long run, this would prove a viable relationship. Besides, he liked clear-cut, definite agreements; ambiguities made him uneasy.

He was sure that Alicia would be delighted to marry him again. His emotions said: She's the one true love of your life;

grab her! But his reason told him that there was no point in remarriage if it was sure to lead to another blowup. The qualities in Alicia that had sundered them before were still, alas, very much in evidence.

He replied to her question: "I brought my last batch of tourists to Angur's Inn. No Ritz, but it beats most of these fleabags."

"I know," she said, scratching at a bite from a Krishnan arthropod. "Jazmurian looks like a dismal place, like Jeshang on a larger scale. Has it any amusements, in case we have to wait over?"

"The ground floor of Angur's is one big night club. They have dancing and entertainers, if you don't mind inept imitations of Terran show biz."

"Dancing?" she said. "Oh, Fergus, I'm looking forward to this!"

Reith suppressed a smile. He had a surprise in store.

"Who rules this city?" asked Marot.

"It's under the Republic of Qirib, which occupies the peninsula in the Sadabao. Until a few years ago, Qirib had a matriarchate. Females were the ruling sex. They had a quaint custom: the queen took a consort; then at the end of each year they chopped off his head, cut him up, and served him at a ceremonial banquet. After that they chose another royal mate."

"Did they get volunteers?"

Reith grinned. "Oh, no; the victims were drafted."

"I should think," said Marot, "that anticipation of this untimely doom would render it difficult to perform one's generative duty."

Reith shrugged. "They assured the people that every egg laid by the queen was of legitimate origin. But Alvandi's daughter turned out to be a Terran girl, whom the queen had obtained as an infant and passed off as her own. The kid was brought up to wear false antennae and all the rest."

"What happened to the matriarchate?" asked Marot.

"It was overthrown by a revolution, led by a Terran named Barnevelt, whose war-cry was 'Equal Rights for Men!' They adopted a republican constitution of Terran style, with an ex-saddler and ex-pirate as president."

Marot gestured towards the house of Jazmurian. "Is this the capital?"

"No. That's Ghulindé, out on the peninsula. Jazmurian's the main seaport of the republic, and scorned by the other Qiribuma as a polyglot, decadent home of crime and corruption. 'Not the *real* Qirib,' they'll assure you."

Alicia put in: "I've been to Ghulindé. I never saw the first President, Gizil the Saddler; but I knew his successor, Vizman er-Qorf. If we stopped off there, I'm sure he'd entertain us."

"Not likely," said Reith. "We're taking the first northbound train we can rustle up the fare for."

Marot asked: "Did this formation of a republic effect a marked improvement in the lives of the people?"

"Hard to say," said Reith. "From what I hear, some Qiribuma, especially the men, say they're better off. But others yearn for the days of that old she-yeki, Queen Alvandi."

"No governmental system ever comes up to expectations," murmured Marot. "At least, such has been Terran experience."

The *Morkerád* approached an opening on one of the piers. Reith knew better than to plague the captain while he was engrossed in warping his boat into its dock. Only when the little ship brought up against the bumpers, and the lines were made fast, did Reith say:

"Captain, when shall we get together with your cousin's agent, to straighten out our obligations?"

Sarf grinned. "Not tonight, I ween! Unloading will swallow the rest of the daylight, and then I'm off to see my wife."

"Your *other*...."

"Hist, not a word, an ye'd thank me for hiding you! Where will ye put up for the night?"

"Angur knows me, so I'm sure he'll take us in even though we're arzuless."

The crew finished wrestling the gangboard into place. With the approach of the ship, a scattering of the usual waterfront populace began to converge on its landing place: longshoremen, porters, sedan-chair bearers, touts, pimps, and peddlers.

Four Krishnans of a different aspect pushed through the crowd and stamped aboard. One was a male in good civilian dress; the other three wore uniforms with crested brass helmets and brazen cuirasses, which flashed in the afternoon sun. This armor was worn over scarlet tunics and pleated kilts, and each soldier bore a short sword suspended from a baldric. Two soldiers were male, but the third, evidently an officer, was a female, whose cuirass was molded to fit her feminine shape. Reith told his companions:

"All the soldiers used to be female, and most of the higher ranks still are. But the ratio is changing, as more males enlist."

While Captain Sarf and the civilian conferred over the ship's manifest, the three in scarlet and brass advanced upon Reith and Marot. The female said:

"*Ohé!* Terrans wearing swords? *Ertsuma* are not exempt from the laws of Qirib! Hold still, ye twain, whilst we render your hangers harmless."

One uniformed male belayed the swords of Reith and Marot into their scabbards by iron wire, wound around the guard and through the suspension rings. Then the other soldier fastened the ends of the wire together with a clamp that confined them within a leaden seal.

"Now," said the female, "if ye be caught with your peace wires unfastened, ye'd better have ponderous excuses ready, as that ye were set upon by robbers. Otherwise 'twill go hard with you."

"I understand, Officer," said Reith. "I've been here before."

The officials went ashore, and longshoremen lined up to file aboard. Sarf said to Reith:

"'Tis a long walk to Angur's. Will ye hire a carriage or a set of chairs?"

"I doubt the ordinary carriage driver would extend credit on the strength of my little plaque. Most of them cannot read."

"Let it fret you not. I'll stake you to your carriage ride. In for an arzu, in for a kard, as they say in Qirib."

Sarf rounded up a carriage, the prospect of seeing his other wife having put him in a high good humor. He loaded his Terrans aboard and paid the driver. Qa'di departed afoot, clutching her incubator in one hand and a sheet of paper bearing the address of an attorney in the other.

Angur's Inn stood in the upper town across a spacious square, facing the end of the railroad platform. A train was being made up at this station, which consisted of a shed between two stub-end tracks of qong-wood, and beyond, a small station building. Several little four-wheeled cars had been rolled into place, and more were being added by a tame bishtar, which pushed with its head at the command of its mahout.

The second story of Angur's three-story inn, upheld by a row of arches, extended out over the sidewalk. Reith led his companions in the front door on the ground floor. Angur, whose exceptionally long antennae gave him somewhat the look of a beetle, sat behind a desk in the small lobby, beyond which could be seen the tables and dance floor of the cabaret, occupying most of the ground floor.

Angur rose to greet the newcomers. "Hail, Master Reit'! 'Tis a small touristic party ye bring this time; but they shall enjoy all the luxe my elegant establishment affords. What accommodations will ye have? Business hath been a smitch slow of late, so I can offer a wide range of choice."

"Have you one double and one single room?"

"Aye. I'll give you Numbers Twelve and Thirteen." Angur took keys from a rack and shouted: "Haftid! Hither!"

An adolescent Krishnan picked up the small bundles of personal gear. The youth would also have picked up Marot's bag of fossils—now shrunken by Marot's expert chipping and prying to little more than half its original weight—had not the Frenchman forestalled him.

"What's in that?" said Angur. "Treasure?"

"Mineral specimens," said Reith. "Doctor Marot is wise in such matters. Show them a sample, Aristide."

Marot raised his eyebrows, but he untied the sack and dug out a couple of fossiliferous stones. Curiosity satisfied, Angur led the trio upstairs to the second deck and unlocked two doors. Reith glanced into the rooms, then took Alicia's bundle and his own from the youth and carried them into the large room. He set them down, saying:

"Here you are, Alicia!"

She hesitated in the doorway, and their eyes met. Then a smile of pure happiness lit up her classic face, as if a ray of the sun had crossed it. Reith knew she had been wondering whether he would forgive his ducking in the Zigros, or banish her to the single room. When they were settled and the porter had departed, she asked:

"Why did you insist on showing the innkeeper Aristide's fossil fragments?"

"If I hadn't, they'd have been sure the bag contained gold, jewels, or what have you. I'd trust Angur, but not his hired help." Reith raised his voice. "Aristide! Will you step in here, please?. . . . We have a couple of hours before dark. What would you two like to do with that time?"

"I should like to go look at the railroad," said Marot. "Perhaps I could arrange for our passage."

"Has Jazmurian a decent shopping district?" asked Alicia.

"I don't think the railroad would give us credit, and there's no use shopping with empty pockets."

"Well then, I shall go look at the trains," said Marot. "I am what you call a railroad bluff."

"Buff, old boy, buff. Find out what you can about fares and schedules."

"And I'll write up my rough notes," said Alicia.

"In that case," said Reith, "I'll leave you for a while. Lock your doors. If you go out, stay close to the inn, and don't wander off into any tough districts."

"Where are you going?" asked Marot.

"To the temple of Yesht, to see if our little Jeshango priest made it."

"Could you buy me some more paper and pencils?" said Alicia. "I'm running short."

"Sure; I have a couple of karda left. See you."

The temple of the Judge of the Dead was a heavy, square structure surmounted by a huge dome. The entrance was below street level, so that to enter, one went down a flight of steps. This, Reith thought, was a shrewd psychological preparation for worshipers of the Lord of the Underworld.

In the entranceway, an acolyte took Reith's name and listened to his inquiry after the Jeshango priest of Yesht. Soon Nirm bad-O'lán appeared in the full green-and-purple regalia of a priest of the Qiribo cult.

"Master—Master—Reit', is it not? 'Twas you and your companion who succored me in Jeshang, wherefore I shall be forever grateful. Come hither where we can talk."

In an audience room, the garrulous little priest described his passage down the Zigros. By way of gossip, he added: "We have here another fugitive from the wrath of the Bákhites, a priest of Dashmok who arrived but a few days since. The jolly Majburo god hath no temple here, but he had a small cult in Jeshang. We have given refuge to the Reverend Ozagh, even though his god be not ours, and heard his breath-stopping tale of violent doings in Jeshang. Shall I hale him forth?"

"By all means," said Reith.

Ozagh appeared in the red-and-yellow habit of his cult.

When Reith questioned him, he said: "As I heard the tale, there were two sets of you bone-diggers at the Zora ranch. Methought they were all of one party. Which is sooth?"

"We were two parties, not working together. The priest Behorj queried my party and departed, seemingly satisfied."

Ozagh wagged his head in the peculiar Krishnan negative gesture. "For some reason I know not—the tales conflict—the Reverend Behorj's men fell into strife with the servants of the other bone-digger. A battle ensued, wherein several were wounded or slain. The surviving bone-diggers were brought to Jeshang for judgment. Most were simple countryfolk, of no interest to Her Holiness. But the leader, a Terran disguised as a human being, hight Foltis I'm told, aroused her suspicion. So she summoned him for further interrogation.

"Since the questioning was done in private, I know not how Master Foltis fared. But I am told that he hath neither been boiled in Lazdai's Kettle, nor been enlarged to go his way.

"I hear Her Holiness hath conceived an interest in further interrogating the other set of bone-diggers to wit: you and your companions. She suspects that the queries of the Reverend Behorj pierced not deeply enough. So she issued commands that you be apprehended upon arrival in Jeshang and brought before her. But you somehow slipped through her fingers, whereat she waxed passing wroth. How didst work this sleight?"

Reith smiled. "I'm sorry, but on this point my tongue is tied."

A knock on the door heralded a young Krishnan in the habit of an acolyte of Yesht, carrying a strip of thin paper covered with microscopic writing. He handed this strip to Nirm, saying: "Father Nirm, this message hath just arrived from our informant at Jeshang by bijar post."

"Thank you; you may go." Nirm frowned over the strip. Then his antennae quivered with excitement. *"Ohé,* Master Reit'! This doth concern you!"

"What does it say?"

"It saith that the Bákhites of Jeshang, resolved to settle the controversial matters whereof we have spoken, have sent persons forth to find you and your comrade, the learned doctor, and to return you to the Great Temple willy-nilly, for interrogation and judgment.

Reith grunted. "I should have foreseen they'd do something like that. What form will this kidnapping take?"

"Alas, the message saith not. 'Tis not likely they'd attempt an armed incursion, in view of the much greater strength in arms of Qirib. More likely, they'll slip into Jazmurian an agent or two, well furnished with coin, wherewith to hire a gang of local bravos to crimp you twain and hustle you to the border. This is a corrupt and lawless town, where such dark deeds are easily set in motion."

"I thank you," said Reith. "We'll take precautions."

Reith hastened back to Angur's, pausing only long enough to pick up Alicia's stationery supplies and to buy a bottle of falat and three cheap pottery mugs. As he and his companions drank the soothing vintage, he reported on his visit to the temple.

"I think we're fairly safe in the inn," he said. "We must of course keep our doors locked—that reminds me, ours isn't at the moment." He rose and took care of the matter, and in addition placed a chair at an angle with the chair back wedged beneath the doorknob. He continued:

"We should go out only under necessity. When we do, we should go no farther from the inn than we must, and Aristide and I should go armed and together. What did you learn about trains, Aristide?"

The scientist replied: "They run on alternate days. We have missed that of today, *helas*. The next departure will be the day after tomorrow, at the third hour."

"Damn!" said Reith. "We shan't be really safe until we board that train."

Alicia said: "Mightn't it be just as quick, and much more comfortable, to go by sea? On a ship I can work on my notes, which I couldn't do in one of those bouncy little cars."

"Let me think," said Reith. "Jazmurian to Majbur by rail is about five hundred and fifty kilometers; by sea it's a little over nine hundred. The train trip takes five days; with good winds and no stops, the sea voyage also takes five days."

Marot asked: "How is the ship so much faster than the train?"

"The train makes four overnight stops, while the ship sails all night."

"And why such a discrepancy in the distances?"

"Both Jazmurian and Majbur stand at the heads of deep

bays, so to get from one to the other you have to sail three sides of a rectangle, around Cape Dirkash."

"Me, I hope you will decide on the train," said Marot. "I am curious about Krishnan railroads and have never ridden one. Besides, I am not a good sailor."

Alicia: "You did all right on the *Morkerád*."

"Ah, but that vessel floated on water so smooth that one could play the billiards on it."

"After you've been bounced around on that wooden track," said Alicia, "you might change your mind. Besides, if we took a ship, we'd probably stop at Damovang, and I do so want to see how Vizman's campaign against slavery is coming."

Reith listened silently, but his muscles tensed. Alicia's mention of the Qiribo President sent a surge of jealousy coursing through Reith's veins. He told himself not to be silly. The Krishnan politician, unlike that blackguard Foltz, had done Alicia no harm. In fact, he had made an honorable offer of marriage, at a time when she was free to wed anyone she liked.

So long as he, Reith, had not offered to remarry her and been accepted, what right had he to object to her seeking love elsewhere? He was being a dog in the manger, he told himself; but the feeling of jealousy persisted. Whatever method of travel they chose, he would try to make sure that they did *not* stop at Damovang.

"What are the relative hazards of the two modes of travel?" asked Marot.

Reith pulled his mind back to their current problem. "The train is safe enough, save for an occasional derailment or upset. As to the sea, it's fair-weather time on the Sadabao. The main thing we'd have to fear would be not storms but calms, which might cost us additional days. These ships carry oars, but rowing merchantmen is slow work.

"There was also an outbreak of piracy a few years ago. Ships had to move in convoys, which meant delays and higher costs. The princes and presidents around the Sadabao claim they've put the pirates down, but I don't know how far to believe them."

Marot continued to argue for the train, Alicia for the ship; while Reith remained judiciously neutral. At last he said: "I personally don't care; but as things stand, the railroad has it. The cost is about the same, and the train is likelier to get us safely to Majbur in six or seven days. I'll get our tickets the first thing tomorrow, as soon as we have the money."

Angur, in his incarnation as *maître d'*, escorted the three to a table on the edge of the dance floor and took their orders. This was a touch of special deference, since the usual procedure was to give orders over a counter directly to the cook.

"One of the perks of a tour guide," Reith explained. "They all hope for future tourists to exploit."

Only a few other patrons occupied the big room. After the waiter brought their dinners, however, more Krishnans drifted in. Marot was raising his eating spears to his mouth when he started so violently that he dropped the food back on his plate and pricked his own chin. "*Sacre dieu*, what are those?" he said.

Reith turned his head. Marching past their table were three reptilian creatures, taller than a man but more slender, who walked on their hind legs with tails held stiffly out behind them to balance their bodies. Heads, a little smaller than human but with bulging crania, rode atop necks thirty centimeters long. Arms much like human ones ended in four-clawed hands. Instead of clothes, the newcomers bore on their scaly hides intricate patterns of spots and stripes, in black, white, and red.

"Those?" said Reith. "Osirians. From the planet Osiris."

"Of the Procyonic system," added Alicia. "Quite a few visit Krishna."

She wore the filmy, nipple-baring dress that Ilui had given her in Kubyab. The sight of Alicia in that dress stirred a cauldron of emotions in Fergus Reith. There was sexual excitement, unsuppressible yearning love, anger at her past treatment of him, sorrow that she was no longer truly his, and relief that he no longer had to brook her volcanic temperament. There were also a half-hidden wish to break out of her spell and forget her, and resentment that he could not seem to do so—at least, not while she was present and visible day after day.

Marot mopped the trickle of blood on his chin and held his napkin (a recent innovation on Krishna, inspired by Terran example) against the wound until it stopped bleeding. "If the dinosaurs had not become extinct on Terra, that is what we might look like today. I mean, that is what the intelligent Terran species, occupying our place in the biota, might resemble."

The three Osirians did not sit at table. Instead, the waiters moved a couple of tables away from a corner, and the Osirians lowered their scaly, baggy bodies to the floor. They squatted facing outward, so that the tips of their tails met in the corner. Waiters set down drinks on the floor before them.

Angur wandered past the Terrans' table, remarking: "Be the victuals to your taste, Master Reit'? Doctor Dyckman? Doctor Maghou?" Assured that Angur's cook had done himself proud, Angur followed the Terrans' glances towards the Osirians. "They're good customers but afeared lest some wight tread upon their tails.

"I mind me some years since, one of that ilk had a drop too much kvad and decided he must needs monstrate to all a Terran dance. So he seized our entertainer, the talented Pari bab-Horaj, spun her out upon the floor, and whirled her round and round. Another couple was dancing a simple *ragsudar*. The alien's tail, swinging like the boom of a ship, smote the man on's arse as he bowed to's lady. His partner, being of the then dominating Balhibiya, wore a sword loose in its scabbard. The man, incensed, snatched his partner's weapon and would most bloodily have slain the tailed one, had not a wandering Earthman dissuaded him with an earthen mug, launched like a dart from a catapult, to's cranium. 'Twas a near thing. Now I tell Osirian patrons they may not dance when the floor's in use by dancers of tailless species.

"Here come our present minstrels. May ye enjoy their performance!"

Five musicians took places in an alcove on the far side of the dance floor. They brought a drum, a harp, a kind of miniature xylophone, and two instruments that looked like woodwinds. The clatter of eating spears died down as patrons turned to listen.

"Ah!" said Marot. "At last I shall enjoy some of the genuine Krishnan performing arts! It is a thing I have long wished; but on this safari, we have been too hurried and harassed."

The harpist signaled the start. All five instruments crashed together in four notes, da-da-da-DUMM; and then in a lower register, da-da-da-DUMM.

"Mon dieu!" cried Marot, clapping a hand to his forehead "They are giving us Beethoven's Fifth! So much for the native arts!"

Alicia said: "Well, he *was* a great composer. I've heard that piece on the Japanese *koto*, the Indian *sârangi*, the Russian *domra*, and Trinidadian steel drums. I've even heard it on Ken Strachan's bagpipes; at least that's what *he* said he was playing."

The musicians worked their way through the first movement only, then rose, bowed, and went out, leaving their instruments. A Krishnan female, wearing heavy makeup, appeared.

Her costume consisted of a spangled, metallic loin garment; a tiara; a complex necklace whose strings of gems spilled down on her bare breasts; and bejeweled sandals. Reith assumed that the hundreds of glittering gems were faceted pieces of colored glass; but they glittered beautifully in the lamplight, crimson and emerald and sapphire and white amid the gold of the spangles.

The entertainer sat down and began talking, telling jokes and stories in so pronounced a dialect, and so filled with local slang, that they went over the heads of the Terrans. The Krishnans seemed to find them uproarious, for they burst into the gobbling Krishnan laugh until they nearly drowned out the speaker. Next, she did a little dance, playing a small metallic instrument that looked to Reith like a kazoo.

When she had ground and bumped and tweetled about the stage, she sat down to a lively cracking of joints, the Krishnan applause. She picked up the harp, struck a chord, and launched into a song:

Mainai zafsin zeglo riáv zeke mináv zelort. . . .

"I have heard that tune somewhere," said Marot.

"You probably have," said Alicia. "It's *The Battle Hymn of the Republic*, by Julia Ward Howe. 'Mine eyes have seen the glory. . . .'"

Marot sighed and shook his head. "It is depressing enough the way our own planet has become homogenized, so that in a given latitude everyone dresses the same world round. Local traditions and customs are virtually extinct, save where artificially maintained as bait to draw tourists. Now I see that Krishna is starting down the same road."

"It'll take some time," said Reith. "I certainly expect enough local differences to keep tourists coming here through my lifetime. After all, nobody forced either Beethoven or Mrs. Howe on these folks."

"No; but I ask myself: is this blending of all cultures good?

Does it rob the individual of his sense of identity?"

Reith shrugged. "Who knows? But I wonder if they'd like *The Battle Hymn* so well if they knew it was an anti-slavery song?" The song ended in cracking of thumb joints and shouts of approval.

The band struck up. Reith listened, then tapped the table: "One, two, three-four-five! One, two, three-four-five! You're *foutu* again, Professor. That's a tango, or else a cha-cha at half speed." He stood up and nodded to Alicia. "Would my lady care to dance?"

"Really? Why, Fergus, I thought you hated dancing!"

"I try to give my clients satisfaction. Come on!"

They began their tango, although nobody else got up to share the floor with them. When they had made one circuit alone, Alicia exclaimed: "Why, Fergus, what's happened? The last time I danced with you, you weren't so bad as some I've known but not very good, either. Now, all of a sudden, you're simply divine! Have you been taking lessons on the sly?"

"To tell the truth, I got tired of being embarrassed, like the time I was commanded to dance with Princess Vázni."

"The one you were forced to marry?"

"Yes."

"Why didn't you stay with her?"

"Vázni's a nice girl in her way, but she's just the opposite of you. She's placid, amiable, loving, sexy, frivolous, stupid, and dull. Mostly dull."

She jerked her head back, missing a step. "You mean I'm not loving or sexy?"

"I don't mean that; but you're certainly neither placid nor stupid. Vázni's only interests were clothes, parties, and screwing. Being a bird in her gilded cage became as boring as a life sentence in a Terran jail."

"Too bad you couldn't have married both of us and divided your time between us, like Captain Sarf and his wives. When you couldn't stand one, you could flee to the other."

"You know, Alicia, that's a *great* idea! But I see practical difficulties. I don't dare go back to Dur. . . ."

"I didn't mean it, stupid! But I admit I'd rather have half a Fergus than none at all. Where did you learn your dancing? I never heard of a school at Novo."

"You know Kristina Brunius, now Fru Lund?"

"Sure," she said.

"Before she left Terra, she'd been an assistant in a dance studio. So I hired her to teach me. I've been working at it for a year."

"Is that *all* Kristina taught you?"

"You mean, did I have an affair with her?"

"Well, yes. Not that it's any of my business."

Reith smiled. "Would it bother you if I had?"

"No—well, yes—just a little bit."

"Is that the proprietary component in the human sexual drive, about which you write so learnedly?"

"I suppose so. Some primitive, atavistic urge."

"I'm flattered that you should be jealous of my post-marital amours, real or imaginary. But in a word, no. I think I could have—she takes a pretty casual attitude, from all I hear—but I was too busy trying to get over you."

"You poor thing! I wish I could make it up to you."

"Just try not to make life harder than it has to be, for the next moon at least. And remember that I have my proprietary component, too."

The music stopped. Amid loud applause from the Krishnans, Fergus led Alicia back to the table. They had barely sat down when two Osirians walked with clicking claws across the dance floor and approached them. Startled, Reith looked up and rose.

One Osirian said something unintelligible; it seemed to be trying to speak Portuguese, the language of the Viagens Interplanetarias, but not getting very far with it. At last the other reptilian alien said:

"Too you speak Inkwish?"

Remembering that the hissing Osirian language had no voiced consonants, Reith finally understood that the first Osirian had been trying to say: *"Dá-nos o prazer desta dança?"* or "May we have this dance?"

"Who wants to dance with whom?" asked Reith.

"I tance with you, pecause I am femay. He tance with your woman because he iss may. We have pait music to pway another tanko, so you can teach us."

Reith could see no physical difference between the two Osirians, but he surmised that they recognized the opposite sex in their own species. The incongruity of their offer almost made him laugh, but he forbore for fear of hurting their dignity. He said:

"We'll try. Do you know the steps?"

He explained the tango beat, demonstrating with Alicia. Then he signaled the orchestra and went into the slinking glide of the dance with the female Osirian.

The little dinosaurs caught on fast. By the end of the first circuit, Reith was enjoying himself. The Osirian, while nothing like so good a dancer as Alicia, was better than some of the oversized women tourists whom, in line of duty, he had been compelled to pull and push around the dance floor, like a tug berthing a liner in a high wind.

The dance ended to thunderous applause and cheers. Angur approached, saying: "Master Reit', an ye need gainful employ, feel free to offer your services here. Could I put on the spectacle of you, your lady, and yon aliens dancing the tango, I'd fill the house every night of the year."

Soon after, Marot, pleading fatigue, retired. But Alicia insisted on dancing every dance until, after midnight, the musicians went home. By that time Reith, too, was suppressing yawns.

In the double room, Reith again unfastened the buttons on the back of Alicia's dress. Soon she was looking up from the pillow, smiling and holding out welcoming arms. She said:

"Thank you, thank you, for a marvelous evening, you dear wonderful man!"

Reith wasted no time in accepting the implied invitation.

Afterwards, Alicia said: "The dancing was a delightful surprise; but I've been looking forward to *this* ever since Kubyab."

"I endeavor to give satisfaction, Doctor Dyckman."

"Fergus Reith, don't you dare be formal with me! I love you."

"And I love you, too."

She looked expectantly at him; this was the first time since their reunion at the Zora ranch that he had used the word "love." But he remained silent. At last she asked in a small voice: "Am I forgiven?"

"For what? My bath in the Zigros?"

"Yes. I'm terribly sorry about that."

"Forget it, Lish. I still love you, even if I'll always be careful not to get between you and the rail of a ship. Kindness to animals is fine, but feeding me to an 'avval is carrying the idea to absurdity."

"Oh, Fergus, you're mean! When I realized what I'd done,

I wept for an hour. You know I hate to cry, and most of all I hate for anyone to see me crying. I hid in the woods—me, Alicia the Superwoman, who always gets what she goes after and never sheds a tear! That's why I was late getting back to the boat, because I was still determined to interview the locals."

"You didn't act very contrite when you came back aboard."

"I was angry again, this time at my last interviewee. He was a rude, arrogant fellow who, instead of giving me straight answers, kept making propositions and crude anatomical remarks. I had to play up to him and be oh-so-sweet to get what I was after; but by the time I finished, I'd have happily boiled him in Lazdai's Kettle. He wouldn't have dared if you'd been along."

"You should have let me go with you when I offered."

"I know; I was just too angry at the time to think clearly. And then later I took my anger out on you and Aristide, which was vile of me. Why do I go through life making these horrible mistakes?"

"I don't know," said Reith. He gathered her into his arms, where she wept softly against his chest. "What I know of psychiatry you could put in your eye without discomfort."

"Damn!" she said, wiping tears with the bedding. "Every time I think I'm living up to my own standards, you come along and spoil my self-image by making me cry." She gave him a playful poke in the ribs. "You're the only one in the galaxy who can do that to me. I can't decide whether I ought to love you or hate you for it."

"Let's settle for love," said Reith. "It's more fun."

The next morning, over breakfast, Reith said: "Aristide, you'd better come with me to the office of Sainian's agent. Wear your sword. Then we'll go straight to the railroad station."

"Oh, good!" said Alicia. "I'm coming, too. When we get our money, we can do some shopping."

Reith said sternly: "No you don't, darling! The shops in Majbur are far better than here, and the prices are lower. Once there, we shall have unlimited credit, and you can wear your feet off running the shops. You'd better stay here, behind a locked door."

"I won't! I'm tired of being cooped up—"

- "We'll discuss it in our room, please."

When they were alone in the large bedroom, Reith found

Alicia emitting sparks. "Fergus Reith!" she said in a deadly tone. "If you think you're going to keep me caged up here. . . . I don't know this town very well, and I want to explore it and ask the people questions. If you don't want me with you, I'll wander around on my own."

"With a gang of kidnappers in the pay of the Bákhites looking for us? Are you crazy?"

"Don't worry about me. They're looking for you and Aristide, not me; and anyway I'll take my chances. I'm going right now, and if you try to stop me. . . ." She picked the pitcher off the washstand and hefted it menacingly.

With a herculean effort, Reith controlled his temper. "Darling, will you just *listen* for a moment?"

"Well?" She poised the pitcher.

"Do you really want to see me boiled in Lazdai's Kettle?"

"No; but what's that got to do with it? If they grab me, that doesn't hurt you."

"You forget. Perhaps they're not after you; but they know about you. They could hold you as a hostage. Presently I'd get a note saying: Reith, unless you give yourself up to us, we will set to work on your female Terran. To show we mean business, we inclose a finger, or a nose, or other detachable part of her."

"You needn't obey their demands!" she snapped.

"But ask yourself whether I *would*. You know me pretty well. I said I wouldn't order you around, and I won't. You needn't break Angur's pitcher over my head in order to walk out that door. But think about what I've said."

Slowly she set the pitcher down. "You win, damn it! Oh, Fergus!" Her speech ended in a wail as she threw herself into his arms. "Why do I do these things?"

Between kisses, he said: "The human mind is a mystery to me—especially yours, my love."

IX.

THE STAR CHAMBER

The mahout astride the bishtar's neck blew a flourish on a shrill little trumpet and whacked his beast with a goad. The links between the cars clanked, and the car in which Reith, Alicia, and Marot were traveling jerked into motion. The train clicked over switch points and out the yard on the single-track line. Flanges groaned, axles screeched, and the wooden frames of the little cars creaked like ships at sea. Ahead, the passengers could hear the muffled thud of the bishtar's six elephantine legs.

The background noise compelled the Terrans, clad in their worn, patched khakis and sharing their car with six Krishnans of assorted ages, to raise their voices. Eventually they fell silent, fatigued by the sheer effort of shouting.

The train rattled and rolled, at a steady fifteen kilometers a Krishnan hour (longer than its Terran equivalent) through the farming country of northern mainland Qirib. As the hours passed, the country grew increasingly rugged and rocky, and the farms more scattered and less prosperous.

"Hey, what's up?" said Reith, awakened from a catnap. The train had ground to a halt in hilly country, covered only by open stands of scrubby trees and bushes. "There's no siding here, for a southbound train to pass...."

As Reith thrust his head out the window, Alicia, looking out the other side, cried: "Who are those people? It looks like a holdup!"

So suddenly did the marauders appear that they might have sprung from the earth. Reith saw one emerge from behind a boulder; others must have lurked behind ground cover until the train stopped and then risen at a signal. Then a yelling mass swarmed towards the train from both sides. They seemed well armed, with an occasional flash of chain mail beneath their nondescript garments and ragged mantles.

"Get our swords, Aristide!" yelled Reith.

As the paleontologist rose to reach for the weapons in the overhead rack, Reith heard intruders burst into the next car aft. One shouted in a Chilihagho accent:

"Keep your seats! Be calm! Ye shall not be hurt! We do but seek certain aliens amongst you."

"Must be Lazdai's boys," growled Reith. "Forget the swords, Aristide. They're still wired into their scabbards, anyway."

"What can I do to help?" said Alicia.

"Pull something over your hair and pretend you don't know us," Reith hissed.

"But I can't desert—"

"You must! You can't do us any good if they nab you, too!"

"My fossil!" cried Marot. "They will destroy it! How can I hide it?" He hauled the bag out from beneath his seat. "Alicia, my dear, pretend that it is a baby, and you are nursing it!"

"But how—" began Alicia, who had tied a scarf over her betraying blond hair. Marot placed the sack in her lap and untied the draw string at the top, whispering: "Please! I beg you!"

"Heaviest damned baby...." muttered Alicia, unbuttoning her shirt. She thrust a breast into the opening in the bag and sat gently rocking the sack and crooning to it as armed Krishnans burst into the car from both ends.

"Ha!" cried their leader. "These twain bid fair to answer the description. Zanzir, where's that warrant...."

Reith stared, with more imperturbability than he felt, at the bared swords pointed at his chest.

"Here we have it!" said the leader. "'A Terran hight Fergus Reit', of good height, with hair the color of copper. A Terran hight Aristide Maghou, of similar stature but stouter build, having black hair flecked with gray, and wearing eyeglasses.' Masters Reit' and Maghou, I hereby arrest you in the name of the Dasht of Chilihagh! Come along! Resist not, or 'twill be the worse for you. Now where is that accursed bag of stones we were commanded to find? Look about, men!"

Several Krishnans searched the car, poking at the luggage in the overhead racks and peering under the seats. None paid attention to the bogus baby in Alicia's lap. One said: "'Tis not here, sir."

"Oh, Hishkak!" growled the leader. "We were straitly commanded to work with all possible dispatch. We cannot linger to take apart the cars, seeking some fribbling bag of stones. Come along, ye twain!"

"What—what—" protested Marot as he was hauled out into the center aisle.

"All shall transpire at Jeshang. Bring them forth!"

The two were hustled out of the car. The raiders assembled, leading ayas; Reith thought there must be over a hundred of them. A glance back at the train showed that, beyond the stopping point, the track had been torn up.

"Here's your mount, Master Reit'!" said a Krishnan. "Ye ride, I trow? Lest ye get any storybook ideas, we'll make sure ye don't try a bolt. Hold still!"

They tied a noose around Reith's neck and another around his right wrist. "Now mount!"

Encumbered by the ropes, Reith mounted awkwardly. With a mounted Krishnan holding a rope on either side, any attempt at flight would be futile. His captors had but to pull up and haul on the ropes, and he would be plucked from the saddle and slammed down with bone-breaking force on the rocky earth.

A Krishnan blew a whistle, and the raiders sorted themselves out into a mounted column. At another blast, the troop set out at a trot to westward. Marot, also roped, rode behind Reith. Rising in his stirrups, Reith had a last glimpse of Alicia, with a scarf on her head, gazing after him. As the cavalcade broke into a canter, she fluttered her fingers in a discreet farewell.

All day they rode and far into the night, not even stopping to eat. Reith surmised that their captors wanted to get out of Qirib as quickly as possible. They pushed the animals hard, cantering, then walking them for a space to breathe them, then cantering again. Avoiding towns and traveled roads, they meandered through wild country, sometimes following a game trail or a long-disused road. They must, thought Reith, have planned this foray carefully so as not to provide Qirib with an excuse for war.

Roqir set. The endless ride continued, although the troop now moved at a walk. Every few hundred meters, they passed a lighted lantern set in the ground to show the returning raiders the way.

Ready to fall off his mount with fatigue, Reith guessed it was near midnight and that they had crossed the border, when the troop emerged into cultivated country, found a good road, and speeded up to a trot. Reith found the aya's trot hard, because the saddle, mounted over the middle pair of legs, transmitted a pitiless jar up through the rider's spine.

A group of houses, washed in the light of two of Krishna's three moons, appeared on either side of the road ahead. Most were dark, but a few windows shone yellow with the glow of candles or lamps. A few minutes later, the ayas' hooves thundered on the timbers of the floating bridge across the Zigros. The riders crossed, two by two, and entered Qantesr on the southern bank.

The troop halted while their commander conferred with a hooded figure. Then the riders guarding Reith and Marot commanded: "Dismount, Terrans! And come this way; ye shall bunk in the schoolhouse."

Reith had only a vague perception of events, so tired was he. When he and Marot were helped down from their mounts, they stood in an apelike slouch, unable to straighten their cramped legs and backs save slowly, a centimeter at a time. Later, when a Krishnan approached them with a plate of food, he found both men already asleep on the schoolhouse floor.

Next morning a Krishnan who entered the schoolhouse with two bowls of hot stew found the Terrans gingerly doing knee bends and groaning over each stiff muscle. The Krishnan said: "What do ye, aliens? Prayers and obeisance to some Terran god?"

"Yes," said Reith with a wry grin. "We are paying our respects to Hercules, the god of muscles. Let's have that food!

I could eat an aya, bones, hide, and all. How much farther to Jeshang?"

"An early start and a brisk all-day ride should fetch us to the Great Temple by this even."

Reith and Marot groaned again, this time in unison.

Roqir had not quite set when Reith and Marot were delivered to the Great Temple of Bákh. Dazed with fatigue, they were hauled from their mounts and hustled through the vast front door of the marble edifice. Inside, they were led through endless halls and passages, where the flames of copper torchères were reflected from gilded ornaments and picture frames and shone on mural paintings showing scenes from the *Book of Bákh*.

At some point, the ragamuffin appearance of their captors gave way to the chain mail and smart black-and-white uniforms of the Temple guards. These led the prisoners to a corridor, somewhere in the rear of the huge building, lined on both sides by rows of barred cells. An officer unlocked a door with a metallic clank; the hinges squealed, and Reith and Marot were thrust inside.

The cell had two small, barred windows, high up, through which the prisoners could see a patch of green-tinged evening sky. Mattresses, three stools, a small table, and a washstand provided the cell's spartan comforts.

As Reith and Marot entered, an Earthman, brooding on one of the stools with his back to the door, rose and faced them. Like Reith, this man was of good height and lean build. The light of the setting sun revealed that he had once been disguised as a Krishnan, but that the disguise had begun to wear off. One of his antennae was missing; one of the false points on his ears was partly broken away; and his skin showed the Krishnan olive-green tinge only in patches. Moreover, the man's jaw was shadowed by a ten-days' growth of heavy black beard, which so changed his appearance that it took Reith a few seconds to recognize Warren Foltz.

As Foltz perceived Reith beneath his coating of dirt and dust, he bounded to his feet, snarling: "You!"

Although a minute earlier, Reith was so fatigued that he thought he could not even swat a fly, he sprang at Foltz like a madman. With bestial growls, the two men closed, punching, kicking, gouging, and clawing for each other's throats. Foltz jammed an elbow into Reith's eye; Reith in turn sank his teeth into Foltz's groping arm as they clinched, fell, and rolled on the rough wooden floor. Reith seized Foltz's throat; while Foltz, making strangled sounds, clawed at Reith's crotch.

"Stop!" shouted Marot, trying in vain to pull the furious fighters apart. The cell door flew open, and a squad of Temple guards rushed in. Seizing the limbs of each combatant, they managed to drag the two maddened Earthmen loose.

At length the combatants stood in opposite corners, breathing hard and bleeding from many cuts and scratches, while a pair of guards held each by the arms. Reith's right eye was bloodshot and half closed, while Foltz's bitten arm showed the pattern of Reith's teeth, each tooth mark seeping blood.

The leader of the detail scowled at his guards. "What ninny commanded that these twain be clapped up together? 'Tis known that there's bad blood betwixt them." He turned to Marot. "What's all this with you *Ertsuma?* If this be how learned Earthmen behave, Bákh deliver us from real Terran ruffians!"

"Sir," said Marot, "you must keep my fiery colleagues well apart, lest they kill each other."

"What ails them?"

"They hate each other, because of rivalry over an Earthwoman."

"Ohé! I begin to understand," said the officer. He spoke to the other guards: "Put the new arrivals in Number Nine, and move furnishings in from the other cells." His lips curled in the Krishnan version of a sardonic smile. "With such mutual hatred, they'll make a lively spectacle at the hearing."

"What hearing is this?" said Marot. "We do not yet know why we have been brought here."

"Why, the hearing wherefor ye've been fetched hither, to answer charges laid against you by Master Foltus."

"When will it be?"

"On the morrow, Bákh willing."

Marot said: "We are exhausted after a strenuous, two-day ride. Could we not have a day of rest and restore our forces?"

"I'll pass word of your request to my superior; but count not upon any easement. The High Priestess wishes to conclude the matter with dispatch."

* * *

Reith slept a one-handed Krishnan clock around and woke stiff and sore but alert. He did a few calisthenics to stretch his aching muscles, wincing at the pain from his bruises, then plunged into a hearty breakfast. Marot studied him appraisingly, saying:

"Fergus, you have the most beautiful *oeuil poché*—I think you call it the blue eye?"

"Black eye. This safari of ours will go down in history as the black-and-blue paleontological expedition. I've never had so many bruises as I've collected in the past moon." Reith frowned somberly. "A couple of years ago, if you'd told me I'd try to kill another man with my bare hands over a woman, I'd have said you were out of your calabash. But something took hold of me. . . ."

"Then, my friend, perhaps you can understand what it is that makes the little Alicia do irrational, contraproductive things."

"You've got a point," said Reith. "But knowing that I have such weaknesses doesn't make her any easier to live with."

The captain of the temple guard, who had conducted them to their cell the night before, entered the cell with brisk authority. "God den, Terrans! Yestereve ye besought the lieutenant to have today's hearing put off, to give you time to recover from your ride. The High Priestess hath given her consent, holding it unjust that one adversary be in the pink of perfection whilst t'other gasps for life. Thus the hearing will take place at this hour on the morrow. May the best Terran win!"

The captain seemed not unfriendly. Reith suspected that the guards would await the outcome of the trial before deciding which prisoners they might mistreat with impunity and which they had better be kind to, lest an exonorated prisoner retaliate against them. Reith said:

"Would it be possible, Captain, for us to bathe and shave? We are unsuitably groomed for such a public event."

He ran his bruised fingers through the coppery stubble that sprouted over his jaw. Krishnans thought Terran whiskers repulsive, having but a few scattered hairs on their own chins. Therefore Earthmen on Krishna were careful to appear cleanshaven, even when, as happened every few decades, beards were fashionable on Earth. The officer replied:

"A bath ye may have, belike; but what's this shaving?"

"Scraping the face with a razor." Reith scratched his cheek. "What is a razor?"

"A very sharp knife, used by Terrans to remove facial hair."

"Nay, we've no such object. I can lend you a pair of tweezers, wherewith to pluck out the offending strands."

Reith sighed. "Not practical with a beard as thick as mine. But the baths will be appreciated."

Cleaned up, Reith and Marot spent the morning discussing the questions they might be asked and the replies they thought they should give. They agreed that, if permitted, Marot should field questions of a religious or philosophical nature, while Reith handled those having to do with Terran activities on Krishna. They shot questions at each other to hone their wits and criticized each other's answers. When Reith began to yawn and let his attention stray, Marot said:

"This may be a bore, my friend, but it is better than being boiled like a lobster."

When the midday meal was brought, Marot asked the jailer: "Would you please inquire of the captain whether we might have a copy of the *Book of Bákh?* We need spiritual enlightenment."

Shortly afterward, the captain appeared with a copy of the *Book of Bákh* under his arm. "Such piety merits praise, O Terrans," he said, handing over the book. "Methinks ye'll fare well at the hearing."

Reith and Marot spent the afternoon listening to each other drone through the first chapter of the *Book of Bákh,* over and over, until they had it memorized.

An enormous golden star adorned the door of the hearing room. The captain of the Temple guard pulled open the door, saying: "Go on in. Ye shall sit to the right, over yonder, where your defender now sits."

The hearing room was spacious, but there was no provision for spectators. Opposite the entrance stood three thronelike chairs, with high backs gilded and elaborately carved. In the largest of these sat Kharob bad-Kavir, Dasht of Chilihagh. On his right huddled an aged, bony Krishnan woman, who Reith surmised was the High Priestess Lazdai. The Krishnan on the left of the Dasht, another ancient wearing spectacles, Reith did not recognize. In a low voice, he asked the captain:

"Who is that in the throne on our right?"

"Chief Justicer Hargao," murmured the captain.

As Reith's glance swept the chamber, he saw Warren Foltz sitting across the room beside an aggressive-looking Krishnan. Eight armed guards were disposed around the room.

Reith and Marot took their seats in the two chairs assigned to them and nodded to the youthful Krishnan who was to act as their defender. The captain faced the tribunal, brought his right fist smartly against his left shoulder in salute, and announced: "Your Altitude, Captain Zurian of the Temple guard begs leave to report that preparations for the hearing in the matter of the three bone-hunting *Ertsuma* are now complete."

"My Altitude thanks you," said the Dasht. "Let the inquiry proceed. Sir Chief Justicer, state the case."

The aged male Krishnan spoke in a creaky voice: "On the fourteenth day of the third month, in the twenty-fifth year of Dasht Kharob bad-Kavir, we are assembled to investigate certain disturbances that have taken place within the Dashtate of Chilihagh during the past moon, in order to decide whether the persons involved, to wit: three aliens from the alleged world called Terra, have committed an offense against the laws of Chilihagh; and, if so, whether they should be tried under the civil law; or dismissed without further proceedings; or expelled as undesirable aliens; or, in the event that they prove suspect of an offense against the True Religion of the Dashtate, they should be remanded to the ecclesiastical authorities for further proceedings under the statutes governing such matters. Sir Prosecutor, proceed."

The Krishnan seated beside Foltz rose, bowed to the tribunal, and turned to face Foltz. He said: *"Ertsu, identify yourself."*

His voice still husky from the effects of Reith's strangling fingers, Foltz spoke: "I am Doctor of Philosophy Warren William Foltz, a native of the city of St. Louis, the nation the United States of America, the planet Terra."

"Explain, in a few words, how you came to be in Chilihagh."

Foltz: "I was a student of the evolution of life on my native planet. I came to this world supposing that life here had followed a similar course from lowly, invisibly small aquatic creatures to various larger forms, including the intelligent species—"

The prosecutor cut him off. "You will have a chance to explain your change of philosophy later." He turned to Reith, saying: *"Ertsu* with the fiery hair, identify yourself."

"My name is Fergus MacDonald Reith, a native of the city of Philadelphia, in the United States of America, on the planet Terra."

"How came you to be in Chilihagh?"

"I was hired as a guide by Doctor Aristide Marot, here beside me, to take him to the Zorian region of Chilihagh, where he intended to pursue his scientific researches."

Similar questioning established that Marot was a native of Lyons, France; and that, being an authority on the evolution of Terran life, he had come to ascertain what parallels with and divergences from Terran evolution had taken place on Krishna.

The prosecutor turned back to Foltz, saying: "Doctor Foltus, narrate the events that led to your being brought to Jeshang under guard."

Foltz shot a nasty little smile across the room. "As I have stated elsewhere, I arrived in your world assuming that evolution here had followed a course much like that on my own planet. In Jeshang, however, I read the *Book of Bákh* and learned that, contrary to the course of events on Terra, here Bákh created all species at once, at the time he established human life; and that all these created species have persevered with only minor changes down to the present."

"State how you came to be involved with these other Terrans," said the prosecutor.

"I knew the work of Doctor Marot on Terra and had met him at scientific meetings. I also knew of his plan to travel to this world to pursue similar investigations. Before I saw the light of Bákh, I knew of no objections to my colleague's plans. When, however, the Truth of Bákh was made manifest to me, I perceived that, for the sake of the True Faith, I must forestall Doctor Marot's well-intentioned activities. Knowing him to be dogmatically committed to the false hypothesis of evolution—false on this world, that is—and surmising that he would seek evidence to support his fallacy in the geological beds of the Zorian formation, I arrived ahead of him.

"As I foresaw, Doctor Marot unearthed a fossil by means of which he meant, with specious arguments, to foist upon the enlightened people of Chilihagh his wrongful theory. I therefore seized the opportunity to destroy the fossil. In the course of this action, I was compelled to have my servants forcibly restrain Masters Reith and Marot, who were understandably distressed at the loss of what they in their delusion deemed evidence of their belief. I took care to apply no more force than was necessary and would have released them unharmed, had not the unfortunate conflict with the escort of Father Behorj taken place."

"How came that conflict to pass?"

"As I have explained, it arose as a result of a mistake. In a heavy rainstorm, my men took the men of Father Behorj's escort for a gang of brigands and shot crossbow bolts at them. I have expressed my profound regrets for this blunder, which occurred without my authority while I was occupied with destroying the fossil."

"It is a serious matter natheless," said the prosecutor. "Five men slain, one of Behorj's escort and four of yours, not to mention numerous wounds."

"Any penalty I must suffer in consequence of this blunder, I will gladly submit to," said Foltz, looking martyred.

"One moment!" The Krishnan seated next to Marot rose.

Dasht Kharob said: "You may speak, Sir Defender."

The defender turned to Foltz. "Doctor Foltus, you have stated that you destroyed this fossil. Yet when the men of Father Behorj's party escorted you back to the site of the excavation, you are reported as having said: 'It is gone! The *zefta* must have come back and carried off the fragments!' So tell us, pray, in what form, if any, this object still exists?"

Foltz shrugged. "My statements were true. I left the rock slab broken into a score of pieces. When I was brought back thither, they were not to be seen. What befell the specimen thereafter, I do not know."

The defender continued: "We have the statements of Father Duriz, that his men examined the cargo of the riverboat *Morkerád* without finding this suppositious bag of stones. We also have the statement of Captain Manyao, who led the raid into Qirib, that his men diligently searched the car wherein these Terrans rode, likewise in vain. Doctor Maghou, can you enlighten us as to the present whereabouts and condition of this evidence?"

Marot gave an expressive French shrug. "I never set eyes upon my specimen after the attack by Foltz's followers."

"Then how account you for its vanishment from the site of your researches?"

Marot paused. "That country is full of little bumps and hollows, all looking much alike. It is easy to mistake one's location. Moreover, it was raining, and light was poor because of the dense clouds. I suggest that Doctor Foltz erred in showing you what he believed to be the site of my work. An error of a few paces would suffice."

The prosecutor addressed the High Priestess: "Your Holiness, if you think it worth the while, we can send another party to scrutinize the banks of the River Zora more closely, in hope of finding these fragments."

"We'll decide anon," said Lazdai. "Having seen how these artful rogues can slip through our fingers, I'd not assume they did not have some ingenious sleight to get their bones past our folk."

The defender turned towards Foltz. "Is it not true, Doctor Foltus, that there was also a personal conflict betwixt you and Master Reef?"

"There was, but this had nothing to do with the question of evolution and the True Faith."

"What, then, was the cause of this conflict, wherein, we are informed, you attacked Master Reef with a sword and would have slain him but for the intervention of his comrade?"

"I had a secretary, an Earthwoman, whom Reith hired away from me by a promise of higher pay. A very able person, she had been keeping my records and managing my crew, and her abrupt departure left me in a difficult predicament. I went to Marot's camp to protest this high-handed action and was attacked by Reith with a pick. When I defended myself with my sword, Marot treacherously assailed me from behind with his hammer."

"Liar!" said Reith loudly.

"Order in the court!" snapped the Dasht. "You shall have your say, Master Reef."

The defender persisted: "Is it not true, Master Foltus, that you and Master Reef were rivals for the personal affections of this secretary, whose name was. . . ." (He consulted a sheet of notes.) ". . . Ah-lee-shah Dah-eek-man?"

"It is untrue so far as I am concerned," said Foltz. "My relations with the lady were purely professional, as employer to assistant. Whether Reith entertained more personal sentiments, I do not know."

Marot whispered: "Fergus, when your turn comes, make

much of the triangle among you, Foltz, and Alicia. Tell the story of your marriage."

"Why?"

"It will shake his tale of having opposed us from lofty religious motives."

Reith scowled. "Look, Aristide, I can't get up in court and accuse her of fornication! It wouldn't be decent."

"It might be better than being boiled."

"No matter what fool things she's done, I can't drag her name in the mud!"

"Oho, who now has the quaint old-fashioned ideas! Statistics show that over ninety-six per cent of all women—"

"I don't care what the statistics say; it's a matter of principle—"

"But, my friend," continued Marot in a stage whisper, "we must be realistic! She is a realist, and I am sure that she would be the first to confess her various *faux pas* to save you. . . . I tell you! You be the discreet, reticent one. But when my turn comes, I bare all, describing the little Alicia's affairs so as to present you in a favorable light. If she learns of this, you can blame me."

Reith grunted. "Order in the court!" said the Dasht.

While Reith and Marot had been carrying on their whispered conversation, the defender had been asking Foltz peripheral questions, fishing for leads and getting either noncommittal answers or protestations of ignorance. At last the defender said: "I have no more questions for the present. Proceed, Sir Prosecutor."

The prosecutor faced Reith. "Master Reef, describe your duties under your contract with Doctor Maghou."

"I promised to guide him, protect him from the vicissitudes of travel, act as translator, and purchase equipment and hire labor on his behalf."

"Had you any concern with the theoretical, philosophical, or religious aspects of his search for petrified bones?"

"None whatever, sir."

"What was your understanding of the difference between Doctors Maghou and Foltus?"

"As presented to me, it concerned a highly technical point in the theory of the evolution of life on this world."

"What point was that?"

"Something about whether all land vertebrates were descended from one line of water-dwelling ancestors or two."

"What is your opinion on this subject?"

"I have none, sir. The question is far beyond my competence."

"Were it fair to say that you favor the idea of the evolution of life on this world?"

"It was the only theory I had heard of, until I became acquainted with the religion of Bákh."

"To what belief do you now adhere?"

"To none. I am a tour guide, not a scientist, and I see no need for me to decide such profound philosophical questions."

The prosecutor paused, then said: "Master Reef, what is your version of the quarrel betwixt you and Doctor Foltus over Mistress Dyckman?"

"She is Doctor Dyckman," said Reith. "I knew her before this expedition. The night after Marot's and my visit to Foltz's camp, Foltz gave Alicia Dyckman a severe beating. She fled his camp and, knowing me from aforetime, sought refuge with me. Foltz invaded our camp the following day and tried to take her back by force; so we fought him off."

"Why did Foltz beat this Earthwoman?"

"She told me that he beat her in a jealous rage, because she and I seemed too friendly to please him."

The prosecutor looked around the hearing room. "We should have the Earthwoman here to straighten out this discrepancy. Why was she not taken from the train when these others were arrested?"

The High Priestess spoke, in a surprisingly deep voice: "The warrant named only those two. No evidence hath been adduced involving this Earthwoman in the question of the Truth of Bákh."

"Still," said the prosecutor, "her presence could greatly expedite this case. Doth Your Holiness know where she may now be found?"

"Nay. If she was on the train with these *Ertsuma*, I ween she hath returned to Jazmurian."

"Whence it were impracticable to fetch her," muttered the prosecutor, "the Qiribuma doubtless being sufficiently stirred up by our pursuit and capture of these two." He turned. "Doctor Foltus! Did you beat this Earthwoman?"

"No. I never laid a hand on her. We had high words when she announced she was leaving, and she rushed out of the tent in a passion. In so doing, she tripped on a tent rope and fell, sustaining bruises. These furnished her with a pretext for saying I had struck her."

Reith controlled his anger with difficulty. The defender spoke: "Master Reef! During your intercourse with Doctor Foltus, did he give any sign of conversion from evolutionism to the Truth of Bákh?"

"No, sir."

"Were such matters discussed during your visit to his camp?"

"Yes, indeed."

"What opinion did Foltus then express?"

"He stood up for his version of the evolution of all life on this world. This was essentially the same as Marot's, differing only in the detail I mentioned before."

"Did Foltus endeavor at any time to convert you and Maghou to the Truth of Bákh?"

"No."

"So his conversion could have been feigned, to get him out of trouble with the state religion and you into it?"

"I object!" said the prosecutor. "The question calls for inference by the witness about matters whereof he hath no personal knowledge."

"Objection sustained," said the Chief Justicer.

The prosecutor took his turn. "Doctor Maghou, what is your present stand on the question of evolution versus the Truth of Bákh?"

"I hold them equally true," said Marot blandly.

"How can that be? *The Book of Bákh* clearly states that Bákh created the universe in three days; so how could life on this world have formed gradually over millions of years, as I understand your evolutionary theory contemplates?"

"It is a question of which words of your holy book are to be taken literally and which figuratively."

"Explain yourself, pray."

"Gladly. I have some slight acquaintance with the *Book of Bákh*. I find that it displays many parallels with the sacred book of the Terran religion that I was reared in, called Christianity. For example, all Terrans but the most primitive and ignorant realize that Terra is of spherical shape; yet many passages in this sacred book, called the Bible, imply that it is flat. It speaks of 'the four corners of the Earth.' It tells of men building a tower by which they hoped to invade heaven, as if the universe were a box, with the Earth as the floor and the heavens the lid. They tell of a prophet's seeing all the kingdoms of the Earth from a high mountain.

"The explanation of our theologians is that, while the book was written under divine guidance, it was expressed in terms intelligible to those to whom it was addressed. At the time this book took shape, most Terrans believed the Earth to be flat.

"Permit me to add that Terran theologians have learned to be wary of disputing scientific facts. Half a millennium ago, a scientist named Galileo asserted that Terra traveled around our sun, and not the sun around the planet, as was then the official belief. The most powerful of the Christian churches forced him to deny this belief and kept him confined to his house for the rest of his life. It transpired that Galileo was right and the official belief wrong; but it took this Church two centuries to admit its error. Christianity has never quite recovered from its loss of prestige in the matter of Galileo."

"Doctor Maghou," said the defender, "can ye shed light upon the contradiction betwixt the other two *Ertsuma* in the matter of Doctor Dyckman?"

"Of a certainty!" said Marot. "I saw the bruises on the poor woman when she arrived at our camp. I assure you, they were not the result of tripping over a tent rope. Although I did not witness the beating, there is every indication that it took place.

"The fact is that Doctor Dyckman was Master Reith's former wife, and they still retain a mutual affection. I shall not be surprised if they eventually re-marry. So, naturally, she took refuge with him when Foltz mistreated her."

"Why had he beaten her?"

"Because, in return for his employment of her services, he compelled her to accept him as a lover. When she and Reith met at Foltz's camp, he observed their tender regards and concluded that they were still in love. So in a jealous rage he beat her."

"How is she Reef's 'former wife'?"

"She obtained a divorce under the laws of Novorecife, after a number of quarrels."

The High Priestess boomed: "Doctor Maghou!"

"Yes, Madam?"

"Was Master Reef, during his marriage to this Earthwoman, a chronic drunkard?"

"I am sure not. I have known him well on my expedition

and found him a careful, abstemious drinker."

"Was he an inveterate gambler?" Lazdai persisted.

"No."

"A wastrel?"

"No."

"A fornicator?"

"I have heard nothing to indicate it."

"Had he beaten her?"

"I am sure not."

"Was he an addict of the *ramandu* or other narcotic?"

"I am sure not."

"Was he involved in crime or corruption?"

"I believe not."

"Is he forever ill-natured and quarrelsome?"

"But no! I can assert from my own knowlege that he is not."

"Was he sexually perverted or deficient?"

"I have no reason to think so."

"In other words, would you term him a man of good moral character, well qualified to act the rôle of spouse?"

"Of a certainty, yes!"

"But, although he was innocent of the vices and faults that, amongst folk of civilized moral standards, would be deemed sufficient reason to dissolve a marriage, his wife divorces him because of some petty quarrels. This confirms my opinion, that you *Ertsuma* are as immoral, casually changing mates every few years on flimsy pretexts, as the promiscous Balhibuma. They, at least, are not hypocritical about it. They have abolished marriage and refer to their nonce mates by the term *jagain,* meaning simply 'he or she with whom I am currently futtering.' Now, perhaps, you can understand why we in Chilihagh regard Terran influence as malignant. Excuse the digression, Sir Prosecutor, and proceed."

The questioning ground on, going over the same ground in an endeavor to clear up the contradictions between the stories of Foltz on one hand and of Reith and Marot on the other. Foltz insisted that he had tried to warn his colleagues of the dangers of subverting the Truth of Bákh and even attempted to convert the other Terrans to that faith; they denied that he had said anything of the sort. Marot repeated the arguments he had already given the priest Behorj for a figurative understanding of the *Book of Bákh:* that, being omnipotent, Bákh could make the 'days' of his creation any length he chose.

The defender and the prosecutor held a whispered conference; then the defender produced a sheaf of papers. "I have here," he said, "the deposition of Ghirch bad-Gargan, a shai-han-herd. To save time, the prosecutor and I have agreed to stipulate that this Ghirch was in the employ of Sainian bad-Jeb, owner of the Zora ranch; that this Ghirch was commanded to stay at Doctor Foltus's camp to observe the proceedings and to assist Foltus in the event of difficulties. He accompanied Foltus on the latter's first visit to Maghou's camp. I shall now read the rest of the deposition:

"'Question: After the visiting Terrans had finished their dinner and departed, what next befell?'

"'Answer: I heard a disturbance from Foltus's tent, as if he and the Terran female were quarreling.'

"'Question: What action did ye take in regard to this disturbance?'

"'Answer: None, sir. They often quarreled, so I thought no more of the matter and went to bed.'

"'Question: Did this Terran female, clept Alicia, regularly sleep in Foltus's tent?'

"'Answer: I believe that was her usual habit.'

"'Question: Did she and Foltus engage in carnal intercourse?'

"'Answer: How in Hishkak should I know, sir? They never did it where I could see them, and I know not what strange customs the *Ertsuma* follow.'"

The defender asked Marot: "Doctor, amongst Terrans, when a male and a female occupy the same chamber overnight, do they normally engage in carnal intercourse?"

Marot shrugged. "Sometimes. It depends on many factors: whether they are permitted by law, custom, or religion; the degree of affection between them; their physical and mental condition; and so on."

The defender resumed reading: "'Question: Did this Alicia flee Foltus's camp during the night?'

"'Answer: I suppose she did. I did not see her about the following morning.'

"'Question: When did you see her next?'

"'Answer: Never, sir.'

"'Question: What befell the next morning?'

"'Answer: I was at breakfast when Foltus came storming

out of his tent with his face scratched. He demanded that I leave my victuals to saddle up two ayas forthwith and ride with him to the other bone-diggers' camp. Well, I was not much pleased; it upsets my stomach when I am snatched away in the midst of a repast. I mind me of the time of the great stampede, when in the middle of dinner—'

"'Question: Yea, yea, Goodman Ghirch; but let us return to your visit to the other camp.'

"'Answer: Aye, sir; begging your pardon. We were halfway to the other camp, and Foltus had been cursing under his breath. Then he pulled to a halt, shouting: "Bákh damn them all to Hishkah!" When I asked what betid, he said he had forgotten to lead a third aya with us, needed to carry another person back to our own camp. He would have turned back, but I told him that my own aya could carry double. She is a big, strong beast, with a white blaze—'

"'Question: Stick to the course, pray.'

"'Answer: Oh, aye, sir. We arrived at the other camp, and Foltus lighted down from his beast and began shouting at Reef, who shouted back. I know not what they said, since they spake some off-world gibberish. The next I knew, they were fighting. Foltus with his sword and Reef with a pick.'

"'Question: Which attacked the other? Which struck the first blow?'

"'Answer: I could not say, sir. Meseemed both were set upon doing the other to death.'

"'Question: What was the upshot?'

"'Answer: Doctor Maghou, yonder, ran up behind Foltus and knocked him senseless with a strange kind of hammer.'

"'Question: What then?'

"'Answer: My orders being to succor Foltus in difficulties, I roped his body to his saddle and led the aya back to our camp. By the time we reached it, Foltus had begun to recover.'

"'Question: What befell next at the Foltus camp?'

"'Answer: I know not, sir. When we reached the camp, I found another of Squire Sainian's men with a message, that I should leave the camp and join the roundup, since one of the herders had been hurt.'

"'Question: Thank you, Goodman Ghirch.'

"As ye have heard," said the defender, "Ghirch's account corroborates that of Reef and Maghou. Doctor Foltus!"

"Yes?"

"What have ye to say to this testimony?"

"That it is a pack of lies," said Foltz. "My colleagues across the room must have suborned Ghirch with money or promises of more lucrative employment."

Asked the same question, Reith and Marot said that Ghirch's testimony was quite correct as far as it went. "The next deposition!" said the prosecutor.

This was an interview with the camp worker Doukh. It settled nothing, because Doukh, obviously frightened, answered "Aye" to every question, even if this answer contradicted a previous one.

"Have you any more depositions?" asked the Dasht.

"Nay, my lord," said the prosecutor. "We endeavored to obtain statements from Foltus's servants about such matters as the relations betwixt him and his secretary, and his alleged beating of her. But those men have all gone into hiding."

Kharob asked: "How could they, when they were brought to Jeshang along of Doctor Foltus?"

"The five brought hither were enlarged by order of Her Holiness, as having nought of interest to say. There were two or three others; but they, too, have disappeared."

The Dasht glared at the High Priestess, who glared back. She said: "Bákh told me that nought was to be gained by holding them."

After further haggling over technicalities, the prosecutor said: "I have no more questions, my lords."

"And ye, Sir Defender?"

"None more, Your Altitude."

"Very well. The Terrans shall be given refreshment whilst my colleagues and I withdraw to consider our verdict."

A Krishnan hour later, when all had returned to the hearing room, the Dasht said:

"The Chief Justicer will announce the verdict. Rise, *Ertsuma!*"

The old lawyer adjusted his eyeglasses and spoke from a sheet of notes: "Whereas the Terran clept Warren Foltus hath been involved in a combat causing the deaths of five of His Altitude's subjects and the wounding of divers others, he hath rendered himself liable to punishment. In view, however, of his sincere conversion to the Truth of Bákh and his help in bringing to book the other two *Ertsuma,* it hath been decided to limit his penalty to summary expulsion from the Dashtate.

"Whereas Masters Reef and Maghou have been shown to be stubborn and fanatical adherents of the false theory of evolution, they shall be released to the custody of the religious authorities, for such disposal as seems best suited to promote the Truth of Bákh."

"Which," said the High Priestess with a crooked smile, "shall be the regular penalty for contumacious heresy, as soon as I can sign the papers. Orders have already gone out, and the Cauldron of Repentance will be ready on the morrow. Take them away!"

In the late afternoon, Reith and Marot were returned to their cell. Their depression was not lightened by the sardonic grin that Foltz flashed at them in the corridor. For hours they sat, stirring betimes to mutter an occasional comment:

"Aristide, wouldn't it have been better to pretend wholehearted conversion? Foltz got away with it."

"I do not think so. It would perhaps have cast doubt on his sincerity; but while that might have put him into the kettle, it would not deliver us."

Reith held his head in his hands. "Remember my saying we'd be safe once we were on the train? How stupid can anyone be?"

"Do not blame yourself, my friend. If the mouse has six holes from which to issue, not even the most gifted cat can foresee which one will be employed. Should we perhaps have fought the Bákhites when they attacked the train, instead of tamely yielding?"

"I thought of that; but I figured the odds were hopeless. I have no illusion that I can cut my way through a hundred foes and escape—and on foot at that."

They scarcely touched their dinners. Darkness had fallen, and a Temple guard was lighting the lamps in the corridor outside, when the cell door was unlocked and two figures came in. The first was a tall person in a hooded cloak; the second, a burly Krishnan carrying a broad-bladed, two-handed sword.

Reith pulled himself together. "To whom do we owe the honor of this visit?"

The hooded figure cast off the cloak and stood revealed as Dasht Kharob bad-Kavir. "Good even, gentlemen."

"Good even to Your Altitude. What now?"

The Dasht said: "Know that I did not concur with this afternoon's voting. To me, your stories were more plausible than those of Doctor Foltus, especially with the corroboration of the shaihan-hand. I would have merely exiled you along with Foltus, but I was outvoted. Her Holiness is taken with Foltus, who hath beguiled her with flatteries and obsequious blandishments. She would have let him off scot-free; but I insisted on my right to expel him.

"She holds that to cast doubt upon the literal veracity of a single syllable of the *Book of Bákh* puts the whole edifice at hazard. Therefore she demands your bodies, to serve as an example to other temerarious Terrans, who might come hither to spread subversive ideas."

"If you're the Dasht," said Reith, "haven't you the power to pardon us, or at least commute the sentence?"

"Not in matters of ecclesiastical jurisdiction, and the extent of that jurisdiction is what the High Priestess saith it be. You know not our local politics."

"Why did the Chief Justicer take her side?"

"He fears an accusation of heresy, should he display unwonted independence of mind. Since you'll not survive to tattle, I can be frank. Lazdai and I have been opposed in many things; but such is her hold on the people that I dare not come out openly against her, lest a mob, incited by her minions, string me up in the main square. I can trust but few, such as Jám here." He nodded at the swordsman. "He's here, first to make sure you try not something desperate, like seizing me as hostage; and second to effect the favor I offer, an you accept."

"And that is?"

"In lieu of the official penalty, Jám will give you a quick quietus. All you need do is assent, kneel down, and bow your heads—and *kchunk!* 'tis all over in a trice. Lazdai will be passing wroth, but I can ride out that storm."

Reith said: "May we have a few minutes to consider this unseductive choice, Your Altitude?"

"Certes." The Dasht and his headsman stepped out of the cell.

"I think we had better accept," murmured Marot. "I have no more fear of death than most; but boiling—*pouah!*"

"I say no," said Reith. "While there's life there's hope; but if we let this guy slice off our heads now, that's the end of it. If a rescue party arrived—and I'm sure Alicia will do her damnedest to launch one—they'd find nobody to rescue."

Marot made a helpless gesture. "Do what you think best."

They called the Dasht back in. Reith said: "Much as we appreciate your offer, Your Altitude, we must decline. We trust Bákh to work a miracle to save us."

Kharob sighed. "I have done what I could to ease your pains. I must own, Doctor Maghou, that I was vastly impressed by your argument about figurative interpretation of the sacred book. If I were more sure of my power. . . . But what will be, will be."

Roqir rose in a clear sky as Reith and Marot, hands manacled, were hustled out to a courtyard behind the Great Temple of Bákh. A wood fire crackled under the Cauldron of Repentance, and gentle plumes of vapor ascended from Lazdai's Kettle towards the greenish sky. Reith paid little heed to the droning of the priests who chanted prayers.

In the midst of these preparations, Marot said: "Your miracle had better occur soon, Fergus. I do not think these preliminaries will continue much longer."

"I can't wave a wand and summon spirits from the vasty deep," snapped Reith. "If I could, we wouldn't be here— what's that?"

Beyond the courtyard, a disturbance arose, the noise of which grew swiftly. There was shouting and a clash of metal on metal.

Into the courtyard burst a swarm of mounted newcomers, with the brazen cuirasses and the scarlet tunics and breeches of the Balhibo cavalry. There were hundreds of them; some had wounds bandaged. In their midst rode one of different aspect, a slender, blond, disheveled Earthwoman in worn khakis.

"Fergus!" she screamed, leaping down from her aya. She flung her arms around Reith, who could not return her embrace until he had hoisted the chain of his manacles over his head.

"I got them to turn out the whole Jazmurian garrison squadron," she panted. "They were furious at the raid, and I stirred them up even more. We had to knock a few heads at the border. Oh, Fergus darling!"

The lovers clung to each other as two Krishnans confronted each other: the tall Dasht and the stout female officer commanding the squadron. Kharob bad-Kavir spoke: "Madam, what is the meaning of this violation of the sovran territory of Chilihagh? I protest this warlike incursion! Who are you?"

"Major Kaldashi, commanding the Second Cavalry Squadron at Jazmurian. It is I who protest the violation of the territory of the Republic of Balhib by a band of marauders from Chilihagh, who carried off two Terran travelers from the Jazmurian-to-Majbur train. There they are!" She pointed to Reith and Marot. "We have no fell designs on your sovranty, my lord. We wish merely the two Terrans unharmed and shall depart forthwith—albeit, had we arrived to find them executed, there might have been more serious consequences."

The Dasht replied: "I yield to superior force. I shall issue commands that you be not hindered or molested on your way out of the Dashtate. I shall send an officer with you to assure compliance with this order."

With the shadow of a Krishnan smile, the Dasht walked off while the major approached Reith and Marot and questioned them about their experience. Soon Dasht Kharob reappeared with the captain of the Temple guard, saying: "Captain Zurian, unlock those gyves!"

As the manacles were removed, Reith said: "Thanks, Your Altitude. I said Bákh would pass a miracle. Where's Foltz?"

"He would have tarried to enjoy your execution, but I sent him on his way with an escort. Whilst I am officially outraged by Major Kaldashi's incursion, I shall turn it to account. I have commanded the arrest of High Priestess Lazdai and her priestly council, for having, on their own responsibility, committed a warlike act against a friendly neighboring nation. The civil government shall at last reassert itself against the usurpations of the Bákhites!"

"Will Your Altitude then restore religious freedom?" asked Alicia.

"Aye. We mortals have enough to do to settle quarrels amongst ourselves, let alone disputes amongst the gods."

At last Reith and Marot were mounted on spare ayas, and the squadron clattered out of Jeshang. Riding beside Marot, Reith said: "At least, I hope this ride won't be at the breakneck pace of the last one."

"I hope so also. It should be shorter, since we came here by a roundabout route." Marot nodded towards Alicia, riding ahead beside the major. "What about her?"

Reith sighed. "If she wants to marry me again, I'd be a swine to refuse her, after she saved my life. But I dread to think what life with her will be like. I've been through all that, enough for two lifetimes."

"At its worst," said Marot, "it will be less painful than the Cauldron of Repentance."

"True, but that would have been over in a few minutes. The other may last for more than a century!"

X.

THE PALACE

Three days later, the squadron returned to Jazmurian. A lieutenant accompanied the three Terrans to Angur's Inn and led their ayas away. Reith paid Angur for baths for himself and his companions, saying to Marot:

"I don't care if you think three tubfuls extravagant! This isn't the French boondocks. If your Institut makes a fuss, I'll pay for the extra two myself."

Later, Reith told his companions: "I must go to the railroad station, to see if the trains are running again."

At the station, the clerk said: "Nay, sir, the break in the track hath not yet been repaired."

"When will service be restored?"

The Krishnan spread his hands. "Bákh knows. The Chili-haghuma not only tore up that stretch of track but also destroyed a bridge. In another eight or ten days, belike."

Reith reported back to his friends at Angur's, saying: "This probably means we'd better go by ship. It's too late in the day to start looking for berths; so we might as well take it easy till dinner and afterwards go to bed early."

"But we ought to dance, to celebrate your escape!" said Alicia.

Reith clapped a hand to his forehead. "Woman! Are you a flesh-and-blood creature, or a mechanical marvel that never runs down?"

"My cogwheels are of the best quality. Come on, Superman! You don't want to admit that a poor, weak woman can outlast you, do you?"

"Whatever I've said about you," said Reith, looking martyred, "I've never once called you 'weak.'"

Next morning in the big bed, Alicia giggled. "And you're the one who feared he wouldn't have enough pep for dancing last night!"

"It's the quality of the inspiration, darling," said Reith.

She drew back and looked at him. "Fergus dear, for one who's just proved himself a super-lover, you look unhappy—troubled. What is it, dearest?"

"Nothing, darling," said Reith, forcing a smile. "Just thinking how to get us safely back to Novo."

This, Reith knew, was not what really troubled him. Ever since the rescue, he had been torn by conflicting urges. She had aggravated his turmoil by giving him long, level, open-faced looks, with raised eyebrows—looks that said plainly: well, when are we going to get married again? Love, covetousness, and gratitude for the rescue urged him on.

On the other hand, his hard-earned caution, and a lively memory of their stormy life together, restrained him. He told himself: she's a wonderful person, but she's still the same tempestuous Alicia. She would boss you, bully you, argue with you, reorganize your life for you and, on the least pretext, lose her temper and scream at you—if she didn't use a blunt instrument on you. In a moon or two, you and this spitfire would be right back where you were before she left you. One traumatic marital breakup is enough!

She said: "Do you know what I wish, darling?"

"What?"

"That you and I had met way back, before either of us had experience of sex, and that we'd gotten married then, and that there'd been nobody but just us ever since. If you believe the books, that's how lots of people used to do it."

"A lovely idea, Lish. But of course, you might not have liked me as a shy, skinny kid with his nose in a book."

"I don't know about that. But I know I was a horrible person to live with. So you wouldn't have liked me, either."

"Maybe; maybe not. Unfortunately, life isn't like a reel of tape, which you can rewind and edit and play over again. I guess we have to act out our current segment of tape, and right now that means getting up for breakfast."

Reluctantly, she unwrapped her arms from around his bony torso and untangled her legs from his.

At breakfast, Reith said: "Our next job is to find a ship for Majbur. Can I leave you two to your own devices for a while?"

Marot: "I shall go look at the trains."

"Lish?"

"I'd like to go shopping, now that we're in funds."

"I don't advise it. This is a tough town for a woman to wander alone."

"Oh, fishfeathers! I've knocked around by myself all over the lands of the Triple Seas. Besides, we've fixed Lazdai's wagon."

"Just listen for a minute, sweetheart!" said Reith earnestly. "I promised not to order you around any more. So I did not say, thou shalt not shop! If you must, go ahead. But I'll be back in a couple of hours; and then, if you like, we can all go out to buy things together."

"Oh, all right. Then I'll work on my journal for a while."

Relieved at avoiding another confrontation with his head-strong amorex, Reith borrowed a scooter from Angur. The harbor master's office was in a cupola atop the customs building, whence that functionary could look out over the neighboring roofs to keep track of the ships that entered and left the harbor. Reith climbed the circular stair to his office and greeted the occupant:

"Hail, good Master Peyuz! Do you remember me, Fergus Reith?"

"Certes! How go your tours? Have ye brought a swarm of *Ertsuma* to gape at our sights, ogle our wenches, and finger our merchandise?"

"I have only two, which is hardly a swarm. We wish to book passage to Majbur forthwith. May I see the list of sailings?"

It transpired that the *Kubitar*, of Captain Gendu, left at noon the following day for Damovang, Majbur, and Darya. "A well-found ship, not above a year old," said the harbor master. Reith asked:

"Does any other ship, leaving soon, *not* put in at Damovang?"

"The next is the *Garm,* bound for Majbur and Reshr; but that sails not till twelve days hence."

Reith chewed his lip. At the moment he was inclined to propose remarriage to Alicia. This morning at the inn, she had been quite reasonable in following his advice. If she kept on improving. . . . But he had a feeling that to stop to visit her native friend, President Vizman of Qirib, would somehow upset the delicate relationship between them. On the other hand, a twelve-day delay would get them to Novo at a date uncomfortably close to the departure of the *Juruá* for Terra. With a sigh he decided on the *Kubitar.*

When Reith found the *Kubitar's* berth, he pushed up the gangboard amid a stream of longshoremen bent beneath bags and boxes. A towering captain, standing at the head of the plank directing stowage, looked sharply at Reith as he approached.

"Captain Gendu?" said Reith. "I am Fergus Reith, a Terran as you see. We are told you expect to sail at midday tomorrow."

"So we shall," growled Gendu, "if landlubbers get not in the way of our lading."

"I regret to trouble you, but have you accommodation for three passengers to Majbur?"

"Oh, that's a different story. Aye, we have, and welcome ye shall be. Chindor!" he shouted at his first officer. "Show this gentleman our passenger cabin." He turned back to his loading.

The passenger accommodations, which occupied the central part of the deckhouse aft of the captain's quarters, were a small compartment with four bunks. There were two on each side and ladders for reaching the upper berths. A door on each side opened on the deck.

"When do you expect to reach Majbur?" Reith asked the mate.

"If the winds hold fair, we can arrive in five and a half days, including the stop at Damovang."

"That's good time."

"Aye, but this be a new ship, with hull unfouled by growths marine and sails new and flat, not stretched into bags by wind and wave. For now, she's the swiftest merchantman on the Sadabao."

Reith paid for three passengers, promising to be on the pier well before sailing time.

Returning from the docks, Reith found Marot studying a wooden rail coach and took him to the ticket office in the station building. He said to the clerk:

"Here are the stubs of three tickets to Majbur, bought about a ten-day ago. We were on the train that was held up short of Kolsafid, and I wish a refund."

The clerk wagged his head. "That I cannot do, O Terran," he said in an arrogant tone. "The rules clearly say that, to obtain a refund, ye must apply within three days of the cancellation."

"What! But my friend here and I were abducted from that train and taken to Chilihagh. How in Hishkak could we apply for refunds from a prison cell in Jeshang?"

The Krishnan spread his hands. "That's your misfortune. Rules are rules, and we cannot make exceptions for every whim of chance."

Reith reddened. "Look here, young fellow!" he roared. "Know that I am Fergus Reith, planetary manager for the Magic Carpet Travel Agency. Doctor Marot is one of my tourists. It is ridiculous for the railroad to let a passenger be kidnapped from a train and then refuse to return his fare. What is your name?"

"I—You have no right to ask that," said the clerk, losing assurance.

"I shall find out, fear not. Who is the highest railroad official in this building?"

"The—the vice-president, Master Lazkar. But he sees none without appointment."

"He'll see me! Where is his office?"

"Really, good my masters, there's no need to roil the waters over this matter. If ye say a refund is in order, doubtless ye know whereof ye speak. How much paid ye?"

Leaving the station with money in his pockets, Reith smiled. "That's the sort of thing we sometimes have to do, Aristide. My trade calls for a thick skin and plenty of brass. I'm a shy, timid fellow at heart, but I've learned to act the blustering bully when necessary. The trick is to know *when* to bluster; one can be in my business for years and still not get the hang of it."

Reith paused to examine the sundial in the center of the square. "Let's collect Alicia and go shopping, to replace the stuff those damned cowboys stole."

They bought toothbrushes and razors. Alicia got a new sewing kit. Marot replaced the flute he had lost at Zora with a Krishnan instrument of similar form. All three obtained wide-brimmed straw hats like those they had seen at the ranch.

Their boots were disintegrating; but Krishnan footgear had to be made to order, and the handwork would take a ten-day. Alicia said: "On the ship, we'll go barefoot until we get to Majbur. But wouldn't it be nice if we could buy new underwear? I don't know about Aristide, but yours and mine are falling apart."

"It is the same with me," said Marot with a self-conscious smile.

"I don't know," said Reith, "whether the Terran culture trait of wearing underwear has spread so far from Novo. We'll see."

They canvassed a number of shops. In each, Reith said: "Good afternoon, madam. Do you have underwear for sale?"

Each time, the clerk would roll her eyes, wag her head, and sadly confess: "Ah, no, sir; there's no underwear here."

Alicia giggled. "It looks as if you two will have to risk exposure when the wind catches those kilts."

The *Kubitar* worked her way out of the harbor under six sweeps manned by the sailors, who then shook out the two big red-and-yellow striped triangular sails. A steady south wind bore the vessel swiftly out into Bajjai Bay, where it overtook and passed a tubby coastal craft.

"When do we reach Damovang?" asked Alicia eagerly, leaning on the rail.

"About mid-morning tomorrow, I think," said Reith.

"Fine! We'll get a good look at Mount Sabushi."

"What mountain is this?" asked Marot.

Reith explained: "Mount Sabushi rises steeply behind Ghulindé, of which Damovang is the port. A thousand or so years ago, some ruler with big ideas ordered Mount Sabushi carved into a seated statue of the war god Qondyor, who held the city in his lap. By now the crag's pretty well eroded away and no more than an odd-looking mountain; but it's still one of the sights on the tourist track."

After dinner, the three companions gathered on the fantail, to watch the red disk of Roqir sink behind the dark horizontal line of the Jazmuriano hinterland. Alicia said: "Aristide, why don't you get that flute thing you bought? You can play while Fergus and I dance."

Reith said: "I thought we'd danced enough at Angur's last night to hold you for a while."

"Don't be an old poop! I want to try out that new Krishnan dance we saw them doing, the one that looked like the Zulu back on Terra. How about it, Aristide?"

"I have not yet mastered this instrument, with its unfamiliar scale...."

"Oh, that's all right! If you hit a false note, we'll never know the difference."

The last ruddy rays of the setting sun saw Reith and Alicia trying out the steps of the *kormez*, to the uncertain tune of Marot's *chari*. The helmsman became so fascinated that Captain Gendu came aft to roar curses at him for letting the ship drift off course.

Reith admitted to himself that, while dancing in general was a chore, with Alicia floating feather-light in his arms, it became a delight. Gazing at her classic features in the light of two moons, he thought: I don't care if she is difficult at times! Nobody else on two planets can be such marvelous *fun;* and the sheer pleasure of being with her, when she is in one of her sunnier moods, is worth a few pains. I'll ask her to marry me the first night out from Damovang, when Karrim's at the full. It's taking a chance, of course, but what the hell....

Then a roll of the ship sent them staggering up against the rail, and Reith's reverie ended in a gust of mutual laughter.

The *Kubitar* dropped anchor outside the harbor of Damovang to await inspection. Not until early afternoon did the ship make fast to a pier. As the gangboard was lowered into place, a brass-helmed Qiribo officer strode aboard.

"Captain Gendu!" said the one. "Have the goodness to present me to Doctor Ah-lee-shah Dah-eek-man."

"That's her yonder, the Terran wench with the yellow hair," said Gendu.

The soldier came to attention before Alicia, banging his fist against his cuirass in salute. "Doctor Dyckman!" he said loudly. "I, Lieutenant Gilan of the Republican Guard, have the honor to present to you the compliments of President Vizman, and his request that you and your Terran companions attend him at dinner and accept the night's accommodations in the palace."

"Well—ah—that's very kind," said Alicia. She looked at Reith and Marot. "Have you boys any objections?"

"Captain!" Reith called. "When do you plan to sail?"

"Tomorrow ere noon, if not hindered," growled Gendu.

The lieutenant gave a tight-lipped smile. "He shall sail when ye have returned to the ship, and not before."

"It looks okay to me," said Reith, with unspoken misgivings in his voice. Marot nodded agreement.

"You may tell the President," said Alicia regally, "that we shall be delighted to accept his invitation. But how did he know that we should arrive on this ship?"

"The President reads the manifests of all incoming vessels," said Gilan, "and saw your name on the list." The lieutenant saluted again, did an about-face, and marched ashore.

"Oh, dear!" said Alicia. "If only I had some new clothes. . . ."

"Rubbish, darling!" said Reith. "In that dress the Sainians gave you, you could run for Miss Krishna and win over any conceivable competition."

"You mean Miz Krishna," she said. "They have such a beauty contest on Terra now, for divorcées only."

"Which class does a remarried divorcée fall into?"

"I don't know. Perhaps it depends on whom she remarries. Come on, let's go ashore and walk a bit before we take a nap!"

The day had been a scorcher in Ghulindé. The presidential palace, innocent of Terran cooling technology, offered little relief. Sweating in his substantial Zorian finery, Reith envied the locals, wearing nothing above the ankles but a square of gauze pinned over one shoulder and allowed to flap and gape as it pleased.

At the palace, the three travelers were led through corridors, past pairs of guards who looked them over and let them pass only when the usher leading them identified them. One hall was lined with statues of former queens of Qirib. During the revolution, someone had gone through the hall knocking off the marble heads, and now workmen were cementing the heads back in place and repairing chipped features.

The three Terrans were taken to a large chamber, at one end of which stood a dining table laid for six. Vizman er-Qorf, President of Qirib, greeted them suavely and kissed Alicia's hand. He proved a large, heavy-set Krishnan, older than Reith had anticipated, ponderoцs of movements and mien.

Vizman introduced his guests to two other Qiribuma: a mature, cigar-smoking female, the Secretary of Commerce; and a small male, presented as Parenj er-Qvansel, leader of the opposition party. They stood about drinking falat while the Krishnans plied the Terrans with questions about their Zorian adventure.

When dinner was announced, Reith found himself across the table from Alicia, who was placed on Vizman's right. Marot sat on the President's left; beside him sat the Secretary of Commerce; then Reith, and finally Parenj, on Alicia's right.

Reith realized vaguely that the food was excellent, but he paid it little heed. For one thing, the Secretary of Commerce, whose name was Kiri, wanted to know all about the economics of guiding Terran tourists. She asked:

"When may we expect you to bring a party of these *Ertsuma* hither, good Master Reit'?"

"I hope," Reith replied, "to include Ghulindé in the itinerary of the next set."

"Indeed?" Kiri leaned toward Reith, thrusting out a bulbous breast, bared by her exiguous garment. But there was nothing sexy about this female; she was all business. "Tell me, how much spending money would your Terrans carry, and what share thereof can our shopkeepers expect to garner?"

Reith struggled to form an estimate, distracted as he was by the sight of Alicia, wholly occupied with President Vizman. The two were speaking in undertones with their heads together. The small Krishnan politician, the leader of the opposition, tried to carry on a conversation with Marot across the diameter of the table.

Eventually the repast was cleared away and kvad poured. A trio of musicians entered, seated themselves, and began to strum and tweetle. A dancer, clad in a few beads, turned a cartwheel into the chamber and launched into an acrobatic dance. She proved that she could, by muscular control, move each breast in a separate circle. The lamplight sparkled not only on her ornaments but also on the drops of sweat that beaded her face and athletic body.

When the dancer departed, a female singer took her place. Reith was glad to escape the inquisition of the Secretary of Commerce, whose mind was as voracious for facts as a yeki for meat. Sweating, Reith picked up his silver goblet for another sip of kvad.

At the sight of the level of the liquid, he frowned. He was sure he had drunk at least one gobletful and perhaps two; but his drinking vessel seemed to remain full no matter how much he drank. He became watchful, vaguely aware that the dancer had reëntered the chamber and was flitting about behind him.

When the singer finished, a flunkey came in and whispered in Parenj's ear. Rising, the opposition leader bowed to Vizman, excused himself to the other guests, and followed the attendant out. From beyond the dining hall, sounds of a scuffle and a shout of protest arose, above the chanting of the songstress. Then these sounds died away.

"It is unfortunate," said Vizman evenly when the singer had finished, "that Parenj should compel me to cause his arrest whilst our Terran guests be in residence. Today I received evidence that he planned an uprising and had arranged for my assassination." The President sadly nodded his head. "He is the fourth such leader whom I have been forced to dispose of. His was the last opposition group."

Reith blinked, wondering if he had drunk more than he intended. The heat had tempted him half-unconsciously to keep sipping. Although his head buzzed and the walls seemed to sway, he managed to ask: "Your Excellency, are you—have you—does this mean that Qirib will become a one-party state?"

"Aye. I fear my people are not yet ready for a government of your parliamentary Terran type. Here, the purpose of politics is to magnify oneself, enrich one's friends, and exterminate one's foes. I have striven to give the Qiribuma a liberal rule, but I have been compelled to defend myself and my party against subversive plots and murderous conspiracies.

"Let us not, however, dwell upon these sordid realities. One of our poets, the eminent Sarhad er-Sandu, will give a reading."

The poet, a lean, stooped, eyeglassed Krishnan, held a scroll in both hands. In a high, thin voice, he announced:

"To begin, I shall read a composition of my own, *The Fall*

of Malayer, telling the tale of this tragic event, all too recently in the minds of all here.

> "The nomad king sat astride his mettlesome beast,
>   And glared from the hill o'er the fertile Surian plain.
> He vowed ere the year was out that he'd hold a feast,
>   And a drink from the Dour of Suria's skull to
>   drain. . . ."

Although the Krishnans' long-winded rhetoric often made Reith impatient, he liked their poetry. It had a fine, rolling swing; moreover, it actually had form, rhyme, and meter, qualities missing from most Terran poetry for a couple of centuries.

Reith found it hard to give the poet his full attention, however, because at the other side of the table Alicia and Vizman continued whispering. Closer, Kiri was asking Marot for his views on the evolution of Krishnan life. Every time the paleontologist started a carefully-phrased answer, the Secretary of Commerce broke in with a comment or another question. She was not the sort to hold her tongue for any mere entertainer.

When Sarhad had finished the poem, he said: "I shall now read from the celebrated epic, *Abbeq and Dánqi.*" He gave a wry smile. "Fear not, gentlefolk; I do not propose to read the entire two hundred and sixty-four cantos. A single canto will, methinks, suffice. This is the forty-first. . . ."

The poet launched into the vast metrical romance. Reith had more trouble following, because the language was an archaic form of Gozashtandou, with many obsolete words. He had once, while a prisoner in Dur, tried to read it himself, but he had never gotten beyond a few cantos.

Between Kiri's ever more strident voice and the difficult dialect of the poem, Reith gave up. Then he found that the dancing girl had slipped into the seat once occupied by the unfortunate Parenj. The girl leaned towards Reith with a beguiling smile and a sinuous wriggle.

"Ye Terrans seem like unto gods to me!" she breathed. "All my life have I heard of your might and wisdom. Would that I could know one intimately, instead of being a mere dancing puppet, turning back-flips for his amusement. For I, too, am a person. I breathe! I love! I rage!"

She glanced at Reith's goblet. "A moment, Master." She slid out of her chair, circled around behind Reith, and reappeared with a bottle. She filled Reith's goblet almost to overflowing.

Reith took a sip to avoid spilling the fluid and watched her undulating body as she returned to her chair. "I have no doubt of your personhood," he said dryly. "But tell me, Mistress— what's—ah—what's your name?"

"Shei, my lord."

"Well, Ss—Sh—Shei, tell me: Have you been sneaking kvad into my goblet every time I set it down?"

She gave a delighted laugh. "My lord must have eyes in the back of 's head! I was commanded to make sure ye never wanted for refreshment."

"How much have you poured for me this evening?"

"How know I? A splash now and then. But hold; ye've emptied one bottle and are halfway through your second."

"Great Qonyor!" muttered Reith. That must, he thought, be the equivalent of over half a liter of Terran whiskey. No wonder. . . .

"Art ill, Master?" said Shei anxiously.

"Yes, little one. I must with—withdraw. Pray present my apologies to the President."

The poet had finished and departed some time since; Reith suspected that the poor fellow had cut his canto short when he saw he was not holding his audience. Shei darted around and whispered in Vizman's ear. When the President nodded and resumed his conversation with Alicia, the girl came back and helped Reith to rise unsteadily. He staggered out with an arm around Shei's neck. Like Alicia, the dancer was stronger than she looked.

Vizman had assigned the Terrans three separate bedrooms. Reith had planned, after the palace had quieted for the night, to move from his own room into Alicia's. Now he reeled into his room and saw the walls waver. He wanted to lie down in his clothes and pass out; but he feared he might vomit and make a mess. He grabbed a bedpost and lowered himself heavily to a seated position on the bed, clinging to the post. While he sat staring stuporously, Shei busied herself with his buttons and buckles.

"Lie down, Master!" said Shei. "Ye will feel better anon."

Reith collapsed on the bed, and Shei pulled off his clothes. The bed, he found, developed the alarming property of whirling round and round, like a small airplane out of control. He was wondering how to bring it out of its tailspin when consciousness fled.

Hours later, Reith opened a sticky eye. A glance at the window showed the night sky paling into dawn. He looked at himself, sprawling naked in a tangle of bedclothes. As he shook his head to clear it, he saw that Shei lay beside him, breathing evenly. When he raised himself on one elbow, the motion aroused the dancer, who came awake instantly. She asked:

"How fares my lord this morn?"

"A slight headache, but otherwise intact. What—what are you doing here?"

"What? Why, good my sir, what think ye?"

"Suppose you tell me."

"I'm here to serve your pleasure. What ye command, that I will do."

For the blink of an eye, Reith was tempted to take Shei up on her offer. But a host of other thoughts crowded this idea out. He looked at her narrowly, asking:

"Shei, did you go back to the party after you put me to bed?"

"Aye, for a little while, to report to the President."

"What happened?"

"He commanded me to return to you, and here I am."

"You don't know what the others did after that?"

"Nay; how could I?"

"Was this—getting me drunk and then spending the night here with me—planned in advance?"

"Why, be ye displeased, my lord?" Her antennae drooped, betokening grief.

"Just answer my question, please."

"Well—ah—the President instructed me to make sure your goblet was kept ever full, and to care for you anon an the drink should overcome you. That I have striven to do."

"I don't blame you," said Reith, thinking hard. "I just wonder. . . ."

After a silence, she said: "My lord, be ye not fain to make love? I'm said to be good at it."

"No. Put on your beads and go your way. I have other things on my mind."

"But—"

"I said go!" Reith spoke in such a grim tone that Shei

grabbed her negligible costume and fled.

Reith got up, wincing at the pain in his head, and closed the door behind her. When he opened it again, he was shaved, dressed, and showing no sign of his excess the night before save a pair of bloodshot eyes.

Peering about, he oriented himself in the palace. His room, along with several others, opened on a hall. The hall was decorated with enormous candelabra, converted to burning natural gas, the common illuminant in Ghulindé. A suit of antique armor stood in a corner. At the far end, a pair of brass-and-scarlet-clad guards stood with bared swords before a double door. This, he surmised, led to the President's private quarters.

Reith gently turned the knob of the next door. In that room Marot, in his ragged underwear, lay atop the bed snoring.

The next room, if he remembered rightly, was Alicia's. This proved empty, and the bed had not been slept in. But a couple of Alicia's toilet articles lay on the washstand.

Reith came out, closed the door, and turned towards the double door at the end of the hall, where stood the impassive guards. The knowledge that he had dreaded and tried to push to the back of his mind struck him like a blow in the solar plexus.

For a long minute he stood bemused. While he hesitated, one of the double doors opened and Alicia came out, walking briskly towards her room. She was reaching for the doorknob when she noticed Reith and halted with a sharp little intake of breath.

"Good morning, Doctor Dyckman," said Reith, keeping his voice under firm control.

"Oh!" she said, her blue eyes becoming large and round. "You—you know, then?"

"What do I know?"

"That I—you know—the President—oh, Fergus! I didn't mean to hurt you, but I had to do this, even though I hated it. . . ."

"Do you mean he took you by force?"

"N-no, nothing like that. But he made me an offer I couldn't refuse."

"What was that? Gold? Jewels? The First Ladyship?"

"No, no! It was a great social good. I'll explain after breakfast. Now we're supposed to join Vizman as soon as we can get Aristide up—"

"Present my apologies to the President; I'm going back to the ship."

"But Fergus, you can't! That would be—"

"I'd better go, or I'm likely to kill the guy as soon as I see him. Good-bye!"

Reith reëntered his room, closing the door sharply. He gathered up his toilet articles and marched out. Alicia had disappeared, but voices came from Marot's room. Although tempted to eavesdrop, Reith resolutely turned away and walked out of the presidential palace, stopping at the cloakroom to recover his sword from the sleepy attendant.

Loading of the *Kubitar* was almost complete when two litters appeared at the base of the pier. The bearers set down their chairs. Marot and Alicia got out, paid off their chairmen, and walked out to the ship. As they boarded, Reith gave them a glance of cold indifference and showed inordinate interest in the operation of a man-powered crane at the end of the pier.

After the ship had been towed out of the inner harbor, the striped sails filled with a steady south wind. Standing at the rail, Reith heard a small voice: "Fergus, I've got talk to you."

"Go ahead, Doctor Dyckman."

"Very well, Mr. Reith. I didn't do what I did on a whim, or because I've suddenly fallen in love with Vizman. Anyway, he's turning into just another dictator. He used to be full of ideals, but I suppose power has corrupted him, as they say."

"That has a sadly familiar sound to a Terran. But go on."

"Neither was it for fun. Krishnan males don't give me pleasure, since they're all through almost before you realize they've started. Other Earthwomen have told me the same thing."

"If you didn't screw Vizman for those reasons, then why?"

"I told you about my giving him Terran views on slavery. He'd prepared an emancipation proclamation and had been waiting to issue it at a suitable time. Well, he offered, if I'd sleep with him, to put it out today, regardless of the political risk. He still wants to marry me; but when I said that was out of the question, he'd settle for one night.

"We figured you'd sleep late after all the kvad Shei poured into you, and I'd be back in my room before you woke up. Then Shei was to stay with you. Did you have fun with her?"

"No. As soon as I was conscious, I sent her packing. I wanted to be true to you, if you know what fidelity means.

Besides, I sensed that something was fishy, and I wanted to get to the bottom of it."

She sighed. "Always austere and rational, that's you. If you'd taken your pleasure of her, then even if you'd found out about Vizman and me, you couldn't have made such a fuss about it. Well, my little plot backfired. Was it so wicked for me to lend my poor, shopworn body to free all those miserable slaves, sweating their lives away in the mines in the Zogha Mountains?"

"Not wicked, exactly. Contraproductive, perhaps."

"How do you mean?"

"You wanted two incompatible things."

"But it's not as if I were your wife, or even your fiancée. You never asked for a commitment. Your position was like the lover of one of Madame Kyumi's girls in the Hamda'. Some have sweethearts to whom they're sincerely devoted; but they don't let that interfere with business; and the lovers accept the necessity. So I had a perfect right—"

"Of course you did. My feelings don't count."

"I didn't know you had any."

"My fault, I suppose, for trying to do the reasonable thing. Thanks, anyway."

"What?" she exclaimed.

"I said, thanks. You've given me the answer to a question I've been asking myself."

She sniffed. "So that's it! See if I care! In fact," she spat, "if you'd asked me, I'd have turned you down and laughed at the look on your face! You never loved me as a person; all you wanted was free cunt. Why don't you go buy yourself a tailed female slave? She'd give you all you really need from any woman!"

Reith assumed a grim smile. "Okay, then, we understand each other. Well, Doctor Dyckman, as you say, you're a free, independent woman. If you want to return to Novo, I'll try to get you there as a simple matter of duty. If you go off on your own, that's okay, too."

His voice rose as his self-control began to slip. "Meanwhile, since you're so fond of extraterrestrial copulation, why don't you go fuck Captain Gendu and his crew, one after another? You might get a book out of it, or at least an article—"

Alicia stamped her foot and screamed: "Oh, *stop* it! Stop

it! Shut up! Aren't things bad enough? You don't have to aggravate them by being bitter!"

Reith started to roar: "And why shouldn't—" He bit back the rest of the sentence and forced himself to assume a blank expression. In a level tone he said: "Me, bitter? My dear ex-amorex, whatever gave you that idea? And what do you mean, 'things are bad'? Far as I can see, they're just fine. Now I'm going to take a nap before lunch. So long!"

Later, when Reith stood at the rail, watching the sea drift past, Marot said quietly: "Fergus, my friend, I do not pry into such matters; but I could not avoid hearing some of your conversation. If there is anything I can do...."

"You can tell me how not to fall in love with a former wife—or, I ought to say, how to fall *out* of love with her. I can't seem to get over her, no matter what she does."

Marot sighed. "The poet Ovid had some advice: Do not see her. Burn her letters and other reminders of her. Keep busy. Engage in the sports. Take a journey. Avoid sentimental books and plays. And finally, find another woman. I cannot improve on these suggestions."

"Most of them are completely impracticable aboard the *Kubitar*. But thanks anyway."

XI.

THE SHIP

For the next two days, Alicia and Reith treated each other with cold formality, seldom speaking save when circumstances demanded. They resumed employment of given names, since "Mr. Reith" and "Doctor Dyckman" seemed silly between two who, whatever their current feelings, had known each other so intimately. But to Reith she was now always "Alicia," never "Lish."

He tried to treat her with the same neutral, impersonal politeness that he had found effective with his tourists; but the contradictory emotions that her presence aroused made this hard. Although he had heard of "love-hate" relationships, this was the first time that one had struck him with all its brutal force.

An old love, he found, dies hard, even when it has been kicked around and trampled. But so do old animosities. He supposed that, for this reason, most divorced couples, even with the best intentions, would find it difficult to be "just friends." Every time they got together, the mere presence of the other would stir up a witch's brew of conflicting emotions in each: loving tenderness from the memory of the good times they had shared; but also rankling resentment of hostile words

179

and deeds from the bad times. Hence each meeting would be likely to erupt either into frantic lovemaking or into a furious quarrel.

The warm south wind carried the *Kubitar* briskly eastward into the broad Sadabao Sea. On the second day from Damovang, the course veered to the north, and the ship hove to for the complicated process of shifting the boom of the lateen foresail from one side of the mast to the other.

For the rest of the day, the *Kubitar* ran wing-and-wing, like some gigantic leather-winged aqebat. As swells crept up behind and forged past, the vessel pitched with the slow, easy motion of a porch swing. Nevertheless, Aristide Marot looked more and more unhappy. He finally fed his breakfast to the piscoids.

"The poor fellow's as green as a Krishnan," said Alicia. "Aristide, why don't you work on your fossils, to take your mind off things?"

"But no! With the ship moving in this manner, some piece might roll overboard. I think I shall go in and lie down."

"My experience," said Reith, "is that it's better to stay on your feet. Then your body remains vertical despite the ship's motion."

"Thank you, my friend," said Marot. "You are a great comfort." But he went into the cabin.

The rugged hills of Cape Dirkash, beyond which Reith and Marot had been snatched from the train by the Bákhites, rose from the sea a few hoda to port. The yellow sun glared on a blue-green sky, and the temperature climbed swiftly. Fanning herself with her hat, Alicia, breaking the near-silence between them, said: "I've never seen it so hot and sticky. Those sailors have the right idea." She nodded towards the Krishnans, who were going about their duties naked but for coats of grease.

Reith had not intended to let himself be drawn into chitchat with Alicia, but the temptation to lecture a willing pupil proved too strong. "It's this running free," he said. "When you go with the wind, the velocity of the ship is subtracted from that of the air. So, if we have a ten-knot breeze and are sailing at five, the wind passes us at five knots, which is practically a calm. Besides, the humidity is a hundred percent at sea level, so of course we're sticky."

"No use being more uncomfortable than we must. Wait here a minute." She disappeared into the cabin and came out with her new sewing kit. "Now take off your clothes, and I'll sew up those rips and tears." She stripped off her own torn khakis and ragged underwear. "Aristide would be embarrassed, but he's asleep in his bunk. Sewing is my only domestic accomplishment—though I daresay I could learn others."

Reith stripped and handed her the garments. Then he got his sword from the cabin and, standing at the rail with his back to her, devoted himself to removing the peace wires that bound the hilt to the sheath. If he let himself gaze upon her splendid pink-and-ivory body, he knew his frustrated passions would become all too visible.

All the long afternoon, Alicia worked away. When she handed Reith back his clothes, he could not resist exclaiming: "But that's marvelous, Alicia! You've made my rags as good as new. Thank you very much!"

"You're welcome, Fergus. Sorry I can't mend everything so easily." She rose and slipped on her shorts. "Now I'm going to pester the captain for some sociological data. See you at dinner." With the grace of a professional dancer, she walked aft to where the gruff, taciturn Gendu leaned on the after rail, with one eye on the sails, another on the helmsman, and a cigar between his teeth.

An hour later, as Roqir winked out behind the hills of Cape Dirkash, Alicia came back to where Reith stood at the rail, staring morosely at the sea. Her face now bore an evasive little smile.

"What now?" said Reith, forgetting for the moment that he was supposed to be coldly furious. "I see that something's happened."

"Nothing much. The captain has asked me to share his bunk tonight, just as Sarf did on the *Morkerád*."

"These Krishnan big shots have good taste in Terran women, anyway. What did you decide?"

"Why? Would you mind? The day before yesterday you practically urged me to give the captain my all."

Reith's lips tightened, his face flushed, and his jaw became rigid. At last he forced himself to say: "I'm sorry I was rude; I was in a bad temper. As to what you do, it's entirely your affair. If you want one more native lover, it's not my place to advise you."

She flinched but forced a smile, coming close and looking appealingly up. "Are you sure? Because if you really don't care, I can go back and say I've changed my mind; that I'll sleep with him after all."

"You mean you turned him down?" Despite his efforts to maintain a poker face, Reith felt his expression lightening.

"Yes. But what difference does that make to you?"

"Of course I—" Reith began with some heat. Then he took a grip on himself. "Look, Alicia, let's get something straight. There are many things you have a right to do, and that are absolutely no business of mine. But, because of what you've been to me, I can't take an objective, cold-blooded view of them. Sometimes they hurt me, or fill me with rage or jealousy or fear. I warned you in Jazmurian that, like lots of other people, I develop proprietary feelings towards those dear to me." Reith was vexed to find his lip trembling and his eyes watering, but he plunged on:

"If you take some crazy risk that may get you killed, I shouldn't care any more than I would about any other Earthwoman; but I'm terrified for you. If you lie down with some blug like that so-called President, I suppose I ought, like some Terran spouses, to say: 'Have fun, kid!' and dismiss the matter. But I'll never be so liberal-minded as all that; instead, I want to kill the bastard. If I'm considered a barbarian in Katai-Jhogorai, that's just too bad."

Reith stared at the waves and composed himself. "I try not to show these feelings or interfere in your affairs. If I don't always succeed, the reason is that I'm not quite the 'cold fish' you once called me during a quarrel. Some day I may think of you as only one more Terran; but that day's not here yet. If I believed in some Krishnan god, I'd pray to him to hasten its coming." Reith hastily wiped his eyes with his knuckles.

Alicia stared at him, then seized both shoulders and kissed him. "You're sweet, under that gruff manner, and I'm glad you care. You deserve a woman with all my better qualities and none of my horrible faults. With this captain, you needn't worry. I used the same gag I did with King Ainkhist."

"Teeth in your personal person?"

"Sure. I said it would be a pity if, in a transport of passion, I bereft him of the pride of the merchant fleet. He was a little puzzled, saying: 'In that case, how do you Terrans propagate, if every male who impregnates a female suffers mortal hurt?' I told him the teeth wouldn't bite the female's official mate."

"But, as I remember, that talk didn't scare off Ainkhist the second time."

"That's true; but the reason was that Percy, unintentionally, had given the game away. So the second time I was in Mutabwk, it was either give the king what he demanded or be flogged to death for *lèse majesté*. Percy swore he'd kill Ainkhist if he got a chance, for dishonoring Terran womanhood. Percy has some of the quaintest ideas you ever heard of outside a nineteenth-century novel."

"Quaint, maybe," growled Reith, "but I'd kill the swine, too."

"Dear Fergus! You and Percy want me to be a delicate, dimwitted, fluttery female like the heroine of one of those old novels."

"That's not the point. I'm no killer, but the thought of my woman's being laid by one of those quasi-men pushes the same buttons in me as if he were human."

She looked sharply at Reith. "What do you mean, your woman?"

"Well, say a woman I care about. Didn't you feel somehow degraded?"

"Yes; because I'd been compelled against my will, not because Ainkhist wasn't human. When you live among Krishnans as much as I have, you forget they're of another species. So, while I wouldn't ask anybody to take vengeance, if I heard that Ainkhist had come to a sticky end, my grief wouldn't overwhelm me. And in the long run I profited from the episode."

"You mean Ainkhist *paid* you?"

"No—yes—well, not exactly. He gave me a valuable necklace; but after we escaped from him, I gave the thing to Percy to give his wife as a homecoming present. I didn't want it; it made me feel like a whore. And don't you dare ever tell Vicky where it came from!"

"Of course not! But how did you profit?"

"I had a whole day in the harem, while Ainkhist went hunting; and I interviewed all the inmates. After I left you, I wrote *Women of a Khaldoni Harem* and sent it off to my Terran agent. Of course it'll be years before I learn whether the book was published and how it made out."

Reith shook his head. "You're the most amazing person I've ever known."

She turned away with a small smile of satisfaction.

*   *   *

Reith had taken one of the upper bunks, to save his companions the trouble of climbing. During the night, a change in the ship's motion woke him. For a confused moment he wondered if they had reached port, though an instant's pause quashed this idea. Carefully he lowered himself to the cabin floor. He lit the candle in the small lantern, put on shirt and pants, and went out.

Thick fog lay like a sable blanket over oily-smooth water. A faint breeze stirred the limp sails, giving the ship just enough way to dispatch a line of ripples from each side of the bow.

Aft, Captain Gendu stood at the taffrail, near the sailor at the whipstaff. Above their heads, a lantern hung from a pole, its feeble yellow light pushing ineffectually at the fog. To starboard, a faint pearly luminescence heralded the coming dawn.

"Fear not; 'twill lift after sunup," growled the captain when Reith came up to him. "Then we may hope the breeze will freshen."

Reith walked the deck to warm his muscles and did a few knee bends and pushups. Little by little, the light in the east waxed stronger and the fog began to turn pink.

"Sun's up," said Gendu. "Twill soon burn off the vapor."

Reith reëntered the cabin, meaning to try to snatch another hour's sleep before full daylight. Marot snored in his bunk; Alicia breathed lightly in hers. Reith set down the lantern and began to remove his trousers when a sound from outside brought him to full alert. It was a shout, which seemed to come, not from aboard the *Kubitar*, but from across water.

Captain Gendu's deep, rasping voice gave an answering shout. Then came cries of crewmen, a patter of bare feet on the deck, and a clash of metal. Something metallic struck wood with a sound like that of an ax biting into a log. Amid a rising babel of voices came a grinding and cracking of strained timbers. The deck jerked beneath Reith's feet, staggering him.

In the seconds between the first shout and the jolt of the ship-to-ship contact, Reith, groping in the dim light, found his sword and stepped to the door on the side whence the noise seemed to come. A glance showed Marot and Alicia sitting up in their bunks and putting their feet on the floor.

"*Qu'est que—*" mumbled Marot, in chorus with Alicia's soprano: "What's this—"

"Hold the other door, Aristide!" shouted Reith. "Alicia, get some clothes on!"

As he spoke, the door in which Reith stood flew open. In the doorway stood a Krishnan wearing a dirty breechclout and a dented, rusty breastplate. The newcomer brandished a curved sword, aiming a forehand cut at Reith's neck.

Reith got his blade up in time to parry, though the shock of the contact with the massive weapon made his hand tingle. The invader next swung a backhand slash, wielding the heavy blade as if it were feather-light. Again, Reith barely caught the sweep on his own sword.

At that instant, Reith heard the other door, behind him, fly open and the sound of entry of more armed Krishnans. A shriek from Alicia cut through a shout from Marot and sounds of struggle.

Reith sent a quick thrust at his opponent's face while the latter was still recovering from his second slash. The Krishnan jerked back out of range, brought his heavy sword up over his head, and started a terrific downright cut, with both hands on the hilt. Reith had an instant of fear that, while he could get his sword up in time to parry the blow, the impact might break his lighter blade.

The Krishnan, however, had forgotten that he was standing in a doorway, with the lintel a few spans above his head. His blade struck the lintel, pierced deeply into the wood, and stuck fast.

Without thinking out his next move, Reith threw himself forward in an extended lunge, aiming for the Krishnan heart region, as if he faced an unarmored foe. The lunge went home perfectly, striking the Krishnan about where the solar plexus would be on a Terran and the heart on a Krishnan.

The point, however, skittered off the steel of the breastplate. Remembering too late the difference between an armored and an unarmored foe, Reith jerked his arm back to send a remise at the Krishnan's unprotected throat. But something hard and heavy struck his skull from behind. The surroundings dissolved in a pyrotechnics of whirling lights. Reith dimly heard the clang of his dropped sword and felt the impact of the deck against the hands and knees to which he had fallen.

Horny hands seized Reith, hauled him to his feet, and hustled him, staggering, out the door, vaguely surprised to find himself still alive. Outside, the brightening light showed that alongside the *Kubitar* lay another ship, of similar length but more slender hull. Three grapnels from the strange ship were sunk in the *Kubitar's* starboard bulkhead. Figures, dimly seen through the fog on the deck of the other ship, held the grapnel ropes and thus kept the ships together.

The deck was crowded with a swarm of Krishnans in motley garb, some wearing bits of armor and all carrying swords, pikes, or axes.

"Fergus!" came Alicia's high voice. "Where are you?"

"Here!" replied Reith, looking about. He located her in the crowd, with a pair of burly Krishnans holding her arms. Another pair held the arms of Aristide Marot; blood ran down one of Marot's arms and dripped on the deck.

"What happened to us?" Reith called.

Marot replied: "I think I made a slight wound on one of our attackers, but another gave me a cut on the arm. Then one ran up behind you and struck you with the pommel of his sword."

Beyond Alicia and Marot, Captain Gendu and his crew stood in a group with the invaders' swords at their throats. Several bled blue-green Krishnan blood from untended wounds. Among the legs of the attackers, Reith glimpsed the bodies of two of Gendu's crewmen. A hoarse voice bellowed:

"Move not! Yield or die! Those who resist no longer shall not be hurt!"

The speaker appeared at the rail of the other ship. Through the thinning mist, Reith perceived the outline of a short, stout female Krishnan, in helmet, cuirass, and kilt.

The rising sun spread a rosy carpet across the still waters, so that Reith could discern the features of individuals.

"Put them on our ship!" shouted the female leader. "We'll scrutinize them when the light waxes stronger. Do I see some *Ertsuma?* With hair of red, yellow, and black, as described in the contract? 'Tis indeed they, praise Maibud! The old witch of Jeshang will pay us more for these creatures than we'd get in a score of ordinary ransoms. Lucky for you scum that ye took them alive as I commanded! Get them aboard! Yare, yare!"

Reith and his companions were hustled to and over the rails of the ships, which ground together with the slight motion of the waves. Reith and Alicia managed to land on their feet on the deck of the other ship, but Marot fell heavily and got up groaning. Gendu and his surviving crewmen were likewise forced over the rails. As the captives reached the deck of the other ship, other pirates seized them and tied their wrists together with stops of light line. Meanwhile other pirates—for such Reith assumed they were—scattered over the *Kubitar* for loot. Reith called:

"Alicia! Are you okay?"

"I don't know that 'okay' is quite the word," she answered, "but I'm not wounded."

"You, Aristide?"

"Except for this cut."

"Let me fix that!" said Alicia. In starting to dress as Reith commanded, she had only gotten as far as a pair of panties. Now, with her wrists bound, she slipped these off and tore them into a couple of long strips; the disintegrating fabric parted easily. Soon she had a bandage around Marot's upper right arm. The pirates neither helped nor hindered her first aid.

"Just a scratch, luckily," said Marot. "It will heal up in a few days. Fergus! What is all this?"

"I'm trying to find out," said Reith. "Captain Gendu! Who are these people?"

Wearily, Gendu explained: "This ship is Tondi's *Haghrib*. That she-devil's the worst pirate captain of the lot."

For the next hour the captives—three Terrans, Captain Gendu, his mate Chindor, his cook, and his nine surviving seamen—huddled unhappily in the bow, while the pirates went through the *Kubitar* and handed their pickings across the rails to the deck of the pirate craft. Tondi supervised the stowage of loot. As each item came aboard, a stout pirate with a wooden peg leg and eyeglasses incongruously perched on his nose entered the accession on a sheet of paper. Then the object was carried down a ladder into the hold.

Standing at the edge of the hatch opening, Tondi shouted down to place the wine jars together, pile the bolts of cloth neatly in one spot, and so on. Presently a pirate appeared at the rail with Marot's sack of fossils, saying:

"Captain, be this the bag of stones the Bákhite said his mistress wanted?"

"Is't the only bag of stones aboard? Well then, this must needs be it. Old Lazdai must be getting soft in the brain, to collect stones; but 'tis all one to us so that she pays us what she promised. Fetch it aboard!"

At last a pirate reported: "Captain, we find nought else save bulk goods of low value: slabs of marble, ingots of lead, farm produce, and the like. No jewels and no coin but a few hundred karda. This is no treasure ship." Reith inferred that the "few hundred karda" were mostly his.

"Then we must needs scour this route until we find more profitable prey," Tondi replied.

"But Captain!" said a pirate who seemed to be a ship's officer of some sort. "Won't the price of these Terrans from the priestess suffice for the voyage?"

"And how if the old puzzel renies her debt to us, once she hath the off-worlders in her grasp? I trust her not. So we'll cruise some more and then seek the rendezvous to turn these creatures over. Loose the other ship and scuttle her!"

When the first curl of dark smoke arose from the *Kubitar's* hold, the pirates pushed the ships apart with boathooks. Oars quickly emerged from their holes to drive the *Haghrib* away from her victim. As the distance increased, the fire on the *Kubitar* blazed more and more brightly through the thinning fog. The sails went up like torches, for an instant rivaling the wan, fog-shrouded sun in brilliance.

Reith heard Captain Gendu mutter: "I told the owners we needed armed guards. But nay, they said; the pirate menace is abated, and good guards cost good silver."

The sun brightened and the breeze strengthened. The last wisps of fog drifted past like homing ghosts. The temperature began to rise.

"Now," barked Tondi, "we'll look over our guests."

With blows, threats, and curses, the pirates dragged the captives to their feet and pushed them into line against the gunwale. Overhead, the beige-colored sails caught the freshening breeze and filled; below, the oars were again withdrawn, releasing the rowers to join their fellow pirates on deck.

Tondi went to her cabin but soon reappeared. She had shed her helm and cuirass and now wore nothing but a short kilt, which had once been white. She was barrel-shaped, flat-breasted, and ugly both by Terran and by Krishnan standards. She looked as if she had not had a bath in years. Her long, greasy hair bore the bluish tint of the Krishnan races dwelling east of the Triple Seas.

She started down the line. The first captive, a sailor, turned gray and his antennae quivered with fear as she examined him. She said: "He'd be useless."

She jerked a thumb. As two pirates seized the sailor and hoisted him up on the rail, he screamed: "Tondi! Ye promised us no harm—" A splash heralded his end.

Tondi gave a snort of laughter and went to the next sailor, who stammered: "T-tondi, I'll gladly join your crew!"

"We already have a full complement." Again she jerked a thumb, and, yelling protests, the sailor was tossed over the side like the other.

The next captive was Chindor, the mate. He said: "Ye durst not drown me, Tondi! My brother's High Admiral of Ulvanagh. He'd hunt you down as far as the Southern Pole—"

"Ye threaten *me?*" screamed Tondi. "Over the side with him!"

"Cursed fool!" mumbled Gendu. "If he'd bragged of 's seamanship, he'd like have bought's life."

"No *Pirates of Penzance* here," murmured Reith to his companions.

The massacre continued until only Captain Gendu and the three Terrans remained. Gendu growled: "How did ye catch us so featly, Captain Tondi?"

"We followed you through the night by your stern lantern."

"Ye showed no lights!"

Tondi gave a scornful snort. "Think ye we're noodles, to warn of our coming?"

"'Twas a clever scheme, anyway, worthy of your repute."

Tondi allowed herself a Krishnan smile. "If ye futter as well as ye flatter, I may not regret sparing your worthless life. Be ye not Captain Gendu, of Goftan and Forá?"

"Aye."

"I know the firm. They'll pay well for one of their ablest skippers. So consider your life prolonged for the nonce; but ye'd better give me a good stroking when your turn comes!"

She passed on to Reith: "Ah, he of the fiery hair! What's your name and business?"

Reith gave the information. Tondi asked: "How be ye in bed? Canst deliver many a mighty stroke?"

"My women haven't complained," said Reith, trying not to show how repelled he felt by her stench.

"Ye shall have your chance to prove your words," Tondi

said, "and woe betide you if ye prove but a bladder filled with air."

"What's this about the High Priestess of Bákh in Jeshang?" asked Reith. "When we left Chilihagh a ten-day ago, the Dasht had ordered Lazdai and her council clapped into prison."

"Ah, but things have changed yet again! The High Priestess and her folk were delivered from jail by a mob of her faithful. Lazdai called for an uprising, and part of the army joined the Bákhites. The latest word is that Lazdai rules the Dashtate, whilst the Dasht and his few loyal followers are besieged in's palace."

"How do you learn these things?"

Tondi laid a finger beside her nose. "Trade secret. My spies are everywhere!"

She turned to Alicia. "Aha, the Terran female we were besought to watch for! I'm told they provide high pleasure for virile human men like my knaves. Lusty though I be, I can't keep the whole shipful happy." She raised her voice. "Men! See ye this *Ertsui?* Who craves to ram his yard into her alien cleft?"

"I!" shouted a pirate, and others took up the cry.

"Line up, then. We must needs do things in an orderly way. Ye two, hold the strumpet down."

Two pirates seized Alicia and threw her to the deck. She tried to kick and bite but, with her hands tied, her struggles were unavailing.

Reith was in agony. His mind raced in an effort to find some way to save Alicia. Then he remembered his talk with Alicia after Gendu had made advances to her. He forced a loud, raucous laugh, as if he had just heard the dirtiest joke of his life.

Tondi scowled. "Wherefore so buffoonish?"

Reith said: "I look forward to the sight of your lusty rouges' losing their privy members. A revenge fit for the god Qondyor!"

"What mean ye, rascallion?"

"Only that, as all Terrans know, the female Terran is provided, in her tunnel of love, with razor-sharp teeth. If her lover please her not, these teeth go—" He closed his jaws with a click. "—and the poor wight's unmanned forever. Many die of this rough usage."

Tondi turned to Marot. "Be this tale true?"

"Of a certainty, mistress. It is the sure defense against unwanted entry, wherewith the gods of the *Ertsuma* have provided the females of my species."

"Absolutely!" added Reith. "That's why rape is unknown among us."

Tondi growled: "Methought rape was unknown amongst Terrans because your females were so hot to be tupped that there's never a need for force. What if the male hold a knife to the female's throat, commanding her to keep her nether fangs sheathed till the deed be done?"

"That would be useless," said Reith. "The action works of itself, whenever the female's inner spirit be unwilling."

"What know ye of this?" Tondi asked Gendu.

"Only what these aliens tell," replied the captain. "But I'm not lief to risk my own precious pintle to make a test of the tale!"

"I know not whether to believe this taradiddle," snorted Tondi. Turning away, she said to her crewmen: "Ye heard these rascals, did you not? Who's fain to put this story to the proof? Tokh! Ye?" She pointed to the first pirate in line.

"Pray excuse me," said Tokh. "I've not been well of late."

After several others had given similar excuses, Tondi burst into a bellowing laugh. "Gods, this is the funniest thing that hath befallen since we flayed alive that fat Majburo merchant! My lusty rogues, unmanned by the mere thought of a toothbearing cunt! For this enjoyment, I'll have you unbound. But ye shall remain here on the deck—" With the point of her sword she scratched a square on the planking. "—and not stir therefrom without express permission. Tokh, ye and Ferdur shall guard them; let none stray. Allow the drab to rise!"

The four prisoners, with hands untied, huddled miserably on the square of deck outlined by Tondi. Another hour passed before Marot remarked:

"I once read a romantic novel about a pirate queen, in the days of the flintlock musket and the muzzle-loading cannon. She was tall, slender, beautiful, and fastidious, with hair as fiery red as yours, Fergus. Any man who approached her lewdly was spitted on her rapier like a pat of butter. Somehow our present hostess fails to match that description."

Reith gave a grim smile. "If there ever were any of those—pirettes, I guess you'd call 'em—on Terra, they probably looked more like Tondi than that fictional heroine."

"Yes. I—" Marot clapped a hand to his forehead. *"Mon dieu!* I have just realized that I have no eyeglasses! If something demands itself to be read, you or Alicia must read it to me. They took my ring camera and film. And my longevity capsules, also, remained on the other ship."

"Alicia has obviously lost her LPs, too," said Reith. "Mine are in my money belt, which I've been sleeping in. These yucks haven't searched me yet. I haven't pills enough to last the three of us to Novo; but I'll share those I have as far as they go."

Alicia leaned against Reith, who put an arm around her. She murmured: "Oh, Fergus, I'm so bruised and miserable! And my beautiful notes, all burned up on that ship!" She began to cry.

Reith, his anger forgotten, hugged and kissed her and stroked her blond hair. Despite her nearness and nudity, he felt no sexual arousal, but only a vast tenderness. If at that moment, despite all that had happened, she had begged him to take her back. . . . But she did not. He said:

"Things could be worse. At least we're still alive, and you weren't gang-raped."

"Much as I'd have hated it, I'd rather put up with that than with the loss of my notes."

Marot said: "I understand, my dear. But whereas you have lost notes, much of which you can reconstruct from memory, I have lost the specimen that I crossed light-years of space to find."

She wiped her eyes with the backs of her hands. "You're right, Aristide. I'm sorry to be a sissy, when you've suffered a worse loss than I. My, this sun's getting hot! I know Roqir doesn't affect human skin so severely as Sol, but I just burn and peel."

"Same here," said Reith, taking off his khaki shirt and wrapping it around her. "Hey, Tokh!" He addressed one of the pirates guarding them. "How about some water?"

When a dipperful had been passed around, and each had drunk a few swallows, they were silent for a while. Then Alicia said: "This is worse than yesterday. Wouldn't some shade. . . ."

"Seaman Tokh!" said Reith.

"Aye?"

"We *Ertsuma* can't endure so much direct sunlight without covering. A full day of this could kill us."

"That were your misfortune, alien. I got you water."

"But if we're dead, you'd get no ransom. Hadn't you better warn your captain?"

"To what avail? We can't turn off the sun."

"I saw you bring our clothing aboard. Could this female have her own garments back?"

Tokh conferred in an undertone with his companion and departed to the cabin. Presently he returned.

"The captain saith to put you all in the hold," he announced. "Come."

They followed the guards aft to where a large wooden grating occupied much of the deck between the bulwarks. The guards yelled for help, and four brawny pirates heaved up the hatch cover. Another picked up a hooked ladder and lowered it into the hole until the hooks caught in the coaming.

"Down ye go!" said Tokh.

"What's down there?" said Alicia nervously.

Reith bent over the edge of the opening. "Seems to be mostly stacks of loot. Gentlemen precede ladies on stairs. Come on!" He backed into the hole, and soon all four stood on the floor of the hold. The pirates pulled up the ladder and replaced the grating.

Reith looked about. Little squares of sunlight through the grating relieved the gloom, and as his eyes adjusted to the dark, Reith found he could see quite well. The hold extended for most of the length of the ship, ending at wooden bulkheads fore and aft. The bare deck stretched around for many meters; but at bow and stern the space was crowded by chests, jars, and crates.

"Their hold's about half full," said Reith, "so they'll plan a few more captures before returning to base."

Alicia discovered a large, untidy pile of garments. She darted to it and burrowed into the heap, throwing kilts, jackets, and mantles aside.

"I'm looking for my own clothes," she said. "Nakedness is all very well in this heat, but I'm tired of getting splinters in me whenever I sit down. Some of these clothes look nice. I wouldn't mind owning this!"

She held up a black kilt of velvetlike material, with a waistband and a hem sparkling with spangles.

"Take it," said Reith.

She slipped on the kilt and continued to hunt. She next

found a little crimson bolero with short sleeves, open in front.

"To hell with my old khakis!" she said. "I like this better. With all this looted stuff, we can have a one-woman fashion show."

Marot said: "You are amazing, Alicia. Nothing keeps you down for long."

Gendu grumbled: "If ye'd talk in a speech that I can understand, instead of that off-world chatter, we might get on better."

"We beg your pardon," said Marot.

"Our next order of business," said Reith in a low voice, slipping back into Gozashtandou, "is to find a way out."

"Ye dream, *Ertsu!*" said Gendu. "We lack a ladder wherewith to gain the deck. Best await our ransoming with such patience as we can muster."

"We certainly shan't escape if we never try," said Reith.

"Besides," said Alicia, "High Priestess Lazdai somehow got word to Tondi that she'd pay well for us. I don't know how they'd get us from here to Chilihagh without detection; but still...."

"I daresay they have ways," said Reith. "In any case, I'm not going to sit still while Lazdai has her kettle fired up again. I'll take a look around, to see what might be useful."

He strolled among the piles and ranks of loot. Towards the ends of the hold, where the light was too dim to make objects out clearly, he fingered the materials. At last he paused at a row of chests, neatly lined up. He opened one and found it full of heavy cloth, perhaps for blankets. Another held plates and tableware. A third was full of rolls of Krishnan paper, each tied up with a colored ribbon.

"They look like wills and deeds, the way they do them up here," murmured Alicia at Reith's elbow.

"They must be from some Krishnan lawyer's archives. Now why should Tondi keep a chest full of legal papers?"

Alicia shrugged. "I suppose she hopes to find someone who'll pay for their return, on a no-questions-asked basis."

The next chest brought a squeal of joy from Alicia. Even the gloom could not conceal the sparkle of a heap of bejeweled necklaces, bracelets, and other gauds. She dug her fingers into the mass and held up piece after piece to the dim light.

"Looks like costume jewelry," grunted Reith. "You won't find any valuable stones there—just brass and colored glass."

"I don't care! I'm tired of being a mere female scientist in dirty khaki. I want to be a womanly woman for a change. How's this?"

Around her neck she clasped an ornate necklace—a lacelike collar of golden filigree in which was set a dazzling array of colored stones resembling emeralds, rubies, sapphires, amethysts, garnets, and Bákh knew what else. Each large stone was surrounded by a circlet of winking diamonds, or at least rhinestones, whence depended a fringe of lesser gems in graduated sizes. She said:

"It looks like the neckpiece worn by that entertainer at Angur's. Do look, Fergus!"

"Very pretty," said Reith absently. "But you'd better hide it before the pirates see it on you."

Alicia danced over to the pile of assorted garments and dug among them until she found a scarf. This she tied around her neck so as to hide the necklace.

Meanwhile, Reith opened the next chest. After an astounded pause, he called in an excited whisper: "Hey, Aristide! Gendu! Come here!"

The chest was half full of swords—fancy weapons with jeweled hilts, and scabbards decorated with gold and silver filigree. The other males drew in sharp breaths. Reith said in a low voice:

"These must have been made for rich lordlings." He picked out a sword, unsheathed it, and gave a disappointed grunt. "Purely a parade weapon—no edge."

Marot handled another. "This one seems sharp."

They hunted through the chest, thumbing each blade. Of the fourteen swords, five proved fighting weapons.

"All very well," grumbled Gendu, "but locked in this crypt, we shall have little use for them."

"Don't be too sure of that," said Reith.

The day crawled past. The prisoners told each other stories and jokes to while away the time and to take their minds off their ever-growing pangs of hunger. Even the glum, irascible Gendu was persuaded to recount tales from his seagoing career. Eventually lack of water dried out their throats and brought their speech to a halt.

When the daylight was fading, a pirate called down: "Come up for dinner, prisoners. 'Ware ladder!"

"Should we take swords in hand and set upon them?" whispered Marot.

"No," said Reith. "It's still daylight, and they'll be watching us. But I'm getting an idea."

Roqir was half occluded by the jagged hills of Cape Dirkash when the pirates directed their prisoners to a section of deck. There, sitting on the boards in a circle, they were served bowls of some sort of stew, on top of which had been dumped a number of rock-hard biscuits.

"Eat hearty, my bullies," said the pirate assigned to watch them. "Twice a day is all the repasts ye shall get."

Marot took one bite and proffered his bowl to the others. "Take it, my friends, if you are hungry. With the *mal de mer*, I could not keep it down."

"Thanks," said Reith. "I could eat enough for three. Take your share, Gendu. Yours, too, Alicia. The trick is to soften the biscuits in the gravy; otherwise you may break a tooth on them."

Tondi appeared. At the sight of Alicia in her spangled kilt, jacket, and scarf, she cried: "Ho, Earthwoman, what do ye in those garments? They're our property by right of conquest!"

"Oh, please don't be angry, Captain!" said Alicia in her most winsome manner. "I was awakened from sleep and didn't have time to put anything on. I couldn't find my own clothes in that pile downstairs, so I took the liberty of borrowing these." She rose and spun around. "Do you like them on me?"

Tondi gave a snort of laughter. "Well, I'll add the value of those fripperies to your ransom fee, and ye may keep them."

She touched Marot's shoulder. "As for you, when ye finish your repast, I'm fain to have you in my cabin. I've never been futtered by an *Ertsu*, and here's a chance to try it. Dost understand?"

"Of a certainty!" He looked a sigh at Reith. *"Je ferai tout mon petit possible; mais, elle pue!"*

When Reith, Alicia, and Gendu had been returned to the hold, Reith said: "We'd better make our try tonight."

"Why?" said Gendu. "We're a man short. Why not wait till all be present?"

"Because tomorrow night she'll have picked you or me for yard duty, and the night after the other of us, and so on.

Moreover, we're now within sight of the coast. Another night we may be out of sight of land."

"What good doth the sight of the coast do us?" grumbled Gendu. "We cannot walk on water, as some Terran god is reputed to have done."

"We'll swim."

"Great Qondyor! Belike you Terrans can swim that monstrous distance; but I cannot swim at all. No proper sailor swims. If a man fall overboard in a storm, he's dead in any case."

"You see that hatch grating?" Reith pointed up.

"Aye. What of't?"

"When they open the hatch to let us come up, they lean it upright against the mast stays. If we could throw it overboard and jump in after it, we could use it as a raft."

"Ye be mad, *Ertsu!* I know somewhat of rafts, and yon thing's too small to bear one of us, let alone four."

"We won't ride upon it. We'll hold it by the edge, to keep our heads out of water, and swim with our legs, pushing it ahead of us."

"The thing must weigh above a hundred Qiribo pounds. Think ye one of us could lift it and cast it forth?"

"I think two could."

"But if I jump over the side, being no swimmer, I shall be dead as soon as I strike water!"

"We'll catch you and pull you to the raft."

Alicia asked: "On the water, how can we keep headed in the right direction? We can't take the ship's compass with us."

"Alicia, with three moons and a sky full of stars to steer by, even I could keep track of our course," Reith replied.

Gendu spoke: "What of the other *Ertsu?*"

"When Tondi hears the disturbance, she'll come boiling out, and Marot will come, too. We'll call to him, and he'll know what to do."

"'Twill never work. Ye haven't even named a way to get us to the main deck. Think ye these villains'll stand about quietly whilst we ascend to the deck and make off with their hatch cover? Belike wishing us a pleasant voyage?"

"All right, what do sailormen fear most at sea?"

Gendu pondered. "A fire. A storm ye can ride out, if your ship be sound and well-handled. But if ye burn, that's the end of you. Therefore the first rule of the sea, for pirate and honest merchantman alike, is: no smoking below decks!"

"And if this ship developed a fire in the hold, what would the crew do?"

"Saw ye not that row of buckets along the bulwark? The sailors'd form a line coming down into the hold here and hand buckets of water along to quench the blaze."

"Well then," said Reith. "We'll set the ship afire. When the smoke rises through the hatch and they hear us yelling, the crew will raise the hatch and lower the ladder. The first who come down will have a surprise awaiting them. Then up we go, and in the confusion we'll throw the hatch cover over the side and dive after it. I ought not to say 'dive,' because one should jump off feet first. If you hit your head on the raft, that might be your finish."

"And what's to hinder the fire from burning us up, or the smoke from smothering us, whilst we await the ladder?"

"I think they'll move lively enough. Anyway, that's a chance we'll have to take."

"A terrible chance indeed. And even if we can swim that distance, a gvám or a sáferir may swallow us at a gulp."

"That's just one more chance—"

"Chance, chance! When ye add these chances, that of survival is like unto that of slaying a yeki with your bare hands. 'Tis a mad scheme. Why not quietly await your ransoms?"

"We have places to go and things to do; and I doubt if the plan's any riskier than life on this craft, with its murderous mistress. No more argument; pick a sword! You, too, Alicia."

Reith chose a sword of medium length and weight. Alicia picked the lightest weapon with a good edge. Gendu gloomily handled the remaining swords and chose one with a curved blade, twice as heavy as most. He swished it through the air, saying:

"Those pretty needle-pointed things serve well enough on land, where the footing is solid. But on a rolling deck, a man hath no use for fancy fencing; his thrusts and lunges go agley. What ye need is something that'll cut deep, whithersoever ye swing it!"

When full darkness came, slightly mitigated by moonlight through the grating, Reith examined his lighter. "Damn!" he muttered. "I forgot I used the last charge of tinder to light the lamp this morning, and I don't have my tinderbox."

Alicia: "These gauzy clothes might do."

"Splendid! Help me to cut some little pieces."

An hour later, the three had laid half a dozen small fires about the hold and piled combustibles around them. For kindling, they used scrolls from the chest of documents and slivers of wood from the chest itself, which Gendu whittled off with his cutlass.

"Ready?" said Reith. "Here goes!"

He snapped the lighter. The fluff of cloth in the chamber caught and blazed up ruddy yellow. With his other hand he touched the end of one of the scrolls to the flame. When the scroll caught fire, he handed his torch to Alicia, who darted away to set one of the blazes. He handed another flaming scroll to Gendu. He lit a third for his own use; but by the time he had it going, his companions had started all six fires.

Reith pressed his sword into Alicia's hand. "Stand behind me now and keep this sticker out of sight until I reach back for it." He coughed in the gathering smoke. "Ready, everyone? Yell 'Fire!'"

The cry of "Fire!" was echoed from the deck above, which soon resounded to the drumming of naked feet. Amid a babel of voices, the grating was raised, letting the full light of the moons into the hold. The ladder slanted down. Reith looked up to see a ring of worried Krishnan faces, tinged yellow by the flames below, which crackled and waxed larger by the second.

"Hurry with those buckets!" screamed Reith, as if in mortal terror. He heard rumblings and splashings and shouts. Presently a pirate backed down the ladder, holding a bucket in one hand.

"Hasten!" shouted Reith, reaching behind him. Alicia thrust the sword hilt into his hand.

The first pirate reached the floor of the hold and stared goggle-eyed at the circle of fires. When a glance assured Reith that the second pirate was halfway down, Reith thrust his sword into the firstcomer's belly, twisted the blade, and tore it loose. The bucket crashed to the deck.

Reith's blade took the second pirate in the ribs. As the Krishnan, with a yell, fell off the last two steps of the ladder, Reith's sword was nearly wrenched from his grasp. Seizing the hilt with both hands, he pulled the weapon free.

Reith then scampered up the ladder. Above him loomed the

backside of another sailor. Hugging one upright with his sword arm, Reith caught the Krishnan's ankle with his free hand and plucked the pirate from his perch. The Krishnan tumbled past him with a shout, spilling his bucket over Alicia; but his yell was cut short by the chopping sound of Gendu's cutlass.

When Reith reached the topmost rung, he found a pirate, holding a bucket, standing agape before him. Reith ran the Krishnan through and sprang out on deck. The other prisoners followed. The unarmed pirates scattered before the three swords, screaming to one another to get weapons from the armory.

A naked, potbellied Tondi flung open the door of the captain's cabin and bellowed commands. Golden tongues of flame licked up above the hatch coaming.

"Get the grating!" panted Reith. "Guard our backs, Alicia! *Aristide!* Where in hell are you?"

"Here!" came a voice. In his ragged undershorts, Marot, carrying something in a sack, shoved Tondi aside and ran towards Reith and Gendu, who struggled with the grating. When a pirate barred his way, the Frenchman swung his bag and smote the Krishnan over the head. The pirate fell to his knees, clasping his skull.

With straining muscles, Reith and Gendu turned the grating at right angles to the bulwark and heaved it up. Marot set a hand under the lower edge and heaved, so that the structure was balanced on the rail. Then over it went with a great splash. Marot's tossed his sack after the grating, on which it landed with a clank.

"Over the side, feet first!" gasped Reith, climbing the rail. "Don't hit the grating!"

A pirate charged the fugitives with a pike. Captain Gendu snatched up the cutlass he had dropped and whirled. A sound of chopping meat, followed by the clatter of the pike and the thud of a body, told that tale.

Alicia swung at another pirate, who dodged back. Then, throwing her sword at the Krishnan, she sprang to the rail.

Reith struck the water feet first, went under, and bobbed up. Alicia's falling body struck his shoulder and knocked him under again. This time he came up choking and coughing.

"G-get away from the ship!" he wheezed. "Where's Gendu?"

"I have him," said Marot's calm voice. "Put your elbows on the raft, Captain, and let us do the swimming."

Marot added the strength of his legs to the vehement kicks

of Reith and Alicia, and slowly the ponderous hatch crept away from the *Haghrib*.

Something whistled through the dark and plunked into the water. "They're shooting!" said Reith. "Faster!" He moved to the side of the raft, holding it with one hand while swimming side stroke.

Another arrow hissed, and the sound ended in a faint thud. "I'm struck!" said Gendu.

Marot said: "It appears to be lodged in your shoulder muscle, Captain. I do not think that it is fatal. We shall remove it ashore."

"I knew...this crazy scheme...my doom," growled Gendu.

Hours passed, while the moons and stars wheeled slowly across the sky. They neared the shore of Cape Dirkash with heartbreaking slowness, as they often had to stop to rest. During the first of these halts, Alicia said: "We must have swum clear to Majbur!"

"Save your breath, Alicia. We could make better time without clothes dragging at us."

"Right! Hold my head out of water."

Reith held up her chin while she struggled out of the scarf, the jacket, and the kilt. He then tried to unbutton his own shirt and trousers, but gave himself a ducking as he fumbled with the wet garments.

"Put your shoulders up on the raft, Fergus," said Alicia. "I'll manage the buttons. . . . There!"

Reith's and Alicia's clothes and Reith's money belt were heaped on the grating. Reith said:

"How about you, Aristide?"

"My undergarment, it does not incommode me."

Rests became more frequent as they tired. At the second stop, Marot exclaimed: "Where is Captain Gendu?"

They peered into the ambient dark and called, but the captain was not to be seen. Reith said: "He must have slipped off and drowned. His wound looked superficial, but I guess the loss of his ship destroyed his will to live."

"Unless," said Marot, "he was taken by one of those sea monsters, like the gvám."

"Oh, lord!" said Alicia. "What if it comes back for seconds?"

"Nothing much we can do about it," said Reith. "All we can do is keep swimming and hope for the best. Let's go!"

They swam again. At the next halt, Alicia said: "Aristide, what's in that bag of stuff you brought out of the cabin?"

"My fossils, *naturellement*."

"*What?*" cried Reith. "How in Bákh's name did you salvage them?"

"That is a curious story. Tondi drank heavily during our assignation, perhaps to steel herself for the ordeal of an interplanetary amour. Hence she told me more than, I suspect, she would have sober.

"It came out that, while we were riding back to Jazmurian, High Priestess Lazdai got word by bijar post to members of her faction in the Temple of Bákh in Jazmurian, offering a fabulous reward for us and the fossils. When the members of this faction, who hope to seize control of the temple in her name, went to look for us, we had already parted on the *Kubitar*.

"But Tondi keeps a spy in Qirib, to apprise her of the sailings of treasure ships, to arrange ransoms, *et ainsi de suite*. Lazdai's faction informed this spy of the offer, and he passed it on to Tondi at their next rendezvous, in a secret cove on the coast of Qirib."

"How'd you make out with Tondi?" asked Reith.

"I upheld the honor of France, although I was tempted to hold my nose while so doing. But that was not the most serious difficulty."

"What was that?" exclaimed Alicia and Reith in unison.

"It was trying not to laugh at a time when laughter might have had fatal results. You see, my friends, the pirate queen had somehow got her hands on the little Alicia's Krishnan dress, the one that shows her *mamelons*. Needless to say, it did not fit; but Tondi was determined to play the glamorous seductress. When I entered, she had split the fabric in pulling it over her circumference, and she demanded that I push the little buttons through all those loops in back. But the edges of the material failed to come within half a meter of meeting. I did not dare tell her so, lest in a rage she have me thrown overboard like those poor sailors."

"What did you do?" Alicia asked.

"I convinced her that the buttons were purely ornamental,

not intended to be fastened. Then she pirouetted before me as she had seen Alicia do, evidently hoping thus to arouse my passions. But so bizarre was the spectacle that I was compelled to disguise my laughter by a violent spasm of coughing. After I had coughed like a terminal case of pulmonary disease, we got down to the serious business of the assignation.

"When I could not repeat my performance every few minutes, I explained that we poor, weak *Ertsuma* had to rest between times. That was when she asked me about the bag of stones; so I told her about fossils. Oddly, she seemed fascinated by my talk of ancient eras and vanished life forms and begged me to tell her more. I was lecturing her on paleontology when your diversion began. I must say for her that she proved a more attentive audience than some undergraduate classes I have addressed on Terra." He glanced back at the blazing hulk of the *Haghrib*, small in the distance. "The fire seems to have defeated their efforts. There goes a mast! I do not think any of these rascals will survive."

"I hope not," said Reith. "Now let's swim some more."

The stars had wheeled across the sky, and the sky itself was growing opalescent with the approach of dawn, when the swimmers heard breakers. Marot said: "I hope we approach a sandy beach and not a stretch of jagged rock. It would be a pity to be dashed to our deaths against a cliff after having endured so much."

"Sounds like a beach surf to me," grunted Reith. "We'll know when we get there."

In the feeble dawn light they staggered out on a smooth, sandy beach. They picked their few possessions off the grating and abandoned it to the sea. Reith and Alicia spread their clothes out to dry and collapsed on the sand beside the already recumbent Marot. Alicia still wore the ornate necklace she had picked out of the chest. Its gems, winking in the growing light, outshone the fading stars.

Roqir was rising high in the greenish Krishnan sky when three armed men on shomals—a tall Krishnan quadruped, somewhat like a humpless camel—trotted along the beach. They halted at the sight of three *Ertsuma*, two nude and one clad in Terran underdrawers, asleep on the sand. At the sound of voices, the younger male awoke.

"Qararuma?" asked Reith blearily.

"Aye," said the rider who, respendent in silvered mail, appeared the leader. "I hight Sir Hulil, and these be my men-at-arms. The burning of a ship off this shore hath been reported. Canst tell aught of this?"

"Can I!" said Reith. "I could a tale unfold. . . ." He touched Alicia and Marot. "Wake up! Help has arrived! Aristide, you may get another train ride after all."

XII.

THE SEAPORT

As the suburbs of Majbur rocked past the train windows, Reith raised his voice above the rattle of couplings, the squeal of axles, the creak of wooden car frames, and the rumble of the bishtar's six huge feet on the cross ties: "We've got to figure out how to get to Novo. Thank Bákh, Majbur is a place where our credit is good. We can buy ayas and ride, or take passage on a riverboat. Those boats move slowly upstream, so we'd probably save a few days by riding."

Alicia groaned. "I'm worn out from all we've been through, Fergus. I couldn't face another long ride until I've rested up."

"Permit me to express identical sentiments," said Marot. "I, too, am exhausted. How long is the passage by boat?"

"Let me think. It's about three hundred and seventy kilometers to Novorecife. At the normal rate of upstream travel. . . ." Reith closed his eyes. "It would take a minimum of nine days. Allow ten or even eleven if we count the inevitable delays, compared to five or six by road."

Marot said: "These people make sophisticated carriages, drawn by ayas. Could we not buy or hire such an equipage here and drive it? It would be more comfortable than the saddle."

"Can you drive one of those rigs?"

"Alas, no. I have never learned this type of manège."

"Same with me," said Reith.

"Why, Fergus!" said Alicia. "I thought you could do *everything*, like Ivan Skavinsky Skavar."

"Sorry to reveal my feet of clay. I'll try to learn."

"Could we not hire a driver?" persisted Marot.

"I suppose so; but to assemble carriage, ayas, driver, and all, and try them out, itself would take several days. What's your deadline for return?"

Marot: "I have space reserved on the *Juruá*. This will be in something more than a moon—perhaps twenty-five days."

"You, Alicia?"

"I have no plans," said Alicia, studying her hands. "If the *Juruá* brings me more grant money, I thought I'd go to Suruskand to investigate their system. If not, I may return to Earth, *if* they have room and I can borrow the fare. Otherwise. . . ." She shrugged, with a long look at Reith, whose face remained impassive. Alicia continued: "If a riverboat leaves soon, we'll have plenty of time to get to Novo before blastoff. Besides, I have a reason for preferring a boat."

"What's that?" asked Reith.

"As soon as I get some pencils and paper, I'm going to start rewriting my notes from memory. A peaceful riverboat is a perfect place for writing. I couldn't do it in a carriage, let alone on ayaback."

The train pulled into Majbur's South Station, amid a squeal of brakes and shouts of the mahout astride the bishtar's neck. The three Terrans climbed stiffly down. They looked anything but prosperous travelers, in their rumpled clothing with Marot's bag of fossils their only baggage.

Reith still wore his khakis, much the worse for wear. His cheeks glowed with a coppery stubble, on its way to becoming a full red beard. Alicia looked like a Gypsy in her bedraggled bolero, skirt, and scarf from the *Haghrib's* hold.

Marot had been forced to board the train in his ragged undershorts. During the overnight stop at Yantr, all three had bought crude leather slippers for their painfully abraded feet; and Marot, with Reith's help, had purchased a second-hand jacket and kilt. Although these patched garments were in their last stage of decrepitude, Marot shrugged off their seediness.

"Dressed like a vagabond," he said, scratching his newly

sprouted pepper-and-salt beard, "none thinks me worth the robbing. Where are you taking us tonight?"

"I'll first drop in on Gorbovast," said Reith. "We need money to square our debt with the railroad and buy us passage home. His office is about six blocks from here."

Gorbovast bad-Sár, Resident Commissioner in Majbur for King Eqrar of Gozashtand, less formally known as Novore-cife's principal intelligence agent and general trouble shooter, proved a small, elderly Krishnan with a face ridged with tiny wrinkles and hair faded to pale jade. When he saw Reith, he cried in English:

"Ah, Mr. Reese! What an exquisite pleasure to see you again! What tale of misfortune dire have you to tell zis time?"

"Tale enough," said Reith. "We've just arrived from Jaz-murian on our way to Novo, flat broke, without shelter, and far from home."

"A pity! I would urge you to use my house as your own, save zat a score of my kindred have come hither to celebrate ze hatchday of my latest grandchild. Still, you must bring your friends to my house for dinner on ze morrow, and tell ze tale of your adventures."

"It'll be a confession of my shortcomings," said Reith with a self-deprecating grin. "Adventures are a sign of incompetence. My tours are successful to the degree that they go smoothly to the point of dullness." He introduced his companions.

"I sought I recognized ze beautiful Doctor Dyckman," said Gorbovast, "from ze time you came here wiz Mr. Mjipa. Let me sink. . . . Am I correctly informed zat you and Mr. Reese are man and wife?"

"Were," said Reith shortly.

"Oh, excuse! So sorry! I did not mean. . . ."

"Forget it, Commissioner," said Reith. "We Terrans have all sorts of bizarre arrangements."

Gorbovast turned to Marot. "Doctor, do I hear a certain Terran accent? *Vous êtes français, Monsieur?*"

"*Mais oui!*" cried Marot. "*Comme j'aime entendre la lan-gue de la civilisation!*"

"*Ah, comme je m'étonne de cette belle civilisation!*" ex-claimed Gorbovast.

Not to be outdone, Reith continued the conversation in his

stiff, bookish French, rusty from lack of practice. "First, we have need of the money. Then we have need of a place to stay until we find the transportation."

"How will you travel?"

"If a riverboat leaves for Novo soon, we want to take passage thereon. Know you the dates of the next sailings?"

"A moment, please." Gorbovast dug into a desk and brought out a fistful of papers, through which he riffled. "Alas, I cannot find that list of departures, Menshu!"

"Here, sir." A clerk emerged from a back room.

"Mount your scooter and hasten to the riverfront. Learn what towboat next leaves for Novorecife and when. Tarry not!"

When Menshu had departed, Gorbovast, still speaking French, said: "How came you from Jazmurian? Did you have difficulties?"

"Bien sûr!" said Reith. "We were abducted between Jaz- murian and Kolsafid—"

"You were perhaps on the train stopped by raiders, who tore up the track?"

"Yes. They took us to Jeshang, and threatened us with the death by boiling, from which Doctor Dyckman rescued us *comme marée en carême.* Then when we tried to voyage here by sea, we were captured by pirates. We sank the pirate ship and swam ashore. Aside from that, it was an uneventful trip."

"Great Dashmok! *Mon dieu! J'ai râm!* I am afire wiz im- patience to hear ze whole story. How came you hither from the shore to which you swam?"

"A Mikardando knight flagged down a train from Kolsafid and persuaded the conductor to carry us on credit. The rest will have to wait, because we are weary and have much to do. We still owe the railroad for our fares."

"I understand. About the money, I must fill out some pa- pers. . . . Seat yourselves, I pray you. . . ."

Gorbovast vanished into the inner office. By the time the clerk returned, Reith's pockets bulged with coin. Gorbovast said: "You had better avoid the waterfront with so much money on your person. Menshu, what learned you touching the riv- erboats?"

"Captain Ozum's *Zaidun* sails the day after tomorrow, sir."

"That's good luck for us," said Reith. "Ozum runs a stout ship, and he's the most honest skipper around. Dashmok must be on our side for a change." Reith smiled at his companions.

"That'll give us a day's shopping, before our host's most welcome dinner. Then off for home!"

"Fine!" said the commissioner. "Menshu, kindly conduct my friends to Khaminé's Inn. Tell Master Khaminé I wish them to be accommodated as a special favor. When you have delivered them safely, hunt down Captain Ozum and pay for three berths on his boat to Novorecife. *Bon soir! À demain, sans faute!*"

At Khaminé's, Reith ordered a single and a double room as before. At the door of the smaller room, he waved Alicia in. She paused, looking hopefully at Reith, and murmured:

"Fergus, is this your way of saying we can never go back to the way things were, before Ghulindé?"

"That's right," he said.

"I'm so sorry, Fergus. It was such glorious fun, being your amorex."

"I'm sorry, too; but I think it's the best—the only way."

"Even if I solemnly promise never to do anything like that again?"

"No. After that hoax you and Vizman tried to pull, with drink and a dancing girl, I could never again trust one of your promises."

"I didn't mean to hurt you. If I'd known Vizman's plan in advance, I could have discussed it with you. Then, if you refused—"

"My dear Alicia, if I'd said 'no!', you'd have replied: 'It's my body, to do with what I please!' And off you'd go in a fury."

"Oh, come, Fergus! I'm not an utter—but anyway, I figured that, if I gave in to Vizman and you never found out, I might help to end a great injustice to those mine slaves. What would be the harm? Vizman first brought the matter up at dinner. I couldn't very well call out: 'Hey, Fergus, the President wants me for his bedmate tonight! Is that okay with you?' I asked for time to think it over, hoping I'd have a chance to discuss it with you; but no, Vizman wanted his answer right away. So I had to decide quickly, and I chose what seemed the right course."

Reith nodded. "No doubt you did what seemed right to you; and now I'm doing what seems right to me. But let's not further hash over this unfortunate business."

"Oh, all right, Mr. neo-Puritan. Any time you can't stand the primal urge any more, you'll know where to find me."

Reith changed the subject in a marked manner. "How about that shopping spree we've been looking forward to? We can buy necessities today and luxuries tomorrow."

"Oh, good!" she cried, seizing Reith by the neck and planting a lush, moist kiss on his lips. "I want a dress like the one the Sainians gave me." Her eyes lit up with the feral gleam of a carnivore stalking its prey.

When Reith returned to the larger bedroom, Marot said: "I infer, my friend, that the affair is now over, *fini?*"

"Yep," said Reith.

"A pity. I shall miss my single bed; for you are given to the thrashing and the groaning in your sleep."

"If you like, I'll ask Khaminé—"

"No, no, do not consider it. I am not serious. But the little one, I am sure she most sincerely repents her dalliance with that *soi-disant* President. She told me all about it after you left the palace. He had cleverly maneuvered her into a position where she had to choose between her ideals and her love for you."

Reith growled: "I might have come to accept her sleeping with Vizman, in time, as I had the Foltz affair. But what really browned me off was her trying to hoax me with the liquor and the dancing girl. There are people you can trust—a very small class—and people you can't. Until that night, I thought she was one of the first kind."

"But you see, Vizman arranged things so that she should have no time to consider the alternatives. When he offered her a seeming way to retain both her ideals and your affection, she yielded to the temptation. Have you never yielded to the temptation?"

"Yes," said Reith, remembering how he had been lured into an affair with Princess Vázni. "It's an unfortunate business all around; but I'm still not going back. If you want to court her, Aristide, feel free."

"You mean to sue in your behalf, like that fellow Miles Standing?"

"Standish, I think you mean. No, I mean in your own behalf."

Marot threw up his hands. "May the good God forbid! If you, with all your experience and force of personality, cannot

domesticate this tornado of energy, how could a naïve old
pedant like me hope to do so? I know my limitations, and I
would never, never attempt such a folly."

A half-hour later, the three ragamuffin travelers were can-
vassing the shops of Majbur for essentials. Knowing the city
and its ways, Reith managed their purchases with efficient
dispatch.

At last they reëntered the inn, cleansed in the public bathhouse, the men freshly shaven and wearing new baldrics and
swords over new jackets and divided kilts. Alicia looked a
legendary princess in a simple lilac tunic of linenlike fabric,
embellished by her necklace and her freshly washed and cropped
shining hair.

The clerk at first failed to recognize the former vagabonds.
When he realized who they were, he bowed so low that he
nearly lost his balance. Reith grinned at the sudden deference
and said: "Kindly show us to the dining room."

Alicia brightened at the sight of a dance floor. "Oh, wonderful! Tonight we can dance as late as we want!"

"Good God, woman," laughed Reith. "I thought you were
all worn out?"

"Shopping invigorates me," she said. "Poor Fergus, if you
are exhausted, you can go to bed right after dinner." She slid
an arm through Marot's. "Aristide and I will have fun tonight,
won't we?"

"My dear Alicia," said Marot, "me, I have not danced in
many years. I warn you, I shall be as maladroit as a bull on
the roof."

"If you two can take it, I guess I can," said Reith. "Don't
want to spoil my image as a superman."

The entrée was a kind of sea slug with tentacles, which had
the unnerving property of continuing to wriggle after being
boiled. When the orchestra struck up with the Krishnan equivalents of harps, flutes, clarinets, and trumpets, Alicia fixed
Marot with her piercing sapphire eyes. "Let's dance!"

"As I have remarked," said Marot in plaintive tones, "I am
hopelessly out of practice...."

"Aristide! You're going to dance, and that's that! Come
along!" She rose and tugged on the Frenchman's wrist.

With a sigh, Marot let himself be cowed into compliance.
He cast an appealing glance at Reith, who replied with a flicker

of a smirk. As they circled the floor, Reith observed that Alicia was such an exquisite dancer that she could make even the awkward scientist look proficient.

As they returned to their table, the orchestra struck up again. Reith rose and bowed. "May I have the pleasure?"

The band played an athletic dance tune; and Reith and Alicia skipped about the floor with two other lively couples. As the music ended and the musicians tuned their harps and polished their wind instruments, Alicia said: "Fergus, think of all the fun we missed when we were mm—you know—because you didn't take those dancing lessons sooner."

"No doubt," he said dryly, "or to put it another way, because we didn't stay married long enough for me to get around to those lessons."

Alicia sighed. "I know, darling; it's all my fault. Let's make the most of our chances from now on."

When the music resumed, Alicia again bullied the compliant Marot out on the floor. As Reith sat watching them, he became aware that he in turn was being watched by a young Krishnan, who was seated by himself across the room.

The watcher wore baggy black trousers tucked into soft-leather boots, and a jacket of heavy green stuff, which he had opened to bare his chest against the heat. A scabbarded sword lay beneath his table. The garb bespoke a resident of the Empire of Dur, north of the stormy Va'andao Sea.

At last the Krishnan rose and walked unsteadily across the dance floor, narrowly missing a pair of dancers. Reith watched his approach uncertainly. Halting, the Duru said:

"I crave pardon, but are you not Sir Fergus Reese, once consort of the Princess Vázni of Dur?"

Reith rose. "Who are you, and why are you asking that question?"

The Duru swayed, staring at Reith. "Ah, I see that you are indeed he. Then, sir, I name you foul traitor, caitiff knave, vile rogue, and recreant treacher. I will now prove my words with steel upon your odious body. Prepare to defend yourself!"

"What in Hishkak?" said Reith. "I don't know what you're talking about. And what am I supposed to defend myself with?"

The Krishnan wobbled drunkenly back to his table, picked up his scabbard, and drew the sword. Shouting: "Now shall you see how a knight of Dur avenges an insult to his sovran lady!" he charged across the dance floor, whirling his blade and causing the dancers to scatter with cries of alarm.

Reith, who had just sat down, leaped up again and snatched up his chair. All the dancers fled from the floor but one. That was Alicia Dyckman who, darting forward, thrust a shapely leg into the Duru's path to trip him. The Duru fell sprawling, his sword skittering across the qong-wood floor. Coming around the table, Reith brought his chair down with a crash on the fallen Krishnan's head.

"What's this? What's this?" cried Khaminé the taverner, bustling forward. "No brawling on my premises! Gorbovast assured me—"

"He's a perfect stranger to me," said Reith, explaining what had happened. "He may have mistaken me for someone. Ask any witness."

"Would ye file a complaint? I like not to call the watch."

"I'll tell you, Master Khaminé. I wish to get to the bottom of this affair. Let me and my friend take this person to our room for a while. Sit in with us if you like. If it's a mere misunderstanding, no official action will be needed. If not. . . ." Reith shrugged.

"Aye, that makes sense," said the taverner. "I'll give you a hand with him. The rest of you, on with the dance!"

"Thanks for your help, Alicia," said Reith.

In the large bedroom, the unconscious Duru was tied to a chair. Cold, wet towels applied to his face and neck finally brought him round. He rolled bloodshot eyes and asked: "Where am I? Gods, my head aches!"

As Khaminé sat down in the other chair, Alicia and Marot took posts on the bed. Reith explained where the Krishnan was and how he got there.

"Now," said Reith, "who are you?"

"Sir Vaklaf bak-Khazir, a knight of Dur."

"What are you doing in Majbur?"

"Studying at the university."

"Why did you attack me?"

"Well—ah—I knew you from pictures in the palace at Baianch. They had a photographer up from Hershid for your wedding to Vázni. Knowing how foully you had deserted the sweet lady, I saw it my duty to administer condign chastisement. 'Twas bad enough that the Regent wed his cousin to an off-worlder; but to let that slimy alien dishonor Krishnan womanhood by deserting her was too unmannerly to be brooked."

"Your sins are catching up with you, Fergus," said Alicia with a barely-suppressed smile.

Sternly, Reith said to the youth: "I take it you hadn't heard the full story of my connection with Vázni?"

"I am aware of the official account."

"Which is about as truthful as any man of experience would expect. Do you wish to hear my telling of the tale?"

"What is your story then, alien?"

Ignoring the Duru's truculence, Reith told how he had brought his first party of tourists to Dur; how the Regent Tashian entrapped him into intimacy with Vázni; how he was forced into marriage, literally at sword's point; and how he escaped. He explained:

"Tashian's motives were clear. He likes being Regent and running things; and he's full of ideas about what's good for Dur. He thought that if Vázni married a Krishnan, there would be offspring, one of which would grow up to become emperor. That would spell the end of Tashian's power. I know, because Tashian asked me if there was any chance of offspring between a Krishnan and a Terran."

Sir Vaklaf sneered. "Why should I believe the tale of a slippery alien over that of the noble Tashian?"

"Believe what you like; but if you dig into the matter, you'll find that I speak the truth. And I must remind you, Sir Vaklaf, that you have put yourself in a most precarious position."

"Mean you to murder me?"

"Perhaps; but there are alternatives. I can have you imprisoned, or expelled from the university, or stripped of your knightly rank. Having been a knight of Dur myself, I know the duelling regulations, and you flagrantly violated all of them."

Vaklaf stared at the toes of his boots. In a less defiant tone he said: "I must have drunk too much kvad."

"Doubtless. I'll let you go without further ado, if you'll agree to answer a few questions and give your knightly word to take no further actions against me."

"I promise, Sir Fergus."

"All right, then. First, Are you in any way connected with the cult of Bákh of Chilihagh?"

"Nay. Do they in sooth worship Bákh there?"

"They do. Did anyone suggest, urge, or offer you money to attack me?"

"You are offensive, sir! A knight of Dur, bribed to assault another? Perish the thought! After all, I am who I am!"

"In my experience, men of your rank come good, bad, and indifferent, like the rest of your species. Next: Where is Vázni now?"

"That's part of the great scandal that you caused! A few months after you fled from Dur, the lady eloped with a young male with whom she had formed an attachment. They settled in Hershid, where Dour Eqrar holds them in protective custody for bargaining with Regent Tashian. That little fussbudget Eqrar performed some ceremony to legitimatize their union. Any day we may hear that their first egg hath hatched."

Reith smiled. "I hope my little Vázni is happy at last. Better a proper mate of her own species than an unwilling alien."

"You may have some reason on your side. But an insult is an insult, and can only be erased in blood!"

Reith sighed. "On my world, a poet once wrote: 'Against stupidity the very gods do strive in vain.' He must have had youths like you in mind. Now swear your oath. . . ."

When Vaklaf had sworn on his knightly honor to pester Reith no more, Reith said: "Untie him, pray, Master Khaminé. Run along to your studies, Vaklaf."

The student went out. Alicia said: "Fergus, would you like to make me very happy?"

"That depends," said Reith warily. "What do you want?"

"Let's go back to the dining room. Since you've become such a splendid dancer, I want all the dances with you I can get."

Reith sighed once more. "Yes, my dear."

The great shopping spree took place the next morning. Marot bought new undergarments and a pair of Krishnan eyeglasses. Since they were poorly ground by Terran standards and not made to his prescription, he found that continual usage made his head ache. "At least," he said, "I am no longer an illiterate." He also purchased another flutelike instrument to replace the one lost in the piracy.

Alicia had formed a passion for a dress as much as possible like the filmy, bare-breasted gown that the rancher's wife had given her. After hours of trudging from shop to shop, Reith's and Marot's feet were sore from Majbur's cobblestoned streets and their knees ached from standing in shops. Reith grumbled:

"I must be getting old despite my LPs. I find a quarter-hour of shopping more fatiguing than a fifty-kilometer hike."

"Oh, you poor little man!" said Alicia. "You, the hero of a hundred fights and flights, worn out from looking at a few dresses? Come on! I'm just getting into my stride. There's a likely-looking shop!"

"Aristide," said Reith wearily, "they've found cures for lots of things, like cancer, alcoholism, and homosexuality; but nobody has found a remedy for the female addiction to shopping."

Alicia darted into the next shop and, by haranguing the proprietor in fluent Majburo dialect, got him to bring out a score of gowns of the type she sought. Eventually she found one enough like the Chilihagho dress to suit. When she tried it on and looked in the steel mirror, she gave a cry of delight, kissed both Reith and Marot, and spun round and round in a little dance of joy.

As they passed a jeweler's window, Alicia paused to stare at the baubles spread out there. Marot said: "Fergus, I see a bench for customers within. If the little Alicia goes in and asks for an appraisal of her necklace, you and I can enjoy a respite from standing."

So pleased was Alicia with this proposal that for once she forgot to take umbrage at Marot's form of addressing her. Reith said: "Okay. I still think it's junk—glass and brass—but I don't mind getting a professional opinion."

Inside, they found a small, wizened Krishnan behind a polished showcase. His face was wreathed in a Krishnan smile, and he bowed obsequiously. "Welcome, my Terran lords! How can your servant serve you?"

Alicia unwound the scarf that hid her necklace, unclasped the necklace, and stretched it across the jeweler's pad of soft black cloth, saying: "Good my sir, have you a pair of earrings that would go well with this?"

The jeweler stared at the necklace through his jeweler's loupe. The only sound was the drip of water in a clepsydra. At last he said:

"I pray you, my lady, do but wait an instant."

He called, and from the rear of the shop an even older Krishnan, bent and wrinkled, tottered out to examine the necklace in his turn. He uttered an unprofessional gasp. The two muttered to each other, and finally the first jeweler said:

"I'll do my best, my lady; albeit I doubt that my finest gems could match those of your royal neckpiece. It is very old and of excellent workmanship. Did it descend to you from some noble family?"

"I have been so told," said Alicia warily. Reith and Marot exchanged startled glances.

The jeweler took out a huge key, unlocked a strongbox that lay behind a panel in the wall, and brought out a small, velvet-lined case. When he opened it, a dazzling array of fine stones sparkled in the sunlight that slanted through the window. He said:

"Though nought in my modest establishment can match your princely mass of jewels, belike these might complement your necklace not badly." From the case he picked a pair of splendid ruby earrings. "A bargain at five hundred karda," he said.

Reith exclaimed in English: "Good lord, Alicia! We can't afford anything like that. Our funds are limited, and—"

"My friend," Marot interrupted, "for the lady who has saved our wretched lives, and more than once, nothing is too costly. I shall pay half, and you can use your tessara for credit."

Reith shrugged. "Oh, all right. But let me bargain; I'm sure I can get them for less."

"Also," said Marot, "it appears that Alicia's necklace is a great deal more than the 'junk' you called it. Let us ask for the appraisal."

Reith haggled the jeweler down to four hundred and fifty karda and produced the jadeoid rectangle in payment. When the necessary papers had been written up, Reith said: "Now, master jeweler, be so good as to tell us the value of the necklace."

The jeweler called the older Krishnan back, and the two peered at the necklace, muttered, and scribbled notes. At last the first jeweler said: "I will give five thousand karda for it, instanter."

With a wry grin, Reith said in English: "That means I could bargain him up to ten thousand, and he could sell the thing for at least twenty. As an amateur gemologist, I guess I'm just a competent tour guide."

"I thank you," said Alicia to the jeweler in her great-lady manner. "But, of course, we do not intend to sell. Tonight we shall dine with King Eqrar's Commissioner, and the earrings and necklace will nicely embellish my gown."

When they were outside again, she seized both Reith and

Marot in turn and kissed them vigorously, causing a few Majburuma to pause and stare. "Thank you, darlings, for my lovely earrings! We'll show old Gorbovast and his people we can put on the dog as well as any of them!"

On the way back to Khaminé's, Reith detoured to show Marot the war galleys in the harbor, the great brazen statue of the god Dashmok, and a couple of the temples. Most of the afternoon they slept away; then, clad in their best, they set out in a hired carriage for Gorbovast's mansion in the suburbs.

Gorbovast's Lucullan dinner had been eaten; the swarm of shrieking Gorbovast grandchildren had been put to bed; and the host of Gorbovast kin had plied the Terrans with questions about their adventures. A brief silence permitted Reith to pose some queries of his own. He asked:

"Commissioner, you know everything that goes on around the Triple Seas. What's the latest from Chilihagh? We've been told that the Dasht failed to make good his revolt against the Bákhites and is besieged in his palace."

"Aye," said Gorbovast. "That's the situation as I last heard it, with one small addendum: his General Gurshman, being a worshiper of Qondyor and not of Bákh, hath joined the struggle on the side of the Dasht. He is said to be gathering the frontier forces in an essay to break the siege of the palace."

"Anyway," said Reith, "it's evident that we still have to watch out for fanatical Bákhites trying to haul us back to Jesh-ang for boiling. Do you know of anyone else, Commissioner, who wants to make life hard for us?"

"Now that you allude thereto," said Gorbovast, "I did, indeed, this very day, receive an inkling of such. It had slipped my mind—a thing that, alas, takes place increasingly as the years advance."

"What happened?"

"An informant averred that one approached him offering money, would he but employ his singular skill upon an alien creature."

"Your Excellency," said Reith, "I'm not so tactless as to ask the name of your informant. But tell me, at least, what his peculiar skill consists of?"

"He is a murderer. Further details I sought in vain from him to elicit: the identities of him who made the offer and him—or her—on whom he was to demonstrate his skill. The 'alien creature' could be your esteemed self; or any of an hundred other off-worlders now resident in Majbur. In any case, my informant said he did decline the offer. But, dear Fergus, I do beseech you and your companions, the utmost prudent care to take."

"That we will," said Reith grimly. "One more question, please: Have you heard news from Qirib?"

"Aye; I had a letter thence but yestermorn. The President hath hanged that last surviving leader of the opposition. Rumor saith he means to change the constitution, his lifelong tenure of his office to assure."

Alicia, regally fair in her new gown, put a hand against her mouth in a gesture of dismay. She started to ask a question but seemed unable to force the words out: "Have you heard— has he—did he issue. . . ."

"She wishes to know," said Reith, "whether slavery has been abolished in Qirib."

"Strange that you should ask! My informant saith that Vizman did indeed draw up such an ordinance, having thereto been persuaded by some Terran passerby. On second thought, howsomever, he judged the time unripe and therefore hath deferred this plan to a future indefinite."

Alicia gasped. Reith was tempted to flash her a triumphant smile, which said: "I told you so!" But love, and pity for the pain she must be feeling, stopped him. Instead, he reached over and gave her hand a light squeeze. With what Reith knew was intense self-control, she turned to their host, saying:

"Sir Commissioner, we shall remember your feast as long as we live. But the hour grows late, and tomorrow we must be up with the bijars to catch our boat up the river. Will Your Excellency pray excuse us?"

Thanking their host profusely, Reith and Marot escorted Alicia out.

On the carriage ride back to the inn, Alicia sat silently, now and then biting her lip, while Marot talked of how much he would have enjoyed leading another Krishnan fossil hunt, with Reith as guide.

"I fear, however," he added, "that the life on this planet is too strenuous for one of my age and temperament. So another hand must undertake the task."

"Not every Krishnan guided tour provides the adventures

we've had," said Reith. "I'd taken half a dozen tours out before you hired me, and only the first had this sort of excitement. The problems on the other expeditions were simple things— you know—tourists losing their belongings, or crabbing about their accommodations, or failing to show up on time, or taking violent dislikes to one another."

Glancing at Alicia, Reith saw the moonlight glisten on a tear. He patted her hand and tried to distract her by saying: "I don't know for sure that anybody's out to scrag us; but we shouldn't take chances. Let's check out from Khaminé's tonight and go straight to the *Zaidun*. Captain Ozum won't like being roused at all hours; but he'll put up with it because I'm an old friend and a good customer."

At the inn, Reith told the coachman to wait. He paid the taverner's account while Marot and Alicia went up to their rooms to pack. A few minutes later he joined Marot and was filling his duffel bag when he heard a piercing scream, followed by a crash. Seizing his sword, he rushed around to Alicia's small bedroom, expecting to find her being robbed, raped, or murdered.

Instead, she was lying prone across her bed, beating the pillow with her fists. By one wall lay the shattered remains of a small vase that had stood on the bedside table. The green and crimson plant and the dirt in which it had been rooted lay among the shards.

"Alicia!" said Reith, grasping her shoulder. "What is it?"

She rolled over and sat up, unmindful of a tear-streaked face. "That bastard!" she said in a choked voice. "That son of a bitch! That turd! To think that I sacrificed my one real love, for *nothing!*"

"There, there," said Reith, gathering her gently into his arms. "I know your intentions were good. But politicians are no more to be trusted here than back on Terra."

"He really did write that proclamation; he showed it to me. I suppose I ought to have...."

"Sure. But when and if he issues it, it'll be on a basis of political calculation, regardless of any favors he might enjoy from a lovely Terran visitor."

"I wish I were dead!" Alicia wept for a while against Reith's shirt front, then straightened up and wiped her eyes. "I'm sorry I broke Khaminé's vase, but I *had* to let off steam. I'll pay for it, of course. If you ever get a chance to do Vizman one in the eye, you have my blessing."

"That's the spirit!" said Reith. "We all do stupid things; the trick is not to make the same mistake twice. I'll bet Vizman planned the whole thing in advance! Otherwise he wouldn't have ordered Shei to get me drunk and out of the way. We walked into his trap."

"I guess we did." She managed a weak smile, followed by a lingering look. "Fergus, do you—suppose—if you'd like—"

"Alicia dear! We've got to clear out fast, *depressa!* I don't know who may be after us this time, though I can guess several possibilities. But the quicker we're aboard the *Zaidun* the better. So pack that bag, *byant-hao!*"

As Alicia rose to carry out Reith's command, there came a knock on the door. The taverner's voice called: "Doctor Dyckman! Is aught amiss? We heard a crash."

"Come in, come in!" said Alicia, hastily wiping her tear-streaked face on the bedding. "Master Khaminé, I fear I owe you the price of a vase."

"What befell?" said Khaminé in the doorway.

"As I was packing to depart, I looked up and saw a ghost. I think it was the ghost of one of the former queens of Qirib. In a moment of panic I threw the vase, which of course went right through the phantom."

Khaminé clucked disapprovingly. "Ghosts in my establishment! If ye say nought of this visitation, I'll not charge you for the vase. More than one innkeeper hath been ruined by a rumor that his hostelry was haunted. These dead queens are doubtless enraged by the fall of the matriarchate and seek revenge on all Terrans, whom they blame for their fall. Goodnight! It hath been a pleasure to serve you and your eminent Terran companions." Khaminé bowed himself out.

XIII.

THE RIVER

When the carriage drew up at the base of the *Zaidun's* pier, a fog was rising from the estuary of the Pichidé. Overhead the moons shone brightly; but a few meters away, people were becoming wraithlike and objects were being swallowed by the mist.

"Watch your step!" Reith warned his companions. "If you don't, you may find yourself in the river."

As they felt their way out on the pier to the *Zaidun's* berth, the bargeman on watch went to rouse the captain. Ozum, in a knee-length nightshirt, ran stubby fingers though his touseled hair and said:

"Nay, nay, no apologies. I know you well enough, Master Reese, to say ye'd not rouse me at midnight without cause. Come aboard, and sprackly!"

"Have you any other passengers?" asked Reith.

"Nay, not hitherto. We sail at sunrise. Take Cabins Two, Four, and Six. I'm back to Varzai's bosom."

As the morning sun dispersed the fog, the *Zaidun,* a much larger riverboat than Sarf's, cast off. Under oar and sail it beat its way up the estuary of the Pichidé. At the eastern end of the towpath, the vessel eased up to the bank while the shaihans were driven ashore and harnessed. The long tow to Novorecife had begun.

The passenger quarters were ten cabins in the after part of the deckhouse, five on a side, all opening on the deck. Since Ozum carried no other passengers, each Terran enjoyed the privacy of an entire cabin.

Alicia, wearing the simple Krishnan tunic she had bought in Majbur, disappeared into her cubicle and came out with a sheaf of pencils and a folder holding a ream of blank paper. Settling herself on deck, with her back against the deckhouse, she began scribbling. When Reith spoke, she laid a warning finger on her lips and went on writing.

As the tranquil passage continued, Reith made another effort to draw her into conversation. But she was in an impatient, irascible mood. Anything that distracted her from recording all she could remember brought a sharp retort.

Marot spent his days chipping away at his fossils and practicing his new musical instrument. "It has a lower register than the other," he said. "I should like to play Hayakawa's *Moonlight on the Ruins,* but I must first transpose all the notes."

Left to his own devices, Reith paced the deck, slept, did calisthenics, played piza with Captain Ozum, and practiced his rusty French on the cheerful Marot.

They were past the halfway point of their journey when, towards dinnertime, Alicia shut her folder with a snap. "That's all I can remember now; although doubtless I'll add details from time to time. Sorry to have been beastly all these days, but the job had to be done."

She went to her cabin. When she came to dinner, it was not in her working clothes but in her new Majburo dinner dress. The rubies gleamed in her ears, and her face bore a trace of cosmetics. Reith whistled, and the eyes of even the austere Marot shone with admiration.

That evening, Alicia and Reith stood at the *Zaidun's* rail and watched the rise of Karrim, a silver shield just past the full and nearly twice the size of Terra's moon, behind the darkling trees along the shore. Alicia slipped an arm through Reith's and tipped her head back in such an inviting way that he could not resist the urge to kiss her.

"You're a gorgeous creature tonight, you witch!" said Reith.

"I endeavor to give satisfaction, Mr. Reith."

"You do, Mrs. R—Doctor Dyckman."

Reith looked embarrassed. Alicia's expression changed; her face crumpled as if she were about to burst into tears. Hastily Reith changed the subject. "Where's the necklace from the pirate ship? I'd have thought you'd wear it."

"I left it with Gorbovast to sell for me on commission."

"You did? When was this?"

"I made the arrangements while you were telling his relatives about our adventures. As an advance on the sale price, he gave me a draft for twenty-five thousand karda."

"Twen—good God! That means he must expect to get at least fifty thousand for it. He's a shrewd judge of such things. What'll you do with all that money?"

"For one thing, I may have to use some of it to pay my fare back to Earth."

A sense of impending loss overwhelmed Reith. Taking a deep breath, he asked: "When will you know?"

Alicia paused. "The decision isn't entirely mine to make."

"Oh," he said, grasping her meaning. Not knowing what to say next, he filled in the silence with more kisses. At last Alicia, recovering some of her bravado, said:

"I bought a bottle of the best falat in Majbur, and I've got it in a bucket of water to keep it cool. Why don't we have a little party with it my cabin?"

"Great idea!" said Reith, not without inner qualms. He ardently wanted to be with her but at the same time feared that events were slipping out of his control.

In the cabin, when they had drunk enough to make Reith feel expansive, Alicia ventured in a small voice: "Fergus, can't we be friends, in spite of everything?"

"I guess so. It's worth trying, anyhow."

"All right. Tell you what! Let's tell each other everything, you know, like brother and sister. No more pretenses or coquettish maneuvers."

"Okay, we'll see how it works. What would you like to know, Doctor Freud?"

"I want to know about your other women."

"Eh? Why, for goodness' sake?"

"As a xenanthropologist, I'm professionally interested."

"I am a social scientist; thou art a gossip; he is a snoop. Okay, if you insist. Do you include Krishnans?"

"Absolutely."

"Then will you be equally candid if I quiz you?"

"Oh, sure. Truth or consequences, agreed?"

"It's a bargain; though I haven't had quite your breadth of experience—"

"Fergus, that's mean! You make me sound like a half-kard whore."

"Sorry; that's not how I meant it. To tell the truth, I've had only four in my life besides you. Of these, three were Krishnans, and with two of them I was coerced literally at sword's point. As a Don Juan, I'm just a wimp."

"No excuses needed. I just want to know what happened between you and how they compared with me in bed."

Reith took a deep breath. "All right, here goes. Believe it or not, I was completely inexperienced when I boarded the *Goyaz* and took up with Valerie Mulroy, that nympho on my first tour. Neo-Puritan background, you know. I knew Valerie's appetite was pathological; but she was still a good, patient teacher."

"You mean it's because of her that you're such a superior lover? If I ever meet her, I'll thank her."

"We all have to start somewhere. She broke me in."

"What about the Krishnans?" asked Alicia.

"It's hard to compare them with human women, because their reactions are different—more passive. One told me they prefer Terrans to their own males, because we keep at it longer. This reputation doesn't make us popular with male Krishnans.

"On the other hand, that witch Shosti insisted she disliked it but did it as a religious duty; she thought I'd beget a demigod on her. With poor Borel's gilded skull staring down at me from a shelf in her bedroom, it was hard to keep my mind on my proper job."

"Your improper job, I'd say. How about the princess?"

"Just a sweet little nincompoop who, if she saw me so much as glance at the bed, would giggle, strip, bounce up on to the mattress, and open the way. Half the time I didn't even want it. I'm damned glad to be out of all their clutches."

Alicia said: "You're hard to please, even with a variety of choices."

"Not really. I considered everything about you practically perfect, until our battles began."

"Now you're trying to make me feel guilty for leaving you!"

"We'd better not start on that, if we want to be friends. What more do you want to know?"

"You said you'd had three Krishnan loves," she persisted. "Was the third one that little chatterbox, Qa'di, on the *Mork-erád?*"

"No; I never followed up Qa'di's hints. It was Gashigi in Mishé. She was just a one-night stand, a couple of moons after you left. Said she wanted to broaden her education. What's an unattached gentleman to do when a lady puts it to him that way?"

"Huh! If I'd taken that attitude towards every gentleman who propositioned me, I'd have had more keys in my lock than Messalina. Do you mean this Gashigi's the *only* one since we—ah—"

"Yes, until you showed up at Zora."

"And only once?"

"Yes. My heart wasn't in it, whatever other...."

Alicia gave a little sniff of laughter, then looked puzzled. "Most divorced men would be screwing everything that would hold still."

"You've spoiled me for most women. Whenever I thought intimacy with someone might be fun, you'd rise up like a ghost and make her seem a hag. After you, any other woman would be like skim milk after the best scotch or champagne. Besides, for a while I hoped you'd come back; and I didn't want the complication of another girl friend."

"If you wanted me back, why didn't you contest the preliminary decree? I might have dropped the suit."

"I thought about that, when I got to Novo and found no Alicia, but a fat envelope of legal papers in my mail box." He paused to organize his thoughts. "I let it go through for three reasons. One: You're old enough to know what you want. If you wanted back, you'd come; if you didn't, legal maneuvers wouldn't make you. Two: If anything would poison our relationship forever, it would be our hiring Novo's two lawyers to battle it out. Each would do his damnedest to make the other's client look like a monster. And three: I didn't want to do anything until I'd talked with you and done some hard thinking. I couldn't see setting myself up for another emotional shellacking. But with you off somewhere in the outback...." He shrugged.

"Poor Fergus! I've treated you abominably, and I'm frightfully sorry." She squeezed his hand. "If I could only make it up somehow. . . . I never meant to cripple you sexually."

"Don't worry about my sex drive. It's normal; it's just that you've been too much in my thoughts. I'd have begun to get over you by now if you hadn't appeared at Zora."

She sighed. "I must say I enjoy being your exclusive sex object, and I think you're wonderful. So why can't we get along? If only. . . ." After a pause, she asked: "Why didn't you go after Qa'di?"

"It would have been embarrassing to get her fired up and not be able to perform."

"What, *you?*"

"Darling, I don't think you understand. When you puncture the male ego, as you often do with that razor tongue of yours, you deflate other things as well. Remember how, when we were married, and we quarreled, and you told me off, I wouldn't make a pass at you for a week or more? It wasn't that I was sulking; I was simply physically unable."

"You poor thing! I had no idea your little ego was so tender. I thought you were punishing me. You seemed so reasonable and self-controlled that petty emotions never bothered you."

"That's my façade," he said. "I hate to admit it, but underneath I'm human. After the Vizman episode, I was in the megrims for days, until the pirates gave me more to think about than feeling sorry for myself."

"You didn't act depressed."

"In my trade, the show must go on. That's one thing tour guiding has taught me."

"Weren't you furious after your ducking? You had a right to be."

"Not for long. I can get as angry as the next one when somebody does me dirt. But when I've cooled down, I say: take it easy, Fergus. That person merely did what he'd been programmed for by heredity and environment. It's as much my fault as his, for not understanding him better."

"I wish I had your godlike detachment. By the day we reached Majbur, I felt so horrible about what I'd done in Ghulindé that I wished you'd hit me or rape me or something."

"Darling, I just don't *do* things like that. I may be a softy, but I couldn't deliberately hurt you, even when you deserved it."

"I wish I could be as good to you. End of inquisition. I guess the party's over."

"Hold it! You haven't answered *my* questions."

"Well?"

"Tell me about you and Foltz."

"Oh, forget Warren Foltz! He was a cold fish—completely selfish, in bed or out of it. That's all you need to know."

"No it isn't, and you promised. How did you get involved with the guy in the first place?"

"I'd just got back from Katai-Jhogorai and found I was broke. Also Judge Keshavachandra had issued the final decree that I'd applied for in a crazy moment. Feeling blue, I was unloading my troubles on Juana Rincón, when she told me about Foltz. He was all set to leave for Chilihagh and needed a research assistant. So I hunted him down. He asked me to have a drink in the Nova Iorque and turned on the charm."

"Was it then that he said what he'd—ah—expect of you?"

"Oh, yes; he was quite frank about it. He said: 'Alicia, you can't expect a healthy man like me to travel with a beautiful woman for moons at a time and not make advances. So to save altercations later, let's understand each other right now. Either I have bed privileges, or we call the deal off.'

"You know, Fergus, I enjoy being told I'm good-looking as much as the next woman. But sometimes I've wished I'd been born really ugly, so I could go about my work without having to fend off tumescent males at every step."

"If nobody ever made a pass, you might not like that, either. So you took Foltz up on his offer?"

"Obviously. I had to decide quickly; and I'm not good at snap judgments. When I'd been with him a few hours, I suspected I'd made another ghastly mistake. But then we were well on our way to Mishé; so I hung on, hoping my suspicions were unfounded. But they weren't."

"Didn't the nature of the bargain tip you off?"

"Not really. Such arrangements are common, and nobody thinks a thing about them. When Lucy McKay went to Ormazd, she took a handsome young photographer, and everyone knew he was hired for night duty as well as picture-taking."

"Did she pay him overtime?"

"Not how it's done, stupid. I'd avoided these liaisons up to then, mainly by going on my research trips alone."

"Poor Lish!" It was the first time since Ghulindé that Reith had used that nickname. "If only I'd been there! Was he good in bed?"

She shook her head vigorously. "No better than a Krishnan. Every three days, like clockwork, he'd shake me awake and say: 'Come here, girl; I want you!' Then wham, bam, thank you ma'am, and back to his fossils and notes. Not a trace of affection in him. He viewed sex as a bothersome biological necessity, to be gotten over with as soon as possible. I once said, if he was so perfunctory about it, what did he need me for? When I suggested the obvious alternative, he slapped me hard enough to knock me down. That time he apologized; but I should have been warned."

"If I ever meet that swine——" growled Reith. After a pause he added: "You hinted that Krishnans aren't much good, either."

"Well, I'm not a connoisseur of Krishan sex——"

"Neither am I. But from what you do know——"

"They're built differently from men, with some sort of reinforcing bone or cartilage. But they're all through in a matter of seconds; then they're back twenty minutes later, and so on. Some human women may like it, but I found it merely frustrating."

"Thanks, Lish. What you tell me hurts, but it's better than always wondering."

"Anything else you want to know about my scarlet past?"

"Oh, come off it! A pale pink past, maybe; and I'm sure you've already told me more than I wanted to know about your experiences. Compared to most women of your age, your life has been practically convential."

"Then you'll admit your experience has been quite as wide as mine, any way you measure it?"

"I guess so," said Reith, patting a yawn. "I think we can turn in now."

Alicia set down her goblet, rose, and sat on Reith's lap. Encircling him with her arms, she gave him a long, passionate kiss. "Fergus dear, are you getting ideas?"

"Well, all this talk of sex does raise one's—ah. . . ."

"Darling, what are ex-wives for?"

"Without any promises or commitments?"

"Without any promises or commitments. I'd adore being

your amorex again. There's only one thing I want more." (Reith knew that the "thing" was a new marriage certificate, but he kept silent.) "Come on, stupid! How explicit must I be?" She began unbuttoning his jacket.

Reith said: "If we're brother and sister, doesn't this seem a little incestuous? And are you safe? Your last FM pill must have run out by now."

"Oh, I begged a couple more off Gorbovast."

Struggling with the loops on the back of Alicia's dress, Reith chuckled. "Gorbovast is the greatest little old fixer on Krishna, but I didn't expect him to keep a supply of Terran contraceptives. Darling, you're beautiful whether you're wearing rags or ball gowns; but when I see just the pure, simple you, I'm speechless!"

From out on deck floated the plaintive notes of Hayakawa's *Moonlight on the Ruins*.

When at last Reith rose and reached for his clothes, Alicia rolled over and buried her face in the bedding, stifling sobs. "Oh, why," she murmured, "do I always throw away my most precious possessions? Damn, damn, damn!" With each "damn" she punched the pillow.

Long before dawn, Reith found himself awake and, as had often happened lately, stewing over the question of Alicia. He did not think her remark during their quarrel on the *Kubitar*, that she would refuse an offer of marriage from him, was seriously meant. If it were, that would make things easy. He could say, will you marry me again? and she could say, no; and he would be free of further moral obligations. But he could not count on her refusal. To offer a marriage that his rational side did not want, and have the proposal accepted, would be another invitation to disaster. . . .

Reith gave up trying to sleep, dressed, and went out on deck. The *Zaidun* was tied up at Gadri for the night. A moon-silvered fog lay over the river, making everything indistinct more than a few meters away.

With a faint gurgle, the current lapped around the pilings of the pier and the hull of the *Zaidun*. In their pen at the stern, the shaihans munched their hay throughout the night. These sounds were the only ones audible to Reith's ears. Even the late-night revelers of Gadri must have gone home.

Reith strolled up to the bow, where the boatman assigned the sentry-go sat on the rail and smoked his cigar. Keeping his voice low so as not to disturb the sleepers, Reith said:

"Hail, Seaman Káj! How goes it?"

"Well enough, Master Reef. And your good self?"

"As well as one can expect. . . ." Reith broke off, listening. A faint sound had jerked him to full alertness, head up, senses atingle, and eyes probing the mist-shrouded darkness. A light patter of feet and a murmur of low voices were not in themselves alarming. But, with the Bákhites, Vaklaf the Duru, and Gorbovast's vague warning, Reith was keyed up to anticipate danger.

"Stand by, O Káj!" he whispered. "Got your cutlass? I'm going for my hanger."

Reith strode quickly back to his cabin, moving silently because, like his companions, he had formed the habit of going barefoot on shipboard. He came out of the cabin pulling his baldric on over his head. Then he paused at the gangway, hand on his sword hilt.

As Reith reached the gangplank, nebulous figures emerged from the fog at the shoreward end. Reith caught shreds of talk in the Majburo dialect: "Go on, faintheart! . . . The sentry first . . . All together, now . . . Seize them alive. . . ."

"All hands out!" bellowed Reith, drawing. "We're attacked!"

Another cry of warning came from the bargeman in the bow. Then a drumming of feet announced the rush to board.

Since the gangplank was barely wide enough for two abreast, Reith sprang up on it, thinking he could make a better stand there than on the deck. He could not count his assailants in the fog, but he guessed that there were at least a dozen.

A moment later, the first Krishnan was upon him. The fellow came straight at him with a dagger in his extended fist. Reith straightened his arm in a stop thrust, and the fog-mazed Krishnan ran upon the point.

Reith shoved desperately, forcing the attacker over backwards. As he jerked his blade free and the knife man slumped to the gangplank, the second assailant stumbled over the body and fell to hands and knees.

Reith slashed in the dark and felt the blade strike home. The wounded Krishnan screamed and pulled back among his fellows' legs. The moonlight and the yellow gleam of the stern lantern showed part of his face hanging down in a bloody flap below his jaw.

"At him! At him!" shouted a voice from behind. "All at once, and you'll have him! Seize his limbs!" Reith recognized the Terran accent and guessed that the gang had been recruited by his old foe Warren Foltz.

Now Reith encountered two attackers on the narrow way, one with a bludgeon and the other with a half-sword. The fellow with the club aimed a blow. Reith jerked back. The end of the bludgeon missed his nose by a centimeter; he felt the wind of its passage.

Pressing forward, he thrust at the club wielder, hoping to drive home before the Krishnan could recover; but his point was stopped by some metal fitting on the fellow's clothing. The recruit with the half-sword thrust at Reith before he recovered, and Reith had to leap back to avoid the blade.

The three combatants feinted, thrust, and swung. The pressure of those behind propelled the attackers forward and forced Reith back. Several times he saw an opening, but he had to guard himself against the other fighter's weapon and could not exploit the opportunity. For their part, his attackers were hampered by lack of space.

Then both attackers moved in unison, the swordsman with a thrust, the club man with a swing. Reith was forced back again. This time his foot met air; he had backed off the inboard end of the gangplank. Down he went in a heap on the hardwood deck, while the club swished through the air where his head had been a few seconds before.

All at once, the deck was crowded with the *Zaidun*'s people. Someone stepped on Reith and fell across his legs. As Reith scrambled up, he found himself crowded by Marot wielding a sword on his left and Captain Ozum swinging a cutlass on his right. Swords clanged, and everyone seemed to be shouting at once.

The attacker with the club disappeared with a loud splash, while the Krishnan with the half-sword lay gasping out his life at Reith's feet. A Majburo voice cried:

"'Tis useless. They're all alert and armed!"

"Let me at them, cowards!" snarled Foltz's voice. As Reith sprang back on the gangplank, Foltz pushed to the front and launched a *flèche* or running attack. He tried to catch Reith's sword in a double bind, whipping the blade around in a circle before thrusting home.

Reith disengaged and straightened up in another stop thrust. As Foltz plunged forward, Reith's blade pierced the deltoid muscle of his right arm. Foltz gasped as his weakened arm dropped, letting the point of his weapon touch the deck. Ozum, reaching out over the rail, chopped at Foltz's calf.

Despite two crippled limbs, Foltz made a resolute effort to shift his sword to his left hand while remaining upright. But Reith caught the wrist of his injured arm and jerked him forward, so that he fell on the deck on top of the dying half-swordsman.

Suddenly the shoreward end of the gangplank pulled away from the pier and dropped, catapulting several of Foltz's gangsters into the river. Leaning on his bloody sword and panting, Reith was relieved to realize that one of the bargemen had cut the mooring lines, setting the *Zaidun* adrift downstream with the gangplank trailing in the water.

Standing on the deck, besides Marot, Ozum, and the crew, Reith saw Alicia. She was holding a boathook and bending over the rail.

"Alicia!" gasped Reith. "What are you doing with that boathook?"

"I pulled the guy with the club off the plank, and I was looking to see if he swam away. I don't see him."

"Most of these city rats can't swim," said Reith, setting a foot on Foltz's sword lest the paleontologist try to pick it up again.

"Me, I rosed one in the arm," said Marot, wiping his blade on the clothing of the half-swordsman's body.

"You mean, you pinked him," said Reith. He nudged the body with his toe. "Who got this one?"

"That was our gallant captain. What shall we do with *this?*"

Marot pointed his blade at Foltz, who sat huddled on the deck, clutching his wounded shoulder.

"If you idiots let him go again . . ." muttered Alicia.

"Let's question him," said Reith. "Help me to pull him into my cabin."

* * *

Oozing blood, Foltz sat on the floor of the cabin with his back to the bulkhead. The three Terrans and Captain Ozum stood guard over him; even Alicia, who had picked up Foltz's sword, scowled at him from where she sat with her weapon ready.

"If you mean to kill me," rasped Foltz, "let's get it over with."

"We haven't decided," said Reith. "First, we have some questions for you."

"You might at least bandage my wounds," said Foltz. "I can't answer questions if I pass out from loss of blood."

"There's merit in that," said Captain Ozum. "Besides, I'm not fain to have my ship beslabbered with's alien blood." He shouted for one of the bargemen, who brought two strips of cloth and bound them around Foltz's arm and leg.

"Now," said Reith, "what have you been doing since our trial at Jeshang? We know something of what's happened, so it won't help you to lie."

"I've been through a lot," said Foltz in a self-pitying whine. "Kharob's escort took me to the Mikardando border. Before they pushed me over the line, they stripped me, leaving me with no money, no clothes, not even shoes. I'd have died if a kindly peasant hadn't taken me in, given me some old clothes, and lent me a few karda to buy food on the long walk to Mishé. There, by claiming that I was a friend of yours, I established credit."

"A friend of mine!" howled Reith. "Why didn't you tell them you were Napoleon or Muhammad?"

"While I was recovering in Mishé," Foltz continued, "from that three-hundred-hoda hike, I heard the Bákhites had risen and shut the Dasht up in his palace.

"As you know, I'd become something of a pet of old Lazdai. Not that I believe her theology, but for obvious reasons I had to pretend to be a fanatical convert." Foltz studied his knuckles. "Since I'd lost everything at Zora, I needed money to get my researches going again—perhaps in a geological formation outside of Chilihagh."

"Get to the point," snapped Reith.

"I'll get there, if you let me say it in my own way. Well, I rode back from Mishé to Jeshang, stopping off to repay that peasant the money he'd lent me, with interest. In Jeshang I found Lazdai in control and wild with rage because you'd slipped through her fingers three times. Anyhow, she offered me enough money from the treasury of Bákh to keep me digging for the rest of my life, if I'd bring the three of you back to Jeshang, along with Aristide's specimen. By the way, do you still have that thing?"

"That's our business," said Reith. "Go on."

"I traced you to Majbur, where I hired a squad of local bravos. But by the time I had them organized, your boat had sailed. So, with Lazdai's advance, I bought ayas for the gang and followed you. I thought that tonight, by a sudden rush, we could overpower you without unnecessary bloodshed."

"How kind of you," sneered Reith, "to save us for the kettle later!"

"I don't like seeing people boiled," said Foltz. "I begged Lazdai not to execute you and Marot, but she wouldn't—"

Smack! Marot reached down and hit Foltz a back-handed blow in the face. "That is for the lying. We had the true story from the Dasht."

Foltz shook his head and wiped a drop of blood from a cut lip. "You're wrong, Aristide. When Lazdai sent me out on his mission, I exacted a promise that you would not be tortured or killed."

Reith and Marot exchanged glances. Marot said: "How could we confirm that story?"

"By going to Jeshang and asking the old witch," growled Reith. "But I don't think we need the truth so badly as all that." He turned back to Foltz. "So what was your objective?"

"With the Priestess's money, I could set up my own institute here and put Krishnan paleontology on a sound basis, not screwing up the facts like my muddle-headed colleague. In the long run, Terran science would benefit."

Marot began to sputter with rage, but Reith cut in: "Well, we've heard his story, some of which is undoubtedly true. So what to do with him?"

"Kill him!" said Alicia. "Think of all the trouble we'd have been saved if we'd done it the first time! If we let him go, he'll only plot more outrages. I know him, to my sorrow, and I know he's one of mankind's most passionate haters."

"Alicia!" cried Foltz. "Is that any way to treat a man who loves you?"

"Love? You?" said Alicia, staring incredulously.

"Yes. I fell in love with you at Zora, though I didn't fully realize it till after you'd left me. I've been hoping to find you again and marry you. And I did save you from starvation by giving you a job, didn't I?"

"By making me your whore! And it's a funny kind of love that plots to deliver me to that she-monster in Jeshang—"

"But my dear Alicia, as my wife you'd be protected—"

"I can just see it," said Alicia in deadly tones. "You get me to Jeshang and say: 'All right, my dear, marry me or prepare for boiling!'"

"Oh, you can't really believe I'd do such a—"

"Shut up and listen to me, Warren Foltz! I've had marriage proposals from two Krishnan heads of state, a king and a president. I have no desire for a Krishnan mate; but I'd infinitely prefer either of those to you. You're a treacherous, fanatical, sadistic, narcissistic, paranoid egomaniac, incapable of loving anyone but yourself. You're a slimy *thing*. You're also the planet's lousiest human lover. And you're not even a villain in the grand manner, but an infantile egotist, so petty as to cut up my one good dress after I ran away. I hate your guts, and I always shall. Do I make myself clear?"

Reith saw the paleontologist wince as Alicia spat out each sentence. He seemed to shrivel, to shrink into himself, and wax older as she spoke. At last he mumbled:

"Well, I can understand why you might be a little prejudiced against me. But I swear things will be different—"

"Shut up!" said Reith. "What to do with him? It'll soon be daylight—"

"Let me suggest," said Marot, "that we vote."

"If ye vote, as they do in Suruskand and Katai-Jhogorai, ye should count me in," said Ozum. "After all, 'tis my ship."

"Okay," said Reith. "How do you vote, Aristide?"

"Death. I hate bloodshed; but a man who wantonly destroys scientific knowledge is worse than a murderer."

Foltz sighed and shook his head. "That's no way to treat a colleague. We men of superior education should stick together against the ignorant masses."

"You, Captain?" said Reith, ignoring Foltz's plaints.

"I say not," said Ozum. "The story of this brabble must soon or late reach the ears of those in high places, and I would not be held culpable for any affray amongst Terrans. I have my living to earn on this river. Ye can demand his arrest under the laws of Gozashtand, in whose demesne the *Zaidun* now rides."

"Alicia?" said Reith.

"Kill him! We've been all through this before. If we let him go, he'll only try to have us killed in one way or another."

"And to think I've loved you!" said Foltz. "How can you kill the man who loves you?"

"I'd rather be loved by a cobra," said Alicia. "How about you, Fergus?"

Reith drew a long breath. "I think we'd better follow Ozum's advice and turn him over to the local authorities. I hope to go on working here, too, so it behooves me to keep my legal skirts clean. I can tie up Foltz with so many charges and suits that he'll be harmless for a long time."

"He'll wheedle and bluff his way out again," said Alicia. "Besides, the litigation would keep us all here till doomsday."

"No; I can get depositions from you and Aristide, to use if you leave the planet. . . ."

Since the four were deadlocked, the arguments went round and round, becoming ever more vehement. Ozum suggested, as a compromise, that instead of killing him they blind him and turn him loose. This proposal evoked another storm of dispute.

Up to that point, considering his desperate plight, Foltz had conducted himself with a fair degree of courageous, cold-blooded self-possession. When he heard the proposal to put out his eyes, however, his features took on an expression of horror. While his captors were too intent on shouting each other down to notice, Foltz suddenly heaved himself up and, though limping heavily, lunged for the door. He bowled over Marot and was out of the cabin before any could stay him.

With a shriek, Alicia leaped after him. Behind her pounded Reith and Captain Ozum, the latter roaring oaths. The two collided as they tried to get through the door at the same instant. By the time Reith reached the deck, he saw Alicia bending over the rail and pushing something down with a pole. He cried: "What are you doing, Alicia?"

"Drowning Warren Foltz," she replied crisply. "He tried to climb over the rail, wounded arm and leg and all. But he slipped on the blood and fell flat into the water. So I grabbed the boathook, and now I'm holding him under."

Reith looked over the side. The sky was paling with dawn-light, and beneath the black surface of the river he could make out a pale human body, whose limbs made feebly struggling motions.

Despite his bias for law and order, Reith did not interfere. Foltz, he thought, was due for a sticky end sooner or later, and what difference if it were compassed by Alicia or another?

"There!" she said in tones of satisfaction. "He's stopped moving."

"My ruthless little superwoman!" said Reith. "Captain, shouldn't we weigh the body down, so it won't bob to the surface and cause a hue and cry?"

"The 'avvals will take care of it, fear not," said Ozum.

The body disappeared, and Alicia retrieved the boathook. Reith and Ozum heaved the body of the half-swordsman over the side, as Roqir's disk began to show scarlet through the thinning fog. Marot said:

"My dear Captain, let us hope that so-called cook of yours can for once furnish a decent breakfast. I could eat one of your shaihans, hide, bones, and all!"

XIV.

THE SPACEPORT

The following day, Marot asked Reith: "Where on Krishna did Ozum get that cook? He is terrible! Me, I am sure I could do the better, despite the unfamiliar ingredients. I will speak to him."

"Better get Ozum's okay," said Reith. "He wouldn't like it if you didn't go through channels."

The next time Reith saw him, Marot was in the galley speaking to Yeshram, the stout cook. Ozum glanced in and went about his business; but Yeshram seemed too awed by his off-planet visitor to say more than: "Aye, sir. Aye, sir. I'll try it, sir."

"For tomorrow's breakfast," said Marot, "we shall learn what in my country we call *crêpes*. They are a kind of very thin—Ah, Fergus!"

"Yes?" said Reith, looking into the galley.

"What is Gozashtandou for 'pancake'? I cannot find it in my phrase book."

Reith frowned. "I don't know of an exact equivalent; but *nánash* comes pretty close."

"Excellent! Master Yeshram, we shall make the crêpe, which is a very thin nánash. We begin with badr powder and shaihan milk. Have you two bijar eggs? First we shall separate the yolks from the whites, because they must be added to the mixture separately. A little salt.... A large spoonful of that sap you use for sweetening...."

Marot finally spooned the thin batter into Yeshram's hot copper frying pan and tilted the pan with a wobbling motion, round and round, so that the sizzling batter ran to all parts of the pan bottom. He picked up the spatula, saying: "Now, my friend, regard! I take the *gâche*, whatever you call it.... There we are! It is simple when one knows. Then we roll it up, so. Now taste!"

Yeshram tasted and gave an appreciative gurgle. Marot continued: "Today you shall pour a crêpe. Tomorrow you will mix the ingredients under my eye. Go ahead, pour!"

Nervously Yeshram picked up the frying pan and the serving spoon. As he spooned the mixture into the pan, which had been heating on his little coal stove, Alicia appeared at the galley entrance, saying: "Move over a little, Fergus, so I can see."

Yeshram began to wobble the pan as he had seen Marot do. "Hey!" cried Alicia, stepping forward. "You're doing it all wrong!"

"Please, Alicia!" said Marot. "You will only confuse him. He must learn by doing—"

"We can't let him form bad habits; poor pedagogy. Let me show—"

"Lish!" exclaimed Reith. "Stop interfering and get out of the galley!"

Bewildered, Yeshram looked from one vehement Terran to the other, pan and spoon immobile in his hands.

"You'll ruin it!" cried Alicia. "Give me that frying pan!"

She grabbed for the handle, but Yeshram refused to let go. As the two struggled for possession, Reith reached into the confined space and seized Alicia's left wrist. "Come *on*, Lish! You'll only make a mess—"

As he spoke, he pulled Alicia towards the galley door. Stubbornly she resisted, trying the while to keep her hold on the utensil. Yeshram, his antennae quivering with fright, suddenly released his grip on the handle. The pan swung wildly, and the hot metal scorched her left arm.

"Ow!" she yelled, and dropped the pan. It landed with a clang upside down on the galley floor.

Reith backed out the doorway as Alicia picked up the pan,

beneath which lay the crumpled remains of Yeshram's crêpe.

"You—you—" she breathed, advancing on Reith with murder in her eyes. Wielding the pan like a headsman's ax, she whipped it up over her head and, with a mighty swing, slammed it down on Reith's coppery hair.

Reith staggered back a step and slumped to the deck, with his back against the rail. He slowly put his hands to his head and groaned.

"Are you mad, Alicia?" exclaimed Marot. "Is it that you wish to give him the concussion? Or perhaps to fracture the skull?"

"Fergus!" she cried. "Are you all right?" As Reith looked up, blinking from unfocussed eyes, she added: "You're so pale!"

Slowly he replied: "I don't know. What happened? You're—you are my wife—Alicia Dyckman Reith. Or are you still my wife? What are you doing here? And that fellow is. . . . Wait. He is Aristide—Aristide—who?"

Marot said: "My poor friend, let me take you to your cabin. You have had an accident."

"Oh, Fergus! Darling!" wailed Alicia.

"Help me up, Aristide," said Reith. The two staggered into his cabin. Reith sat down on his bunk, while Marot poured water into a basin and dipped a towel. He wiped the blood from Reith's hair and saw that the scalp was broken and oozing. The flesh beneath had begun to swell into a fine goose egg.

"How are you now?" asked Marot.

"My head aches," said Reith. "But I'm beginning to remember. It was that damned pancake. . . ."

Alicia had followed the men into Reith's cabin. Peering at the wound, she exclaimed: "Oh, Fergus, I'm so horribly sorry! What can I do—"

Reith raised his head and gave her the level, slit-eyed, expressionless stare with which a man confronts an enemy. In an even, coldly precise voice, he said: "What you can do is to stay out of my sight. I never want to see you again."

Stifling a sob, Alicia ran to her cabin and closed the door.

Reith presently began fumbling with the money belt beneath his shirt. He said to Marot: "While I think of it, here are enough LPs to last you and Alicia for the rest of the trip." He held out a fistful of capsules. "You give her her half; I don't want to be the one to give them to her."

"How many does that leave for you?" asked Marot.

"Never mind that!"

"My friend, I insist; or I will not take them."

"Well, truth to tell, that's all there are. My share's finished."

"But I cannot accept—"

"You can and you will!" said Reith. "I'm the youngest of the three of us, and it won't hurt me to age at the normal rate for a couple of days."

"No, I beg you! Keep half for yourself, and I will give the rest to Alicia. I, too, can do without for a little while. We arrive at Novorecife in two or three days."

At last they compromised. Alicia should receive her full ration, but the men would use the precious longevity pills only on alternate days.

After the frying-pan incident, Reith and Alicia said nothing to each other beyond a curt "Good morning." Alicia doggedly added to her notes, rarely speaking save to ask Marot: "What was the name of that place where . . . ?" or "Remember that Krishnan who . . . ?" or "What day was it that we . . . ?" When Marot could not answer the question, he sometimes got the information from Reith; but Alicia never spoke to Reith directly.

In one of his morose moods, Reith sat on a chest on deck and watched the familiar banks of the Pichidé creep past. Marot said: "Cheer up, my old one! Despite its hardships and hazards, our safari has been a great success."

"Huh? It's nice for you to think so; but I don't see that we've accomplished a damned thing."

"Ah, but we have! Your Ozymandias is a significant step in understanding the evolutionary development of Krishna."

"I know that's important to you," said Reith gloomily. "As for me—well, I just can't feel passionately involved."

"In addition," continued the genial scientist, "we broke the religious tyranny of the Bákhites. We pried open the door to admit the truth of evolution to Chilihagh. This is one key—the thin end of the wedge, as you say—to starting the scientific revolution here."

"You think that's a good thing?"

"But of course! Policies based on irrational myths cannot in the long run benefit their believers. People need a solid grounding in the science, to achieve their desires by logical action."

"Well," said Reith, "during the last few centuries, a substantial fraction of our fellow Terrans have abandoned the 'irrational myths' of the major religions for what they consider scientific materialism. But I don't see that it's done a damned thing for their manners and morals. If anything, they've become worse. Maybe they need cults and doctrines like Lazdai's to make them behave."

Marot brushed the objection aside. "You are a born pessimist, my old one. Then, having amassed an amazing lot of data on Krishnan societies, your little Alicia came close to abolishing slavery in Qirib. At least the idea of emancipation has been launched there. Besides, in this wild place, merely to have survived is a triumph."

"Okay, then, we're a success," said Reith lugubriously.

Marot smiled. "I know; your personal problems weigh upon you. *Ça passe.* Come and show me how to play that game they call *piza.*"

When the *Zaidun* tied up at Novorecife, Reith bade a warm farewell to Captain Ozum, waved to the deck crew, shouldered his bag, and went ashore with Marot. Carrying a folder of pencilled notes as well as her bag, Alicia caught up with Marot and tugged at his arm. "Aristide!"

Marot paused; Reith tramped on up the path as if he had not heard. "Yes, my little one?" said Marot. "Excuse, I forget that you dislike the expression."

"How is he?"

"In health, as good as ever, save for that lump on the cranium. That will soon depart."

"Well—I wonder—could you give him a message?"

Marot shook his head. "No, my dear, I regret to say that I will not. If you wish to convey a message, speak or write yourself. You have seen the results of ill-advised meddling. Me, I avoid it."

"Oh, please! I only want to tell him how sorry I am."

"No, dear Alicia, for his sake I will not. With you for a friend, my poor Fergus has no need of enemies."

"Oh, Aristide, what a cruel thing to say! You know I love him!"

"My heart is torn, but there is nothing I can do. I am not a marriage-and-divorce counselor."

Following Reith, Marot strode resolutely up the path, leaving Alicia with her bundles at her feet and hands pressed against her eyes.

The *Juruá* came down in flame and thunder. When the landing pad had cooled, the towering landing ramp wheeled itself out and extended its upper section like a tentacle.

As passengers began to trickle down the long slope, bearing their hand luggage, Fergus Reith awaited them at the foot of the ramp. He recognized the tour leader by the yellow paper sunflower pinned to his coat and stepped forward to greet him: "Mr. Svoboda?"

"Mr. Reith?" said the man with the sunflower, smiling. "Glad to know you. Let me introduce Mr. Kovacs, Mrs. Powanda, Mr. Mahler, Mr. and Mrs. Bratianu, Miss Nagy, Mrs. Markovici, Dr. Wyszkowski, Mr. and Mrs. Novotny...."

Reith shepherded his new gaggle of tourists through customs and saw to their billeting in the part of the compound reserved for incoming travelers. Henceforth Svoboda, who spoke no Krishnan languages, would (Reith noted with satisfaction) be responsible for the groups' internal problems. Reith was in charge of the external ones, including itinerary, transportation, quarters, food, and sights of major interest.

For several days, organizing the new tour preëmpted Reith's attention. He had to escort his charges, a few at a time, through the Outfitting Shop. Novo's physician, Marina Velskaya, gave each one a physical checkup. Ivar Heggstad, the trainer, put the men and the more active women through muscle-hardening exercises.

During this busy time, Reith caught not even a glimpse of Alicia, towards whom he made a determined effort to remain coolly impersonal. Yet, as his resentment of her assault with the frying pan cooled, his bitterness faded before a host of tender memories and recollections of how stoutly she had stood by him in danger.

Reith had an informal understanding with Herculeu Castanhoso, the station's chief security officer. Before each tour group set out under Reith's guidance, Castanhoso would take them on a couple of small excursions, up the Pichidé to Rimbid and down to Qou. This would give Reith a chance to clean up unfinished paperwork and iron out last-minute details.

Reith also dropped in on Li Guoching, the communications officer. After he had told some of his adventures, Reith added:

"What's the latest from Chilihagh? They were having a civil war."

"The Dasht won, but by a fluke of fortune."

"Indeed? Do tell."

The stout Chinese drew on his potent Krishnan cigar. "Kharob had Lazdai and her leading priests arrested, but a mob of Bákh-ites delivered them. Soon Lazdai controlled all Jeshang but the palace, where Kharob held out with his partisans. General Gurshman collected a force from the frontier garrisons and marched on Jeshang. Someone loyal to the Dasht opened the gate for them.

"The two forces met in the main square of Jeshang. After much shouting of threats and anathemas, Lazdai ordered a charge. Her forces much outnumbered the loyalists, including those who had been besieged in the palace, and who had broken out and joined Gurshman.

"But Lazdai decided to lead the charge in person, bran-dishing a sword like legendary Queen Dejanai. The ancient bag of bones, however, had not been on an aya for nearly a century. When her mount bounded forward, she fell off and was instantly killed by the impact of the cobblestones. The Dasht set up a cry of 'Bákh has spoken!' and the insurgents fled helter-skelter. Their leaders' heads now adorn the main gate.

"Kharob has disestablished the Temple of Bákh and declared his realm friendly to all gods regardless of their overlapping claims."

Reith chuckled. "Foltz's attempt to kidnap us wouldn't have done him any good after all. He'd have arrived in Chilihagh to find our friend the Dasht in control."

In telling of Foltz's abortive raid on the riverboat, Reith had said nothing of his death at Alicia's hands. He had simply said that Foltz had fallen into the river during the fight and drowned. As far as he was concerned, this would remain the official story.

Sitting in his quarters one evening, Reith was calculating the expenses of his expedition with Marot, as far as he could reconstruct them. He heard a knock and called: "Come in!"

Alicia, wearing a simple Terran street dress, black with a white collar, entered hesitantly. "May I sit down?"

"Of course, Alicia. What have you been doing with yourself?"

"Tidying my records for microfilming. How about you?"

"Getting my next tour organized; and you can bet we won't stop at Ghulindé! I'm also giving myself a crash refresher course to polish my rusty German. Half these Middle European tourists of mine speak German but no English, and I'm damned if I'll tackle Magyar or Czech or Românian. *Was kann ich für dich tuun?*"

Alicia hesitated, nervously twisting her fingers. "This isn't exactly a business call."

"Well?"

"I have a reservation on the *Juruá* tomorrow."

"You *have?* I didn't know you'd decided to go Earthside."

"Well, I did, more or less. I—I didn't think you'd want me to go off without saying good-bye."

"Of course not! I'd certainly want to see you off; but it would seem a little cold, just to shake hands at the ramp and say: *'Boa viagem!'* "

"Look, Fergus—I don't know how to say—what I mean is—"

"Take a deep breath, count ten, and spit it out."

She paused. "Well—what I mean is, if you asked me to marry you again, I'd jump at the chance. I can still cancel my passage."

Reith chewed his lip. "I thought something like that was in the wind."

"Well, are you going to ask me?"

"I've been thinking about that very thing. Ever since Zora, in fact, I've thought about little else—except when we were being chased by pirates, fanatical priests, and mad paleontologists."

She brightened hopefully. "And what did you conclude?"

Reith looked at Alicia, sitting in his favorite chair and looking like a goddess in Terran street clothes. His heart sank into his bedroom slippers, but he knew he could not stall any longer. "I'm sorry, but I'm afraid the answer is no. I know we'll never be good for each other."

Alicia's shoulders sagged, and she drooped like an unwatered flower. "After all we've gone through together? Don't you love me any more?"

"I still love you with all my heart. It might make things

easier if I said I didn't; but you've always been square with me." Except with Vizman, he thought.

"Then what prevents us from making another try? You know I love you, too."

"Because, darling, no matter how passionately we love each other, we simply cannot live together."

"You mean all those wretched quarrels and arguments?"

"Yes; not to mention my ducking in the Zora and the frying pan. I don't want to be a battered husband."

"I'll try to control my temper," she said. "I'll really, really try."

"I know you've tried, but you haven't succeeded, have you? The moving finger writes, et cetera."

"If you really loved me, how could you be so cold-bloodedly rational about us?"

"Just using my brain to save my hide, as sensible people do," he said.

"Maybe you should have been the scientist instead of me. I'm too emotional. . . . Darling, I'm sure I could change my ways. I'll do anything you want. Before, I wouldn't have children because of my career. Well, I'll even give *up* my career and settle down as a housewife, and mother as many children as you want."

Reith sighed. "A pretty picture, Lish; but I know you too well. After a moon or two of housewifery, you'd get itchy and either tear off on some expedition or break a vase over my head."

"I have a confession to make," said Alicia.

"Yes?"

"On the *Zaidun,* when I said I was safe, I lied. Well, not exactly; I said I'd begged FMs off Gorbovast—and that was true. But I didn't say I'd taken them. I hoped you would get me pregnant, so you couldn't let me go. But I'm not. Fergus, if you won't have me as I am, I'll undertake a basic personality change."

"How?" he asked.

"If you'll wait for me, I'll board the *Juruá,* go back to Earth, and put myself under Moritzian deep therapy. It takes a year, and it's drastic and painful; but they say it can actually change a person's basic traits."

He shook his head. "Won't work, Lish."

"Why not?"

"The time factor. It would take maybe a year and a half by subjective time—your time. But by objective time, my time, you'd get back to Krishna twenty-odd years after you left. By that time, I might be dead, or the patriarch of my own family, or a Krishnan sultan with a harem."

"I may take the Moritzian therapy anyway, since my present personality seems contraproductive. Maybe when I'm all fixed up, I'll come back with another research grant, to see how Krishnan society has changed."

"I'll always be glad to see you. But that's all."

She straightened her shoulders and, with a flash of her old intransigence, said: "Or maybe I'll settle down with a nice, dull, conventional husband—though I'll never love him the way I love you."

"The husband for you, darling, is a meek, submissive rabbit of a man, who'd let you boss, bully, and dominate him; who'd obey orders and let you make all the decisions; and who'd worship you even if you kept a stable of lovers."

"Good heavens!" she exclaimed. "I couldn't respect a man like that, and he'd bore the hell out of me! I want one with guts and character, a man like you."

"Thanks; but the trouble is, you want two incompatible things. A man of guts and character wouldn't permit you to push him around, the way you do with everybody who lets you get away with it. Can't have your cake—or as the Krishnans put it, you can't go swimming and expect to stay dry."

"You mean it's okay for husbands to domineer but not for wives?"

"Not at all. A man can be fair-minded and still refuse to be bulldozed. If either spouse, male or female, is domineering while the other is subservient, they may get along; but if both are dominant types, the marriage will be one long Donnybrook—while it lasts."

"Should I wave my alabaster body at Aristide on the way home? He's a good, kind man, even if he's the unsexiest Frenchman I ever met. He's about as exciting as one of his fossils; but at least he'd be a quiet, undemanding husband."

"You could try, though I doubt he'd take the bait. He once told me he knew he could never cope with a 'tornado of energy' like you and had better sense than to attempt it. But you don't really need a husband, Lish."

"What, then?"

"You need success in your career, and an occasional lover to flatter you and satisfy your sexual needs."

"Oh, to hell with my sexual needs! You make me sound like the cliché of the modern career woman, who cuts a new deal every day and screws a new man every night. I've told you sex as mere recreation doesn't interest me. You know all about my wretched little affairs, and you know I was never promiscuous, in spite of what some people say about field anthropologists. You're the only one I ever enjoyed it with, because we had love. Without love, it's just exercising the lower abdominal tissues.

"Besides, no money came on the *Juruá*. So either I marry you, or get a job here, or go back to Terra."

"What's wrong with a local job? I could pull wires."

"It would waste all my special knowledge, training, and experience."

"With the money from your necklace, you wouldn't have to work at all, for years anyway." Reith got up and paced the floor, back and forth in front of her.

She shook her head. "I don't see hanging around Novo for years, doing nothing useful and hoping you'll change your mind; I know you too well. Seeing you now and then would just tantalize me with false hopes. If I can't have you, roped and branded, I'll go back to Earth and try to pick up the pieces there. In time I suppose I'll get over loving you. But I'm not going to sit forlornly in my casement window, waiting for my knight in shining armor who never comes riding by."

"Oh, come! Any time you go sit in a casement window, you'll have a whole squadron of knights singing canzonets and roundelays beneath it." Reith halted his pacing before Alicia and made motions of strumming a guitar. She said:

"I want only one man, and you're he. There are so many things we can do as a couple that we can't do alone."

Reith smiled. "Like the tango?"

"That's only one. You know how much more effectively we work together than separately. It's a case where one and one makes more than two."

"But hitting each other with blunt objects isn't my idea of working together."

"Oh, dear! I don't suppose you'll ever forget that frying pan."

Reith gingerly touched his scalp. "You wouldn't, if it had

been your skull. But I've forgiven you long since, if that's any comfort."

"But forgiving isn't forgetting, is it?"

"It never is, unless you hit the victim hard enough to cause permanent amnesia."

Reith sat down; this time Alicia got up and paced. She asked: "Isn't it true that, a couple of times on the way back from Zora, you almost proposed to me?"

"Yes," admitted Reith.

"Then, when did I blow it? You were so loving and tender at the ranch house in Kubyab, the day after the battle, that I thought I had you for sure."

"You almost did. To answer your question, it wasn't any one thing that blew it but a whole series of incidents. At times you seemed to be controlling the virago in you so well that I thought there might be hope for us. But every time I wavered towards proposing, you'd do something outrageous, like the rumpus over the visit of the Bákhite priest, or your tryst with Vizman—"

"I've regretted the Vizman thing every day since—because of what it did to us, not because it was altogether wrong in itself."

"Maybe it wasn't wrong in the abstract; but it sure gave a kick in the balls to my masculine ego. Most people have love affairs at some time or other. But if one is seriously courting somebody, one doesn't go frigging in the rigging with a third party practically under the loved one's nose, and then expect the courtee to like it. That's just Human Nature 1A. You of all people ought to know that, having written a thesis about it. Anyway, by the time we arrived here, you had finally convinced me that, much as I love you, to marry you again would be a dreadful mistake."

Alicia sat down on the corner of Reith's desk. "By the time of our last night together, on the boat, you'd made up your mind, hadn't you?"

"Let's say, ninety-five percent. The frying-pan incident made it an even one hundred."

"So I've got to spend the rest of my life being miserable?"

"Oh, rubbish! With your looks, brains, charm, and energy, you can get anybody you want."

"Damn it!" she cried. "I don't just want anybody. If I'm all that good, why can't I have the one man I really want?"

"Because marriage between us is like a beautiful yacht, all fresh paint and shining brasswork, that won't float. We've been all through it and know how it works—or rather, doesn't work. You're an adorable creature, but I can't take the treatment you deal out to the one who adores you."

She pounded her knees. "Fergus, why can't I make you understand how miserably sorry I am for all those incidents? Every time I lose my temper, or make an idiotic decision, I go through hell afterwards."

"I know; you're always frightfully sorry after you've done something that can't be undone. That doesn't stop you next time."

Not yet ready, even then, to concede defeat, she argued further. She proposed that they live together on a trial basis; that Reith come back to Earth with her; or that he marry her but keep a mistress to comfort him when Alicia was difficult. To all of her suggestions, Reith turned a deaf ear. At last she cried:

"Oh, damn! Why must you be so realistic?"

"If I had been truly realistic, darling," he said gently, "I'd have come to a firm decision much sooner and stuck to it. But I couldn't leave you broke in the middle of nowhere, and you're such a damnably desirable woman."

They sat in silence for a time. At last Alicia gave a long sigh. "Well, if I can't change your mind, wouldn't you like to make love, just one last time?"

Reith shook his head, although in her prim black-and-white outfit she seemed more desirable than ever. "No, dearest love. It would only make the parting harder." He rose. "I'll see you at breakfast. Good-night, Lish." He did not voice his real reason for rejecting her suggestion: a lively fear that, if she renewed her importunities while he lay in her arms, he would weaken and yield after all.

Wordlessly, Alicia fled the room. When he was alone, quietly, and for the first time in many years, Reith wept.

In the cafeteria, Reith and Alicia were dawdling over their breakfast. They said little but stared at each other as if to store up memories of every detail of the other's appearance. At last Reith said:

"Besides all those xenological treatises you're determined to write, why don't you compose a personal memoir of your years on Krishna? You've had adventures enough for three. The book could be a best-seller."

"But I'd have to tell the world how horrid I was to you!"

"Actresses are always confessing how beastly they were to their husbands and lovers, of whom they seem to have hundreds apiece. Or you could blame me for all our troubles; or tactfully skim over the parts about us."

"Oh, Fergus, I couldn't bear to blame you...." But even as she spoke, her sapphire eyes took on the gleam of a writer who sights a viable book idea. "I may try it at that. I'll confess all my follies. Would you mind if I published it under the name of Alicia Dyckman Reith? I have a sentimental attachment to the name."

"Use any name you like, darling. I'd be honored."

"And I'll dedicate it to—to 'My once and future—'" She broke off, pressing her lips together, her eyes brimming with tears. Then she glanced at the wall clock. "I'd better get out to the boarding ramp. Coming to see me off?"

At the foot of the ramp, Reith drew himself up. "Good-bye, Lish, and the best of luck. I hope your books on Krishna set Terra afire."

"Thanks. Oh, Fergus dear, you haven't changed your mind?"

"No. This is it."

"Then good-bye." They kissed, an endless, ardent kiss, clinging to each other.

"I'll come back some day," she said at last. "And as long as I live, I'll remember our great adventure together, and what a fine person you are, and what a splendid lov—" Her voice broke and she turned away, dabbing at her eyes with a hand-kerchief.

With head up, Alicia ascended the ramp, very slowly, as if she were mounting a scaffold. Reith, with a knife twisting in his entrails, watched her go. Within him rose a surge of emotion, a burning wish to call out: Alicia, come back! We'll work something out! He tried to suppress the urge, knowing it to be irrational and self-destructive. It would be an invitation to another disaster. But the emotion grew and swelled until, like a tidal bore racing up a river, it swept away all prudential considerations. As she turned to wave, and even while he told himself: stop, you fool! he filled his lungs to shout.

At that instant, a familiar voice said: "Ah, *mon ami!*" Marot held up a small bag of fossil fragments, each freed from its surrounding burden of stone. "See our Ozymandias? Some pieces were doubtless lost when Foltz broke up the fossil, but I think there are enough left to settle the dispute. I shall name it *Parodosaurus reithi*, meaning 'Reith's transitional lizard.' It will go down in history as one of the most important discoveries in Krishnan biology. I will see to it that you are given credit for, first, finding it and, second, for getting it back to Novorecife through ghastly perils.

"If you return to Terra, *mon cher*, you must come to see me in Paris. Perhaps we shall go out on a dig together. *Au revoir!*"

Marot kissed Reith on both cheeks and strode briskly up the ramp. Alicia had already disappeared into the lock.

Back in the customs building, Reith ran into Kenneth Strachan, the civil engineer. Strachan was in his professional-Scotsman mood, larding his speech with "braid Scots." "Ye dinna look happy, ma billie! Parting from the little blond dynamo, eh?"

Reith nodded. "Ken, if there's a more miserable feeling than learning that the one great love of your life is someone you can't possibly live with, I hope I never know it." He blew his nose, muttering: "If that damned Frenchman hadn't come along. . . . but maybe it's just as well he did."

"Ah, stuff!" said Strachan. "I dinna believe in the one great love of your life. It disna exist; it's an invention of romantical storytellers. Man, there'll be anither along in a minute! Why, a braw pair of lassies came in on the *Juruá* to work here, and incidentally to look for husbands."

"Wait till you meet your true love," said Reith. "You'll sing a different tune."

Strachan waved away the notion. "Tell you what. Next to a glass of guid Scots whiskey, which canna be had on this world, there's nocht like a guid fuck to cheer a man up. I know a bonny little hoor in the Hamda', so fasteejus she makes her clients bathe before she screws 'em. I'll introduce ye—"

"Wouldn't help," said Reith. "The way I feel, I'd be as limp as a wet noodle. Anyhow, I've got to round up my new batch of tourists. We've supposed to start down the Pichidé tomorrow, and Captain Zarrash's *Chaldir* is two days overdue. I must keep my charges busy till he comes."

"That's the spirit!" said Strachan. "This might be considered a happy ending after all."

"How do you figure?"

"Weel, from all I've heard and seen about the pair of ye, as miserable as you were at the parting, you'd have been a sight unhappier yet if you'd tried to live together again."

"Ken," said Reith with a wry laugh, "if that's your idea of a happy ending, may Bákh preserve me from an unhappy one! Have you seen Svoboda around? You know, my opposite number on this next tour? I've got to find him. . . ."

AWARD-WINNING
Science Fiction!

The following titles are winners of the prestigious Nebula or Hugo Award for excellence in Science Fiction. A must for lovers of good science fiction everywhere!

☐ 77420-2	**SOLDIER ASK NOT,** Gordon R. Dickson	$2.75
☐ 47809-3	**THE LEFT HAND OF DARKNESS,** Ursula K. LeGuin	$2.95
☐ 06223-7	**THE BIG TIME,** Fritz Leiber	$2.50
☐ 16651-2	**THE DRAGON MASTERS,** Jack Vance	$1.95
☐ 16706-3	**THE DREAM MASTER,** Roger Zelazny	$2.25
☐ 24905-1	**FOUR FOR TOMORROW,** Roger Zelazny	$2.25
☐ 80698-8	**THIS IMMORTAL,** Roger Zelazny	$2.75

Prices may be slightly higher in Canada.

BEST-SELLING

Science Fiction
and
Fantasy